Violet glanced at her watch again as Landon came back with the coffee.

"Still timing me?" he asked, sitting down.

"No. I was just thinking that there's a call I should make soon."

"Go ahead, if you want."

He might be making an effort to be accommodating. Or he might be interested in who she was calling. She hadn't quite made up her mind yet about Mr. Landon Derringer.

"I'll wait until I've seen your mysterious friend," she said.

He glanced at the door. "You won't have long to wait. She's here."

The door swung open, and a woman stepped inside. Slim, chic, sophisticated. And other than that, Violet's exact double.

LONE STAR PROMISES

Marta Perry

AND

Brenda Minton

**Previously published as *Her Surprise Sister*
and *Her Rancher Bodyguard***

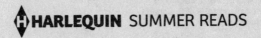 HARLEQUIN SUMMER READS

Special thanks and acknowledgment are given to Marta Perry for her contribution to the Texas Twins miniseries.

HARLEQUIN® SUMMER READS

PLEASE RECYCLE
THIS PRODUCT IS RECYCLABLE

ISBN-13: 978-1-335-17996-8

Recycling programs
for this product may
not exist in your area.

Lone Star Promises
Copyright © 2020 by Harlequin Books S.A.

Her Surprise Sister
First published in 2012. This edition published in 2020.
Copyright © 2012 by Harlequin Books S.A.

Her Rancher Bodyguard
First published in 2016. This edition published in 2020.
Copyright © 2016 by Brenda Minton

This edition published by arrangement with Harlequin Books S.A.

For questions and comments about the quality of this book, please contact us at CustomerService@Harlequin.com.

Harlequin Enterprises ULC
22 Adelaide St. West, 40th Floor
Toronto, Ontario M5H 4E3, Canada
www.Harlequin.com

Printed in U.S.A.

CONTENTS

A lifetime spent in rural Pennsylvania and her Pennsylvania Dutch heritage led **Marta Perry** to write about the Plain People, who add so much richness to her home state. Marta has seen nearly sixty of her books published, with over six million books in print. She and her husband live in a centuries-old farmhouse in a central Pennsylvania valley. When she's not writing, she's reading, traveling, baking or enjoying her six beautiful grandchildren.

Books by Marta Perry

Love Inspired

Brides of Lost Creek

Second Chance Amish Bride
The Wedding Quilt Bride
The Promised Amish Bride
The Amish Widow's Heart

An Amish Family Christmas
"Heart of Christmas"
Amish Christmas Blessings
"The Midwife's Christmas Surprise"

Visit the Author Profile page at
Harlequin.com for more titles.

HER SURPRISE SISTER

Marta Perry

This story is dedicated to the Love Inspired sisters who worked on this continuity series. And, as always, to Brian, with much love.

When I consider thy heavens, the work of thy fingers, the moon and the stars, which thou hast ordained; What is man, that thou art mindful of him? and the son of man, that thou visitest him?

—Psalms 8:3–4

Chapter 1

What could she possibly say to a father who had walked out of her life when she was an infant? *Hi, Dad, it's me, Violet?*

Violet Colby's fingers tightened on the steering wheel. What was she doing miles from home in Fort Worth, trying to follow an almost nonexistent clue to her birth father?

A sleek sports car cut in front of her SUV, horn blaring. Shaken, Violet flipped on the turn signal and pulled into the right lane. City traffic had frazzled whatever nerves she had left.

A coffee-shop sign ahead beckoned to her. That was what she needed—a short respite, a jolt of caffeine and a chance to reassess her situation.

She found a parking space, fed the meter and pushed open the coffee shop's glass door, fatigue dragging at her. The aroma drew her irresistibly in, and a few moments later she was sitting at a small round glass table, a steaming mug and a flaky croissant in front of her. She hadn't bothered to read through the long list of specialty coffees the shop offered. All she wanted was caffeine, the sooner the better.

A woman brushed past her, the summer-print dress and high platform sandals she wore making Violet uncomfortably aware of her faded jeans and scuffed cowboy boots. It wasn't that she hadn't been in Fort Worth before, but she usually took the time to dress appropriately for a trip to the city, a five-hour drive from the Colby Ranch. This time she'd bolted out of her mother's hospital room, exhausted from long nights of waiting and praying for her mom to open her eyes.

She hadn't been able to take it any longer. That wasn't the Belle Colby everyone in the county knew, lying there motionless day after day. Belle Colby was energetic, vibrant, always in motion. She had to be, running a spread the size of the Colby Ranch and raising two kids on her own.

Not now. Not since her mare had stepped in a hole, sending Belle crashing to the ground. And Jack, Violet's big brother, was so eaten up with guilt for arguing with their mom before the accident that he was being no help at all.

Violet broke a corner off the croissant and nibbled at it. Her family was broken, it seemed, and she was the only one who could fix it. That's what she'd been thinking during those lonely hours before dawn at her mother's hospital bed. The only solution her tired brain could come up with was to find their father—the man Belle never talked about.

Now that she was here in Fort Worth, where she'd

been born, the task seemed futile. Worse, it seemed stupid. What would it accomplish if she did find him?

She didn't belong here, any more than the sophisticated-looking guy coming in the door would belong on the ranch. Swanky suit and designer tie, glossy leather boots that had certainly never been worn to muck out a stall, a Stetson with not a smudge to mar its perfection—he was big-city Texas, that was for sure.

That man's head turned, as if he felt her stare, and she caught the full impact of a pair of icy green eyes before she could look away. She stared down at her coffee. Quickly she raised the mug, hoping to hide her embarrassment at being caught gaping.

It didn't seem to be working. She heard approaching footsteps and kept her gaze down. A pair of glossy brown boots moved into her range of vision.

"What are you doing here?"

Violet looked up, surprised. "What?"

"I said, what are you doing here?" He pulled out the chair opposite her, uninvited, and sat down. "I told you I'd be at your apartment…" He slid back the sleeve of his suit to consult the gold watch on his tanned wrist. "In five minutes. So why are you in the coffee shop instead of at your condo? Are you trying to avoid me?"

Okay, he was crazy. That was the only answer Violet could come up with. She groped for her bag, keeping her eyes on his face. It looked sane enough, with a deep tan that made those green eyes bright in contrast, a square, stubborn-looking jaw, and a firm mouth. His expensively cut hair was sandy blond.

He didn't *look* crazy, but what did that mean? Or maybe this was his idea of a pick-up line.

Her fingers closed on her bag and she started to rise.

His hand shot across the table and closed around her wrist. Not hard, but firmly enough that she couldn't pull away without an undignified struggle.

"The least you can do is talk to me about it." He looked as if keeping his temper was an effort. "Whatever you think, I still want to marry you."

Violet sent a panicked glance around the coffee shop. The customers had cleared out and even the barista had disappeared into the back. People walked by on the sidewalk outside, but they were oblivious to the drama being played out.

"Well?" He sounded impatient.

Her own temper spiked. "Well, *what?* Are you crazy?" That probably wasn't the smartest thing to say, but it was what she felt. "Let go of me right now before I yell the place down."

His grip loosened and he looked at her, puzzlement creeping into his eyes. "Maddie? Why are you acting this way? What's wrong?"

Relief made her limp for an instant. He wasn't crazy. He'd mistaken her for someone else.

A flicker of caution shot through her relief. If this someone else was a woman he'd proposed to, how could he mistake Violet for her?

"My name isn't Maddie." She said the words in a soft, even tone, the way she'd speak to a half-gentled horse. Maybe it worked on humans, too. "I think you've confused me with someone else."

His fingers still encircling her wrist loosely, he studied her, letting his gaze move from her hair, probably escaping from the scrunchy she'd put on her ponytail ages ago, to a face that was undoubtedly bare of makeup at this stage of the day, to her Western shirt and well-worn jeans.

Finally he shook his head. "You're not Maddie Wallace, are you?"

"No. I'm not." She pulled her wrist free. "Now that we have that straight, I'll be going...."

"Wait." He made a grab for her wrist again, and then seemed to think the better of it when she raised her fist. "I'm sorry." He gave her a rueful, disarming grin. "You must think I'm crazy."

"The thought did cross my mind." A smile like his could charm the birds from the trees. Maybe it was worth sitting still another minute for. She had to admit, she was curious.

"It's uncanny." A line formed between his eyebrows. "But I think..." He let that sentence fade away. "Look, my name is Landon Derringer. Here's my card." He slid a business card from his pocket and put it on the table in front of her. According to the card, Landon Derringer was the CEO of an outfit called Derringer Investments.

Of course, that didn't prove anything. "Not that I'm skeptical, but I could have a business card made up that said I was the queen of England."

He chuckled, the sound a bass rumble that seemed to vibrate, sending a faint tingle along her skin. "Fair enough. But if you'll be patient for a few minutes while I make a call, I think you'll find it worthwhile."

She gave him an assessing gaze. Her brother would probably say she was naive to trust this guy, but then Jack and everybody else at Colby Ranch tended to treat her as if she were about ten. Oddly enough, that decided it for her.

"All right."

The guy—Landon—gave a crisp nod. "Good." He flipped open a cell phone.

In normal circumstances she would think it impolite to listen to someone else's phone conversation. But nothing about this encounter was normal, and she intended to hear what he said. This encounter had one thing going for it: it had taken her mind off her troubles, at least briefly.

"Maddie? This is Landon. Just listen, will you?"

This Maddie person must not be eager to talk to him, judging by his tone.

"I'm over at the Coffee Stop, and there's someone here you have to meet. I think she might have some answers about that odd package you received last week."

He paused while she talked, and Violet could hear the light notes of a female voice, but not the words.

"No, this is not just an excuse to see you." He sounded as if he were trying to hold on to his patience.

More waiting, while the voice went on.

"Okay," he said finally. "Right. We'll be here."

He clicked off, and then met Violet's raised eyebrows with another flash of that smile. "Five minutes. It won't take her any longer than that to get here. Her apartment is just down the street a block or so. And you'll find meeting her interesting, I promise."

She glanced at her watch. "Okay. I'll give you five minutes, no more."

"Good." He rose, taking her coffee mug. "I'll get you a refill. And you look as if you could use something a little more substantial than that croissant."

"What do you—"

But he'd already gone to the counter. She was tempted to pull out a mirror and look at herself, but that

would betray the fact that she cared what he thought.
Anyone would look frazzled after as many sleepless
nights as she'd had.

She glanced at her watch again as he came back
with the coffee.

"Still timing me?" he asked, sitting down.

"No. I was just thinking that there's a call I should
make soon." She'd have to check in at the hospital to see
if there'd been any change. And try to track her brother
down, if she could.

"Go ahead, if you want."

He might be making an effort to be accommodating.
Or he might be interested in who she was calling. She
hadn't quite made up her mind yet about Mr. Landon
Derringer.

"I'll wait until I've seen your mysterious friend,"
she said.

He glanced at the door. "You won't have long to
wait. She's here."

The door swung open and a woman stepped inside.
Slim, chic, sophisticated. And other than that, Violet's
exact double. Violet's breath stopped. It was like being
thrown from a horse, the wind knocked out of her. This
couldn't be true, but it was. The evidence stood right
in front of her.

Landon rose as Maddie turned toward them. She
took a step, her cautious smile fading as she looked
from Landon to his companion. Her eyes widened; her
face paled.

"Maddie, are you all right?" He kicked himself mentally. He should have given her more of a warning.

She nodded and walked toward them as slowly as if

she were wading through water. When she reached the
table, he pulled a chair out and she sank into it, never
taking her eyes from the other woman's face.

He was having a bit of difficulty with that himself.
He looked from one to the other, feeling almost dizzy.
Same long, straight auburn hair, same chocolate-brown
eyes, same delicate features. Aside from the obvious
differences in style and clothing, it was like looking at
mirror images.

"Who are you?" Maddie ignored him when she
spoke, all her attention on the other woman. He'd been
careful not to ask the woman's name, since she'd clearly
been suspicious of him, and he waited, curious, to see
how she responded to Maddie.

"Violet Colby." She said the name, seeming per-
plexed for a moment, as if wondering if she really were
who she thought she was.

Small wonder. How could anyone react when con-
fronted by an exact duplicate?

The stranger—Violet—seemed to shake herself, as
if in an effort to regain control. "Who are you? Why…"
She glanced from Maddie to Landon. "Is this a trick
of some kind?" Her voice sharpened with suspicion as
she looked at him.

"How could it be a trick?" he asked, spreading his
hands to indicate innocence. "When I saw you sitting
here, I thought you were Maddie. You're identical. I
couldn't make that up."

Curiously, Maddie's expression was equally suspicious as she looked at her duplicate. "I don't believe it.
Are you the person who sent me that note?"

Violet looked confused. She shook her head, the long
ponytail swinging, tendrils of hair freeing themselves

to cluster on her neck. Maddie hadn't worn her hair that way since she was about fourteen, when she was in the middle of her horse-mania stage. It made him feel for a moment as if Violet were a kid.

Careful, he warned himself. *You don't know anything about this woman, and Maddie's family has money and position.* This could be some sort of elaborate scam, and if so, it was his duty to protect Maddie. He'd promised her brother he'd look after her.

When Maddie didn't speak, Violet seemed to feel more of a response was called for. "I don't know what you're talking about. What note? How could I send you anything when I didn't even know you existed until just this moment?"

They could go on dancing around the question all day, it seemed. He'd always rather go straight to the heart of the matter.

"Look, it's obvious that you two are identical twins. Just look at yourselves. Maddie, did you bring the note?"

He expected a flare-up from Maddie at his assumption of authority, but she just nodded and fished in her bag. The shock of this encounter seemed to have knocked the stuffing out of her for the moment.

Maddie drew out a much-creased piece of notepaper and pushed it across the table. Violet spread the note flat and bent over to read it.

Landon didn't need to look at the page again to know what the note said. The words had been revolving in his mind since Maddie received it a couple of weeks ago.

I am sorry for what I did to you and your family. I hope you and your siblings, especially your twin, can forgive me as I ask the Lord to forgive me.

No signature, and the ink was a bit faded, as if it hadn't been written recently.

"I don't understand," Violet said, pushing the paper back to Maddie. "Where did this come from? Why would you think I had anything to do with it?"

"Because you're obviously the twin referred to in the note," he said, watching her closely. But he couldn't see any indication that she was faking. Her puzzlement and distress seemed natural.

"Let me tell it," Maddie said, interrupting. "It's my business."

Not yours, in other words. But he couldn't be pushed away so easily. In the absence of her father and brothers, Maddie needed someone to watch over her, even though she didn't think she did.

"This letter appeared in my mailbox a couple of weeks ago." Maddie touched the note. "It was tucked into a new Bible, with no indication of who it was from." She shrugged. "It upset me at first. It seemed so weird. But then I assumed it had just been sent to the wrong person. I don't have a twin." She paused. "Anyway, I didn't think so."

"I didn't think so, either." Violet paused. "They do say that everyone has a double somewhere. Maybe it's just some sort of odd…" Her voice died off, probably because she realized how ridiculous that was.

"The obvious solution is usually the right one," Landon said. If he didn't keep pushing, they'd never come to a conclusion. "Would you mind telling us about your family, Violet? If you were adopted—"

She was already shaking her head. "I know what you're thinking, that we could have been split up as babies and adopted by different couples. But it can't be.

Everyone says I look just like my mother." A shadow crossed her face when she spoke of her mother…distress, fear…he wasn't sure what.

"What is it?" He reached impulsively for her hand. "Is something wrong with your mother?"

Violet took a deep breath, seeming to draw some sort of invisible armor around her. "My mother was in an accident a few days ago. She had a bad fall from a horse. She's been in a coma in a trauma center in Amarillo ever since."

"I'm sorry." The depth of her pain touched him, even though she was trying to hide it. "But…what are you doing here in Fort Worth, then?"

Violet's lips trembled for an instant before she summoned up control. "I…it was a crazy idea, I guess. But I thought maybe I could find my father."

"Find your father?" Now it was Maddie's voice that shook a little. "Is he missing?"

Violet rubbed her temples, and he thought she was fighting tears. "I don't know. I've never known who my father was. I was sitting there in the hospital, praying that Mom would open her eyes, and suddenly I was longing to see my father." She gave a shaky laugh. "I suppose I wanted someone to walk in and tell me it was going to be all right. Stupid, isn't it?"

"Maybe not so stupid," he said. "It brought you here, didn't it? But why Fort Worth?"

"Because this is where I was born. My mother did tell my brother that when he kept badgering her about it, although then she closed up and wouldn't say any more. I thought I might find some records."

"Do you know which hospital?" At least that was something that could be checked. Landon would welcome some positive task that would lead to unraveling this puzzle.

Violet shook her head. "Mom always clammed up whenever we asked her about it. So eventually I stopped asking. My brother, Jack, was more interested in finding out than I was, but she just always said we were better off not knowing."

"I can run a check on hospital records. What's your birthday?" He pulled out his cell phone. The firm of private investigators his company sometimes used would know how to access that information.

"January 26th." They made the reply almost in unison, and then looked at each other, some sort of bond seeming to form in that moment.

"You don't need to do any checking," Maddie said. "It's obvious, as you said. We're sisters." She reached across the table, touching Violet's hand. They looked at each other, faces breaking into identical smiles.

It couldn't help but warm his heart, but his rational mind sounded a note of caution. All they knew about this woman was what she'd told them.

A couple of college boys came into the coffee shop, discussing baseball loudly as they approached the counter. Maddie gave them an annoyed look.

"We can't talk here," she said. "Violet, you just have to come back to my condo. There are a million things I want to ask you. All right? Will you come?"

Violet seemed to hesitate for a moment. Then she nodded. "Okay."

Landon rose when they did, and Maddie gave him what was obviously a dismissive smile.

"Thank you, Landon. I appreciate what you did to

bring us together. I'll talk with you sometime soon." She turned away, heading for the door.

Violet was obviously startled by Maddie's action. She started to follow and then turned back, giving him a shy smile.

"Thank you, Landon. If I hadn't run into you, I might never have known I have a twin." She held out her hand, and he took it.

They stood for a moment, hands clasped, and it seemed to him they were making a promise. Confused by the sudden emotion, he smiled and stepped back. He'd been summarily dismissed, and he couldn't very well barge into Maddie's condo to see what they did next.

But as he watched them walk out the door together, he knew this couldn't be the end of his involvement. Even if Violet were as genuine as she seemed, the situation still had the potential to explode, hurting the whole Wallace family. And if Violet were playing some game of her own...

Well, even though their engagement had never been more than a formality, it was his duty to protect Maddie, and that was what he intended to do.

Chapter 2

Violet hurried outside to catch up with Maddie, her palm still tingling from Landon's touch. That wouldn't do, she lectured herself. According to the dapper CEO, he wanted to marry Maddie.

Still wanted, he'd said. That implied there'd been an engagement between them, didn't it? So what had gone wrong for them?

On the face of it, Landon Derringer was quite a guy—obviously handsome and sophisticated, apparently wealthy and successful. Still, Maddie knew him better than she did. There could be very good reasons why she'd changed her mind about marrying him.

Maddie waited on the busy sidewalk and gestured down the street. This part of Fort Worth seemed to be a mix of businesses, professional offices and apartment buildings.

"My condo is only a couple of blocks from here, so I

walked. But maybe you want to take your car and park it there in the garage, rather than leave it on the street."

"Yes, thanks." Violet went quickly to the SUV and opened the door to be greeted by a blast of heat. Texas-in-July heat. She switched on the ignition, turned the air on full blast, and rolled the windows down as Maddie got in. "Sorry it's so stifling. It should cool off pretty fast."

"No problem. I was born here, remember? I'm used to it." Maddie shook her head, her silky hair swaying. She wore it in a shoulder-length cut that had obviously been done by a professional, since the style fell back into place with every movement.

Violet couldn't help touching her ponytail. Would her hair look that way with the right cut? Maybe so, but she couldn't afford to find out. Anyway, the ponytail was a lot more practical for the life she led.

She checked the rearview mirror and pulled out into traffic. In the mirror she could also glimpse Landon Derringer, still standing by the coffee-shop door.

"We both were born here," Violet said, still trying to understand what was happening to her. "Do you think your friend will really be able to find the records?"

"Probably. He has the connections, if anyone does." Maddie's nose crinkled. "I wish he'd butt out, but knowing Landon, he won't."

Violet hesitated for a moment before asking the question in her mind. "When he first saw me, Landon thought I was you. He said he still wanted to marry me. You, I mean." She was probably blushing.

Maddie shrugged, a quick, graceful movement. "I ought to tell you about it, I guess. Landon and I were engaged, but it was a mistake. Now we're not. End of story."

It couldn't be all there was. Violet knew there had to be a lot more to the engagement and the breakup than that, but if Maddie didn't want to tell her, she wouldn't pry.

"Just past this next corner," Maddie said. "Turn right into the basement garage."

Violet followed her directions, turning into an underground parking garage. She parked the car where Maddie indicated and walked beside her, their footsteps echoing on the concrete floor. They stepped into an elevator that lifted them soundlessly to the third floor.

"Right over here." Maddie pulled out keys as she spoke, going quickly down the carpeted hallway to the second door. She unlocked it and led the way into a condo.

So this fancy place was where her twin lived. It looked like a magazine spread.

"This is lovely." Violet stepped into the living room, which had a dining area on one end and an open counter, beyond which was a small kitchen. Spacious and trendy, with sleek leather furniture and vibrant paintings on the walls, the living room had a bank of glass doors leading onto a balcony that overlooked the city.

Maddie looked around, as if surprised by her comment. "I guess it is. Dad helped me buy this place when I decided to get out on my own."

Dad. The casual word echoed in Violet's mind. Was Maddie's father her father, too? He must be, for them to be identical twins. She realized she was still trying to wrap her mind around that one fact.

"What's your father like?"

Maddie crossed the Berber carpet to a glass-topped table that held a series of photos in silver frames. She picked one up, holding it out.

Violet took the photo and stared at three pictured faces. The older man had to be Maddie's father. *Her father.* He had a chiseled face and dark brown eyes with a somber expression. Remote—that was how he looked.

The other two were younger. She stared at one of the pictured faces and felt the room spin around.

"Who is that?" She pointed to the face.

Maddie looked at her oddly. "Are you okay? That's just my older brother, Grayson."

Violet shook her head, pulling her cell phone out of her bag and flipping through the photos until she found the one she wanted. "This is my older brother. Jack." She handed it to Maddie, knowing she'd see what Violet meant at once. The faces were identical.

Maddie stared at the photo for a long moment. She sank down onto the nearest sofa, looking shell-shocked. "I feel as if I've wandered into a science-fiction movie."

Violet sat down next to her. "Me, too. Two sets of identical twins? It's…it's just crazy."

"That's the right word for it," Maddie agreed, shaking her head in disbelief.

"Who is the other person?" Violet pointed to the third man in the framed photo.

"My younger brother, Carter." Maddie looked at her. "Please don't tell me you have an identical younger brother. That would be too much. I'd be ready for the funny farm."

Violet managed a smile. "I don't have any younger siblings at all."

"That's a relief." Maddie flushed. "I mean… I didn't

mean that I'm glad you don't have younger siblings. Or that I'm not glad to have found you. It's just…"

"Yes. I know." Violet rubbed her forehead. Maybe if she weren't so tired, she could think this through better. "So what do we make of this? We must have the same parents in order to be identical, to say nothing of Jack and Grayson being identical. So my mother and your dad were together at one time, and they had two sets of twins. That's what we're saying, isn't it?"

"I guess so." Maddie was staring at the photo she'd identified as being her younger brother. "But that must mean Carter is my half brother. I remember when he was born. It never occurred to me that Mom wasn't my mother, too."

Violet could hear the hurt in Maddie's voice, and it seemed to echo in her heart. There were too many complications for her to grapple with. "What about your dad? He has to know the answers to this. Can't we go and see him?" Her heart gave an extra thump at the thought of actually seeing her birth father.

But Maddie was shaking her head. "He's not within reach, I'm afraid. Dad's a doctor. Right now he's on a mission trip, and he said he wouldn't be in cell-phone range most of the time. Not that we talk all that much, anyway." Maddie shrugged. "If you're picturing an old-fashioned, doting, emotionally engaged father, forget it. Dad's more involved with his patients than with his kids."

"I'm sorry." She reached out to touch Maddie's hand, responding to the pain in her voice. "But there must be some way of reaching him in an emergency. We'll go nuts if we don't find some answers."

"I can send an email. He is able to pick those up

occasionally. But before I do that, tell me about your mother. *Our* mother. You said we look like her."

Violet flipped through the cell phone photos again, stopping at one she especially liked. Belle was leaning against a corral fence, wearing her usual jeans, plaid shirt and boots, her head tilted back, smiling with that pleasure she always seemed to take in whatever she was doing at the moment. Violet touched the image. She'd give a lot to see her mom looking like that again. She handed the phone to Maddie.

"Oh." Maddie touched the image, just as Violet had. She wiped away a tear. "We are like her, aren't we? It's funny to look at her and know what I'll look like in twenty years or so. She's beautiful."

"Yes. But right now—"

"You said she'd been in an accident." Maddie rushed her words. "How bad is it?"

"Bad." Violet swallowed the tears that wanted to spill out. "Her horse stepped in a hole, and she fell. Mom has a head injury. They were able to get help right away, but it was serious." Her voice thickened. "At first they didn't think she'd live, but she was tough enough to survive the surgery. Now…well, now they don't know if she'll ever wake up."

Maddie's hand closed on hers, the grip tight and imperative. "I have to see her. Please, Violet. She's my mother, and I've never seen her, and if she doesn't make it…" Her voice broke. "Can I go back with you?"

The enormity of the request hit Violet. If she took Maddie home with her, took her to see her mom, how on earth was she going to explain her?

"I know what you're thinking," Maddie said softly.

"That would bring this craziness out in the open for sure. But if I don't see her—"

"It's okay." She'd figure out the explanations somehow. "Why don't you pack a bag? You can follow me back to the ranch. You probably want your own car there."

Maddie jumped to her feet. "It won't take me a minute. Make yourself at home. Help yourself to the fridge. You must be tired and hungry."

She was, probably too tired to drive all that way, but she didn't really have a choice. She couldn't stay away any longer, relying on other people to run the ranch and look after her mother.

She scouted through the contents of the refrigerator, feeling a little odd to be helping herself. But that was what Maddie had said, and she did need something to keep her going. Maddie's tastes seemed to run to fresh fruit and cheeses, judging by her fridge.

Maddie was back in minutes, carrying a suitcase.

"That was fast." Violet was still eating the yogurt she'd found on the top shelf. It was lemon, her favorite, making her wonder if she and Maddie had similar tastes.

"I used to travel for my job, so I got pretty good at packing in a hurry." Maddie glanced toward the laptop on a corner desk. "I'll email Dad, just telling him it's important that he contact me right away. And I guess I'd better email Landon as well. I'll take my laptop with me so I can stay in touch."

Violet waited, trying not to look interested in what Maddie was typing. It was obvious that Maddie still cared about Landon, or she wouldn't be letting him know what was going on. Probably their broken engagement would be mended eventually. Someday she might be taking a part in her sister's wedding.

Violet was unpleasantly surprised to discover that she felt an odd twinge at the thought of Landon and Maddie getting married.

Violet and Maddie drove straight through to the ranch, stopping only to eat once. Maddie wanted to go right to the hospital, but once Violet had found there was no change in her mother's condition, she knew she had to get a decent night's sleep.

Relief flooded through her when she finally drove through the imposing stone gateway to the Colby Ranch. The three entwined *C*s at the top of the gate's arch seemed to welcome her home.

She pulled up in front of the sprawling brick-and-stone structure that was the main house, aware of Maddie's car behind her. When she still hadn't been able to reach Jack, Violet had phoned Lupita, the housekeeper, cook and second mother who kept the house running like a well-oiled machine, telling her to prepare the guest room.

Violet hadn't said whom she was bringing. The effort to explain over the phone had seemed way too much to her. Thank goodness Lupita, with her usual gentle wisdom probably sensing that questions weren't welcome, hadn't asked.

"This is it," she said as Maddie joined her on the wide front porch.

"It's huge." Maddie glanced around. Mature trees and a wrought-iron fence surrounded the ranch house, with grasslands and rolling hills stretching out in the distance. Behind the house, outbuildings dotted the property: barns, greenhouses, storage sheds, the cottages occupied by Lupita and her husband and that of foreman Ty Garland, and the bunkhouses. Colby Ranch was a busy place, so busy that it was sometimes hard to find a moment alone.

"I'll show you around tomorrow." She picked up Maddie's suitcase. "Right now let's get you settled and see what Lupita's fixed for supper."

"I think you're the one who needs to settle." Maddie linked her arm with Violet's. "You've been running at full speed since the accident, haven't you?"

"Pretty much." Violet pushed open the heavy oak front door and led Maddie into the center hallway. The pale tiled floor gleamed in the fading light, and there were fresh flowers, as always, on the massive oak credenza against the side wall. The staircase swept upward to the second floor in front of them. Through the glass doors at the far back end of the hallway, solar lights cast a glow over the courtyard.

"I'm home," Violet called as she always did when she entered the house. "Lupita, are you here?"

"*Si, si,* I'm coming." Lupita emerged from the kitchen at the back of the house, wiping her hands on the apron she'd wrapped around her plump waist. "It's about time you were getting home." The tone was gently scolding and filled with love. "You must—"

Another step, and she had seen Maddie. She stopped, black eyes wide and questioning, and Violet thought she murmured a prayer in Spanish.

"Lupita, this is Maddie Wallace." What else could she say?

Fortunately, there seemed no need. Lupita rushed to them and wrapped her arms around Violet, enfolding her in a loving hug. "So," she said softly. "I was right. There was a sister."

Violet pulled back, thoughts tumbling. "You knew I had a sister? Lupita, how could you keep this from me?"

"No, no, I didn't know." She patted Violet's cheek. "Don't fuss, little one. Once when your mother was sick, she rambled. She spoke of her baby girls, calling for them. So I thought there had been another. But I never thought to see her, not in this life."

"You thought I had a sister that died," Violet said, suddenly understanding.

Lupita nodded, turning to Maddie. She walked to her, taking Maddie's face in her hands and studying her for a long moment. "You are home," she said. "I am glad."

She turned, reverting to briskness probably to hide her emotion. "You must be starved, both of you. Wash up and get to the table. The food will be there by the time you are." She bustled back to the kitchen, wiping her eyes with the tea towel she held.

Maddie looked a little dazed. She put her hand to her cheek. "I didn't expect that kind of a welcome."

"Lupita's been with us since we were kids. As far as she's concerned, we're her kids, too."

"Do you think she knows anything more about us?" Maddie set her bag on the credenza. "Wouldn't she have tried to find out more from your mother, if it happened as she said?"

Violet shrugged. "Lupita always tells the truth, but sometimes she leaves things out. For our own good, she'd say. If she knows anything else about us, I'll get it out of her eventually."

By the time Lupita had stuffed them full of her special chicken enchiladas with black beans and rice, topped off with a scrumptious peach tart, Violet was feeling vaguely human again. She leaned back in her seat. Lupita always said that trouble and an empty belly were bad companions, and this time she seemed to be right. But even though she felt better, Violet was still too conscious of the empty chairs at the table.

Maddie, who'd demolished her piece of peach tart, was staring at the framed portrait on the dining room wall. "Who is that? Another relative?"

"That's Uncle James." Violet smiled at the pictured face, the weathering and wisdom of years showing in skin like crinkled leather. Kind blue eyes seemed to smile back at her. "James Crawford. He wasn't actually a relative, but that's what Jack and I always called him."

"Who was he, then?" Maddie eyed the portrait curiously.

"He owned this place. Mom came here as housekeeper when I was three and Jack was five. He took us in and made us feel as if this was our home, too. He didn't have any family, and soon he was treating us like kin. I really don't even remember a time when he wasn't part of our lives."

"So he left this place to you?" Maddie sounded faintly disapproving.

"Not just like that," Violet responded, sensitive to criticism on that subject. Other people had talked about that, she felt sure, but Belle had ignored them. "Over the years, Uncle James needed more and more help. Mom took over the bookkeeping, and as his health failed, she took on increased responsibility for every aspect of the ranch. Eventually Uncle James insisted on making her a partner, and when he died, we found that he'd left the rest to her."

Violet's confidence faltered. Had Uncle James known

the truth about them? Had he known about their twins? She suspected that even if he'd been privy to her mom's secret, he never would have told. Honor was everything to a man like Uncle James.

Violet pushed her chair back as one of Lupita's numerous nieces came in with a tray, the young woman's gaze wide-eyed and curious when she looked at Maddie. Word of this event would be all over the ranch in minutes and all over the county in a day. Violet was resigned to that happening.

"Let's take our tea into the living room so we're out of Lupita's way." She stifled a yawn. "I hope…"

Her voice faded as she heard boots coming from the direction of the kitchen. She rose from her chair. If only it was Jack…

But it wasn't. Ty Garland, the ranch foreman, paused in the hallway, hat in his hands.

"Sorry to bother you, Violet." He seemed to be making an effort not to look at Maddie, which meant he'd already heard about her arrival. "I was hoping you knew when Jack would be around. There's a couple of things I need to talk to him about."

"I wish I knew the answer to that, too, Ty." She glanced toward Maddie to find her looking at Ty appreciatively. Maybe Maddie was practically engaged, but she certainly noticed the tall, dark and handsome Ty.

Sighing, Violet decided she'd better make introductions.

"Maddie, this is Ty Garland, our foreman. Ty, this is my…this is Maddie Wallace."

Ty nodded, falling silent as he did so readily, especially with strangers. And Maddie, with her elegant looks and bearing, was definitely different from anyone around here.

"It's nice to meet you, Ty." Maddie smiled up at him from where she sat. "It sounds as if you have a lot of responsibility around here."

"Yes, ma'am." Ty eyed Maddie warily, making Violet wonder what he was thinking.

Maybe she'd better get this conversation back to business. "What was it you needed to talk to Jack about?"

Ty turned to her with something like relief in his dark eyes. "Well, for starters, we had planned to go to the livestock auction on Saturday, and I was just wondering if that was still on."

She tried to think what day it was, but her brain seemed to have stopped working. Still, she could trust Ty to know what to do.

"I don't know that you can count on Jack, with Mom still in the hospital. Why don't you just use your own judgment, okay?"

"Sure thing. I'll go and see if they have what we're looking for." He let his gaze stray toward Maddie. "Night, ma'am. Violet." He strode toward the back door, settling his Stetson squarely on his head.

"Nice to have such a good-looking cowboy around," Maddie said once the door had closed. "Is there anything special between you two?"

"Definitely not." Violet shook her head. "Ty's a great guy, but like everyone else around here, he treats me as if I'm about twelve or so. Maybe younger. He seemed to appreciate you, though."

"Please." Maddie shuddered. "I'm through with men. One broken engagement was enough for me." She picked up her cup and started toward the living room.

The front door burst open. Jack came through, as brash as ever. He tossed his hat in the direction of the hook on the credenza, catching it perfectly. He caught sight of Maddie first, as she stood directly under the hall light.

"Hey, Vi, where did you disappear to—" He stopped. Blinked. And looked past Maddie to where Violet stood. And looked again. "What is going on here?"

"Jack, this is Maddie Wallace." Violet went and stood next to Maddie, letting him compare them one against the other. "My twin."

Jack stared. With a pang, she noted the lines of strain around his light brown eyes and bracketing his firm mouth. He was taking his mom's injury hard, blaming himself, and she feared this discovery was going to make things worse.

He shook his head. "It can't be."

"It is." Violet took his arm, feeling the muscles tense under her hand. "Come into the living room and sit down. We'll talk about it."

Unwillingly, he nodded and let himself be led to the overstuffed leather couch. He slid down into it, looking almost boneless. But the tension was still there, in the lines on his face and the tightness of his jaw.

"Okay, I'm not going to argue the point of whether or not you're twins." He stared at Maddie. "I can't. This isn't just a resemblance…you're identical. How did you find her?"

"Maddie," Maddie said, her voice tart. "My name is Maddie, and like it or not, I'm your sister."

Jack looked taken aback for an instant. Then he managed a strained smile. "Sorry, Maddie." He shook his head, looking as if he'd taken a fall. "What does this mean? Vi, if you have a twin we've never even heard of, then maybe nothing we think we know about our past is true. What if I'm not really your brother?"

"You are. I know that." Violet clasped his hand, her heart hurting for him. "Maddie, show him the photo."

Maddie got out the framed picture she'd brought along and handed it to Jack. He stared for a long moment at the face that was the image of his own.

He put the picture down carefully, lunged from the couch, and strode across the room, looking as if it weren't big enough for him. Violet recognized the signs. When he was hurting, Jack had to be alone. Usually he'd take one of the horses and ride until they were both exhausted.

"Jack…" Her voice was filled with sympathy, but she didn't know how to make him feel any better about this. He'd already been struggling with guilt over the quarrel he'd had with his mom right before her accident.

He held up his hand, obviously not wanting to hear more. "Don't, Vi. I don't get it. How could Mom keep this from us all these years? I feel like my whole life is a lie. Is my name even Jack Colby?"

She didn't have an answer for that. It might be Wallace, she supposed, but they didn't even know if that was right.

"I don't know," she said carefully. "Maddie's father is away. She's trying to get in touch with him. When she does, maybe he'll have some answers."

Jack spun, facing them, his hands clenched into fists. "So you expect me just to wait while some stranger decides to tell me about my own life? I can't do that. I've got to—" He stopped, shook his head. "I've got to get away until I can clear my head."

"Jack, don't." *Don't go away and leave me to face this alone*—that was what she wanted to say.

"I have to." He was already headed for the door. "I'll take my cell phone. Call me if there's any change in Mom's condition." He yanked open the door and charged out. The door slammed behind him.

Violet fought down a sob. Her family really was breaking apart, and her efforts to smooth the waters had only made things much, much worse.

Chapter 3

Landon's mind was still on that encounter with Maddie's unexpected twin when he arrived at his office the next morning. The long arm of coincidence had really extended itself when he'd walked into that coffee shop yesterday.

Or maybe it wasn't coincidence at all. He stopped in there often, sometimes with Maddie. Maddie was there even more often alone, living as close as she did. Still, he couldn't quite see why Violet would take such a chancy way of approaching Maddie, even if she had known of her existence.

Despite his caution, he had trouble imagining that Violet was anything other than she seemed. She'd been genuinely shaken at the sight of Maddie. He didn't think she could have faked that.

Odd, that Violet could be so like Maddie in appearance and yet so different in other ways. Violet gave the impression of a woman with a warm heart combined with a strong will. Sometimes that could be a dangerous mixture.

He pushed open the door to the office, which was discreetly lettered Derringer Investments. The firm had little need of obvious advertising. Their clients came to them by word of mouth—by far the best way, as far as he was concerned.

"Good morning, Landon." Mercy Godwin, his secretary, receptionist, assistant and good right arm, was at her desk ahead of him as always. Mercy's row of African violets on the windowsill made an unexpected display of color in a place of business.

He'd agreed she could have one plant in the office, back in the mists of time when they were just starting out. Somehow the number of violets had multiplied along with their clients.

"Morning, Mercy." Sometimes he wondered how she timed her arrivals. No matter how early he walked in, she was already there.

"Your schedule is fairly clear today." She frowned at her computer screen, as if daring it to come up with an event she didn't remember. "Dave Watson called. He'll be here in about fifteen minutes."

Mercy didn't ask why the private investigator was coming in. Never displaying curiosity was one of her admirable traits. In her fifties, plump and graying, she was a childless widow whose life revolved around her work. He wasn't sure what he'd do when she decided to retire.

He'd actually contacted the private investigator before he'd left the coffee shop yesterday. The sooner his doubts about Violet Colby were put to rest, the better. Dave would start with the whole question of whether or not the twins were born in Fort Worth. Apparently he had results already.

"That'll give me time for a quick look at my email first. I took a break from business yesterday."

Taking a break in this case had meant driving out to the ranch where he boarded his horse and setting off on a long ride, followed by a late swim and an early bed, with all connection to the outside world strictly forbidden. He'd adopted the weekly ritual when he'd realized that if he didn't take a breather from the tyranny of constant communication on a regular basis, he'd burn out before he was forty.

Nodding to Mercy, Landon went on into his office. Simple and understated, it suited him. His business was almost entirely electronic, and costly decorating was unnecessary, besides not to his taste. Sinking down in his leather desk chair, he scanned quickly through his email, mentally classifying the messages in order of importance as he did so, until one name stopped him cold.

Maddie. According to the time, she must have sent the message about an hour after they'd parted the day before. He clicked on it.

I've decided to go to Grasslands with Violet for a visit. Thanks for finding her. I can take it from here.

Please forget about proposing. We both know that what we feel for each other isn't enough to build a marriage on. You only proposed out of some notion that you need to take care of me, but you don't. I'll take care of myself.

I'll call you when I get back. In the meantime, I think it's better if we're not in touch.

Landon sat frowning at the message for a long moment. Maddie had gone off with a woman she'd known for all of an hour, and she didn't say when she was coming back. He didn't like this one bit.

Maybe Maddie was right, and his relationship with her wasn't a good basis for marriage. He'd promised her brother Grayson he'd look after Maddie when all the Wallace men were away, so he'd been trying to do that. The proposal had sprung out of sympathy and caring at a time when she'd been distraught, crying on his shoulder over the loss of her promising job and the lack of support she felt from her family. Somehow he'd thought proposing would make things better. It hadn't. That was one time when his sense of responsibility had led him astray.

Frustration tightened his nerves. Never mind his reasons. He still cared about Maddie's welfare, and she needed someone to watch over her.

She'd probably dismiss that as an old-fashioned ideal, but he'd felt that way since he'd started hanging around with her brother when they were in their teens.

The Wallace kids had lost their mother, their father was absent more than he was present, and in Landon's view, Grayson hadn't done enough to take care of his little sister.

Pain gripped Landon's heart at the thought, and he seemed to see his own sister Jessica smiling at him, looking at her big brother with so much love. His guilt, never far away, welled up. He hadn't taken care of his little sister. If he had, she'd never have gotten into a car with a drunken teenager, never been in the crash, never ended her life far too soon. Maybe that was why he felt such a need to look after Maddie.

A tap on the door interrupted the memories before they could cut too deeply. He looked up with a wave of relief. "Come in."

Dave Watson lounged into the room, deceptively casual in jeans, a T-shirt and a ball cap. He managed to look like a good old boy interested in nothing more than the Cowboys' prospects for the upcoming season. In actuality, Dave was as shrewd as they came and in Landon's opinion, the best investigator in Fort Worth.

"Hey, chief. How's it going?" Dave wandered across the room and slumped into the visitor's chair.

"You tell me." Landon studied the private investigator's face, but Dave didn't give anything away. "Do you have results already?"

Dave shrugged. "It wasn't exactly a challenge. No twin girls were born in any hospital in Fort Worth on the date you gave me."

"You're sure?"

The P.I. just looked at him in response. It had been a silly question. Dave wouldn't report unless he was sure.

So that left the question hanging. Had Violet been lying, or just ill-informed? Either way, Landon didn't like it.

He came to a quick decision. "I want you to expand the search. Same date, but take in Dallas and the surrounding area, okay?"

"Will do." Dave raised an eyebrow. "Is that all?"

"For now. I might need more later." Landon shoved back from his desk in a decisive movement. "I'm going out of town for a few days. Call my private cell number if you find anything."

Maddie might think she'd ended things between them, but she couldn't end his sense of responsibility for her. Regardless of whether Violet was on the up-and-up or not, he had a bad feeling about this situation. Either way, Maddie could end up hurt. It was his job to see that didn't happen.

"Was this the best facility to deal with her care?" Maddie asked the question as they walked through the hospital lobby in Amarillo the next morning.

"It has the highest-rated trauma center in this part of the state," Violet said. "Luckily, Jack saw the accident, so he called for help on his cell phone right away. Doc Garth was there in minutes." She'd be forever grateful for that. Without Doc's prompt care, her mom might not have made it as far as Amarillo. "As soon as the doctor realized how bad it was, he had her airlifted here."

Maddie nodded. "I didn't mean my question to sound critical. Really. I've spent most of my life in the city. The ranch seems so remote in comparison."

"I guess so. It's just home to me." She smiled as they got on the elevator. "You can't imagine how stressed I was driving in Fort Worth traffic. I can drive from the ranch clear into Grasslands without passing another car."

An older woman got into the elevator after them, doing a double take as she looked from one to the other. Violet wasn't sure how to respond. So this was a taste of what it was like, having an identical twin.

If they'd been raised together, would they have dressed alike? Would they have had their own private jokes and secrets that no one else was allowed to know? Sorrow filled her. It was strange, to be mourning the loss of something she'd never had. Did Maddie feel the same, or didn't it bother her?

The elevator doors swished open, and Violet's stomach lurched. The hospital was nice enough, as hospitals went. She led the way down the long corridor toward her mom's room. Bright, cheerful, with none of the antiseptic odors she remembered from a brief hospital stay when she was six.

Despite that, Violet's spirits were dampened each time she came through the doors. No matter how cheerful she tried to be, just in case her mom was actually hearing her, fear hung on her like a wet, smothering blanket on a hot Texas day.

"It's the next room down," she said, and tried to pin a smile on her face when she saw the apprehension in Maddie's eyes. "It'll be all right. One of the nurses told me that coma patients can sometimes hear what's said, even if they can't respond. So she may know you're here. Know we've found each other."

"I hope so," Maddie murmured, and Violet had the sense that she was praying silently. Whispering a prayer of her own, Violet squeezed her hand and walked with her into the room.

Sunlight streamed across the high hospital bed, and machines whirred softly. Belle was motionless, lying much as she had been when Violet left yesterday. A lifetime ago, it now seemed.

"Mom?" Violet covered her mother's hand with hers. How odd it was to see Belle's hands so still—she was always in motion, and even in conversation her hands would be moving.

No response, and Violet fought to keep that fact from sending her into a downward spiral.

"One day when I say that, you're going to open your

eyes and ask what I want." She kept her voice light and gestured for Maddie to come closer.

Maddie's face had paled, and tears glistened in her eyes. She seemed to be searching Belle's features, maybe looking for herself there.

"I brought someone to see you, Mom. You're going to be so surprised. It's Maddie. Can you believe that? We've found each other, after all this time." She gave her sister an encouraging smile. "Say something to her."

"I'm so glad to see you." Maddie's voice wobbled a little on the words. "I didn't know. I never guessed that my real mother was out there someplace. Not until I walked into a coffee shop in Fort Worth and saw Violet sitting there."

Violet stroked her mother's hand, willing her to hear. "We look exactly alike, Mom. Did you realize we would? I suppose we must have, even when we were babies."

The enormity of the whole crazy situation struck Violet, and suddenly she couldn't control her voice. She couldn't keep pretending that this deception was okay.

"Why, Momma?" The words came out in a choked cry, in the voice of her childhood. "Why didn't you tell us?"

But her mother didn't answer. Maybe she never would. For the first time in Violet's life she faced a problem without her mother to advise her. The loneliness seemed to sink into her very soul.

And then she felt an arm go around her. Maddie drew her close, her face wet with tears for the mother she'd never known. As they held each other and wept, Violet knew she'd been wrong. She wasn't alone.

It was late afternoon when Violet finally got to Grasslands that day. She wouldn't have bothered going to town after driving back from Amarillo, but she was responsible for the Colby Ranch Farm Stand, and she had to be sure things were going smoothly.

Maddie had opted to stay at the ranch rather than come into town with her, and Violet couldn't help feeling a bit of relief at that decision. The two of them had attracted enough second glances in Amarillo, where no one knew them. Violet could just imagine the reaction in Grasslands, where every single soul could name her. She'd have to figure out how she was going to break the news to friends and neighbors, but at the moment, it was beyond her.

She hurried into the cinder block building on Main Street that housed the farm stand. The stand had grown and changed a lot since it had been nothing more than a stall along the side of the road. She liked to think she'd had something to do with that growth.

Jack had never shown an interest in the produce fields and the pecan grove, and his only reaction when assigned to weeding or planting duty had been a prolonged moan. Belle had never listened to that, and when they were growing up, they'd both learned how to do every chore that was suitable to their ages. It had been good training for the future.

Violet had never understood her brother's distaste for farming. From the time she could trot after Ricardo, Lupita's husband, she'd gone up and down the rows with him, learning where the soybeans grew best and which types of tomatoes to plant. She'd never been happier than when she had her hands in the dirt.

She took a glance at her short, unpolished nails as she pushed the door open and grimaced. That was certainly one way folks could tell her apart from Maddie, whose perfectly shaped nails were a deep shade of pink.

Violet stepped into the large, cool room that formed the main part of the building, with storage facilities and refrigerated lockers in the back room. This place was home to her, just as the ranch was. It might not be fancy, but it was the product of her hard work and vision.

"Violet!" The exclamation came before she was a step past the door, and Harriet Porter came rushing to give her a vigorous hug.

Harriet, tall and raw-boned, admitted to being over sixty, and most folks thought she was pretty far over, but age didn't slow her down a bit. She could manage the farm stand with one hand tied behind her back.

"Honey, I'm so glad to see you. How's your momma? Is there any change?"

Violet had to blink back a tear at the warmth of the welcome. "Not much change, I'm afraid. The doctors say she's stable, but…" She lifted her hands in a helpless gesture, not knowing any more positive way to say it.

"I'm sure sorry about that." Harriet gripped her arm. "Belle's a fighter, though. Don't you forget. She'll come out of this, you'll see."

Violet could only nod, because her throat was too tight for anything else.

"Mind, now." Harriet shook her finger at Violet. "Don't you let it get you down, y'hear? We grow strong women in Texas, and your momma is one of the best. I reckon the good Lord knows how much we need her here."

Not as much as Violet needed her, but that went without saying.

"How have things been going? I'm sorry I haven't checked in with you more often."

"Honey, don't you think a thing about it. You know I can deal with the stand for as long as you need. And the kids are doing fine."

Harriet had a revolving procession of local teenagers who worked for the stand, carting produce and stocking bins. Harriet always referred to them collectively as "the kids," but she took an interest in each one. They'd get the rough side of her tongue in a hurry if they didn't pull their weight, but she was a staunch defender when any of them needed help.

"That's good." Violet was already sending an assessing gaze around the interior. It was nothing fancy, that was for sure, with concrete floors and cinder-block walls, the produce stacked on long tables or in bins. It was spotless as ever, but Violet noticed a few empty spaces on the tables. "No sweet corn?"

Harriet's gaze grew dark. "That Tom Sandy tried to palm off corn that must have been picked two days ago on us. I told him what he could do with his stale corn. Why, the sugar would all be turned to starch in it by then. I'd rather do without than put that out. Our customers expect the best."

True, but it really would be better if Harriet didn't antagonize one of their suppliers. That had been a change Violet had implemented, buying from some other growers instead of selling only their own produce. It gave them a wider assortment of stock, but managing those growers was time-consuming, and it was a job only Violet could do.

"I'll talk to Tom," she promised. "Is anybody else giving you any problems?"

Harriet shook her head. "We sure could use more tomatoes, though. Folks keep asking, but with the weather, there just aren't enough to be had."

The weather was a constant worry. This year they'd had too much rain in the early spring, making it hard to get the plants in, followed by a prolonged hot, dry spell that had turned the soil to stone. The plants were looking better now, though, so they'd have plenty before long, she hoped.

"I'll make some calls," she said. "Try and find somebody who has them ripening now."

"Just do it when you have time." Harriet patted her arm. "I know it's rough, running back and forth to Amarillo every day. At least you have Jack to help you."

Violet managed a noncommittal smile at the reference to her brother. If he had any sense, Jack would get himself back here before folks noticed he was gone.

She was saved the task of responding by the approach of Jeb Miller. Despite Jeb's youth, he'd won the hearts of most of Grasslands in the five years he'd been pastor at Grasslands Christian Church.

"Violet." He grasped her hands in both of his. "I'm so glad to see you. I must have missed you when I went to the hospital yesterday."

"Yes, I... I had some things I had to take care of." Thankfully, Harriet had retired from earshot, probably thinking to give Violet some private time with her pastor, or she'd have been asking where Violet had been.

"I was sorry to see there was no change." With his red hair, freckles and youthful grin Jeb might not be the classic image of a minister, but he had a warm voice that matched his warm heart. "I prayed with Belle, and I trust she was able to hear and be comforted."

"Thanks, Jeb. I don't know what we'd do without you."

He shrugged, as if to dismiss the need for thanks. "Folks have been wanting to bring food out to the house, but Lupita keeps saying that's not needed. I hope you know your whole church family stands ready to do anything that will help. The prayer chain is going strong."

"I'll let you know if anything else comes up." It was on the tip of her tongue to confide in Jeb about Maddie, but she restrained herself. That was a conversation better held in the privacy of the reverend's office.

"Now, I'm sure you haven't had a minute to think about Teen Scene staffing for this weekend—"

"Oh, my goodness." She stared at Jeb in consternation. "I'm afraid it went clear out of my mind."

Surprising, since the Teen Scene program was her baby. An effort to provide Grasslands' teens with a wholesome alternative for entertainment on Friday and Saturday nights, it made use of the church gym and adjoining lounges for activities. One of her challenges was to keep it staffed with adults she could count on.

"I'm sorry I forgot about it. I'll get right on it—"

"No need for that." Jeb grinned, shoving his horn-rimmed glasses up on his nose. "It's already done. And don't you think about coming back until life settles down a bit. We'll muddle along, I promise."

"I'm so grateful." There were the tears again, threatening to break loose. "It won't be long."

"Well, don't worry about it." He glanced over her shoulder toward the racks. "I need to pick up a few things, and then I'd best drop in the office again and catch up on paperwork. I'll be interviewing people for the secretary's position tomorrow, and it scares me half to death."

"You'll do fine. Anyway, you know what you'd tell anybody else, God has the right person picked out already. You just have to identify her."

As Jeb grinned and moved away, Violet took another look around. Everything seemed to be going all right, other than the stocking problem. And she could make those calls from home, or in person, when it came to Tom Sandy. Waving to Harriet, she headed toward the door.

Outside, she paused for a moment to adjust her hat to shield her eyes from the sun, whose rays still shimmered from the concrete. She took a step toward her car and stopped.

She must have started to hallucinate. Either that or it really was Landon Derringer, Maddie's almost-fiancé, walking down Grasslands' main street, coming straight toward her.

Chapter 4

Violet stiffened, remembering Maddie's short description of her relationship with Landon. What was Maddie going to think when she realized the determined CEO had followed her here? There surely couldn't be another reason why a man like Landon was in a place like Grasslands.

"Violet." He touched his hat brim in greeting. "We seem to make a habit of running into each other."

"In very unlikely places." She managed a smile. "You don't seem to have any difficulty today in telling us apart."

A faint smile touched his wintry green eyes. "I should have realized you weren't Maddie at first sight yesterday. The hair is different, of course, and the clothes."

"Of course." She was a country bumpkin, in other words, in comparison to her glamorous twin.

He lifted an eyebrow. "That wasn't an insult, Violet." He seemed to have no trouble in divining her thoughts. "I like the way you look…sort of casual and windblown."

"More like hot and dusty at the moment," she said briskly. What did she care what Landon thought of her appearance? "What brings you to Grasslands?"

"I'd think that would be fairly obvious," he said.

Clearly the man enjoyed sparring with her, but she wasn't falling for it. Especially since she had much more important things on her mind. Odd, how much more confident she felt facing him today than she had yesterday. She was on her own turf now, and he was the outsider here.

"Does Maddie know you're coming?"

A faint frown line creased his forehead. "Not exactly. I was going to call her, but then I decided it was better just to come." He nodded toward the store. "When I saw the sign with the Colby name, I figured this was a good place to ask for directions. Does your family run this place?"

"Not exactly," she said, echoing his words. "The family owns it. I run it."

"You?" His surprise wasn't very flattering.

She tilted her head back to look up at him. "You know, Landon, I'm beginning to understand why Maddie broke up with you. If you're hoping to win her back, you might want to try being a little less condescending."

She had the pleasure of seeing Landon speechless for a moment. Then he grinned appreciatively.

"Score one for you. I apologize, Ms. Colby. I didn't mean to imply anything about your capabilities by my remark. Will you forgive me?"

She felt herself weakening. He certainly got a lot

of mileage out of that smile, and he probably knew it. "You're forgiven. Just don't make the same mistake with Maddie."

"I'll try not to." He studied the sign over the door. "I don't think you actually mentioned the Colby Ranch yesterday. Is it a truck farming operation?"

"Don't let my brother hear you say that. As far as he's concerned, it's a cattle ranch, and the truck farming is just a sideline."

"It must be quite a sideline to warrant a store that size." Landon nodded to the building, coming a step closer to her in the process.

"We do all right." She shouldn't let herself be pleased that he sounded impressed.

She was beginning to feel a bit confused. Landon surely was here to see Maddie, wasn't he? So why was he spending all this time chatting with her? He was leaning against the building as if he had all the time in the world.

"Something wrong?" he asked, apparently a little uncomfortable at her scrutiny.

"Not wrong, exactly. Just wondering why you're here. What do you want in Grasslands?"

"Did you expect me to let Maddie just wander off with her newly discovered twin and do nothing about it?"

Those green eyes of his could have a dangerous glint in them, she discovered.

"According to Maddie, you two are not engaged any longer. I'm not sure that her actions are any of your concern."

If he'd seemed relaxed a moment ago, all that was

gone now. He frowned at her, and tension seemed to vibrate in the air between them.

"I've known Maddie since she was still a kid," he said. "Even if we aren't engaged any longer, that doesn't mean I can turn off caring what happens to her."

He sounded honest enough, and Violet found herself warming to him. Still, she owed him honesty in return, and she didn't think he'd want to hear it.

"If you really care about Maddie, I admire that," she said. "But I'm not going to do anything to upset her, either. She's had a hard enough day, seeing her mother for the first time in a hospital bed. I won't do anything to hurt her, like showing up with you in tow if she doesn't want to see you."

"You're feeling a bond already, aren't you? That twin thing people talk about."

She couldn't tell if he approved or disapproved. "We're still just getting used to the idea," she said shortly. "The point is that unless there's some good reason for your being here, I don't think you should pursue Maddie if she doesn't want to see you."

His eyebrows had lifted a bit at her tone. Maybe he was surprised at her quick partisanship, but Maddie was her sister, after all.

"What about if I have results from the hospitals in Fort Worth? Don't you think she'd want to hear about that?"

"You've found something out already?" She could feel the energy bubbling in her, ready to burst out. "How did you do that? I thought those records would be sealed. I wasn't sure the hospital records office would even let me look."

"It helps to have a good private investigator on the

payroll," Landon said. "I put him on the job right after we spoke yesterday."

"Did he…is there…?" She was almost afraid to ask, for fear of being disappointed. She shook her head. "I shouldn't ask. You want to tell Maddie first, of course."

Landon must have been able to read her emotions pretty easily. His face gentled with sympathy, and he reached out to touch her hand. "I wouldn't tease you with information like that, Violet. I don't play games."

Her skin seemed to be warming where he touched, and she found it disconcerting. She moved back slightly, putting a bit more space between them. "What did you learn, then?"

"The investigator found out that no identical twin girls were born at any hospital in Fort Worth on your birthday."

"Oh." She felt herself sag with the disappointment of it. "I guess there aren't going to be any easy answers, then."

"I'm not giving up that quickly." Determination filled Landon's voice. "I've told him to check Dallas hospitals, too, and extend the search to surrounding communities. It's possible that your mother mentioned Fort Worth but it's actually one of the outlying areas. And Maddie—" He stopped as an idea seemed to hit him. "That was dumb. I never thought to ask Maddie if she knows what hospital she was born in. How stupid could I be? I guess I was so bowled over by seeing you that my brain stopped working."

"I hadn't thought of that, either." She rubbed the nape of her neck, trying to ease the tension. "Honestly, if we're going to figure this out, we're going to have to think it through. So far I've just been reacting."

"There's a lot more emotion involved for you than there is for me," he said. "But you're right. We ought to talk it over and work out the options to investigate."

She drew back a little more. "I wasn't actually including you in that *we,* Landon."

"Right." He sounded rueful. "You were talking about yourself and Maddie. But I'm not going to stop trying to help, so doesn't it make sense to pool our resources and work together?"

"It makes sense when you put it that way, but I'm not sure Maddie will agree."

"Well, suppose you take me to her, and we'll ask her?" There was that smile again. It almost broke through her common sense. Almost, but not quite.

"I'll take you out to the ranch," she said slowly. "But only if I have your word that you'll leave without argument if Maddie says so."

"Agreed," he said promptly. "My car is right across the street. I'll follow you."

Violet nodded, taking out her car keys. It made sense. She just hoped she was doing the right thing.

Landon hopped into his car and pulled onto the road behind Violet, not wanting to give her time to change her mind. But she didn't seem to be having second thoughts, and soon they were out of Grasslands and on their way to the ranch.

Not that it took very long to get through Grasslands. The town was about what he had expected: a small community with shops and businesses catering to the residents of the surrounding farms and ranches.

Acres of grassland stretched out on either side of the two-lane blacktop road, with low hills in the distance under the huge blue bowl of the sky. The few houses were built well back from the road. Pretty country, the sort of place he'd think would bore Maddie stiff in a day or two at most, if not for the novelty of having discovered her twin.

Thanks to him. What would have happened if he hadn't walked into the coffee shop at just that time? Or if, having seen Violet, he'd gone quietly on his way and never mentioned it to Maddie?

He couldn't have, naturally. But the results were, in a sense, his responsibility, so he couldn't just walk away from the situation.

Each minute he spent with Violet went a long way toward dispelling whatever suspicion he'd entertained as to her motives. Too bad it also had such an unsettling effect on her emotions. Still, even if she were being completely honest, somebody hadn't been. Somebody had split up those children, and finding out who and why might lead to heartache.

What if Maddie ended up devastated by what she learned? It would be his fault for bringing Maddie and Violet together in the first place.

Ahead of him, Violet's right-turn signal blinked. She slowed down and turned on a gravel road that led through impressive stone gates and under an arched sign with three intertwined *C*s. This, obviously, was the Colby place.

The gravel road stretched, straight as a ruler, between barbed-wire fences along pastureland on either side. It ran about half a mile, he'd guess, before ending at a two-story brick house. Good-sized, the house had a porch across the front and what seemed to be wings going back on two sides. Outbuildings scattered behind it like so many Monopoly houses dropped on the land.

Violet pulled up on the gravel sweep in front of the house, and he drew his car in behind her. A fine layer of dust from the lane settled immediately on his hood.

He got out, wondering if Violet had taken the lane at that pace deliberately to mar the glossy finish of his car. But she was waiting for him, and she didn't seem antagonistic. In fact, she looked at him with a question in her eyes.

"I was wondering—I assume you know Maddie's father and her brothers?"

He nodded, jingling his keys in his hand for a moment before slipping them into his pocket. "I can't say I know her father very well, but I do know him. A doctor, busy as most doctors are, I guess. Grayson and I are the same age, and we've always been good friends. Carter was just a kid then, tagging along, but he's grown into quite a guy."

A question in those chocolate-colored eyes deepened. "Have you talked to either Grayson or Carter about all this?"

He shook his head. "Grayson's a cop, and he's on an undercover operation right now, which makes it virtually impossible to contact him. And Carter's in the military overseas. Hasn't Maddie talked about them?"

"Not much." She went through a wrought-iron gate, started toward the porch and he fell into step with her. "I'm not just being curious. Maddie sent an email to her dad, but he hasn't answered. She doesn't seem interested in contacting her brothers, but I thought maybe they should know about all this."

He frowned, thinking about it. "Maybe she feels she

should tell her father first. And since neither Grayson nor Carter can do anything about it right now, maybe she's right about that."

"She really is alone, then," Violet said softly, her eyes shadowed.

"Are you worried about Maddie?" he asked, trying to get a sense of what was behind the comment.

"I can't help but feel responsible." She paused, her hand on the handle of the heavy-looking front door. "If I hadn't started off half-cocked looking for my father, I wouldn't have found Maddie. So if we end up getting hurt by what we find, I'm responsible."

He couldn't quite suppress a smile. "Oddly enough, I was just saying that very thing to myself—that I brought you two together, so if it goes badly, it's my fault."

She smiled back, somewhat ruefully. "Guilt trips. Maybe we should stop overanalyzing things. My mother always says if God puts you in a situation, it's for a reason."

"It sounds like your mother is a wise woman. Suppose we move ahead and find out what that reason is?"

Violet nodded, opened the door, and led the way into the Colby house.

The front door opened into a wide hallway, floored in a white tile that gave it a spacious look. The center hall led back to glass doors opening onto a patio area, where he could see pots and hanging baskets of flowers. He'd been right about the wings. They formed the sides of the patio, turning it into an enclosed courtyard, open at the back.

"This way." Violet nodded toward an archway on their left and led the way into a comfortable-looking living room.

Maddie was curled into an overstuffed chair in the corner, seeming relaxed and at ease, a photo album open on her lap. She glanced up, saw him, and all relaxation vanished. She swung her feet to the floor and stood, looking distinctly unwelcoming.

"Didn't you get my email, Landon?" Her tone was sharp. "I thought I was clear that I didn't want to see you just now."

Before he could speak, Violet crossed the room to her sister.

"Don't be mad that I brought him," she said softly. "I found him in Grasslands, looking for you."

"Well, he shouldn't have been." Maddie's eyes snapped, but at him, not her sister. "I told him there's no point in proposing again, and I'm not going to let him push me into getting married."

"I don't think he'd do that." Violet's voice was coaxing, but with a note of confidence that had been missing the day before. This was her place, of course, and that made a difference.

"Violet's right," he said, giving Maddie a rueful smile. "And you were right, too. We don't have a good basis for marriage, and I'll never mention it again, I promise."

He felt a sense of relief that the words were out in the open. Maddie had always been like a little sister to him, and he loved her that way, but marriage between them would have been a disaster.

Still, he'd made other promises—to Grayson, that he'd look after Maddie. To himself, that he'd never repeat the mistake he'd made with his own sister. He wasn't released from his need to take care of Maddie, especially when he was the one who'd inadvertently led her to this other family of hers.

"Landon has something to tell you," Violet said. "Something his private investigator found out. He promised that if you don't want to hear him, he'll leave right away."

Maddie looked at him for a long moment. Finally, she nodded. "All right, Landon. Sorry if I was rude."

"It's okay." He glanced around. "Mind if I sit down?"

"Please." As if reminded of her responsibility, Violet turned into a hostess, plumping the woven Indian design pillows on the couch and gesturing for him to sit. When he did, she perched on the sofa at the far end, as if careful not to align herself with him against her twin.

"I put my private investigator onto finding out about the hospitals," Landon said. "He has better access than you or I could hope to have. Unfortunately he came up empty. No Fort Worth hospital has a record of twin girl births on your birthdate."

Maddie looked a bit shaken at that news. She'd probably been praying for a quick answer to the puzzle. He swept on, telling her of the instructions he'd given Dave to widen the search.

"There are other things he can try," he concluded. "State birth records and newspaper files, for example. It would help if you know where your parents said you were born."

Maddie's forehead puckered. "Dad never spoke of it that I can remember. As for Mom—" She hesitated, maybe reflecting on the fact that the woman she'd called Mom hadn't actually been that. "Well, you know she died in a car accident when I was still small. I'm sure she told me I was born in Fort Worth, but I don't think I've ever known which hospital."

"Your birth certificate doesn't say?" He pursued the question, thinking he should have mentioned checking that first thing, not that she'd given him the opportunity.

Maddie looked stricken. "I can't believe I didn't think to get it out yesterday. But I don't remember that it mentions the hospital. The birth certificate certainly doesn't say anything about a twin."

He turned to Violet. "What about yours?"

"I haven't seen it in years. Not since I was filling out college applications, I don't think." Violet pushed a strand of hair behind her ear, tugging on it a bit as if that would help her think.

"Can you get it out now?" It would be interesting to see who Belle Colby had listed as the father of her child.

But Violet was already shaking her head. "It's in the safe deposit box at the bank, and Mom's the only one who has access. We're hitting a lot of dead ends, aren't we?"

"Your mother didn't put you or your brother on the access list?" His tone sharpened. That sounded as if Belle Colby had something to hide. Otherwise, she'd probably have changed that access, which was certainly the practical thing to do. How could she know that her daughter wouldn't need her birth certificate some time when she wasn't available?

"I guess it would have made sense to give one of us the ability to get in the box. She probably just didn't think of it." Violet didn't look convinced of her own words.

Maddie stirred restlessly. "There must be some way

to get around this. With Violet's mother—our mother—in a coma, the bank ought to be a little flexible."

"It's a question of state law, not the bank's choice," he replied. The subject had come up a time or two in the course of his business, when a client couldn't get access to financial documents because his or her partner was incapacitated. "You'd have to go to court and show need, as well as a reasonable expectation that the person holding the box would never be able to—"

He stopped, realizing that his passion for exactitude had led him onto dangerous ground. Violet looked distraught.

"Anyway, it's time-consuming and not very practical right now," he concluded hastily.

"I should talk to Grayson, I guess," Maddie said, with an air of wanting to get off the painful subject quickly. "The trouble is that he told me not to try and contact him until he finished up a job he's on." She turned to Violet. "Grayson's a detective, did I tell you that?"

Violet shook her head. "No, but Landon mentioned it."

"He did, did he?" Maddie's expression spoke volumes of what she thought about him talking to her sister about her.

Violet seemed to realize she'd said the wrong thing. She picked up a framed photo from the end table and handed it to him.

"That's my brother. Jack."

He studied the face and gave a low whistle under his breath. It was Grayson's face, staring out at him. "You didn't tell me your brothers were identical as well."

"We didn't realize it until I went to Maddie's condo," Violet said.

"Is your brother here?" Landon glanced around, half-expecting a replica of Grayson to walk through the arch.

"He's…he's away for a few days." Lines of strain deepened around Violet's eyes. "Anyway, I guess if you're going to help us, you need to know what we do." She glanced at Maddie and then looked quickly away. "I mean, you'll need to pass the information on to the investigator."

There were way too many crosscurrents of emotion loose in the room right now: Maddie's annoyance at him for butting in, which was at war with his need to keep her safe, the efforts of both women to adjust to knowing that everything they thought they knew about their parentage was a lie, whatever was going on between Violet and her brother, even his own feelings about Violet, ping-ponging between suspicion and…

And what? He'd almost said attraction, but that was ridiculous. He hardly knew her.

"I'll pay the private investigator," Maddie announced, a challenge in her voice.

"Fine," he said, avoiding a fight. "I'll have him send the bill—"

He cut off at a step from the hallway. The woman who paused in the archway was middle-aged, Hispanic, with graying hair and a gaze that went unerringly to Violet.

"You should have told me we have a guest," she scolded gently. "No matter…there is plenty. I will put on another plate."

"You don't need—" he began, and stopped when Violet went to put her arm around the woman.

"Lupita, this is Landon Derringer, a…friend of Maddie's. Landon, I'd like you to meet Lupita Ramirez. She runs the house. And us." Violet gave the woman a loving smile.

"It's a pleasure to meet you, Mrs. Ramirez." He crossed to the hallway. "I'm sure you have your hands full. I can get something to eat in town."

She looked offended. "It would be a sad day when the Colby Ranch table could not accommodate a guest. Supper in five minutes."

She hustled back into the hall, presumably toward the kitchen. Violet glanced up at him and smiled.

"You have to stay, you know, or we'll never hear the end of it."

"I guess we can't let that happen." He looked into her face, caught by the warmth that emanated from her, as welcome as a wood fire on a cold winter day.

Whoa, back up, he reminded himself. *You just broke up with her sister.* Oddly enough, that didn't seem to make a bit of difference.

Chapter 5

Violet pushed the pillow up against the headboard of her bed, trying to get more comfortable. Her vision blurred as she tried to concentrate on the laptop screen, and she'd begun to think she couldn't answer one more message of sympathy. So many people were worried about her mom, so many were praying for her recovery. Surely God was listening to all those petitions.

Sighing, she set the laptop aside and rubbed her eyes. Landon had left soon after supper, saying he'd be in touch after he'd spoken to the private investigator again. She'd tried to give him an opportunity to speak to Maddie without her hanging around, but her twin had been quite determined not to let that happen. Apparently, Maddie really was serious about not picking up their romance again.

The more Violet saw of Landon, the more she thought he was right for Maddie, but Maddie just didn't see it that way. Violet touched her wrist, reliving the warmth that had swept through her when Landon touched her. She hadn't had that instant response to a man in...well, ever. The guys she'd dated in college had been boys in comparison, and since she'd come home to run the produce business, romance hadn't been in the picture.

She smiled, thinking of Jack's reactions when she'd turned down one of his buddies who'd asked her out.

"You're too fussy," he'd said. "You want to end up alone? It's time you were getting serious about someone."

She'd just grinned. "You're two years older than I am, remember? I'll get serious when you do."

That had ended it, as far as Jack's marital advice was concerned. But Landon—

She cut that thought off before it could go anywhere. Landon was totally unsuitable for her in too many ways to count. She wasn't going to think about him anymore.

Rolling off the bed, Violet shoved her feet into slippers. She'd go downstairs and get a snack. Then maybe she'd have enough energy to answer a few more emails.

The upstairs was quiet. Maddie's door was closed, and no light shone beneath the crack. Her sister must have gone to sleep already.

Moving quietly, Violet went down the stairs. The light in the first-floor hall was always left on, and she found it reassuring as she tiptoed down. The house was empty without her mom, no matter how many people were here.

When she reached the hallway and headed back toward the kitchen, Violet realized she'd been wrong. The television was on in the den at the back of the house. Maddie was curled up in a corner of the saggy, comfortable old sofa, watching the news.

"Hi."

Maddie jerked, turning. "Violet, you scared me! I didn't hear you coming."

"Sorry." She held up one foot. "Slippers don't make enough noise, I guess. I thought you were asleep already."

Maddie shook her head, curling her feet under her. "I never go to bed this early, no matter how tired I am. What about you?"

"I'm usually asleep by ten. I get up early so I can do the outside work before it's too hot." She gestured toward the kitchen. "I was going to get a snack. Do you want something?"

"What are you offering?" Maddie wrinkled her nose. "I know I shouldn't, after that meal Lupita fixed, but something sweet would taste good."

"It probably sounds silly in the middle of July, but I love a cup of hot chocolate in the evening," Violet confessed.

"Me, too." Maddie smiled. "Maybe it's a twin thing."

"Maybe so." She waved her hand when Maddie started to get up. "Stay put. It won't take a minute to fix, and we might as well have it in here where it's comfortable."

It was more than a minute, but not much. Violet put the mugs of cocoa on a tray along with a plate of homemade oatmeal cookies and swiped a paper towel over an errant splash of cocoa on the quartz counter that Lupita kept gleaming.

Maddie still sat in the same position when Violet went back into the den. She put the tray down on the coffee table and sat down on the couch.

Maddie sipped cautiously at the steaming cocoa. "Mmmm, perfect."

Violet leaned back, smiling. It was nice to find they had something in common, despite their different upbringings.

"You and your mother seem to be very close," Maddie said, frowning down at the mug she held. "Was it always like that between you?"

"Pretty much," Violet said cautiously, not wanting anything she said to hurt Maddie. "You can talk about her as *our* mother, you know."

Maddie nodded. "I know. Sometimes it comes out so easily, and other times it just seems to get stuck. Crazy, isn't it?"

"That's how I feel about our father, so if you're crazy, I am, too. The normal rules don't seem to apply when you find out something that changes everything you think about who you are."

Maddie's expression was sober, but she reached out to touch Violet's hand. "At least we're not alone in this. Back to our mother…what kinds of things did you do together growing up? Baking cookies, that sort of thing?"

"Actually, I remember doing those kinds of things with Lupita. Mom was so busy helping Uncle James run the ranch that she was outside most of the time. I did lots of things with her, of course, learning to work the ranch. Jack, too. Mom's job was here where we lived, and we worked right along with her."

Violet's voice warmed as she thought about those times. Maybe it sounded strange in comparison to how Maddie lived, but when you grew up on a ranch or a farm, that was how things were. The whole family worked together and everyone's work had value to the family.

"What about you?" she asked. "Did you have a good relationship with your stepmother?"

Maddie's smile was a bit sad. "I didn't know Sharla wasn't my birth mother. She loved all of us a lot, and she did all the mom things." She hesitated. "I think she felt she had to do more because Dad was gone so much. Whenever we questioned it, or got mad because he wasn't there for a school play or a football game, she'd remind us that he was a doctor and sick people needed him."

"She sounds like a lovely person," Violet said gently.

"I missed her more than I can say after the accident. I was quite young when she died. Now…well, everything's so confused in my mind, but it doesn't change the fact that Sharla loved me. I can hang on to that fact."

"Do you think she knew the truth? I mean, obviously she knew that she wasn't your birth mother, but do you think she knew that you and Grayson each had a twin?"

Maddie looked startled. "I don't know. I hadn't even thought of that, but there was never any indication that she knew. If she did, she kept Dad's secret very well."

Violet picked up an oatmeal cookie and then put it back again. "Besides our parents, there's someone else out there who knows the truth, whether Sharla did or not. The person who sent you that note and the Bible."

"We really are on the same wavelength." Maddie pulled out the object that had been out of sight between her body and the arm of the couch…the Bible. It was a small Revised Standard version, with a white, soft leather cover—the sort you could buy at any bookstore. She opened it, taking out the letter.

"There was no information on the packaging as to where it came from?"

"Nothing. No return address at all, just my name and address in block printing. But you're right—the person who sent this knows all about us." Maddie shook her head. "I suppose there could be someone…some relative or close friend of our parents who knew the truth."

"True, but that doesn't account for the writer asking for forgiveness, does it? Why the implication that the person did something bad to our family? That almost sounds as if he or she was responsible for our parents splitting us up."

Violet found her head aching at the thought of what had been done to them. On second thought, maybe it was her heart that ached.

"You can't have any more questions than I do," Maddie said. "In fact, I never did dismiss that note from my mind, even though I kept telling myself it was meant for someone else. It was just too odd. Now I know why I couldn't forget."

Violet touched the leather cover of the Bible. "Is anything written inside?"

Maddie shook her head. "I've gone through it three or four times. Nothing. And why didn't you get the Bible and note as well? I mean, if this person was responsible for splitting us up, he or she hurt you and Jack as well. Why just send it to me?"

That hadn't occurred to Violet. "I don't know. Maybe you were easier to find, for some reason."

"I guess so." Maddie was looking down, seeming to stare at the Bible. "I'm in the phone book, so anyone who knew my name and that I lived in Fort Worth could find me." She hesitated. "You could have, Violet."

Violet stared at her twin for a long moment as the meaning of her words sank in. "You think I sent the Bible? That I planned this whole thing?"

Maddie pressed her lips together. "I don't want to think that. But I can't ignore the fact that you could have."

"I could have if I'd known you even existed, but I didn't. Can't you see that I'm at as much of a loss as you are?" Violet discovered that there was something worse than all the unanswered questions. It was realizing that Maddie didn't trust her.

She started to get up, knowing that if she sat there any longer she'd start to cry. Maddie grabbed her arm.

"Violet, don't go. I do believe you. But once in a while the doubts creep in, and I wonder if I can trust anyone. My whole life has been turned upside down."

"Mine has, too. Remember?" She wanted to be angry, but she understood what Maddie was saying. "Sometimes the doubts ambush me, too. But you're my twin. I keep coming back to that. Not trusting you would be like not trusting myself."

"I know." Maddie's voice was small. "I just felt like I had to say it, instead of letting it eat away at me. I'm sorry if I hurt you."

"It's all right." Violet managed to smile, wanting to show there were no hard feelings. But that wouldn't be true. The hurt still lingered. She had to remind herself that twin or not, it was going to take time to build a relationship between them.

Landon drove toward the ranch house the next morning, his thoughts shifting from the business that had kept him on the phone for several hours to the problem that lay ahead of him: convincing Maddie to go back to Fort Worth.

The ability to concentrate fully on the issue of the moment was one of his strengths, but it seemed to be deserting him just when he needed it most. Violet's image kept coming between him and his need to do what was best for Maddie.

How could he have mistaken Violet for Maddie, even for a moment? Now that he knew them both, he could probably identify them if he were blindfolded. Despite the external similarities, Maddie and Violet each had a distinctive personality that was all her own. Violet had a glow about her—a welcome warmth that seemed to draw him closer each time he saw her. He'd known instinctively that whoever was at fault in this tangled situation, it wasn't Violet.

And the tangle had gotten worse, judging from the call from Dave.

His fingers tightened on the wheel as he made the turn into the lane. Dave, with his customary thoroughness, had gone the extra mile in trying to find out what he'd been asked, checking birth records in Belle Colby's name as well as in Brian Wallace's. That had led him farther than even he had expected.

"Belle Colby doesn't exist," he'd said flatly.

"What are you talking about? The woman is in a hospital in Amarillo. She's real, all right." He'd been impatient, eager to get on with the business at hand.

"She may be real, but she's not Belle Colby." Dave's sureness rang in his voice. "I've checked and cross-checked. Whoever she is, she has a manufactured identity. It's a good job, but not quite good enough."

"Can you find out who she really is?" Landon had focused in on this new issue.

"I don't know." Dave would never promise what he couldn't deliver. "It's easier to find out who someone isn't than who they are, if you get my drift."

"Do your best. Put more people on it if you have to. I need to know what's going on here."

"Will do." Dave had clicked off, needing nothing more to put a full-scale search into operation.

And Landon had headed straight for the ranch. Whatever was going on, he wanted Maddie out of it. He glanced at his watch. If they'd already left to go to the hospital—but no, Violet's SUV and Maddie's compact were parked on the gravel sweep in front of the house. He pulled in behind the vehicles and got out, urgency riding him.

Violet might know nothing at all about her mother's past. But if she did, her instincts were wrong, and she'd been deceiving them. Either way, that didn't alter the fact that by staying here, Maddie was getting involved in something that was probably way over her head.

Violet pressed soil firmly around a pepper seedling that had been disturbed by something during the night. She'd have to double-check the fence to see how the unwelcome visitor had gotten in. If she—

A shadow fell across the plant. Startled, she looked up. Landon was a tall, dark outline with the sun behind him.

She stood quickly, pulling off her gloves. "Landon. I didn't expect to see you this early." Sometime in the wee hours of the night she'd formulated the words to something she wanted to tell him, but she hadn't expected to have the opportunity this early.

"I thought I'd stop by before you and Maddie headed out for Amarillo. At least, I assume you're going to see your mother today?"

There was an undertone to his words that Violet couldn't quite identify. Disapproval? But that was ridiculous. He couldn't disapprove of Maddie going to see her injured mother.

"I needed to get some work done here before it's too hot, so we'll go after lunch. Maddie is in the house if you want to see her."

He didn't move, glancing down the rows of plants. "So this is your domain, is it?"

"Part of it." She waved a hand to the other planted fields. "At the moment we have several kinds of peppers, tomatoes, okra, black-eyed peas and green beans. And the pecan groves, of course."

Following the direction she was pointing, Landon looked toward the pecan groves in the distance. "You have an impressive operation here." That sounded somewhat reluctantly admiring. "You never wanted to do anything else with your education? Teach, for instance?"

Violet shook dirt from her gloves. "Something where I wouldn't get my hands dirty, you mean?"

"Am I sounding condescending again?" Landon gave her a trace of a smile.

"Maybe just a little." She glanced at the rows of plants. "This is satisfying. Plants are predictable, unlike people. Given the right circumstances, they'll flourish."

"Speaking of which, isn't it too hot to be planting now?" he asked.

It was a more intelligent question than she'd have expected from someone who looked as if he couldn't tell the difference between an asparagus plant and a weed. "We plant peppers a couple of times a year. The plants we set out in July give us a fall harvest."

His eyebrows lifted. "You sound like an expert. Did you study horticulture?"

She couldn't help the chuckle that escaped. "Actually, I majored in English literature. I can't say that knowledge of Shakespearean sonnets improved my gardening abilities, but it has enriched my life."

Violet had surprised herself with her answer. She usually turned off that question with a joke, but somehow she'd found herself telling Landon what she really felt.

He was studying her face, his expression grave. "I see the Colby family is full of surprises."

If her cheeks had reddened, maybe he'd think it was from the sun. "Yes, well…" This was her chance to say what she'd been rehearsing, so she'd better do it. "Before you go in to see Maddie, there's something I wanted to say."

Wariness settled on his face. "Yes?"

"I know I've given you a hard time once or twice." That was probably an understatement. "But it's good of you to go to so much trouble to help us. And if you're here because you're trying to get Maddie back, I don't want to stand in your way."

Landon just stood looking at her for a long moment. Then he shook his head. "We're not engaged any longer," he said flatly. "To be honest, I think it only happened because Maddie was feeling vulnerable. She'd lost her job, and with her family away, she needed someone to turn to. And I proposed because…"

He stopped, and she didn't seem to be breathing while she waited for whatever else he was going to say.

Landon shook his head. "It's complicated. Maddie always felt like a younger sister to me. Grayson's in a dangerous line of work, and he asked me to promise to take care of her." A faint smile crossed his face. "I'm sure he didn't mean I should propose to her. I don't love Maddie that way, and she's made it abundantly clear she doesn't feel that way about me, either. I think we're both relieved to be un-engaged."

"But you're still here," she pointed out.

"With all that's happened, I expect she's still vulnerable. So I'm still keeping my promise." His gaze seemed to be probing her thoughts. "At a guess, you're probably pretty vulnerable right about now, too."

She had to shake off the sudden longing to lean on him. "Me? I'm fine. I mean, worried about Mom, of course, but otherwise, I'm okay."

Again, he paused, and she had a sense that he was censoring several things he might say. "I hope so," he said finally, and then he turned and walked toward the house.

Violet looked after him for several minutes. Then, shaking her head, she got back to work. But she couldn't quite dismiss Landon from her thoughts. He'd sounded odd…as if there was an undercurrent she couldn't reach beneath everything he said.

Well, she didn't need to understand him, she scolded herself. He was Maddie's friend, not hers.

In another fifteen minutes she'd finished with the pepper plants. There was certainly plenty to do elsewhere, but if she was going to get a shower and be ready to leave for Amarillo after lunch, she'd better get on with it.

Returning to the house, she crossed the courtyard to the back door and went in quietly, taking off her work boots in the hall.

Maddie and Landon were in the living room, judging by the murmur of voices. Hopefully she could slip up the stairs without disturbing them.

She reached the bottom of the staircase when Landon's voice rang out sharply.

"Listen to me, Maddie. You have to come back to Fort Worth with me now. These people aren't what you think."

She was frozen for an instant, unable to think, only to feel pain. She'd begun to trust Landon. She'd believed he trusted her. And all the time he'd been planning to take her sister away.

The pain surged into anger, and the anger propelled her into the living room. Maddie and Landon stood facing each other, tension in the air between them.

"What are you doing?" The words burst out of her. "I thought you were our friend. Why are you trying to take Maddie away?"

Maddie crossed the few feet between them and put her arm around Violet's waist, facing Landon with her. The gesture of solidarity warmed Violet's hurting heart.

"What *are* you doing, Landon?" Maddie asked. "You said you wanted to help me. Us."

Landon's face had grown rigid. Forbidding. "I am trying to help you." Clearly he was talking just to Maddie. "I'm not saying you have to cut off ties to Violet, but you'd be better off at home until we can sort all this out."

"You don't have the right to tell me what to do. Nobody does. I'm a grown woman, and I can make my own decisions."

After the previous night's doubts, Maddie's support touched Violet's heart. She wanted to speak, wanted to tell Landon just what she thought of his actions, but maybe this was between Landon and Maddie.

"If your father or Grayson were here, I'm sure they'd agree with me." Landon took a step toward Maddie, holding out his hand.

"They're not here, and even if they were, I wouldn't leave without a good reason." Maddie's eyes sparked with anger. "So unless you can explain yourself a little better, I think you're the one who should leave."

"You want a good reason?" Landon, apparently finding his patience stretched beyond endurance, snapped. "Fine, I'll give you one. Dave looked into the anteced-ents of the woman named Belle Colby, and you know what he found? He found that Belle Colby doesn't exist. So whoever is lying in that hospital bed in Amarillo, her name isn't Belle Colby. And maybe Violet already knew that." He strode past them and paused at the front door, frowning at Maddie, leaving Violet alone. "Whenever the two of you decide to listen to common sense, get in touch with me. If I'm not at the hotel in town, I'll be back in Fort Worth."

The door slammed behind him, adding an exclama-tion mark to his words.

Chapter 6

"Do you think it's true?" Maddie broke the silence that had stretched between her and Violet for most of the miles to the hospital as they were pulling into the parking lot.

"I don't know." Violet switched off the ignition and rubbed her temples, feeling as if her head were about to explode. "I don't think Landon was lying. But he's wrong to think I know any of this." Landon's attitude was a separate little pain in her heart.

"Landon." Maddie said the name explosively as they walked toward the hospital entrance. "I'm just plain mad at him. I've told him it's over between us. Why does he have to keep butting in?"

The hospital doors swished open and then closed behind them, giving Violet a moment to compose her thoughts.

"He still cares what happens to you," Violet said, keeping her voice mild with an effort. It was only too obvious that Landon didn't care what happened to her. That shouldn't hurt so much. She pushed the elevator button. "You've known each other for a long time. If he were in trouble, you'd want to help him, wouldn't you?"

"I suppose so," Maddie admitted. "But he's a friend, not a big brother. Or a boyfriend."

They stepped onto the elevator. "That's how Jack is," Violet said. "Always thinking he has to take care of me because he's the big brother."

Except for now, when she really needed his help.

"Jack's not being very helpful from wherever he is at the moment." Maddie's voice was tart. She darted a look at Violet. "Sorry. I know you're close to him, but honestly…"

"He's picked a bad time to go AWOL." She had to smile, although it wasn't funny. "We could use Jack, but he's not here. And you don't want Landon, but he won't go away." She wouldn't let herself think about wanting Landon.

"Men," Maddie said, a wealth of meaning in the word. The elevator doors opened and they stepped out onto their mom's floor.

There wouldn't be any change; Violet knew that. Still, she couldn't stop hoping every time she walked in the door. Today might be the day her mom woke up.

It wasn't. Violet's disappointment was mitigated a little by the fact that Maddie didn't hang back this time. She went straight to her mother's bed and pulled up a chair, bending over to touch a passive hand before she sat down.

"Hi," she said. "It's me, Maddie. Violet and I are both here with you."

"That's right, Mom." Violet bent to kiss her mother's cheek. "I think you have a little more color in your face today."

Actually their mom was ashen beneath her tan, but she had to have hope, didn't she?

Maddie rose, moving restlessly to the window. "Landon always said that private investigator of his was the best in the business." Obviously Landon's revelations were eating at her, just as they were at Violet.

Violet moved away from the bed to join Maddie at the window. Probably, Mom couldn't hear their words anyway, but she didn't want to take the chance. She'd been thinking of little else since Landon slammed out of the house, so they may as well talk about it.

"Well, even if Mom changed her name, that's not a crime." She kept her voice down, her back to the bed. "Maybe she had a good reason. Maybe she was upset and wanted to make a fresh start." But she knew even as she said the words that they didn't make a whole lot of sense.

"If she changed her name, that means she changed yours, too." Maddie looked at her, and for a moment Violet had the dizzying sensation that she was looking in a mirror. "Did you think of that? Maybe you're really Violet Wallace."

She tried the name out mentally, not liking the idea. "I've always been a Colby. I think I'll stick with that, even if…" She paused, and then shook her head. "Mom could have changed our names legally, you know."

"True." Maddie pressed her lips together for a moment, probably in frustration. "If only she'd wake up, she could answer all of this for us. What do the doctors say about the coma?"

Violet turned to stare at her mother's face. The familiar features looked much as they always did, except for the pallor. She might just be sleeping, but she wasn't.

"At first, after the surgery, they kept her in an induced coma. The doctors said it was important to the healing process. When they started lessening the medication, they said she should start to wake up, but she didn't." Her voice choked. "There's still hope."

"Sure there is," Maddie echoed loyally. "You hear about things like that all the time. I read an article about how people sometimes wake up after months, even years, in a coma."

Months. Years. The words broke through the protective shell Violet had been cultivating for the past week. The shell had been her only defense against the fear that she might never have her mom back again, but it was suddenly too heavy to bear. She couldn't do it any longer. The tears came, flooding down her cheeks faster than she could wipe them away. She buried her face in her hands and wept.

"Violet, I'm so sorry." She felt Maddie's comforting arms go around her. "It will be all right." The soft words echoed what her mom used to say to her. "Don't worry. It will be all right."

Violet cried until it seemed she had no tears left. Finally, she moved to the chair and leaned back, exhausted. Empty.

Maddie handed her a cool, wet washcloth, and Violet pressed it to her eyes.

"Thanks," she muttered. "Sorry I fell apart."

"It's okay to cry. Don't you think I have? Sometimes you just need to."

"I guess." She sighed, mopping her eyes again. "I'd rather have answers." She looked at her mom's unresponsive face. "It's just so hard to keep being hopeful, you know? I keep praying, but then I find myself wondering if God's listening."

"Do you think..." Maddie began, and then she hesitated.

"What?" Violet looked up, blinking a little. Her eyes were sore from crying, and she probably looked a wreck, but she didn't suppose Maddie would care.

"You mentioned something about running into your pastor yesterday. I was thinking that maybe we could talk to him."

"Jeb's someone we could trust with the whole story," she said slowly. "But that would mean we'd..."

"We'd have to come out in the open about me," Maddie finished for her. "I understand. People would talk." She gave a rueful smile. "I've already figured out that Grasslands isn't like Fort Worth."

Violet clasped her hand. "You know what? I don't care how much people might talk. Let them. I think it's time I made an appearance with my twin."

Maddie rewarded her with a warmhearted smile, and Violet felt ashamed that she'd ever thought of keeping their relationship quiet. Everyone on the ranch knew, of course, but however much they might talk among themselves, they wouldn't say anything to her.

Well, so what if she had to face some awkward questions? She knew what her mom would do in that situation. She'd meet the questions with a confident smile and go her own way. It seemed as if her daughters could do the same.

"I've wanted to talk to you about Maddie, but it's all been so complicated."

Violet sat back in the comfortable, sagging rocker in

Pastor Jeb's office later with a sense of relief. The story had been told, and she didn't have to worry about how it would be received. Jeb's heart was big enough to listen to almost anything, as far as she could tell. For him, judgment was always best left to God. The pastor's job was to point people to Him.

"I'm glad you told me. It really is incredible." Jeb's gaze traveled from her face to Maddie's. "You two are identical on the outside."

"The outside?" Maddie looked taken aback.

Jeb smiled. "I don't suppose God sees folks the way we mortals do, do you? 'Man looks on the outside, but God looks on the heart,'" he quoted.

"I've been holding back, afraid to bring everything out into the open," Violet admitted. "I guess God knows that, if He knows my heart. But we've decided we can't keep this a secret any longer. We need to know the truth."

"Good." Jeb smiled. "Folks are going to talk about your long-lost twin for a while. You know how Grasslands is. But I think you'll find most of them wish you well, even if they do talk. And if anyone here knows anything that will help you, I'll pray they come out with it."

The telephone rang. Jeb reached toward the receiver but the ring cut off abruptly, followed by the low murmur of a voice in the other office. He shook his head. "I keep forgetting I have a secretary now. She must have come in while we were talking."

A hesitant tap at the door was so timid it almost sounded like a faint scratch. "Come in," Jeb called.

The door opened, and the woman who stood there peered inside hesitantly. "I'm sorry, sir, but—" She stopped, catching sight of Jeb's visitors. Her eyes widened, and she grasped the edge of the door frame.

"It's all right, Sadie, you haven't developed double vision," Jeb said. "This is Violet Colby, and her twin, Maddie Wallace. I'd like you both to meet Sadie Johnson, our new church secretary. She's new to Grasslands, as well, so I hope you'll make her feel welcome."

"It's so nice to meet you, Sadie." Violet stood, starting to hold out her hand, but Sadie had backed against the door, arms folded across her chest, grasping the dull gray cardigan she wore in spite of the heat. Small and fine-boned, she looked like a waif in her baggy, oversize clothes. Anxious green eyes stared at them from behind glasses that were too big for her face.

Violet contented herself with a warm smile of welcome instead of a handshake. She recognized the signs. Jeb was a sucker for a stray, and Sadie certainly looked lost. She only hoped the woman could type, because Jeb would never have the heart to fire anyone.

"Welcome to Grasslands," Maddie said. "I'm a newcomer, too, so I know just how it feels."

Sadie gave a slight nod, still staring at them, standing in the doorway as if mesmerized.

Jeb cleared his throat. "I think you had a message for me, Sadie."

That brought Sadie's gaze to his face. "Oh, yes, sir. Pastor. That was Mr. Watson on the phone. His mother is feeling poorly, and would you stop by."

She still stood in the doorway, as if stuck there. Jeb dealt with the situation by taking her elbow and walking her back to her desk.

"I'll have to go." He glanced at them. "You know

Mavis Watson. She thinks she's dying about once a month, but..."

"But you go, anyway." Mavis Watson might well outlive all of them, but Violet knew Jeb too well to think he'd postpone a visit. "Thanks, Pastor Jeb. I'm glad we told you." Violet glanced at Maddie.

Her sister nodded. "We'll be all right. Just keep our mother in your prayers."

"All of you," Jeb corrected gently. "I'll be praying for all of you."

Once outside, Maddie and Violet parted to run a few errands, agreeing to meet back at the car in half an hour.

Violet turned right and walked quickly toward Grasslands' only hotel. She'd leave it to Maddie to make peace with Landon or not, as she chose.

But talking to Jeb had cleared her mind. She might not like Landon's attitude or even his motives, but if he really wanted to learn the truth, she could hardly fault him for that. After all, she wanted answers as well. Maybe, if she caught him in a good mood, they could even sit down and have a rational discussion about his private investigator's findings.

She crossed the street, but before she reached the hotel, she realized she wouldn't have to go in and ask for Landon. He was jogging down the trail that led through the park.

Landon had told himself that a good workout was what he needed to brush the cobwebs away and let him focus. But after a few circuits of the jogging trail in the park, he knew what was bothering him had nothing to do with mental fog and everything to do with guilt.

Guilt had been a constant companion for years now,

sometimes going into hiding, only to jump out at him when something reminded him of his little sister. Maddie had pushed those buttons when she'd leaned on him, all upset over what her future was going to be after she'd lost her job. And in that case, guilt had pushed him into exactly the wrong path. He didn't want to marry Maddie any more than she wanted to marry him.

He dropped to an easy jog, letting his pulse rate slow. He shouldn't have blown up at Maddie and Violet that way. Losing his temper wasn't the right method for handling anything.

Individually Maddie and Violet each had an odd effect on him. But both of them together seemed to magnify his feelings of guilt and responsibility—to say nothing of the unsettling attraction Violet held for him. It was Maddie he'd promised to protect. So why was it Violet he wanted to put his arms around?

Slowing to a walk, he headed for the bench where he'd left his towel and discovered Violet was there, apparently waiting for him.

He stopped in front of her, picking up the towel to run it over the back of his neck. Violet had the advantage over him this time—she looked cool and collected, while he was red, perspiring and out of breath, to say nothing of feeling guilty. He had to trust his instincts, and they told him clearly that Violet had been as shocked as Maddie at the revelation about her mother.

"I'm glad to see you. It saves me going back out to the ranch to grovel and apologize. Are you still speaking to me?"

Violet smiled, some slight tension in her face easing. "I think maybe the apologies should go both ways.

I know you're trying to protect Maddie. And that was quite a bombshell you dropped on us."

"It felt like a bombshell when I heard it, too." He sat on the bench next to her. "So I overreacted. Look, I'm sorry for being suspicious. You really didn't have a clue about all of this, did you?"

"Not a one." She ran her hands along her arms, as if she felt a chill in spite of the heat of the day. "So many lies—how do we even begin to untangle them?"

"I wish I had the answer to that question. The investigator won't give up, but…" He spread his hands wide.

"Honestly, sometimes I just feel so…so angry. How could our parents do this to us? And then I feel guilty for being angry, especially with my mother lying in that hospital bed."

His hand seemed to tingle with the need to touch her. He longed to pull her into his arms to comfort her, the longing so intense it was hard to resist. But he had to. This wasn't the time or place. "Sometimes it's natural to be angry. I'd guess that your parents had a good reason for what they did, but you and Maddie were still hurt. They probably never imagined a situation where you'd find each other this way."

"I guess not." Violet's hands were clasped in her lap, as if she needed something to hang on to. "Mom certainly couldn't have foreseen a situation where she'd be incapacitated. She's always been so strong and capable."

"Do you think there's anything else Maddie could do to get in touch with her father?" Landon found it hard to believe that the man, mission trip or not, could be so completely out of touch in a world of cell phones and computers.

"I don't know." Violet's troubled gaze met his. "I

haven't wanted to push her. She seems sensitive where her father is concerned."

"Your father, too," he reminded her.

"I know. Or at least I guess I know." She bit her lip, as if undecided. "Landon, do you think we're right to dig into the past? What if…well, if it's better left alone?"

One part of him wanted to agree that she should leave it alone, but it was probably already too late for that. "You mean what if you find out something you'd rather not know?"

Violet nodded. "I'm glad to have found my twin. I'd never want to take that back. But it seems as if everything we learn just leads to more questions, like this business of why Mom changed her name. Sometimes I feel as if digging into our past is like digging into a minefield," she said.

He couldn't help but smile a little. "Waiting for something to go boom? I know the feeling."

"Maybe we'd be better off not doing the digging." Violet rubbed the long, graceful slope of her neck, as if the tension had knotted the muscles there. For an instant his fingers warmed with the longing to do that for her, and he had to fight off that feeling.

"Some people are satisfied with comforting lies. I have a feeling that you're someone who'd rather know the truth."

"Maybe I'm more the ostrich-in-the-sand kind of person." She managed a faint smile. "You haven't known me very long, after all."

"Not long in terms of time," he admitted. "But it's been a pretty intense few days. You can learn a lot about a person by seeing him or her under stress."

She looked at him, as if measuring how honest he

was being. Well, he deserved her doubts. He never should have tried to push Maddie into leaving or insinuated that Violet knew about her mother's secret past.

His cell phone rang before he could say anything else. It was Dave. Maybe he had more answers.

"Dave. Anything new?"

"A few more details. Can you talk?"

He glanced at Violet, but if he meant what he'd just told her, he couldn't start hiding things now. "Yes, go ahead."

"I finally got hold of copies of birth certificates for both girls."

"And?"

"Maddie Wallace's seems pretty straightforward, except for one thing."

"And that is?"

"She and Grayson were both adopted by Brian Wallace's wife when she married him. So that made the wife—whose name was Sharla—their legal mother. But she wasn't their birth mother."

"At least that fits. What about the younger brother, Carter?"

"Carter is the child of Brian and Sharla Wallace, born about a year after their marriage."

The fog was beginning to lift a bit. He glanced at Violet. She was obviously waiting. "What about Grayson and Maddie's birth mother? Were you able to find a name?"

"It took a lot of digging, but we came up with it, finally. Isabella Wallace. I couldn't find a maiden name, which would help in tracing her. Still, there's one interesting thing. Isabella. The nickname *Belle* might be from that."

"You said you found birth certificates for both of them," Landon said slowly, trying to process everything that the P.I. was divulging. "What about Violet?" He heard her suck in a breath and wished this call had come any time other than when she was there, waiting.

"Violet Colby's lists her mother as Bethany Colby and her father as Jason Colby, deceased. Her place of birth is supposed to be Fort Worth General."

Landon frowned. "That doesn't seem to fit."

"That's because Jason Colby didn't exist, either. The whole thing's a fairy tale from beginning to end. And the hospital records have been doctored, as well." Dave sounded satisfied. The tougher the case, the better he liked it.

"How would Belle Colby have been able to do that?" As Violet had said, every answer brought more confusion, it seemed.

"Good question," Dave said. "All I can tell you is that she has a new identity, and it runs back pretty far. We're still tracing it. I assume you want us to keep going?"

"Definitely." He might, a time or two, have been tempted to wash his hands of the whole tangled mess, but he couldn't stop now. He was in way too deep.

"One interesting thing has come up in the records about Belle Colby," Dave said. "She shows up in Grasslands when Violet would have been about three or so. She took a job as a sort of housekeeper/secretary to the owner of what's now the Colby Ranch. Elderly man, name of James Crawford." He took a breath. "She and the kids apparently lived there on the ranch, and when Crawford died, he left everything to her—lock, stock and barrel."

"All right." He tried not to think about what that

might say about Violet's mother. "I'll see if I can get any information on that. Meanwhile, just keep digging."

He hung up, and turned to see the questions in Violet's face. They were questions he had to answer, and once he had, he somehow had to persuade both Violet and Maddie to let him continue to help them. He'd thought he was coming here to protect Maddie, and that was a big enough job. Now he had to protect Violet, too, and that might be a tall order.

Chapter 7

Violet walked along the rows of tomato plants, trying to concentrate on her work, not on that conversation with Landon the previous day. The information his private investigator had come up with simply managed to cloud the issue, rather than clarify it.

At least she felt as if the quarrel with Landon had ended. They'd all three overreacted, but in the long run, they wanted the same thing—the truth. Unfortunately, that seemed to be in short supply right now.

She stopped by a row of Roma tomatoes. The Romas were especially productive this year, but she always had to keep an eye on them. Too much or too little rain at the wrong time could spell disaster.

"Going to be a good harvest this year, even if it's a little late." Ricardo, Lupita's husband, rose from inspecting a plant.

With an inward qualm, Violet realized that it took him longer to get up these days. Still wiry and strong,

Ricardo would not admit that, just as he would never admit needing help with anything, and his age was a closely guarded secret. He had that in common with Harriet Porter, the farm stand manager.

"It does look good. All the canners in the county will be busy making sauce and salsa." She lifted her straw hat and wiped her forehead with the back of her arm.

"Your momma—how was she yesterday?" Ricardo's dark eyes seemed to grow even darker.

Not surprising. He adored her mom, treating her like a much-loved sister instead of his employer. And she relied on him and Lupita, as well. They had been her support system when she was bringing up her kids without a father.

"No change." She pressed her lips together to keep them from trembling. "We mustn't give up hope, though."

"We will never do that," he said. He glanced toward the house. "Your sister went alone to see her this morning?"

Violet nodded. "If I'm at the hospital, I feel guilty because I'm not here. And if I'm here, I feel guilty because I'm not there. I think Maddie wanted to spend a little time alone with Mom, so she went today."

"That will be good for your sister, I think." He leaned over to pull a weed that had dared to pop up under the leaves of the tomato plant. "I have not talked to her very much, but Lupita says she is a good person. Like you, but different, too."

"We keep surprising ourselves at how alike we are in some ways, despite being raised apart." She hesitated. "I just wish I could understand. Why did they break us up that way?"

Ricardo's face, creased by all the years he'd spent in the sun, radiated sympathy. "You will know one day. Until then, you already know that your momma is a person of deep faith. She would not do anything without a strong reason."

The words reassured her. Ricardo, with the patience and wisdom that came from dedication to growing things, had put his finger on the important aspect of the puzzling situation.

"You're right." She looked at him, her heart filled with gratitude. "I do know that about Mom, no matter how bad things look on the surface."

The sound of hooves attracted her attention and she turned to see Ty riding along the edge of the field. She waved, and when he pulled up she walked over to him.

"How are things going?" She shielded her eyes with her hand, looking up at him.

His strong-boned face seemed to tighten a little, unsettling her. If there was bad news she didn't want to hear it, as selfish as that might sound. She had enough to deal with at the moment.

"No problems," he said, his tone as laconic as ever. "Nothing I can't handle."

"Good." But was it? She had a sense of things left unsaid, but she didn't know quite how to approach it. She liked and respected Ty, but it was her mom and Jack who worked with him.

He took the decision out of her hands by touching the brim of his hat. "See you later, Violet." He rode on, leaving her unsettled.

"Ty is a good man."

Violet turned, surprised that Ricardo had come up behind her. She nodded. "He does a fine job as foreman." She waited, sensing that now Ricardo had something else to say.

"People get restless when they don't know what is going to happen," he said carefully. "It makes them worry and wonder, and they don't do their jobs so well."

She was surprised at the turn this conversation had taken. "You mean Ty?"

"No, not Ty. And not my people." He gestured toward the three or four men in the soybean field, most of them relatives of Ricardo or Lupita. "But the cowpokes... I hear them talking. Wondering what will happen to their jobs. To the ranch. Thinking maybe they should be looking out for a new place."

The blow was unexpected, and for a moment she couldn't think how to respond. The cattle part of their operation was always handled by Jack and her mom, along with Ty.

"Well, the ranch isn't going anywhere, that's for sure," she said finally. "Do you think it would help if I talked to them?"

Ricardo shook his head. "It should be Jack. Your brother must come home and take on his responsibilities."

He didn't add the obvious—that she should call him.

"He was upset." She knew her voice sounded defensive.

"You were upset as well, but you did not run away." His voice was firm. "Jack must come home," he repeated.

She'd wanted to give her brother more time—time to deal with his anger and guilt, time to realize he had to come back on his own.

"I'll think about it," she said. "I promise."

What if she called him and he refused to come back? He wouldn't do that, she assured herself hastily. Jack would come if she needed him.

Unaccountably, her thoughts strayed to someone else who hadn't left. Landon had every reason in the world to go back to Fort Worth and his business, but he hadn't. He'd stayed to help.

Landon had spent several hours on work that day, eating a take-out sandwich for lunch. His hotel room wasn't the most comfortable of surroundings, but it was cool and clean, and most important, it had the internet connections he needed. He could conduct business there as long as he had to.

Thanks to Dave, he now knew a good bit more about Maddie and Violet's parentage. In his opinion, and he knew in Dave's, it was highly likely that the Isabella who had apparently been Brian Wallace's first wife was indeed Belle Colby. But until they made that actual link, he had no proof of anything.

Still, Violet had seemed to take it for granted after she'd heard what Dave had reported. She would have talked to Maddie when she got back to the ranch. With any luck, Maddie would have forgiven him for trying to tell her what to do. Maybe.

He walked out the front door of the hotel to feel a blast of heat strong enough to make him want to retreat inside again. But something far more interesting drew him forward, because both Maddie's car and Violet's SUV were parked by the Colby farm store. Apparently Violet had come out in the open about her twin sister. How was she explaining that unexpected acquisition?

He crossed the street and approached the store. If

Maddie was still angry, she'd at least have to be polite to him in a public place.

Landon stepped inside, pausing for a moment before he spotted Violet at the counter. As he moved toward her, she looked up and saw him. Her face warmed.

"Landon, hey. I thought you were probably hard at work." Her face grew suddenly more serious. "What is it? Have you found out something new?"

"No, nothing." He leaned on the counter, keeping his voice down. "I'm just appreciating the values of telecommuting. Give me a phone and an internet connection, and I can work from anywhere."

"I'm sure it's inconveniencing you, staying here," she said. "If you need to go back to Fort Worth…"

He touched her hand briefly. "I'm in this for the duration." He lowered his voice still further, not wanting anyone else to hear that admission. "Are you okay with that?"

He smiled into those deep brown eyes, hoping to see an answering smile in return. She studied him for a moment that felt as if it lasted an hour.

Finally, she nodded. "I'm glad for your help. But I can't speak for Maddie."

"I know. Is she still angry?"

Violet shrugged. "I told you. I won't answer for her."

"Right." He glanced around, looking for something that would let him continue talking to Violet and refusing to think about why that was so important. "It seems as if you're having a big day today." At least three times as many people were inside the store than he'd noticed the last time he'd glanced through the window.

"That's thanks to Maddie, although I'm not sure she's enjoying it." Violet wrinkled her nose in distaste.

"Maddie?" He was startled. "Why? What did she do?"

"She's here, that's all." Violet gave a rueful smile. "We decided it was time she made a public appearance, so when she got back from visiting our mom at the hospital this morning, she came in to work. We'll let everybody satisfy their curiosity and hopefully get over it."

"You think they will get over it?"

"No," she admitted. "I'm quite sure they won't move on that easily. We'll be the talk of the town until some more interesting topic comes along."

"How's Maddie taking it?" He'd think something like that would send her fleeing back to Fort Worth, if anything would.

Violet refused to be drawn. She just smiled. "Go and see for yourself. She's working the back counter."

Landon walked back through rows of vegetables, piled high in glossy, colorful stacks. People were buying, he noticed, along with satisfying their curiosity. They could hardly come in and go away without a purchase. Still, he doubted that the additional income would balance the embarrassment.

He found Maddie, as Violet had said, at the cash register in the rear of the store. Several people stood at the counter. Oddly enough, when he approached, they melted away, suddenly taking an interest in sweet corn or okra. Maybe they recognized him as a stranger.

Maddie eyed him warily. "Landon. I might have known you'd show up."

"Sorry I chased away your customers." He leaned on the counter, keeping his voice low again. He wasn't eager to add to the supper-table conversation in Grasslands tonight.

"They'll be back," she said, sounding resigned. "Everyone wants to talk to me, apparently. But why are you here?"

"To apologize. I already made my amends to Violet. She was kind enough to forgive me for overreacting yesterday. I hope you'll do the same."

"She doesn't know you as well as I do," Maddie said. "She wasn't the one you were bossing around."

He might have realized this would be more difficult with Maddie. "I'm sorry I overreacted to what I found out about your mother. And I had no right trying to tell you what to do. My only excuse is that I was worried about you. I didn't want you to get hurt."

He wanted those words back as soon as they came out. Maddie was bound to resent his assumption that he ought to protect her from hurt.

To his surprise, she just looked at him as if measuring the amount of his remorse. Maybe Maddie had matured in the face of all she'd learned in the past few days.

"All right," she said finally.

That doubled his surprise. "All right?" He had a feeling there must be a catch.

She nodded. "Violet and I agreed that finding out the truth is best in the long run, even if it's painful. Believe it or not, I respect your abilities, Landon. You and your investigator can find out more than Violet and I possibly can on our own. So we accept your help."

Little Maddie really had grown up. "Thank you, Maddie. You won't mind if I hang around Grasslands for a while, then?"

She frowned at that idea. "You're not thinking of proposing again, are you?"

Her suspicious expression actually made him smile. "Maddie, believe it or not, I'm convinced. You and I were never meant to be anything more than friends, and I was wrong to propose to you. All right?"

She nodded. "And I was wrong to accept." Her smile flickered. "I'm glad to be your friend, Landon, but I'm not getting married until I find someone I can't live without. But I'm still not sure it's necessary for you to stay here while this is going on."

She wouldn't be impressed if he told her that he still felt responsible for her, so he needed another good reason to stay. "It seems to me the truth lies somewhere in Belle Colby's past, and she's spent most of her adult life here. It only makes sense to do what I can in Grasslands and help you and Violet as well."

She looked at him speculatively. "Do you really mean that?"

"Sure." What was in her mind?

"Fine, then I have a job for you."

"Hauling cartons of vegetables?" He was only half-kidding.

"Violet and I are volunteering at the youth center her church runs tonight, since the scheduled people can't make it. We need a male volunteer. That's you."

She looked at him with a smug smile, obviously sure he'd try to get out of it.

"Fine," he said. "Just tell me where and when."

Violet gave up her post at the door to another Teen Scene volunteer and walked back through the church social rooms. She felt as if she was always on the alert when the program was running. Opening the church to area teens two nights a week had been controversial, with some members of the congregation ready to pounce on any problem, no matter how slight, as a reason to shut down the program.

All seemed to be running smoothly tonight, other than the last-minute replacement of volunteers when Ted and Judy Fisher got unexpected houseguests from out of town. Maddie was in the kitchen serving popcorn, hot dogs and lemonade to the kids, who always seemed to arrive hungry. Wearing jeans and a plaid shirt of Violet's, her hair pulled back, she fit in surprisingly well. And if the kids were openly curious, it didn't seem to bother her.

Violet smiled at a noisy game of air hockey that was in progress and just missed being hit by an errant Ping-Pong ball from the ongoing, informal tournament. She liked seeing the kids being active, and the variety of activities available gave everyone a chance to shine.

The door to the gym stood open, emitting the squeak of sneakers on the hardwood floor. She walked in and stood for a moment, watching. One side of the gym had a low balcony area, where it was possible to have tables and chairs. The door to the outside was also there, where a volunteer checked kids in and out.

So this was where Landon had disappeared to. He dribbled down the court, moving with an almost effortless grace, and eluded a muscular guard. For an instant she thought he'd take the shot himself, but he passed off to an undersized kid who looked momentarily surprised and then sank the basket.

Landon bent over, hands on his knees, breathing hard. In a moment, amidst a lot of good-natured kidding about his advanced age, he came off the court.

"Not bad," she said. "You almost kept up with them."

"Are you kidding?" He braced his hands on the low

wall that separated the balcony from the gym floor. "They nearly ran me into the ground. Kids that age have more energy than they know what to do with."

Violet nodded, letting her gaze wander over the kids. It was a nice mix tonight, and...

"Don't let me bore you," Landon commented.

"I'm sorry." She smiled ruefully. "Maybe I take things too seriously, but I always want to be sure everyone's feeling accepted here."

Landon nodded. "I understand that. Kids are too ready to put up walls. They like to categorize each other—this one's a nerd, that one's a jock."

"And some other terms that are a lot more derogatory," she added. "They can be mean, but I think when they are, it's usually out of their own insecurity."

He studied her face. "Is that personal experience talking?"

"Was I ever mean to anyone? Probably, although Mom came down pretty hard on that sort of talk."

"Were you ever picked on?" He tilted his head slightly, and the overhead light emphasized his strong, regular features.

"Not picked on like the stories you hear now, especially with all the cyber-bullying going on. Grasslands is a small enough community that everyone knows everyone else, so it's tough to get away with that sort of thing for long. Still, it's harder to be a teenager now than it was even ten years ago."

"Maybe so." He didn't look convinced of that statement. "I remember some nasty stuff going on when I was a teen, though. Drinking, drugs."

"That's why this program is so important," Violet went on. "Not just to give the kids something to do,

but to give them adults who care about them enough
to volunteer their time."

Landon was frowning slightly, and she wondered
why. Maybe, in the privileged life he'd had, he'd been
immune to the problems other people took for granted.

"I'd think a town the size of Grasslands could afford to have a community center to provide this sort of
outlet for the kids. A professional staff would be better
equipped to handle problems."

"Than my group of well-meaning volunteers?" she
asked, irritation edging her nerves. Who was he to come
in and criticize their efforts?

"Well, wouldn't that be better?" he asked. "If a professional can do the job, why rely on untrained people
who let you down at the last minute?"

"This isn't Fort Worth," she reminded him, gritting
her teeth in an effort to keep from saying something
she'd regret. "Like it or not, this is the only game in
town for these kids. If you don't feel you want to participate, I'm sure we can manage without you."

She started to turn away, but he stopped her with a
hand on her wrist. She tried to deny the wave of warmth
that flooded through her.

"I wasn't denying the need you're trying to meet,
Violet." His voice was low, with an intensity that startled her. "Believe it or not, I had plenty of grief of my
own when I was their age. Maybe you're right. I don't
know the situation here. If I'd had someone who cared
enough—" He broke off, looking past her. "Is that girl
crying?"

Violet yanked her attention away from Landon to
look in the direction he nodded. Sure enough, Tracey
Benton was huddled in a corner, trying to keep her tears

to herself. Slight and small, she bent over so that her long, dark hair swung in front of her face.

"Tracey. I'll see to her," she said, pulling her hand away from Landon's. "Thanks."

Maybe it was just as well that the interruption had occurred. She went quickly toward Tracey. She'd been getting way too wrapped up in Landon's intensity. Still, she wished Landon had finished what he was saying.

When Tracey saw her coming she tried to turn away, but Violet put her arm around the girl's shoulders and led her toward the tiny room they used for an office. It wasn't the first time she'd found tears streaking Tracey's olive skin. Maybe tonight would be the time she finally broke through to the girl.

Closing the door, she settled Tracey in the only comfortable chair and gave her a bottle of water and a handful of tissues. She pulled a folding chair up so that they were knee to knee.

"It's okay to cry," she said, remembering when Maddie had said those words to her.

"I'm okay." Sniffling a little, Tracey moved as if to get up.

Violet captured Tracey's hands in both of hers. "Tracey, I said it was okay to cry. It's also okay to talk to someone about what's wrong."

Tracey didn't speak. She freed one hand to brush a strand of glossy black hair behind her ear. Her gaze met Violet's for a moment and then flicked away.

Please, God, give me the right words. Let me help her.

"I'm your friend, Tracey. I'll listen to anything you have to say, and I won't repeat it to anyone. I'll help you any way I can."

But Tracey was pulling herself together, withdrawing

once again. "I'm okay, Ms. Vi. Honest. I just…somebody said something that hurt my feelings. That's all."

Before Violet could say anything else, Tracey jumped up and fled from the room.

Violet watched her go with mixed feelings, mostly doubt. Tracey's explanation might be true. The child of a Hispanic mother and an Anglo father, Tracey probably had more trouble finding her place in the difficult world of adolescence than a lot of kids.

But she had a sense that Tracey was dealing with something more than the usual teasing.

Rubbing her forehead, Violet followed her slowly, burdened down by the weight of her failure. Maybe Landon had it right. Maybe she was kidding herself, trying to do something that ought to be handled by a professional.

Chapter 8

"Are you going to Amarillo today?" Maddie paused in carrying her breakfast dishes to the kitchen, glancing toward Violet with concern in her face. "You look tired. Maybe you ought to stay home."

Violet smiled, trying to look a bit perkier than she felt. "I'm fine. I just didn't sleep well last night."

Maddie set the dishes back down on the table and slid into the ladder-back chair next to her. "Are you worrying about your...our mother?"

"Not exactly. I mean, I keep trying to give that fear over to the Lord, but I suppose it's always there in the back of my mind."

"What, then? Landon?" Maddie gave her a shrewd look. "I saw him talking to you last night."

"Of course I wasn't thinking about him," she said, more sharply than she'd intended. "Landon's not...well, anyway, I was thinking about one of the girls at Teen Scene last night. Tracey—pretty, about fourteen, with long, black hair?"

Maddie shrugged. "That description could fit about half the girls there."

"I guess. Anyway, I've found her upset several times, but I haven't been able to get her to open up to me. It happened again last night, and once again, she wouldn't talk to me. It made me feel so useless. Maybe Landon's right, and—" She stopped.

"Landon, huh?" she smirked. "I might have known he'd have something to do with it. What did he say?"

"Nothing that bad. He implied that professionals could do what we're doing with the teenagers a lot better, and after my failure to get through to Tracey, I began to think that maybe it's true."

"And maybe it's not." Maddie patted her hand. "Landon might just be prejudiced because he's donated a lot of money to youth center programs over the years, all of them run by professionals. And he's a businessman—his first instinct is always to call in the professionals. He's not thinking about the fact that Grasslands isn't Fort Worth."

Violet smiled, her spirits lifting at her twin's support. "That's just what I told him. I didn't know about his charities, though, or I'd have been more careful what I said. I think that's admirable."

Maddie clapped her hand over her mouth for an instant, making a face. "Don't say anything, or he'll know I told you. He keeps things like his charities secret, and the only reason I know is because he recruited Dad to help with some kids who needed surgery."

"I won't say anything, but I don't see why…" Often wealthy people made more of a show of their philanthropy.

"It's got something to do with his sister, I think,"

Maddie said, her forehead wrinkling. "Jessica was his younger sister, and she died in an accident when she was a teenager. I imagine he does it in her memory."

"That's so sad." Violet had been wrong about him then, imagining a trouble-free, privileged life for him. She should have known better. Even in the best of circumstances, people didn't get out of their teen years unscathed, and losing a sister was a terrible loss.

"Jessica was about my age, but I didn't know her since she went to a different school. I do know that Landon was never the same after she died."

"No, I guess he wouldn't be." She wouldn't be, if she lost Jack or Maddie.

Maddie stood, gathering up the dishes. "I'll take these back to the kitchen. You never did answer my question. Why don't you stay home today and get some rest?"

"If I stayed home, I wouldn't get any rest," she said ruefully. "Saturday is always a busy day at the store, and I'd feel I had to go there if I don't go to the hospital. Anyway, since I missed visiting Mom yesterday, I don't want to miss today."

"Okay. I just need to change. How soon will you be ready?" Maddie glanced at her watch.

"Say about an hour. I still have to check in with Ty and Ricardo, and there's something I want to look for in the attic. Does that work for you?"

"Fine by me." Maddie vanished in the direction of the kitchen.

Violet headed upstairs. Sometime in the night she'd tried to comfort herself with memories of the way things used to be. She'd thought of something that might be a comfort to her mom, if she could find it.

When they were little, Belle used to snuggle Violet and Jack in a knitted throw she called the story shawl. They'd cuddle together on her bed or Jack's, the shawl around them, while Belle told them bedtime stories. She could still feel the warmth of the shawl and the music of her mom's voice lulling them to sleep.

Belle wouldn't have thrown away something that meant so much to them. The shawl was probably in a trunk in the attic, stored away with other mementos of their childhood.

If she could find it, she'd take it to the hospital with her. Nobody knew what her mom was aware of. Maybe she'd find some comfort in that shawl. Violet had a feeling she would, anyway, even if Belle didn't.

Switching on the overhead bulb, she headed up the attic stairs and emerged at the top, glancing around to orient herself. Thanks to the overhead light fixture and the windows at either end, the attic was bright enough to search for something easily. And it was clean, of course. Lupita wouldn't hear of any part of her domain not receiving a periodic cleaning, even one as little-used as the attic.

For the most part, the boxes and plastic bins were marked, thanks to Belle's passion for organization. Some of the older trunks dated to her Uncle James's parents' time, and every once in a while her mom threatened to put everyone to work sorting them, looking for items that should be donated to the county historical society. So far, Violet and Jack had managed to evade that task, mainly because they were all too busy.

Slipping around boxes marked Jack's School Projects and Violet's 4-H Awards, Violet came to the trunk she thought most likely. She knelt on the floor and lifted the curved lid, wondering if God minded a selfish prayer that she be able to find the shawl.

The first few items were of more recent origin: a doll she'd won at the county fair one year, carefully wrapped in plastic; a colorful serape Jack had brought back from a trip to Mexico; two graduation caps, one white and one black. Traditionally the boys graduating from Grasslands wore black, while the girls wore white.

She put them carefully aside, smiling at Jack's probable reaction if he realized how many mementos of his youth were preserved up here. She lifted out a patchwork quilt and there, at last, was the shawl. Someone had wrapped it in a sheet, then in plastic, to protect it.

Violet pulled the shawl free of the wrappings, eager to feel it in her hands again. The yarn was soft and worn, cushiony to the touch, and she seemed to see her own small hand clutching it tightly.

Tears stung her eyes and she blinked them back. She shouldn't wallow too much in the past in front of Maddie, reminding her again of all that she had missed with Belle. But she could give herself a few minutes to remember. She drew the shawl around her shoulders despite the heat, and felt the security it had always given her. She could use that sense of security right now.

But Maddie would be waiting, and she still had things to do before they could leave for Amarillo. She leaned forward to put the other items back into the trunk and realized that there was still something in the bottom—a flat manila envelope, faded with age.

Violet picked it up, her fingers telling her that it wasn't empty before she'd even opened it. There was just one enclosure, and she drew the item out carefully, turning it over to look at it.

Her heart seemed to stop for an instant, and she couldn't catch her breath. The photo was old and faded, its surface cracked and marred. But she could still make out the image. Belle—a much younger Belle—stood in front of a small house. She held an infant in her arms and had a toddler by the hand. It had to be her and Jack with Mom in that picture. But that wasn't what reduced her to uncontrollable tears.

A man stood next to Belle. She'd only seen Brian Wallace in photos, but his looks hadn't changed that much with age. He, too, held an infant in his arms and a toddler by the hand.

It was her family—her whole family, all together.

Landon went up the stairs at the Colby house quietly, his ears still burning from Maddie's sharp words. She'd taken him to task for what he'd said the night before, telling him in no uncertain terms what she thought of him. She'd followed up her lecture by demanding that he apologize to Violet, saying he wouldn't be welcome here if he didn't make this right.

If he hadn't been the target, he might have enjoyed seeing Maddie assert herself so thoroughly. He'd always thought Maddie needed protection, but he'd begun to feel he was the one who needed protection from her.

Well, he hadn't intended his words to hurt Violet. That was the last thing he wanted to do. Apparently, from what Maddie had said, there'd been an incident with one of the teens, presumably the one he'd seen crying. Violet felt, probably thanks to what he'd said, that she should have been able to handle it better.

He still thought the teen center should be in professional hands, but his words had been careless, criticizing when he hadn't completely understood the situation. As Violet had said, this wasn't Fort Worth, and they didn't have the city's resources.

Maddie had told him he'd find Violet in the attic. The door to the stairway stood open, so he assumed Violet was still up there. He went up quietly, caught between guilt and annoyance that he had to apologize to her once again.

It took only a quick glance to find Violet when he reached the top, and the sight rocked him back on his heels. She sat on the floor in front of an old trunk, looking down at something in her lap, and she was weeping, her slim shoulders shaking with the depth of her sobs.

His heart seemed to be twisting in his chest. Quickly, before he could think about what he should or should not do, he went and knelt next to her.

"Violet." He said her name gently, his throat thickening at her pain. "What is it? Can I help?"

She gestured toward the item in her lap, seeming unable to speak through her sobs. Taking that as an invitation, he bent over to look. It was a photo—old and faded. He had no trouble recognizing Brian Wallace, though. Clearly the photo was of Brian and Belle with all four of their children.

There were no more questions about who Brian's first wife had been. He could have Dave stop pursuing that missing link, although they still didn't know the Why.

"I'm sorry," he said softly. "You just found this?"

Violet nodded. "They…they look so young. So happy." The sobs overtook her again.

He couldn't help it. He drew her into his arms, stroking her hair. She wore it loose today, and it flowed through his hand like silk. He murmured any sort of nonsense that came into his head that he thought might be soothing.

It probably wasn't a good idea, holding her this way, but at the moment he didn't care. He dropped a light kiss on the top of her head.

"I understand," he said. "You've just had too much to bear lately, and now this. You don't have to be brave all the time, you know." He stroked her shoulders, feeling them shake with her weeping.

Violet drew back a little, sniffling as she tried to contain her tears. "I'm sorry. I didn't mean to fall apart. When I looked at the picture, I realized something." She pressed her palm to her chest. "There's always been an…an empty place in me. In my heart. Now I know what it was. It's the space where my father should have been."

His own heart seemed to be ripping apart. "I'm sorry, so sorry for what they did. It wasn't fair to you." He wanted to touch her cheek, but he held back, fearing he'd cross a line and not be able to get back.

"I can't let myself go like this. I can't. Mom and Jack always tried to take care of me. Now I have to be the strong one."

Landon felt an irrational surge of fury toward her missing brother. "You have Maddie," he said soothingly. "And me."

Violet wiped her eyes with the back of her hand. "You're kind, Landon. But you've done enough. I can't involve you in my grief."

"I think it's too late for that," he murmured, and he knew it was too late for him, as well. He caressed her cheek, and then cradled her face in his hands.

Violet's eyes widened, and her breath seemed to catch. He could feel her skin grow warm against his palms.

Unable to resist, he lowered his face to hers and kissed her. Her lips were soft and warm, and she leaned into the kiss as if it were the most natural thing in the world.

Landon's pulse thundered, and the longing to draw her more fully into his arms was so strong he could barely fight it off.

But he did…he had to. He drew back, but even as he did so, he knew he could no longer pretend he didn't have feelings for Violet.

He brushed his fingers gently along the sweet curve of her cheek and then sat back on his heels. He couldn't seem to stop looking at her the way she was at this moment… her cheeks pink, her lips soft, her eyes a little dazed.

He cleared his throat. "Is this where I should say I'm sorry?"

She shook her head, turning away as if to hide her face. "No." She put her hand against her cheek in what seemed an instinctive gesture. "But maybe we should go downstairs and forget about what just happened."

He took her hand and helped her to rise. "We can go downstairs. As for forgetting—that's something I can't promise."

Violet felt reasonably sure her cheeks were red when they reached the living room and found Maddie curled up in the corner chair that seemed to have become her favorite. She'd already dressed for the trip to Amarillo in tan pants and a silky turquoise top. Next to her twin, Violet felt grubby and disheveled.

Maybe Maddie would assume Violet's flush was

from the two flights of stairs. But from the way Maddie glanced from her to Landon, Violet doubted it.

What had she been thinking of, letting Landon kiss her that way? Worse, kissing him back? True, Maddie insisted that her relationship with Landon was over, but Maddie was angry with him right now. What happened when she got over that?

"Look what I found in the attic," she said hurriedly, before Maddie could speak.

"A shawl?" Naturally Maddie focused on the larger object Violet held.

"This." Maybe she should try to soften the impact, but she couldn't think how to do that. "I found it in the bottom of Mom's trunk."

Maddie took the tattered photograph, holding it carefully by the edges. She stared at it for what seemed a long time, and her eyes glistened with tears.

"Our family," she murmured, her voice growing husky. "It's all of us." She stood and threw her arms around Violet, enveloping her in a fierce hug. "Our family," she repeated.

Violet held her tight. "It's going to be all right." Her voice sounded husky, too. "Now that we know for sure, we'll figure the rest of it out."

The precious photo trembled in Maddie's hand, and Landon rescued it. "Maybe when the two of you are finished being so mushy with each other, we can figure out if there are any clues in this photo."

Maddie released her, blinking the tears away. "That's Landon. Always businesslike."

"I see that," Violet agreed. But Landon hadn't been so businesslike in the attic just a few minutes ago.

"Do you have a magnifying glass, Violet?" He

sounded calm and practical, but there was something in his eyes when he looked at her that brought the blood back to her cheeks.

"I think so. Let me look for it." She hurried out of the room, relieved to be away from his disturbing presence for at least a little while. There should be a magnifying glass in the desk in the den, but even after a prolonged rummage she couldn't locate it.

Lupita must have heard her, because she came out of the kitchen, wiping her hands on a towel. "Violet? Are you looking for something?"

"I thought there was a magnifying glass in the desk, but I can't find it."

"It's here, in the kitchen drawer." Lupita produced it in an instant. "I use it to read the small print on labels. Why do you need it?"

"We've found something." She linked her arms with Lupita's. "Come and see."

Now that her first emotional response had passed, Violet felt excitement rising. Who knew what this discovery might lead to?

They went into the living room arm in arm. Maddie and Landon were standing together at one of the end tables, looking down at the photo, and a strand of Landon's blond hair had fallen onto his forehead. She should not be feeling an urge to press it back into place.

"Let me show it to Lupita," she said.

Landon and Maddie stepped back, and she led Lupita to the table. "Look."

"Ah." Lupita let out a long exhale. She looked from Violet to Maddie. "There you are—such beautiful babies." Her eyes filled with tears. "If only we could have known..." She stopped, shaking her head.

"I know," Violet said softly. "But at least Maddie and I are together now. Maybe soon we'll know why they separated us to begin with."

Violet took the glass and bent over the picture, eyeing it carefully. "Magnifying it doesn't really help much. The quality of the picture has deteriorated. It probably wasn't very good to begin with."

Maddie took the magnifier. "Let me see." She studied it for a long moment, but then she shook her head and handed it to Landon.

Violet tried not to smile. Landon had obviously been itching to get his hands on the magnifying glass and see for himself, not content to take their word for it.

Finally he straightened, shaking his head.

"Isn't there something we can do with it?" Maddie asked impatiently. "Can't we use some photo software to make it clearer?"

"That's not a job for an amateur with a fragile photo like this one," Landon said. "I know a little about it, but not enough. But I do know someone who could at least restore the photo and make copies for you, even if he can't bring out any more details. Will you let me take it back to Fort Worth with me and have him work on it?" He was looking at Violet for permission. "I promise I'll take good care of it."

Much as she hated to part with the photo, that solution made sense. "All right. Are you going back to Fort Worth right away?" She tried to sound as if it didn't matter to her when he left.

"Tomorrow," he said. "I do have to go back then so I can meet with a new client on Monday morning, but I'll be back as soon as I can. Maybe I could take you two out to dinner tonight, if you like."

Violet exchanged glances with Maddie, but she didn't seem to object. "That would be nice. But it will have to be on the early side. I need to be at Teen Scene again tonight."

She gave Landon a defiant glance, wondering if he had anything else to say on the folly of inexperienced volunteers working with teens.

But he just nodded. "Great. I'll make a reservation, then. Any suggestions?"

She smiled. "There aren't a lot of options in Grasslands, trust me. Sally's Barbecue is probably best. She'll be pleasantly surprised to have someone actually call her for a reservation." Obviously, Landon was accustomed to far more fancy restaurants than anything Grasslands had to offer.

Landon nodded, glancing at his watch. "I'd best get out of your way so you can head up to Amarillo. I'll meet you at Sally's at around 5:30, if that gives us enough time before Teen Scene opens."

Us, he'd said. She decided not to read anything into that. "It's fine," she said. "We'll see you there."

Chapter 9

Violet was smiling as she unlocked the side door at the church that evening. After the emotional strains of the day, supper with Landon and Maddie had been surprisingly relaxing. She and Maddie had come straight to the church after supper, but Landon had stopped by the hotel to change into something more casual.

"That was fun, wasn't it?" Maddie, entering the church in her wake, seemed to be on the same wavelength. "Landon was more relaxed than I've seen him in a long time."

"You sound as if you've gotten over being mad at him." Violet tried to keep her voice casual as she switched on the lights.

"I guess I can never stay mad at him for long," Maddie said. She gave Violet a second glance as they went down the stairs to the gym area. "Why?"

Violet shrugged. "He's a nice guy. I know you said your engagement was over, but…"

"I meant it," Maddie said firmly. "Why is that so hard to believe? Yes, he's a great guy, but he's not the one for me. The only time we even kissed was that night he proposed, and there wasn't a single spark. We were both dumb to even consider marriage. Landon was trying to help me, because that's who he is, and I was feeling sorry for myself and lost. But I'm not anymore." Suddenly she grabbed Violet's arm and pulled her around to face her. "You're interested in him, aren't you?"

It might have sounded accusing, but Maddie's face was lit up, her voice filled with mischief.

"No, no, I…"

Violet let that trail off, because Maddie was grinning at her knowledgeably.

"Come on, admit it. You're interested."

"You're not upset?" She clutched her sister's hand, looking into her eyes. "Please, Maddie, you have to be honest with me about it."

"Upset?" Maddie rolled her eyes. "Why would I be upset? I think it's great. I don't want Landon for a husband, but I wouldn't mind having him for a brother-in-law."

"Stop." Violet made a gesture of covering her ears. "It's nothing like that."

"Then what is it?" Maddie teased. "Come on, you can tell me. I'm your twin."

She shouldn't, but the urge to confide in someone was just too strong. "We…well, we kissed. That's all. It doesn't have to mean anything."

Maddie shook her head decisively. "I don't think Landon would kiss you unless it meant something. Not under the circumstances."

"That's just it. This isn't the right time for…well, romance. Not with everything that's happening."

"There is no right time," Maddie declared. "Promise me that you won't discourage Landon just because of what happened between him and me."

Someone was knocking at the outside door she hadn't unlocked yet, maybe Landon.

"All right," Violet said hastily when she saw the unrelenting look on her sister's face. "I promise. Now let go. I have to open up."

Maddie grinned triumphantly. "Don't forget. And tell me everything."

She wouldn't promise that, Violet decided as she hurried to the door. Not everything. She unlocked the door and swung it open, prepared to face Landon.

But it was Sadie Johnson, the new church secretary, standing there peering in anxiously.

"Sadie, hi. Come in, please."

Sadie sidled a few inches forward, clutching that drab sweater around her. She wore it like a protective coating, it seemed to Violet.

"I won't take up much of your time. He… Pastor Jeb, I mean…he asked me to come by and see that you have all the help you need tonight. He said to tell you he can come if you need him."

Maddie had moved next to her, and Violet felt sure Maddie hadn't missed the awed note in Sadie's voice when she said Jeb's name.

"Come on inside, Sadie." Maddie put her arm around Sadie and propelled her onto the balcony that overlooked the gym floor. "So tell us, do you like working for Pastor Jeb?"

Violet gave an inward sigh. Apparently there was no end to Maddie's matchmaking urges.

"He's…it's very nice," Sadie said, her eyes wide behind the oversized glasses.

She had lovely eyes, Violet realized, a deep, translucent green. What a shame that they were hidden behind those ugly glasses.

"Pastor Jeb is a sweetheart," Maddie declared.

Sadie blushed, but didn't answer. Violet decided she'd better intervene before teenagers started piling in on them. That would probably scare Sadie to death.

"I think we're okay for volunteers. Tell Pastor Jeb I'll call for help if I need it." In fact, Tim and Lynn Cole had just come down the stairs, and Violet waved to them. "Thanks for coming by, Sadie. I'd love to have coffee with you one day next week so we can get better acquainted."

She didn't have a spare minute in her schedule at the moment, but the spirit of welcoming newcomers had been thoroughly inculcated by Belle and Lupita between them.

"That…that's nice of you, but I don't think I can. I mean, my new job…" Sadie let that trail off, maybe realizing how silly it sounded.

"I'll call you," Violet said, and turned away to check in three teenage boys with a basketball who were eager to hit the court. When she looked back, Sadie was gone.

"She likes him," Maddie whispered in her ear.

Violet smiled, shaking her head. "Pastor Jeb has that effect on women," she said. "When he came the number of female volunteers for church activities soared, according to Mom."

"I'm not surprised," Maddie replied. "He's sweet.

And Sadie could be attractive if she'd do something with herself."

"Don't matchmake," Violet warned. "That always backfires." She pointed to the small table and chair next to the door. "Here's your duty station. Get names when kids come in. They can leave anytime they want, but they have to check out with you. Mark down the time. Once they leave, they can't come back in."

The rule had been Pastor Jeb's idea, and it was a good one. It discouraged kids from telling their parents they were at Teen Scene and then heading for less worthwhile activities.

"Yes, boss." Maddie gave her a mock salute. "I'll man the gates until relieved. Landon should be here soon."

She sounded a little too innocent with that comment, Violet decided.

"Don't you dare say anything to him about what I told you," she warned.

"Wouldn't dream of it," Maddie replied, but her eyes twinkled. Deciding that saying anything else would just invite more teasing, Violet fled.

Landon glanced at his watch. Another hour and the teen center would be closing. He wasn't exactly longing for this evening to be over, but he had to confess to a sense of…what was it? Inadequacy? As much as he'd done to support missions to teenagers, donating generously and serving on the boards of two projects, he'd never had quite this up-close an experience.

It was one thing to donate money in Jessica's memory. It was quite another to see her face in the young girls who pressed together in close-knit circles, giggling, talking, eyeing the boys who pretended to be oblivious of them. Being here brought his grief to the surface—grief and guilt. If he had paid more attention to Jessica, she might be alive. He'd known from an early age that they couldn't count on their parents for that attention. He should have intervened.

He didn't belong here, Landon thought suddenly. He could play a pick-up game of basketball with the boys, of course, but what good did that do?

Maddie seemed to have adapted to this activity with surprising ease, he realized. Right now she was at a corner table, talking to a slight young teenager over a couple of sodas. The girl had long, glossy black hair and a delicate face. It was the girl he'd seen crying.

Was this the girl Maddie had meant in her tirade against him this morning? The one about whom Violet was worried? If so, Maddie seemed to be making some progress with her.

He sensed someone beside him and turned to see Violet watching the pair, just as he was.

"Maddie seems to be fitting right in," he said.

"You sound surprised." Violet glanced up at him and then looked quickly away.

But not before he'd seen the warmth in her gaze. It gave him a totally irrational urge to put his arm around her.

He restrained himself. "Well, volunteering in a small-town teen center is a far cry from her glamorous job as assistant at *Texas Today* magazine."

"Maddie has unexpected depths," Violet said, smiling a little, but then the smile slipped away. "She talked to me about losing her job. That really devastated her."

"Do you recommend corralling a bunch of teenagers as a cure?" he asked.

Violet's head tilted as she seemed to consider the question. "I don't know about that, specifically. But I know it's important to feel that you're doing something useful, and she is."

"You make a good point." He let his hand brush hers between their bodies, trusting that no one else could see. The kids probably shouldn't see their chaperones holding hands. "Is that the girl Maddie said you were worried about?" he asked quietly.

She nodded. "Tracey Benton. The family is fairly new in the area. They moved here from somewhere in south Texas."

"Trouble at home, do you think?" He glanced at the girl, who was smiling at something Maddie had said.

"I'm beginning to think so. Usually if they're upset about friends or boys, they'll come out with it, given half a chance. Something tells me this is family trouble."

"You really care, don't you?"

She glanced up, obviously surprised. "Of course."

"Even if the girl doesn't let you help her?"

Violet shrugged. "She still shows up every time we're open. As long as she's here, we have a chance to minister to her. There's no way of knowing how and why God might work through us."

Landon was silenced by the words. He made careful, thorough studies of any organization before he donated to it, as meticulous as if he were making a business investment. Violet's haphazard approach was foreign to his nature, but he still couldn't help but appreciate it.

"Well, Maddie seems to have things in hand here,"

Violet said. "I'm going to relieve Lynn on the door. It gets busy when a lot of kids start to leave at once."

She moved off, and Landon stood looking after her. Violet kept surprising him, showing him different aspects of herself that both startled and delighted him.

He checked out the kitchen to make sure the volunteer there didn't need any help, then walked back through to the gym, telling himself he wasn't necessarily doing that because Violet was there.

Violet was there, all right. She stood at the door, her body language eloquent. She was barring entrance to three teenage boys who loomed over her.

He walked quickly toward her, thinking of nothing but the need to protect her. As he came up to the group by the door, she was lecturing the kid who was obviously the ringleader of the trio. Taller than Violet by a half a foot, he teetered a bit on the heels of his Western boots, hat pushed back on his head.

"You know the rules, Sam Donner. Once you leave, you can't come back in."

"But I just went out to check on Danny, here." He shoved the kid next to him. "Danny forgot he was supposed to meet us here."

"You went out looking for beer," Violet said, her tone uncompromising. "And you smell like you found it. Now leave before I call your parents."

It hung in the balance for a moment. Violet's assumption of control seemed to be working. Then the taller of his two buddies prodded Sam in the ribs. "You gonna let her talk to you like that? You said we could have some fun here."

That gave the kid a bit of courage. He took a step toward Violet, opened his mouth, and closed it with a snap as Landon moved Violet aside with one hand and grabbed Sam's collar with the other.

"You've been asked to leave, fellas. I think you probably want to do just that, don't you?" He pulled up on the collar, the slightest movement making the kid stumble. Violet was right—he'd been drinking, and the smell of it churned Landon's stomach, sending memories tumbling through his mind. "Right?" He yanked the collar a bit harder, judging that none of them really wanted a fight, especially not with someone more than their size.

"Landon," Violet murmured, but Landon didn't take his eyes off the kid's face.

"Right, right, we're going." The kid tried to manage a smile, not quite succeeding. Landon let him go, and he stumbled backward out the door. "Come on. We'll find our fun somewhere else." He turned with an assumption of arrogance that didn't quite fly and shuffled off with his friends.

Landon closed the door on the heat and humidity, his stomach still churning. He turned to Violet to find her looking at him with fury in her eyes.

"What do you mean by interfering?" she snapped. "If I'd needed help, I'd have asked for it. Which I didn't."

Violet was still fuming inwardly as she finished the routine of closing Teen Scene down for another week. If she'd been able to say everything she was feeling at the time, she'd probably have simmered down by now.

But she hadn't, both because she wouldn't do that where there was a possibility of the teens overhearing, and because it just wasn't in her nature to blow up at anyone. How could Landon move her to both longing and fury so easily?

Maybe she didn't want to look too closely at the answer to that question.

Violet walked back through the gym, making sure everything had been cleaned up. She had it on good authority that a couple of church members had taken to checking out the rooms on Sunday mornings, ready to complain about the program if they found anything amiss. She was determined that they wouldn't.

The gym was fine, the kitchen cleaned up and everything put away. The games room and social room seemed to be in order as well. She began locking doors, making her way around methodically while wondering where Maddie had gone. She must have already headed upstairs.

Everything secure, she turned off the lights and started up the stairs. Still no Maddie. Violet stepped outside and locked the door.

She turned, looking automatically for Maddie's car, but the space was filled instead by Landon's vehicle, with Landon standing beside it.

He straightened, probably reading the annoyance in her face even in the glow from the light above the door. "Don't be mad," he said quickly.

"Where's Maddie?"

"I asked if she'd let me bring you home so we can talk."

It wouldn't have been hard for him to persuade Maddie, given her obvious desire to bring the two of them together.

"It's late, Landon. I don't want to talk right now."

"But I do." He stepped toward her, and as he came into the circle of light, she was shocked by the pain in his face. "Please, Violet. Take a walk with me. I've got to get this out of my system before I bury it again."

The grief in his voice struck her heart so hard she felt it like a physical pain. Wordless, she held out her hand to him. He clasped it, holding on tight, and they turned and walked along the side of the church toward Main Street.

Landon stopped when they reached the street, as if unsure where to go. Then, still clasping her hand, he led the way across to the green, serene and quiet, its linden trees spreading their branches like arms in welcome.

The bench in the center of the green bore a plaque saying it was donated in memory of Uncle James, and that seemed comforting. Landon sat down next to her and Violet waited, half-afraid to hear what he had to say.

Crickets rasped their monotonous sound, and a light breeze tickled the hairs on her nape. A car went by, its radio playing a country-western song, and then they were alone.

"You think I shouldn't have interfered tonight with those boys. Maybe I shouldn't have, but…" He paused, seeming to search for words. "It's not something I talk about, but you deserve to hear what drives me. We've gotten too close, and everything that's happened since I came to Grasslands has been bringing up memories."

Painful memories, judging by the look on his face, and her heart was swept with the longing to wipe away that pain. If all she could do was listen, then she would. "Tell me," she said quietly.

His fingers tightened on hers. "I don't know if you can understand a family like mine. Two parents, plenty of money, two healthy children…from the outside we must have looked like the perfect family."

He fell silent, and she realized she'd have to prompt him to keep him going.

"Not so perfect on the inside?" she asked gently.

He shook his head. "Don't get me wrong. Our parents weren't abusive or anything of the kind. They just didn't have any time for us."

"Us?"

His hand moved restlessly, and for a moment she thought he'd jump up and run away from telling her. The desire was so strong in him that she could feel it.

"Jessica. My sister, three years younger than I." His voice softened. "She was such a beautiful little kid—blond curls, big blue eyes, such a sweet, innocent smile. Anyone would love her. Our parents just…" He shrugged. "Dad was totally involved with his business. Our mother was totally involved with her social life. We were left to a succession of housekeepers to take care of. I figured out early on that if anyone was going to look after Jessica, I'd be that person."

Maddie had said his sister died when she was in her teens. A cold hand seemed to grip Violet's heart. "Something happened to her, didn't it?"

He was staring straight ahead, and his profile was sharp and forbidding…and as still as if it was carved from rock. He swallowed, and even in the semidark she could see the movement of his Adam's apple.

"She was just fourteen—the age of some of those kids tonight. Mom and Dad were off on a trip to New York, leaving the housekeeper in charge. Jessica had been driving me crazy all week, wanting to go with me to a football game and party." He scrubbed a hand across his face. "I told her I wouldn't because the kids would be too old for her, but the truth was that there was a girl I was interested in, and I didn't want my kid sister tagging along. So I went off without her."

He took a ragged breath. "As soon as the housekeeper dozed off, Jessica slipped out. She left me a note, saying she could find parties on her own and she'd tell me all about it the next day. But she didn't." He stopped, and she saw the muscles work in his neck. "She got into a car with a drunken kid. He ran right into a bridge abutment. He walked away with barely a scratch. She died a few hours later at the hospital, with nobody there but me."

She hurt so much for him that she could hardly breathe. So much pain, so much guilt—it flowed from him in heavy, suffocating waves, nearly burying her.

She couldn't speak, but she had to. She put her hand on his arm, the muscles so tight that they felt like steel cables. "Landon, it wasn't your fault. You—"

"I should have taken care of her. I didn't. She died." His voice was flat.

"You weren't her parent." She tried again. "Just her brother. Just a kid yourself. You couldn't have known what would happen."

"I should have taken her with me. She loved to go places with her big brother." He turned to her then, his face tortured. "But I didn't. I let her go off on her own and get in a car with a kid who was blind drunk."

"That's why you reacted so strongly to Sam and his friends." He'd seen her threatened by a drunken kid, and he'd jumped in to protect her in the way he hadn't protected his sister.

"I had to protect you. Just like I was trying to protect Maddie when I proposed to her. But nothing can make up for what I did to Jessica."

"Landon, I understand. I do. But you weren't responsible. Even if you had been, even if you'd been driving that car, you must know that Jessica would have forgiven you in an instant. That God forgives you." She smoothed her hand along his arm, hoping the simple human touch would comfort him.

He shook his head. "God may forgive me. But I don't forgive myself."

"Don't, Landon." Her voice shook and she tried her best to steady it. She couldn't pretend to have the strongest faith in the world, but this she was sure of. "You can't turn away from forgiveness that way. If you can't forgive yourself, how can you accept God's forgiveness?"

He looked at her bleakly. "I don't know. Maybe I can't."

She touched his face, smoothing her palm along his cheek, feeling warm skin and the faint stubble of beard. A muscle twitched in his jaw as if in protest to her touch.

Then he made an inarticulate sound and pulled her into his arms, holding her fiercely, as if she was his only anchor from the pain that was sweeping him away.

She wrapped her arms around him, holding him close, thinking of how he had held her in those moments after she'd found the photo of her family. She didn't know what he felt for her. She only knew that at this moment he needed comfort, and if that was all she could ever give him, at least she would give him that right now.

Chapter 10

Violet sat in church on Sunday morning, her gaze focused on Pastor Jeb. He stood tall in the simple, pale oak pulpit, his red hair like a flame where a shaft of sunlight from an upper window struck it. Around them, Grasslands' faithful crowded the plain, uncushioned pews of the simple sanctuary, its stained-glass windows the only ornamentation other than the painting of Jesus in Gethsemane above the communion table.

Having Maddie sitting next to her was a new experience, and her heart filled with thankfulness that she was reunited with her twin after all these years. It still seemed impossible that they should have found each other. Still, with God, all things were possible.

She wasn't quite so thankful for the attention they were arousing. People were too polite to turn around and stare openly in church, but those seated behind her and Maddie had a clear view. She could almost feel the numerous eyes on the back of her neck.

Violet brought her wandering thoughts back to the sermon, but Pastor Jeb's words about the power of prayer for even the smallest things in life sent them careening off on another tangent. Of course, Landon's grief over his lost sister wasn't small. It loomed large in his past, still coloring all that he thought and did.

He was taking all the responsibility for what happened to his sister on himself. That was a natural reaction to so painful a loss, but she'd think time and distance would have helped him see that other people bore responsibility, too.

His parents, for instance, to say nothing of the housekeeper who'd dozed off and let Jessica go out that fateful night. Then there were the people who'd given that party and obviously not provided enough supervision, and of course, the drunk driver himself.

And finally, Jessica. Much as it would pain Landon to think about it, a fourteen-year-old should be old enough to exercise caution about getting into a car with someone who was obviously drunk.

She couldn't have said any of those things to Landon last night. Maybe she never could. Landon had been silent as he drove her back to the ranch, as if the effort of telling her had exhausted all his words. She'd been as quiet, not knowing what to say that would do any good. It seemed that the odd way they had been brought together had led them into a closer relationship than would normally be possible in such a short period of time. She'd betrayed her deepest emotions to Landon, and last night he'd told her things he might never have told anyone.

Maybe it was too much, too fast. Maybe that was why he'd been so uncommunicative. Doubts swept through her. Maybe he'd been having regrets about saying anything at all to her.

When they'd reached the house, he'd walked her to the door, told her he'd be back in a few days at most, and given her a quick, hard kiss. Then he'd gotten into the car and driven away.

At least now she knew why he'd reacted the way he had to young Sam and his buddies. How could he do otherwise?

They stood for the closing prayer, and then Pastor Jeb raised his arms as if to encircle all of them in a hug. "God be with you until we meet again."

Somehow her heart eased as she repeated the words in her heart to her mom, to Jack, to Landon, even to the father she hadn't met.

The postlude rang out, and she and Maddie began to edge their way out of the pew. Their progress was impeded by all the people who wanted to satisfy their curiosity by having a word with them.

That was an uncharitable thought, and she scolded herself for it. These people were her neighbors and her church family. Of course they were interested, but they were well-meaning, too. Most of them honestly just wanted to welcome Maddie to their midst.

Glancing back toward the double doors, Violet noticed someone else who was in church for the first time that day. Tracey sat in the corner of the back pew, looking around as if unsure what to do next.

Violet murmured an apology in Maddie's ear and, ignoring her reproachful expression, deserted her, slipping back along the aisle. She nodded and smiled as people spoke to her and evaded the hands that reached out to her. She wanted to get to Tracey before the girl had a chance to disappear.

Violet reached the back of the sanctuary just as Tracey slipped out the door, taking advantage of a large woman who'd stopped to talk to Pastor Jeb to slide past without greeting him. Violet followed her, touching Tracey lightly on the shoulder.

The girl turned, her eyes wide and startled.

"Hey, Tracey, it's so nice to see you here today. I'm glad you decided to worship with us this morning."

Tracey nodded, her expression guarded. "I just thought I would. I mean, since I come here for Teen Scene, the church didn't seem so strange to me."

That was exactly the argument she'd used to sway some of the board members into starting the ministry, and she was glad to hear the reasoning coming from Tracey's lips. Tracey had obviously dressed carefully for her first appearance in church, discarding her usual jeans and T-shirt for a yellow cotton sundress. Her dark hair shone against the sunny color.

"I'm glad you feel at home here." She hesitated, wanting to ask but not wanting to offend. "Would your parents like to come, do you think?"

Tracey shook her head, looking down. "Mama prays a lot, but she said no when I asked her. And Daddy doesn't hold much with church people."

"Calls us a bunch of do-gooders?" Violet grinned. "That's okay. We're glad you're here, anyway." Other people were flowing out of the sanctuary now, and she edged Tracey over onto the grass, away from them, not wanting to be interrupted now that the girl was finally opening up to her.

"I wish they'd come," Tracey said in a sudden burst

of confidence. "They'd like Pastor Jeb. Nobody could help liking him, don't you think?"

"I'd say so. I'm sure he'd be happy to go and visit them, if you think that might help."

Tracey shook her head decisively, her black hair flying out with the strength of the movement. "Please don't ask him that, Ms. Vi. It…they argue too much already. I don't want to make it worse." She clamped her lips together, as if wishing she could have those words back. "I didn't… I shouldn't have said that."

"It's okay." Violet touched her hand lightly. "I'm your friend, Tracey. You come first with me, not your parents. It's tough if they're fighting a lot, I know. Any time you want to talk, I'm here."

"I'm okay," Tracey said, trying to smile. "Lots of kids have parents who fight." She hesitated. "Ms. Vi, if my mama decided to go back to Mexico, would I have to go with her?"

For an instant it took her breath away. So that's what Tracey had been worrying about. She prayed silently for the right response.

"Do you think your mother plans to do that?"

Tracey shrugged, face downcast. "I don't know for sure. But I heard her say something about going back one time when she and Daddy were quarreling, and it made me scared. Would I?"

Unfortunately, Violet had no idea to the legalities of a situation like this. "I think that you and your daddy would have something to say about it, Tracey. It wouldn't be right for her to just take you away. Do you want me to find out what the law is about that?"

Tracey's eyes went wide with fear. "I don't want to get into trouble, or to get Mama into trouble."

"No, no, you wouldn't. I wouldn't mention your name. I can just find out what you should do if that happens. Okay?"

She didn't move for a moment, long enough for Violet to wonder if she'd said all the wrong things. Then Tracey threw her arms around Violet in a quick hug.

"Thank you," she whispered into Violet's ear. Then she turned and rushed off in a swirl of yellow.

"You're working overtime," Landon observed as he opened the door to his condo to find Dave leaning against the doorjamb. He stepped back, gesturing for the P.I. to come in.

"You told me to go all out," Dave reminded him. He stood for a moment in the living room, looking out the bank of windows that gave a view of downtown Fort Worth. From this height the city spread out like a magical place, especially at this hour, when dusk drew in and the lights came on.

"Quite a view." Dave relaxed onto the black leather couch. Everything in the room was either black or white, and Landon realized he was comparing it unfavorably with what he'd seen of the Colby ranch house. Here, everything was new, sleek and impersonal. There, the furnishings might be a bit worn, but there was welcoming warmth to the casual earth tones and bright accents.

He sat down opposite the PI. "I don't suppose you came here to admire the view. What's up?"

"After I got your message about the photograph, I quit chasing shadows. Like you said, it's obvious that the woman known as Belle Colby was Wallace's first wife and the mother of the two sets of twins."

"You got the photocopy I sent you?" At Dave's nod,

he went on. "I turned it over to Phil O'Hara at Optical Graphics. If anyone can do anything with it, he can. But I'm not sure it gets us any further. It can't explain why they split up the twins, or why she's been living under an assumed name."

Dave reached out to toy with the chain of the pewter lamp on the glass-topped end table. "That's how I've been thinking, too. So I started at this end, trying to trace Belle Colby back as far as I can."

Landon nodded, a little discouraged. Even if Dave did produce some answers, what difference was it going to make at this point?

"Right. You told me before she seemed to have done an expert job of creating a new identity."

"It's beginning to look like more than that." Dave sat forward, his lean face expressing as much concern as he ever showed. "We've run into a blank wall, period. Belle Colby and her kids appear on the grid in Arkansas when the little girl was about a year old and the boy three. Oh, their identities are impeccable on paper, all right. Too impeccable."

"So what does that mean?" He had the sense that Dave was building up to something.

Dave spread his hands. "That means we know it's phony, but I doubt very much that we can ever get past it."

"So that's a dead end." He leaned back and realized he was thinking of Violet and Maddie, sitting on either side of their mother's hospital bed, waiting and praying for her to wake up.

"I'm not sure it makes a whole lot of difference, anyway," he said slowly. "Belle Colby may regain consciousness and tell the twins what they need to know.

And Brian Wallace is bound to reappear from that mission trip of his at some point. He must know the answers as well."

"You want me to give it up, then?" Dave asked.

Landon knew from Dave's expression that he hated admitting defeat.

"Let's not write it off entirely," he said. "If anything else surfaces, you'll be in position to look into it."

"Okay, will do." Dave stood, and Landon walked with him to the door. "Sorry I couldn't come up with all the answers."

Landon managed a smile, even though he didn't feel much like it. "I don't suppose we ever get all the answers. As long as we have enough to go on with."

He kept thinking of that after Dave left, and he walked restlessly over to the windows. It was darker now, and the lights shone more brightly. Out there, people were going home to families, going out for the evening, meeting friends. He could call someone or go out somewhere, but he couldn't kid himself. The only place he really wanted to be was a five-hour drive away.

He hadn't spoken to Violet since he'd dropped her off Saturday night. After he'd told her things he never talked about to anyone, not even Maddie.

He hadn't had a choice. He'd seen her face when he dealt with that drunken kid—she'd been angry that he'd interfered, but it was more than that. She'd looked at him as if she didn't know him, and he couldn't handle that feeling.

When he'd told her about Jessica, Violet had reacted with warmth and caring, but she hadn't been able to understand his guilt, not fully. He wasn't sure he did himself.

His email ding sounded, and Landon was relieved to return to his desk, shutting out the disturbing thoughts. He sifted through several unimportant items and saw a message from Phil O'Hara—a message with an attachment.

If nothing else, he might have a decent photo of her family to give Violet. He clicked on the attachment. The photo came up, startling him with its clarity. Phil really could work wonders.

Landon looked more closely, noticing details he hadn't been able to see even with the magnifying glass. One detail in particular. There was a mailbox in the background, with the address stenciled on it. 21 Riley Street.

He leaned back in the desk chair, staring at the address. If the twins had been born in Fort Worth, that was probably a Fort Worth address. It wouldn't be that hard to find.

If he gave this to Maddie and Violet, he knew exactly what would happen. They'd take the bit between their teeth and charge into action, going to the address, asking questions, demanding answers.

He couldn't imagine what those answers might be, but everything in him revolted at the idea of sending those two rushing into that situation. He couldn't forget the implication of what Dave had found out. Belle Colby hadn't just split from her husband. She'd been involved in something so serious that she'd been forced to create a whole new identity for herself and two of her children. Something that might be heartbreaking to her children if they learned it from someone else—maybe even something that could be dangerous.

He couldn't do it. He clicked reply and typed a request, confident that Phil would be able to do what he wanted.

Violet and Maddie would have the photo of their family to cherish…but it wouldn't include that telltale address. He picked up the phone. In the meantime, Dave had something new to investigate.

Violet was on her way out the back door when the phone rang Wednesday afternoon. She turned back to answer it, unable to suppress a sliver of concern. Maddie had gone alone to see Belle, and if she'd found something wrong—

Violet picked up quickly. It wasn't Maddie. It was Pastor Jeb, and he sounded upset. He got right to the point.

"Someone broke into the Teen Scene area during the night. We didn't find the damage until just now. I've called the sheriff and he's on his way over. I thought you'd want to be here, too."

"I'll be right there." She was already reaching for her bag and her keys. "How bad is the damage?"

"Bad," he said soberly. "There's the sheriff now— I'll have to go."

Violet hung up. Her feet seemed glued to the spot. She didn't want to go. Didn't want to see what had been done.

But that was cowardly. She grabbed her bag and hurried out the hall, calling to Lupita that she'd be back later and not stopping for questions.

She raced out to the SUV, but before she could unlock it, she spotted the cloud of dust that meant another vehicle was coming down the lane. She looked, shielding her eyes.

The car pulled up next to her and Landon smiled at her. The smile faded as he saw her expression. "Violet? What's wrong?"

"Vandals. At the church." She began to feel that her tongue wasn't connected to her brain. "I'm sorry. I have to go."

"Get in. I'll drive you."

"You don't need—"

"You're upset. You shouldn't be behind the wheel. I'm coming anyway, and it makes more sense to let me drive you than to have me follow you."

Wordless, she went around the car and slid into the passenger seat. She'd resent his assumption of authority if not for the fact that he was probably right.

"I don't know why I feel so shaky at the news. It's not nearly as important as Mom's injury." She clasped her hands together.

"That's probably why." Landon went out the lane at a speed that had gravel spurting up, pinging against the underside of the car. "You've been running on nothing but nerve for too long. This is one thing too many."

She rubbed the back of her neck. He might have something at that. The least thing seemed to have the ability to drive her close to tears lately.

"Do you know how bad the vandalism was?" he asked.

"No. Just that it was in the area we use for Teen Scene. Do you think—surely none of the kids who come would do that!"

"No point in jumping to conclusions until you learn more." Landon reached into the back and grabbed something. Bringing it between the seats, he put a brown-paper-wrapped package in her lap. "A present for you."

She looked at him, but his gaze was on the road unfolding ahead of them. His clean, spare profile was unexpectedly dear to her.

She shifted her gaze to the package, afraid of giving herself away, and loosened the tape on it. She smoothed the paper back.

It was the photo of her family, restored to a condition that was probably better than it had been originally. The faces were clear—Belle smiling at the camera, Brian looking down at the little boy whose hand he held. Jack? But it could as easily be Grayson.

"Oh, Landon." Her voice choked. "It's wonderful. Thank you so much."

"It's nothing," he said, and there seemed to be a faint reservation in his voice. "There are copies in the back for Maddie, Grayson and Jack as well."

"That was so thoughtful of you." She longed to clasp his hand in thanks, but that probably wasn't a good idea when he was driving.

He shrugged. "Forget it. I knew the right person for the job, that's all."

They were in town already, heading for the church, and her nerves tightened at the thought of what waited there. She tried to shake off the worry, looking at Landon instead.

"You haven't told me what you're doing back in Grasslands. You didn't need to drive all this way in order to deliver the photographs."

"I'm more trustworthy than the mail," he said lightly. "Besides, as I told you, I can run my business from anywhere, as long as I have an internet connection."

"And you find Grasslands an inspiring place in which to work?" she asked, trying to match his light tone.

He pulled into a parking space by the side door of the church and turned to give her a look that brought a flush to her cheeks. "I find it very inspiring," he said, in a voice that had suddenly grown husky.

Violet slid out quickly. "We…we'd better go inside." And she better figure out a way to control both her face and her voice before she saw anyone else.

Sadie met them in the hallway, looking more mouse-like than ever, eyes scared behind her glasses. "Pastor Jeb said to meet him downstairs," she said, glancing from Violet to Landon.

"Thanks, Sadie. We'll go right down." Somehow she always felt she had to be reassuring when she spoke with Sadie, but the effort made her feel a bit more under control.

Violet hurried down the stairs, aware of Landon close behind her. The Teen Scene's troubles really weren't his concern, but it was comforting to have someone on her side.

A chill struck her. Landon had expressed disapproval of the project the first time he'd come. Maybe he wasn't so completely on her side in this.

She was in the social room before she could analyze his reaction any further. She stopped, shocked. Vandalism, Pastor Jeb had said. She'd expected a few broken windows, maybe some pieces of furniture thrown around. This was more like wholesale destruction.

One couch had been slashed, its stuffing hanging out forlornly. The other had been splashed with red paint. The artist hadn't stopped there with the paint—it was splattered liberally over the rug and splashed on the walls, then used to write a few ugly words. The television had been smashed, leaving shards of glass on the floor.

Looking through the open doorway to the game room, she could see that the Ping-Pong table was broken—the legs wrenched off so that it tilted listlessly against the wall. A step forward showed her more of the room—the board games tossed from their shelves and scattered on the floor, the air-hockey table smashed almost beyond recognition.

Landon's hands came down on her shoulders, steadying her. "It sounds as if the pastor is in the gym," he said. "Maybe we should go in there."

She nodded numbly and let him propel her past the damage and into the gym. Pastor Jeb was there, talking with Sheriff George Cole, but he looked up to give her a reassuring smile. Coming to her senses and realizing they hadn't met, she introduced Landon to the two men.

"Landon is a friend of my sister's from Fort Worth," she added. "He helped us out at Teen Scene this past weekend."

Sheriff Cole eyed him for a moment, but then he nodded. "Glad you have somebody with you, Violet. This is an ugly thing to see, especially after you put so much work into the place and all."

She nodded, not wanting to think about all the hours of scrounging up cast-off furniture and begging for donations to cover the cost of paint and equipment. "Who could have done this? How did they even get in? We locked up when we left Saturday night, I know we did."

"Broke in that door with a crowbar, looks like," the sheriff said. "The pastor was telling me that's the door you use to let kids in here, that right?"

She nodded, not sure what he was driving at.

"Seems like it might have been done by someone who'd been here for that program of yours. They'd naturally come to that door. Anyone intent on doing damage to the church would head for the sanctuary, I'd think."

That made sense, much as she hated to admit it, and she looked at Sheriff Cole with renewed respect. He'd been on the force here for as long as she could remember, a sturdy, solid symbol of the law.

"I'd hate to think the kids we host would do something like that. Why would they want to destroy the place they come to for fun?"

Sheriff Cole shrugged. "Teens can take offense easily sometimes. Get the idea you weren't treating them right, or weren't doing enough. Or they were being just plain mean. Anyone you've had a run-in with?"

Her brain didn't seem to be working. It was Landon who spoke.

"There were three guys we had to kick out on Saturday night. They'd been drinking, and Ms. Colby wouldn't let them come back in. They didn't take it well."

"I don't think they'd do this," she protested, but of course she couldn't imagine anyone she knew doing such damage.

"You know the names?" The sheriff had his pen poised over his notebook.

She hesitated, not wanting to be the one to set the police on the kids.

"The ringleader was Sam something," Landon said, clearly not feeling any such reluctance. "I don't think I heard the others' names."

"Never mind, I can fill in the blanks. Sam Donner, along with his buddies Danny and Kevin, was it?" His keen eyes fixed on Violet's face, requiring an answer.

"Yes, that's right," she said. "But I still feel—"

The person who'd just entered gained their attention by the simple expedient of pounding his cane on the wooden floorboards. They all swung toward the sound.

Davis Stuart swept them with an ice-blue gaze, his eyes bright in his leathery face, his hair snowy under the Stetson he always wore. Violet could almost hear Pastor Jeb sigh. With Davis as the chair of his church board, the pastor didn't have many easy meetings.

"This has turned out exactly as I said it would," Davis said, "and you have no one to blame but yourselves for the results. Let riffraff into the Lord's house, and this is what you get. Maybe now you'll realize that it's time for this ridiculous project to end."

Chapter 11

Landon eyed the newcomer cautiously. Whoever he might be, he seemed to think he was important, in his own eyes, at least. The man had white hair and was immaculately dressed. He wielded that silver-headed cane like a weapon instead of an aid to walking.

"Davis." Pastor Jeb sounded resigned. "What brings you here?"

"I heard about the vandalism to my church, of course." His use of the pronoun seemed to indicate that the church belonged to him.

Violet had stiffened, as if preparing for an attack. Annoyance surged through Landon. Violet was already struggling enough. She didn't need more pressure. He took a step closer, wanting to help but not knowing how.

The movement seemed to draw the attention of the older man. He shifted his glare from the pastor to Landon. "Who's this?" he demanded.

"Landon Derringer, Davis Stuart," Pastor Jeb said

briefly. "Landon has been helping us out with Teen Scene."

Stuart sniffed, seeming to think the introduction unworthy of comment. Landon walked to the man and held out his hand, determined not to let Stuart's rudeness affect his actions.

"Mr. Stuart. It's a pleasure to meet you." Actually, it didn't seem to be much of a pleasure, but courtesy helped oil the wheels of most human action, he'd found.

Looking thrown off his stride, Stuart shook hands briefly. Then he clasped his hands on the knob of his cane.

"Well, Pastor?" His tone sharpened. "How do you expect to pay for this mess? Or is Ms. Colby going to do it, since the whole misguided project was her idea?"

Landon could almost feel Violet wince. The Colby family seemed to do well enough, but he suspected that, like most ranchers, their finances were tied up in land and stock and equipment.

"It's a church project," he pointed out. "Surely the insurance will cover any loss."

Pastor Jeb looked stricken. "I wish that were so. But the insurance is really meant to cover us in the face of major destruction, like a fire. The deductible is so high that we can't count on it for something of this sort."

Of course. Like a lot of cash-strapped organizations, they'd taken every cost-cutting measure they could find, most likely.

"I don't know what your interest is, young man." Stuart's bristling white eyebrows lowered. "But the insurance won't cover the damage, and believe me, I intend to make sure that the church council doesn't sink any more of our funds into this misbegotten project. Throwing good money after bad, that's what it would be."

Landon was momentarily distracted by the old cliché, since Stuart said it with such determination.

"But we have to make repairs," Violet protested. "The kids will expect us to be open on Friday night."

Stuart reddened angrily. "Kids! Hooligans, more likely. They've done this, you can be sure of that."

"Now, Davis." The sheriff looked like a man who had dealt with Davis Stuart before. "You can't jump to conclusions like that without proof. This is a police matter. We'll find the guilty parties. That's our job."

"You won't need to look any farther than those young hoodlums who were here on Saturday night," he said, undeterred by the sheriff's wisdom. "There will be no more money spent on them by this church, I tell you. If Ms. Colby's so eager to entertain them, let her find another place."

"Teen Scene is a ministry of Grasslands Community Church." Pastor Jeb surprised Landon by the firmness in his tone. Apparently he was willing to go up against the local power broker for what he believed in. "We have no intention of deserting the program. Even if the guilty parties were in the building because of the teen program, and we don't know that, it wouldn't justify denying the program to all the other kids."

"Fine." Stuart's voice grated, and he thudded the cane on the floor for emphasis. "Just remember that I control the majority of the board. See how far you get without funds."

Violet was looking at Pastor Jeb, her eyes filled with gratitude, and the expression tugged at Landon's emotions. Maybe this program would be better run by a team of professionals, but it was pretty obvious Grasslands couldn't afford that. And Violet had sunk her heart into it. It wasn't fair to desert her when things went wrong.

Landon cleared his throat. "As it happens, I'm associated with a charitable foundation in Fort Worth," he said. "We provide grants for worthy projects that minister to teens. I feel sure we'd be willing to fund the necessary repairs to get the Teen Scene up and running again."

Davis Stuart was looking at him with ill-concealed hostility. Clearly he was used to running things in this church, if not the whole town.

"What's the name of this foundation?" he snapped. "Its board might not be so eager to help if I had a word with them."

"The Jessica Derringer Foundation," Landon said evenly. "Coincidentally, I *am* the board. I can assure you, the money will be here. Repairs can start immediately."

Stuart glared at him for another moment. Then, apparently conceding defeat, he turned and stomped toward the door, where he paused for one final remark. "I hope you know what you're getting yourself into, young man," he growled. He went out and let the metal door bang behind him.

"Well." Pastor Jeb said the word on a long exhale. "Davis was certainly in top form today." He turned to Landon, holding out his hand. "I'm not sure that we've done anything to merit your support, Landon, but we're mighty glad to have it. I can't thank you enough for your generous offer."

"Forget it," he said quickly. He turned to Sheriff

Cole. "Sheriff, how long until your investigation is finished and we can start work in here?"

The sheriff considered, patting his paunch absently. "Well, I reckon we can get done in here this afternoon. You can start first thing tomorrow, if you can get a crew in here that quick."

"We will," he said confidently. "Thank you."

Pastor Jeb put his hand on Sheriff Cole's shoulder. "Let's have a look at the rest of the damage, shall we?" He steered him toward the games room. "Violet, are you coming?"

"In a minute," she said, looking up at Landon with a question in her eyes. As soon as the other two were out of earshot, she asked it.

"Why?" she said simply. "I thought you didn't approve of our program. That you felt it should be run by professionals, not well-meaning amateurs."

"I realized something after I shot my mouth off that way," he explained. "I realized that I trust your judgment. And I'm willing to put my money where my mouth is."

Her eyes sparkled with unshed tears. "Thank you, Landon. Thank you."

Over supper, Violet had been telling Maddie about the vandalism, capping it with the story of Landon's charitable act.

"I couldn't believe he would offer to pay for the repairs, after what he'd said about our amateur efforts." Violet led the way into the den, where she and Maddie had formed the habit of sitting after supper. "It was so unexpected."

"Landon can be unexpected," Maddie said. She

curled up in the corner of the sofa and pulled her laptop from the table onto her lap. "I suspect you had something to do with his change of heart."

"He did say he trusted my judgment." She gave Maddie a searching look. "You're sure that you don't mind—"

Maddie shook her head, smiling a little. "How many times do I have to say it? Landon was always like a big brother to me, and that's all he'll ever be." She leaned across to tap her knee. "Trust me on this. Landon never looked at me the way he looks at you."

Maddie turned to her computer, and they were silent for a few minutes as she checked her email. Violet leaned back in her corner of the sofa, thinking about Landon.

There had been little chance to talk to him alone after his offer. Once the sheriff had gone, they'd been closeted with Pastor Jeb and a few other members of the teen center board, assessing the damage, deciding what repairs were needed, talking to carpenters and plumbers, making plans.

She'd been impressed, seeing Landon in action that way. He'd taken full part in the planning, making it clear that he didn't want them to stint on the repairs but to get them done both quickly and thoroughly. He'd even managed to get Grasslands' only plumber to promise to make the bathroom repairs a priority. She wasn't sure how he'd managed to do that, and she spared a moment of regret for whoever had expected the plumber tomorrow.

"Finally," Maddie said suddenly. "I got an email from Carter."

Carter, the younger brother. Well, half brother, it seemed now.

"Is he all right?" Carter seemed a rather shadowy figure to her.

"Fine, apparently." Maddie was scanning the message. "He never talks about what he's doing. Well, I suppose he can't. The military doesn't want their officers to be giving away anything on what might be an unsecured wireless connection."

"What does he say? Did you tell him about…well, about us?"

Maddie shook her head. "It seems way too complicated to explain in an email. He'd have a million questions, and just be frustrated because he couldn't ask them."

"I suppose you're right," Violet said reluctantly. Somehow this would be a bit more real if Maddie's dad and brothers knew about it.

"So I told him I had some big news to share, but it would wait until he could call me. I asked if he'd heard anything from Dad. He says not for over a month, so that's no help."

"You've emailed our dad again?"

"Again and again," Maddie said. "And I've left messages on his cell phone. He has to be someplace where he doesn't have access, that's all I can figure."

"Isn't there some central organization that's in charge of this mission trip of his?" It seemed so odd that he'd be completely out of touch.

But Maddie shook her head. "He used to work directly with an organized group, but as he got to know more people in some of the impoverished areas, he went off on his own."

"So…he hasn't been around much for you?" Violet asked the question cautiously, wanting to know but not wanting to sound critical.

Maddie closed the computer with a snap. "I guess it does sound funny. I mean, in comparison to how close you've always been to your mother."

"Yes, I suppose it does." Violet seemed to see Belle sitting where Maddie was, leaning forward, her face alight with love, eager to hear about her day. Here, not in the hospital bed in Amarillo.

Maddie's forehead wrinkled. "You know, I guess when you're a kid, you just accept the way things are. We always knew that Dad's work was very important and that he had to be away."

"You never questioned that?" It didn't sound as if she'd missed a lot by not having Brian Wallace in her life.

Maddie considered. "Sometimes you hash over your relationship with your parents with your friends, especially when you're in college. I always had the feeling that Dad was sort of protecting himself from getting too close." She looked at Violet, her face serious. "I guess now I know why. Whatever happened between Mom and Dad, it had to be big, and I think it has affected Dad's relationship with us ever since."

"I wish I'd known him," Violet said softly.

"You will." Maddie grabbed her hand. "Just like I'll know Mom. He'll come back, and she'll wake up. You'll see."

Violet nodded. She had to believe that, but there was a lump in her throat.

"I know what," Maddie said. "Let's write letters to them, telling how it felt to find each other. You can write to Dad, and I'll write to Mom. Then, even if it's a while before they can read them, they'll know how we felt."

"That's a good idea." Violet smiled, but she suspected Maddie would do the same thing she would. She'd leave out the part about feeling angry and betrayed over all they'd lost.

One day, they'd be able to sort this out with their parents, but she didn't think it was going to be easy.

Violet and Maddie reached the church early the next morning. Violet had already consulted with both Ty and Ricardo, reassured by their ability and willingness to handle what needed to be done on the ranch.

But there had been an undercurrent to their conversations that she hadn't been able to dismiss. People who depended upon the Colby Ranch for their livelihood were too aware of the uncertainty of life in the Colby family right now.

Jack should return. She knew that...everyone knew that except, apparently, Jack. Ricardo had looked at her with sorrow in his eyes, even though he hadn't spoken of her brother. He was wondering why she hadn't called Jack to insist that he come home.

She'd have to. She knew that, but still she delayed, praying that he'd come back on his own.

The area outside the door into the church gym was crowded with vehicles—two pickup trucks, the plumber's paneled truck, a delivery truck from the lumberyard and another from the hardware store. Landon stood at the door in consultation with Pastor Jeb.

"Wow," Maddie murmured. "Looks as if someone's been working overtime."

"I wonder what Landon did to get all these people here already this morning." Violet felt faintly uneasy, as if she'd unleashed something she couldn't control.

"Don't ask," Maddie said, getting out of the car. "Just appreciate."

That was probably good advice. Now to follow it.

When they approached the door, Landon glanced at them, his face relaxing in a smile. "Have you come to supervise?"

"We've come to work," Maddie declared. "We're not going to sit back and let you have all the fun."

"The carpenters and plumbers are just getting started." There was a note of protest in his voice. "Maybe if you waited until later—"

"We're going to see Mom later. We'll start in the kitchen," Violet said firmly. "The only damage there was the graffiti. We'll get busy painting." She'd taken the precaution of bringing paint, brushes and rollers, and she didn't intend to be left out. This was her project, after all.

She was ready for a battle, knowing Landon's protectiveness, but she didn't get one. Maybe he knew better.

"Okay, sounds good," he said. "Need any help carrying stuff in?"

"We'll take care of it," Maddie said. "You get back to supervising, or whatever it is you're doing."

Chuckling, Landon turned away to answer a question from the plumber, and they went inside to check out the kitchen and bring their equipment in.

The spray paint on the walls and cabinets might have sent Violet's emotions spiraling downward again, but Maddie seemed determined not to let that happen. She kept up a steady stream of chatter while they scrubbed and wielded the brushes and rollers, forcing Violet to respond and keeping her from focusing on the destruction.

After only an hour, they had begun to see progress. The old kitchen, unused except for the teen center program, hadn't been repainted in years, and it seemed to come to life under the impact of fresh, new color.

"You know, this paint is making a huge difference." Maddie stood back, hands on her hips, surveying their progress. "I like the earth tones in here."

Violet looked at her and couldn't help grinning. "They're pretty becoming on you, too." Maddie had paint everywhere, including a streak down one cheek.

"Better watch out, or I'll decorate you as well," Maddie warned, flicking the brush at her.

"You two girls getting paint on the walls or just each other?" Harriet said from the kitchen doorway.

Violet stared. It wasn't just Harriet from the farm stand. Beyond her was a group of teenagers, peering around her to get a look at the kitchen.

"Sure is a mess." Joey Thomas hopped up onto the kitchen pass-through to get a better view.

"Get off there," Harriet chided. "You're going to make sure it's not a mess much longer. Maria and Janey, you set up a table in the gym with the lemonade and food we brought. Some of you boys find a table they can use. The rest of you, get in here and get busy. Painting, not messing around," she warned.

The kids scattered promptly in obedience, leaving Violet with no response but to stare at Harriet.

"But...the store?" she questioned.

"Don't you worry about a thing," the older woman

said, tying a bright bandanna over her wiry hair. "I left Julie in charge. She might only be eighteen, but she knows what she's doing. I'll pop back later to check on her, but everything's fine. Now let's get busy."

Blinking unexpected tears out of her eyes, Violet murmured a silent prayer of thanks and turned back to the painting.

By the time she and Maddie had to start cleaning up to go to the hospital, with all those hands working, the kitchen was nearly done. Violet walked back through the gym, marveling at the people who were hard at work. Plenty of kids from Teen Scene, people from church, others she didn't even know—all of them had pitched in to help.

Her throat tightened. Some of these people lived hand-to-mouth, she knew. They might not be able to help with money, but they were giving their labor and support, and that meant more.

She walked on into the social rooms in search of Landon, weaving her way through people intent on their work. She found him in one of the restrooms, in consultation with the plumber. He glanced up.

"Violet, glad you're here. We're planning to run a vanity all across this wall. Joe here says he can do either a white laminate cabinet or natural wood. Which would you rather have?"

The two men stood looking at her, waiting, and her throat seemed too tight to speak.

"But...you don't have to do that. We can just keep that single basin. It wasn't damaged."

"As long as we're in here, we may as well do it right," Landon said.

"That's true enough, Violet." Joe Tyler, quite naturally, was eager to do the whole job. "You'll be a load happier with it in the long run."

Her gaze was fixed on Landon's face. "I know you… your foundation…is willing to pay for repairs, but I… we shouldn't take advantage of your generosity…" She stumbled over the words.

Landon stepped over Joe's tools, took her arm, and piloted her out of the restroom and into the adjoining hallway, empty at the moment.

"Listen," he said, holding both her arms in a warm clasp. "This is what the foundation was set up to do." Pain moved in his eyes for an instant. "Whenever we pick up a project, I think about what Jessica would have liked. Then I do it."

"But the expense…" She gazed up at him, still troubled.

He shook his head, his brow furrowed. "It's just money, Violet. Those people donating their time and labor are doing far more, believe me."

A little reassured, she smiled at him. "Only people who have plenty say things like, 'It's just money.'"

"True." He smiled back, his face easing. "The Bible says that the love of money is the root of all evil. I've given that a lot of thought since I became a Christian. I see people like my parents, who let money lead them into an unending pursuit of pleasure, only to be dissatisfied in spite of their possessions."

She nodded. "I guess I can understand that, but most people around here are just trying to get by."

"I decided a long time ago that money is a tool and it can be used wisely or foolishly. The foundation lets me use what's been entrusted to me wisely, I hope." His green eyes suddenly twinkled. "Now, please, let Joe get on with his work. Laminate or wood?"

How could she argue, given the depth of his feeling? "Natural wood, please," she said, returning his smile.

Chapter 12

The hospital was beginning to look too familiar, and Violet found she resented that as they walked down the hallway toward Belle's room. No matter how kind the staff was, and they were very kind, her mom should be at home, where she belonged.

"Violet?" Maddie touched her arm as they started into the room. "Are you all right?"

She nodded, trying to smile. "It's just hard to keep up a cheerful front all the time. You know?"

"I know." Maddie clasped her hand. "Every time I come in, I think this will be the day. This will be the day when she opens her eyes and looks at me, and she knows right away who I am."

Violet squeezed her hand, and they went into the room together.

There was no change. She saw that immediately. Belle lay exactly centered in the bed, the sheet drawn up and folded back at the top. Someone had taken the time to put her shoulder-length hair into two loose braids, and they formed dark auburn ropes against the white pillow.

"Mom, hi. Maddie and I are here to visit." Her attention was caught by a vase of red roses on the table next to the bed. "Wow, Mom. You must have an admirer. These roses are gorgeous. Did Jack send them?"

There was no answer, of course. She plucked the card out from the roses and opened it.

You are in my prayers. Landon Derringer.

She glanced across the bed at Maddie. "They're from Landon."

"I told you he could be surprising." Maddie clasped Belle's hand. "Would you like to smell the roses, Mom?"

"That's a good idea." Hadn't she read something about people still being able to smell, even when their other senses weren't working properly? Violet pulled one of the long-stemmed roses from the vase, careful of the thorns. She held it under her mother's nose. "There. Doesn't that smell lovely?"

"The color is gorgeous, too. It's such a deep, vibrant red. Landon sent them. He's a friend of mine from Fort Worth. Violet probably won't tell you this, so I will. She's crazy about him."

"I wouldn't go that far," Violet said, putting the rose back in the vase. "But he is…well, really special."

She turned away to pull the usual chair up by the bed, and Maddie did the same on her side of the bed.

"So," Maddie queried once she was seated, "how many guys have you called *really special* besides Landon?"

Violet wrinkled her nose. "Okay, none. But that doesn't mean anything will come of this relationship."

"Of course not." Maddie looked a tad smug. "We'll

just wait and see. But if Mom were awake, what would she be saying right now?"

"I know exactly." Violet smiled at her mother's unresponsive face. "She'd say, 'Violet, just be sure when you give your heart to someone.'"

Maddie smiled as well, but then the smile faded. "I wonder if she felt really sure of Dad."

"She must have, don't you think?" Violet stroked her mother's hand. "But sometimes things happen that people can't control."

Maddie nodded, gazing at her mother's face. "How old is she, anyway? I never thought to ask that."

"Forty-three her last birthday."

"Really? That means she was only sixteen or seventeen when Grayson and Jack were born. Did she ever talk about that?"

"Just once, when I did some arithmetic and came up with that figure. I tried to use it as a lever when she didn't want me to go to some party with the older kids." Violet sighed ruefully, remembering that conversation. "Mom looked at me and said she didn't want me following in her footsteps in that regard. And she didn't let me go to the party."

"I wonder how much their youth had to do with their marriage breaking up." Maddie touched her mom's hand where a ring might have been at one time. "They were awfully young to be the parents of twins."

"That must have been hard. It wouldn't be surprising if they weren't mature enough to make a go of marriage." *Wake up, Mom. Answer the questions for us. Please.*

The door swung open, letting in a doctor whose swift pace didn't alter until he glanced up and saw them sitting there. It was a man Violet hadn't seen before, in his fifties probably, with a pencil-thin moustache and an air of authority.

"Are you Mrs. Colby's children?" He glanced from one to the other. "Yes, I see that you are. You both resemble your mother very much, don't you?" His smile warmed a face that Violet had initially thought rather frosty.

"I'm Violet Colby," she said. "This is my sister, Maddie Wallace."

"Nathan Fremont," he said. "I've been thinking I should have a word with Mrs. Colby's family. Are there any other family members?"

"My brother, Jack." It was far too complicated, Violet decided, to bring up Brian Wallace and his sons.

"Your father is not in the picture?" he asked.

Violet shook her head. "Not now. You can talk to us about anything concerning our mother's care."

She could read the reluctance on his face, and a chill hand seemed to grip her heart. "Is something more wrong with Mom?" She had to choke the words out.

"No, nothing like that," Dr. Fremont said. "It's just usually the spouse who deals with the decisions that have to be made in this sort of case."

"What decisions?" Maddie sounded as scared as Violet felt.

He looked from Maddie to her. "Your mother is stable now, I'm sure you realize that. However, there's been no further progress in some time."

"That doesn't mean there won't be," Maddie said quickly.

He nodded. "True. But there comes a point when we have to accept the fact that there may not be any—that your mother may be in a persistent coma from which she won't recover."

Violet pressed her lips together, shaking her head. "I can't believe that. I won't."

"I understand." His voice was gentle. "You should always hang on to hope. The point is, however, that she no longer needs the type of specialized care we provide here. You need to start looking for another place— probably a nursing care facility, if there is one close to your home."

Violet could only stare down at her hands clasped in her lap. Maybe she should have expected this, but she hadn't. Everything in her objected. Surely there was something else the hospital could do. But the doctor had made it clear that there wasn't, and Violet felt herself sinking under the weight of the responsibility.

"How long do we have to make that decision?" Maddie seemed to sense that she'd have to take charge now. "We need time to find the right place for our mother, and we'll need to talk to our brother before we can make any arrangements."

"Of course." He sounded relieved. "We're not rushing you, but it is something that must be done. You should look into different facilities, ask around, talk to people who have used those facilities. We can discuss it again in a few days."

A few days—Violet's mind rebelled. She couldn't possibly be ready to make a decision that soon, not when it felt like giving up hope that her mom would get better.

The doctor seemed to take their silence as agreement. He nodded and walked away, maybe eager to leave now that he'd delivered his unpalatable news.

Maddie walked around the bed and touched Violet's shoulder. "It's not giving up," she said with that quick understanding that seemed to exist between them. "We'll find a good place that can provide all the therapy and support Mom needs. Maybe it will even be better."

Violet appreciated what Maddie was trying to do, but there was one immediate thought in her mind. She couldn't give Jack any more time to come to his senses.

"I have to call Jack." She got out her cell phone, and then realized she couldn't use it here.

"Why don't you go down to the lobby to call? Or even outside? I'll stay here with Mom."

"Yes, that's what I'd better do." Violet stood. "Thanks, Maddie. For…for sharing the burden."

"Hey, that's what twins are for, right?" Maddie gave her a little shove toward the door. "Go on, make the call. It's time Jack came home."

Everyone was agreed on that, Violet reflected as she rode down on the elevator. Everyone except, possibly, Jack himself. Well, he was out of options.

Not wanting to make the call where anyone might overhear, she went out through the sliding door, feeling the heat weigh her down as she reached the sidewalk. Walking a little distance from the main entrance, she found a bench in the shade and called.

She half expected the phone to go directly to messages, but instead Jack answered immediately.

"Vi? What's wrong? Is it Mom?" Fear filled his voice.

"There's been no change," she said quickly.

"Thank God," he murmured.

"But something else has come up. You have to come back."

"If this is about Maddie and her father—" he began.

"No." She cut him off. "It's about Mom. The doctor says that they can't do anything else for her at the trauma center." It was a struggle to keep her voice even. "We have to make arrangements to move her to a nursing home."

Silence for a moment, and she knew he was fighting against accepting that, just as she was.

"I don't know anything about nursing homes. Can't you and Maddie handle it?"

"Stop being selfish," she snapped, her temper frayed to the breaking point. "You went off and left me to deal with everything. This is one thing too much." Her voice shook suddenly. "I need you to come home, Jack. I need my big brother."

Silence for a moment.

"Hang on, Violet," he said, his voice gentle. "I'll be home tomorrow."

Landon was back at Sally's Barbecue again, and he had to confess he was getting a little tired of the menu. If he spent much more time in Grasslands, he'd have to make some other arrangements.

Was he going to spend much more time in Grasslands? A few weeks ago he'd have laughed at the idea. But then, a few weeks ago he hadn't known Violet.

At any rate, he expected a bit more from supper tonight. Not that Sally would have changed her menu, but he'd caught Violet on her cell phone when she was returning from Amarillo and convinced her to have dinner with him.

She'd sounded distracted, and he frowned as he parked his car. He'd had to resort to saying they needed to talk about the progress at Teen Scene before she'd agreed.

He couldn't help but smile as he thought about that phone call. He'd been able to hear Maddie's voice in the background, urging her to go to dinner with him. Maddie had to be the most generous former fiancée in history.

Landon had just gotten out of the car when Violet's SUV pulled in. She got out, wearing a turquoise sundress that made her creamy skin glow in comparison. Her hair wasn't in its usual ponytail—it hung to her shoulders like auburn silk. She took his breath away.

"Violet." He went to her quickly. "You look lovely."

She lifted her eyebrows. "Because I look more like Maddie?"

"No," he said truthfully. "Because you look like yourself."

The color came up in her cheeks. "I don't know what to say to that."

He took her hand and they walked toward the restaurant. "You don't have to say a thing, except that you enjoy being with me as much as I enjoy being with you. If it's true, of course."

"It is," she said softly.

By the time they were seated, Violet seemed to have recovered from her embarrassment. They ordered, and then he took a second look at her face. Happiness lurked in her eyes, surprising him.

"You look as if you've had good news. Is your mother better?"

"No, not that. I wish..." She let that trail off. "I'm just pleased because Jack is coming home."

Jack, the missing brother. "So he called you?"

"No. I called him."

The waitress arrived with platters of barbecue, and

they were silent while she set them on the table and re-filled their water glasses, exchanging some lighthearted banter with Violet and glancing at him with curiosity.

When she'd gone, Violet picked up her fork and then put it back down again. "You didn't ask why I called Jack," she said.

"I had a feeling you were going to tell me." At least, he hoped she trusted him that much.

"Maddie and I talked to the doctor today. He wants us to make arrangements to move Mom to a nursing home."

He studied her face. The flicker of joy when she spoke of her brother coming home had vanished.

"Were you surprised by that news?" he asked, carefully neutral until he knew just what she was feeling.

"I guess I shouldn't have been." She turned the tines of her fork on the red-checked tablecloth. "But it feels like giving up. Like admitting that there's no hope."

He touched her fingers lightly with his, and she stopped mutilating the tablecloth.

"If you move her, you can have her closer to you, right? Closer to her family and friends, where people can drop in on her every day?"

"Well, yes, I guess so." She considered that, and the misery seemed to lighten. "If we could have her at a skilled care center somewhere in the county, she would be right in the center of things again."

He nodded, wanting to encourage a cheerful outlook. "I'm no expert, but I'd think the more her surroundings were like home, the better it would be for her."

"But what about the therapy she's been getting at the hospital? I'm not sure what a nursing home provides, but it's probably not on a par with a city hospital."

"It's worth looking into, isn't it? I'd think you could

arrange to bring a therapist in to work with her, if necessary, couldn't you?"

She brightened. "That's true. The county health service has therapists on staff."

"There you go." His fingertips brushed hers comfortingly. "You'll see. This will work out all right. Your mother will have a better chance of recovery if she's closer to home."

"You're right." Her smile was brilliant. "Thanks, Landon. You've made me feel better."

The urge to speak, to tell her how much she'd come to mean to him, was so strong he could barely control it. But he had to control it. Violet was vulnerable now, her life turned upside down by a succession of events that would try anyone. He couldn't put the weight of his emotions on her, as well.

"Any time," he said.

"You know, I'd just been wishing Uncle James were here for me to talk to about it. But you're almost as good as he was in making me feel better."

"Uncle James? I thought you didn't have any relatives."

"James Crawford. He wasn't really our uncle, but we called him that. He owned the ranch when our mother came to Grasslands to work for him."

It looked as if the subject he'd wondered about was coming out into the open without his even asking any questions. "You must have been very close to him."

She nodded, her eyes misty. "He treated us like family. And when he needed help running the ranch, Mom pitched right in. By his last illness, she was pretty much running the ranch. I don't think anyone was surprised when he left the ranch to us. We were the only family he had, even though we weren't blood kin."

Even allowing for Violet's natural bias, the story made sense, and the doubts he'd been harboring about Belle Colby drifted away. Surely nobody could fool the whole community for years, and he hadn't heard anyone say a negative word about Belle since he'd gotten here.

Violet shook her head, seeming to come back from her memories. "Now, about the teen center. You wanted to talk?"

"We're making good progress, but I don't think we can expect to open tomorrow night," he said. "Pastor Jeb suggests having a grand reopening on Saturday evening. If we can put in a full day on Saturday, everything should be ready."

"In other words, you're talking about paying people overtime just to get the work done by Saturday night." She looked troubled, that sense of economy getting the better of her again.

"Look at it this way. If we delay for another week, it gives the kids too much opportunity to fall into other ways of spending their weekends. Right now they're enthusiastic, feeling good about helping get the place back in order. We want to take advantage of that enthusiasm."

Her gaze met his with a softness that nearly made him forget his good resolutions. "All right," she said. "You've given me no arguments left to make. We'll do it your way."

He touched her hand again, ignoring the food in front of him. "You won't be sorry."

The next morning, Violet hurried out toward the corral behind the barn. She wanted to catch Ty before he headed out on his day's rounds. To her surprise, she found Maddie already up and outside, leaning against the board fence that surrounded the corral, watching him. Apparently, Maddie had developed an interest in horses. Or possibly cowboys.

Ty was saddling his favorite horse, and it was impossible to tell from his stoic expression whether he was paying attention to Maddie's banter or not. Maybe it was just as well that she'd come out to interrupt them.

"Enjoying a morning walk?" she asked her twin innocently.

"Something like that," Maddie said, smiling.

"Mornin', Violet." Ty crossed to her, the horse keeping pace with him. "Something you wanted to talk to me about?"

"Good news," she said. "Jack will be home today. And we'll soon be moving my mother to a medical facility closer to home, too."

"That is good news." Ty looked as if a weight had slipped from his shoulders.

"Will you pass that along to all the boys?" she said, her voice casual. "I think they ought to know."

"Yep." His gaze met hers, and she knew he understood her perfectly. "They'll be glad to hear that, for sure." He touched his hat. "See you later, Violet." His gaze slid to Maddie. "Ms. Wallace." He swung into the saddle.

"Maddie," she said.

"Right. Maddie." He shifted his weight slightly. The horse, accustomed to his every move, turned obediently.

Maddie watched him ride away, a bemused expression on her face.

Violet touched her twin's shoulder. "Lupita has breakfast ready."

"Okay." She fell into step with Violet. "Guess I am hungry, at that."

"Going out for an early walk will do that to you," Violet said, amused.

Maddie didn't seem to be paying attention to the teasing. Her forehead wrinkled. "You know, I was thinking maybe I should head back to Fort Worth."

"What?" The comment hit her in the heart. "Why? Maddie, I thought you were happy here."

"I am," Maddie protested. "I'm not talking about going for good. But I left so quickly and there are things I should do. Bills to pay, clothes I should pack…" She shrugged. "Anyway, you'll be busy with Jack coming home, so maybe this is a good time."

Violet caught her arm as they went in the back door, stopping her in the hallway. "You're thinking about leaving because of Jack, aren't you? Because of the way he reacted to seeing you."

"Well, he wasn't exactly thrilled, was he?"

"He was just shocked, that's all," Violet said, struggling to find a middle ground in her loyalty to her siblings.

Maddie wrinkled her nose. "He could have done without having a new sister, believe me."

"I couldn't," Violet said, putting her arm around Maddie's waist. "Now that I know I have a twin, I can't lose you."

Maddie gave her a quick, fierce hug. "Me, too," she said. "Okay. But I will have to go back sometime, you know. There's the little matter of earning a living. I can't just stay here."

"You can stay as long as you want." Jack stepped out from the kitchen with a beaming Lupita right behind him. "It's time I got to know my new little sister, isn't it?"

"Jack." Tears sprang to Violet's eyes, and she threw herself into his arms.

He lifted her off her feet in an enormous bear hug. "Vi, sugar, it's good to see you."

"You, too." She blinked back tears. As he set her on her feet she slugged his shoulder. "That's for staying away so long."

"Yeah. Sorry." His gaze slid away from hers in embarrassment. "That wasn't the most mature thing I ever did, I guess." He turned to Maddie, looking at her a little uncertainly. "Got a hug for your brother, Maddie?"

Maddie smiled, tension easing out of her face. "Sure thing." She held out her arms, and the two of them hugged awkwardly.

That was natural for them to feel ill at ease, wasn't it? It would take time for Maddie and Jack to form a bond. They didn't have what Maddie called the "twin thing" going for them.

It would take time and patience. She just hoped they had enough of each.

Chapter 13

Lupita smiled with joy as she carried more food than they could possibly eat to the table. Obviously, Violet thought, the prodigal son was being welcomed home. Lupita would never admit to playing favorites, but she'd always had an extra-soft spot for Jack.

Maybe that was because Jack and Belle had so often been at loggerheads. Belle had expected a lot of Jack, so frequently reminding him that he was the man of the family.

Perhaps that was why Jack had developed such a need to know who his father was. While Violet had been content with things as they were, Jack had always wanted to know.

Jack had argued with Belle about that very subject the day of her accident. She'd ridden off, furious with him, and he had seen her fall. Small wonder that he'd had such a struggle with the answer to his question falling into Violet's lap.

She and Jack had changed places, it seemed. He didn't want to talk about their parentage, no doubt because he felt so guilty over Belle's accident. And now that she had Maddie in her life, she felt she had to know the rest. Violet's gaze caught the wise eyes in the portrait of her Uncle James. If he were here, would he know how to deal with this tangled situation?

"Are you really going to eat all that?" Maddie was eyeing Jack's heaped-up plate with amazement.

"You bet," Jack said between forkfuls of burritos filled with Lupita's special scrambled eggs. "I haven't had a decent meal since I left."

An awkward silence fell as all three of them were probably thinking of that night when Maddie had come and Jack had gone. Jack put his fork down and looked at Maddie.

"Listen, Maddie, I'm sorry. I didn't treat you the way I should. When Mom gets better, she'll probably smack me one upside the head for being rude."

"It's okay." Maddie's face relaxed and she grinned at him. "I understand. And if you catch me staring rudely at you, it's just because you're a dead ringer for Grayson."

Violet thought it took an effort, but Jack managed a smile. "So we're as alike as you two are?" He waved his fork between the two of them.

"Identical," Maddie said. "Same brown hair, same eyes." She grinned. "Women are tempted by those golden-brown eyes, you know that?"

Jack shook his head, but Violet laughed.

"He knows," she teased. "He just doesn't want to admit it."

"So when am I going to meet this twin?" Jack wasn't

quite convincing in his effort to sound as if he looked forward to that with any enthusiasm.

"I wish I knew. Grayson's a cop. He's doing undercover work right now, and until this case is wrapped up, I can't contact him. He doesn't even know about Mom."

Jack was trying to act as if this were a normal situation, but Violet saw his face tense for a fraction of a second when Maddie referred to Belle that way.

He turned to Violet. "Maybe you'd better tell me more about this business of moving Mom. You sounded pretty upset about it yesterday."

"I was. I guess I still am, but we should have been expecting it. The trauma center is only set up to handle the more immediate care after an accident. I should have realized they'd expect us to move her at some point."

"I don't see why," Jack said. "They're the specialists, aren't they? Isn't that the best place for her to be?"

"That was my reaction, too, at first," she admitted. "But Landon pointed out—"

"Landon? Who's Landon?" Jack was frowning.

How could so much have happened in such a short period of time? It seemed incredible that Jack didn't know Landon.

"Landon is a friend of Maddie's from Fort Worth." She gazed at Maddie, sending her a silent message to keep quiet about whatever she thought of Landon's relationship with Violet. "He's the one who saw me and recognized that we were twins. He's been staying at the hotel for a few days, kind of…helping us out."

"Wait a minute." Jack's frown deepened. "I don't get any of this. What were you doing in Fort Worth to begin with? What kind of a friend is he? A boyfriend?" He looked at Maddie for an answer to that.

"Just a friend," she said easily. "More like a big brother. He's been Grayson's pal since high school."

"I still don't understand why he's hanging around," Jack muttered. "But go on. You were saying something about transferring Mom."

Violet decided to leave Landon's name out of the conversation. His presence was just confusing the issue, and if Jack learned he'd been engaged to Maddie and was now interested in Violet, he'd think…well, she didn't know what he'd think, but it wouldn't be good. And there was certainly no way she could explain her own confused feelings.

Landon was installing a shelf bracket in the games room when he felt someone watching him. He turned and the chair he stood on wobbled.

Violet grabbed it and smiled up at him, making his heart turn over. "Don't you know chairs aren't safe to stand on? You should be using a ladder."

"All the ladders are already in use." He gestured toward the open door to the gym, where Pastor Jeb could be seen putting up new basketball hoops. "Besides, how many times have you stood on a chair to reach something?"

"Too many," she said, making a face at him. "It sounds as if Joe is still working in the restroom."

Actually, prolonged mutters were coming from that direction, where Joe and his helper were setting the new vanity in place.

"I've discovered that it's better to stay away until Joe finishes what he's doing," he said. "Then he wants you to come and admire it."

"Can I admire the shelves in the meantime? They

look good. I didn't realize you were working on the project. I mean—" She stopped, maybe thinking that sounded insulting.

He grinned, far from offended. "As opposed to throwing money at the project, you mean? I like to get my hands dirty once in a while."

He tried to lean back to get a view of the shelf and nearly tipped the chair again, so he jumped down. "What do you think? Is it even? We only seem to have one level around here, and someone keeps borrowing it."

Violet stood back, hands on her slim hips, surveying the shelves he'd put up. "Great," she said finally. She swiveled, taking in the whole room—fresh paint on the walls and woodwork, a new Ping-Pong table, the newly painted bookcases. "I can't believe it," she said softly. "I wouldn't have imagined it could look like this after what happened."

"It's amazing what a crew of volunteers can do."

Landon glanced around as well, realizing that he had a more profound sense of satisfaction about this project than about the modern youth center he'd spearheaded in the city. Maybe that was because he'd actually become involved here. He knew the kids who'd enjoy this space. He knew the adults who cared enough to make this happen. And he knew Violet, whose heart was wrapped up in this place.

She looked at him, eyes shining, and in that moment he thought there was nothing he wouldn't do for her.

"I still can't quite believe it. The place looks almost ready to open tonight."

"Not until tomorrow," he said. "Joe promises the restrooms will be ready tomorrow night if he has to work right through supper. And I gather that's a big sacrifice for him." He grinned, trying to defuse the emotion that was building in him. "So tell me, did your brother get home all right?"

She nodded, turning away. "He arrived this morning. Everyone is relieved to have him back. Especially Lupita. I thought she'd never stop cooking. That's her way of expressing love."

But something was wrong—he could hear it in her voice. "What is it?" he asked gently.

She looked at his face, a little surprised, and then she shrugged. "Maybe I was expecting too much from his return. He's really making an effort to get to know Maddie, so that's good. But..." She fell silent.

"But," he prompted.

"I guess I thought he'd be more supportive about moving Mom." She picked up a table-tennis ball and rolled it in her palm. "He doesn't even want to discuss it. He just keeps saying that Maddie and I would know more about that than he would."

He made an effort to suppress his annoyance at a man he hadn't met. "Most men feel helpless when someone they love is sick or hurt." He flashed to a memory of sitting in that hospital corridor for an interminable amount of time, waiting to hear about Jessica. He knew about that helplessness.

"It's not that," Violet said. "Or if it is, that's not the main thing. He was quarreling with Mom right before she had her accident. Demanding to know the truth about our father. That's ironic, isn't it?" Her voice trembled a little. "Anyway, I'm sure he's just feeling so guilty that he hasn't been able to face it."

Landon took her hands in his, wanting to make this

better and knowing he couldn't. "I'm sorry," he said. "Give him a little time. He'll come through for you."

She tried to smile. "I hope so. He's a good person, really he is. It's just—" She stopped, as if she couldn't go on.

His fingers moved, caressing her hands. She met his gaze and he saw her eyes darken. Her breath touched him and he leaned closer, ready to feel her lips—

"Hey, Violet, there you are." Sheriff Cole walked into the room, his rolling gait making him look as if he were on the deck of a ship. "Wait until you see what we found."

Violet turned toward the sheriff, hoping she didn't look as if she'd just been on the verge of being kissed. Or had she? Landon was trying to comfort her—that was in his nature.

She focused on Sheriff Cole. "You found something? Do you know who did it?"

"Knowing's one thing. Proving is another. But we do know something. Come on." He beckoned, and they followed him through the gym and out the door.

Once outside, the sheriff led the way along the building to a narrow passage, about eight feet wide, which ran between this section of the church and the sanctuary.

"There." Sheriff Cole pointed. "Cigarette butts on the ground. Empty beer cans in the basement window well. I'm guessing they gathered in here, drinking and pumpin' themselves up to trash the place."

"You think it was Sam and his buddies, don't you?" She hated to think of the vandals as people she knew.

Still, this was Grasslands. Whoever did it, it had to be someone she knew.

"That'd be my guess," the sheriff concurred. "But like I say, proving it is another story."

Landon stirred restlessly. "There would be finger-prints on the cans. DNA, too."

Sheriff Cole stared at him for a moment. "Well, that's true, I reckon. But we don't have the facilities for that sort of thing. We can use the state police lab, but if I told them I wanted to track down three kids for vandal-ism…well, they'd laugh me out of there in no time flat."

"We don't want to do that anyway," Violet said quickly. "We're trying to show these kids Christian values. We want to give them something to do so they won't turn to beer parties for their entertainment."

"It might be too late for these three," Landon said, looking a little disgruntled. He wanted to fix things, of course. That was what he did.

"It's never too late," she said.

"I don't know." Sheriff Cole shook his head as he stepped back into the sunlight. "Much as I hate to admit it, that kid Sam is a tough one. His dad took off some time ago, and his momma can't seem to keep a rein on that boy."

"Have you asked him about the vandalism?" Landon said.

Violet's thoughts were headed another direction en-tirely. Could she have handled that situation with Sam any other way? She had to follow the rules, of course. They'd set them up for just such a situation. Still…

"I talked," Sheriff Cole said shortly. "Got nothing but a smart answer for my trouble. Reckon I'll have a word with the other boys' parents, though. Might discourage them from following every dumb idea that Sam Donner has."

Violet nodded, but somehow she doubted that would do much good. The other two boys probably felt like big deals when they followed Sam's lead.

"You know, it might help if we could get someone who's…well, closer to their age, to talk to the kids."

The sheriff patted her shoulder. "You do that, Violet. No harm in getting at the problem from all sides, so to speak. Truth is, though, some kids just have to learn the hard way." Shaking his head, he moved toward his car.

"Pastor Jeb seems to have a good rapport with the kids," Landon pointed out. "Maybe he could talk to them."

"He could," Violet said, wondering how Landon would react to the idea that had popped into her head. "But I was thinking of someone else. Why don't you talk to them?"

"Me?" Landon stared at her. "I'm no good at things like that. Pastor Jeb's the one you want."

She looked at him steadily. "Pastor Jeb hasn't experienced personal loss that resulted from driving drunk. If you talked to them—"

"No." He took a step back. "I'm sorry, Violet." His voice cracked. "I know you mean well, but I can't do it. Please, forget that idea. Okay?"

There was so much pain in his eyes that she hated herself for having brought it up. "Of course. I'm sorry, Landon."

"It's all right." He forced a smile. "We'd better get back to work."

Chapter 14

Maddie glanced at her watch as they got into the car after their fourth nursing center visit on Saturday afternoon. "I think we'd better call it a day. By the time we get home we'll need to get ready for Teen Scene."

Maddie sounded as down as Violet felt.

"You're right, I guess." She slid into the passenger seat, and Maddie backed out of the lot and headed down the main road.

Violet rubbed her forehead. Good thing Maddie had volunteered to drive on this excursion. As down as she was feeling, she might have run them right off the road.

"Discouraged?" Maddie glanced at her.

"Very. I didn't realize it would be so hard just to find a place that had room for Mom. Let alone one that we like and that has the facilities she needs."

"There are still a few left on our list." Maddie was trying to sound upbeat. "We'll find the right one. I'm sure of it."

"You know, I might have envisioned needing to do this nursing facility search sometime in the very distant future. I sure never thought I'd be doing it at this stage of the game." Violet rubbed her temples again. "And the costs—I had no idea. Of course, Mom didn't think of having insurance that would cover nursing care. She's still a young woman. Why would she?"

"Nobody wants to consider all those somber possibilities," Maddie said. "That's only human nature. But don't worry about the costs. If we find the right place, we'll grab it, regardless of cost. I know Dad will want to help. He'll want her to have the best."

Violet nodded, but in her heart she wondered. They still had no idea what had caused their parents to take such drastic action in splitting them up. Maybe Brian Wallace wouldn't be so eager to rush to his ex-wife's aid.

Had Belle and Brian even been married? They'd been assuming so, based on the original birth certificate for Maddie that Landon's researcher had found. But that was one of the things they still didn't know for sure.

She didn't want to say that to Maddie. One problem was enough at a time. Now they had to find the right place for their mom.

"What about that nursing home next to the clinic in Grasslands? I notice you didn't have it on the list to visit today." Maddie frowned, concentrating on passing a pickup pulling a horse trailer.

"We can stop in there on Monday. It's a nice place—very clean and homelike, and convenient to the clinic right next door. But it's so small. Most of the patients are there because they're elderly and can't take care of themselves anymore, without family that can help. I thought one of the bigger places would be more likely to have the kind of therapy Mom needs."

"Maybe we're not going to find the perfect place." Maddie sighed with resignation. "We'll just have to figure we'll make up for whatever is missing. We can always bring in a therapist to work with her if need be."

"That's what Landon said." Her thoughts shifted to Landon—something they did too frequently these days.

"Speaking of Landon, I gathered you didn't want me to say anything to Jack about your romance." A smile tugged at Maddie's lips.

"It's not a romance," she protested. "Or at least—well, maybe it could be, but everything's so complicated right now. Can you imagine trying to explain to Jack that Landon used to be engaged to you and now he's paying attention to me?" Her head spun at the thought.

Maddie chuckled. "He'd probably head for the horsewhip." She reached across to touch Violet's arm in a comforting gesture. "Sorry. I'm just kidding. Don't listen to me. And don't worry about Jack. Your love life isn't his business, anyway. And Landon can take care of himself."

Those words started a train of thought that Violet didn't welcome. Landon could take care of himself under almost any circumstances, she felt sure of that. He was strong and confident, a man of solid faith and character.

Except in one particular area of his life. His response to her suggestion that he talk to the kids about drunk driving had shown her only too clearly that he hadn't dealt with his sister's death at all.

Or more likely, it was his guilt about her death that he hadn't dealt with.

Landon was a man with an overly developed sense of responsibility. Normally she'd find that admirable. But in this case, she suspected it was crippling him.

Landon made a final check of the restrooms, being sure everything was in order, and walked back through the games room. Funny how this place had become so familiar to him in such a short time. He almost felt as if he belonged here, though the contrast couldn't be greater to the huge church he attended in Fort Worth.

Violet was in the games room, although he couldn't see her face, since she seemed to be looking at something underneath the Ping-Pong table.

"What are you doing?"

She got up quickly, narrowly missing bumping her head. "Landon, I didn't know you were here already. I was just making sure the brackets were secure. In theory there's nothing on this table but the net. But I can't tell you how often I've found kids sitting, leaning, or climbing on it."

"And are they? The brackets, I mean." He moved closer, smiling at her. Her face was flushed from bending under the table, and her hair was escaping from its ponytail. She looked adorable.

"They're fine." She gave the table a little shake. "All is well here, and everywhere else. Maddie's dealing with the kitchen, and aside from the smell of fresh paint, it's ready to go."

"Good." He glanced at his watch and saw that they had a few minutes before the other volunteers started arriving. "How did the nursing home search go today?"

Her expressive face told him, even before she put it in words. "Nothing good enough yet. But we're not giving up. Maddie and I will hit every care facility in the county if we have to. We're going to find it." Those deep brown eyes seemed to darken with worry. "I just wish Jack would get involved. I know he hates to think of Mom sick, but…" She hesitated. "Well, he's my big brother. I know I've always complained because he treated me like a baby, but this is one instance where I'd like to see him taking the lead."

The annoyance Landon had felt over Jack's behavior bubbled up again. "Big brothers are *supposed* to take the lead." The words came out more harshly than he'd intended. "That's their responsibility."

Violet looked at him, her eyes startled and a little wary at his tone, and he was angry with himself for putting that look on her face.

"Jack's always been good at watching out for me," she said. Naturally she'd defend him. "He just feels so guilty over his quarrel with Mom. He can't help but think that had something to do with her accident."

Landon discovered that he was gritting his teeth to keep from saying what he thought about Jack's actions. Suddenly, he couldn't do it any longer.

"I don't care how you dress it up, Jack's behavior is selfish. He's let you deal with everything while he wallows in his guilt. You shouldn't make excuses for him."

"Wallows?" Violet's voice rose, and the concern in her face turned to anger. "I don't think you have room to criticize Jack for his actions."

"What do you mean? I'm not like Jack." He rejected that idea quickly.

"Aren't you?" Violet planted her hands on her hips. "You've done the very same thing. You've blamed yourself for your sister's death, never giving a thought to all the other people who shared responsibility for what happened. You've let your guilt affect the rest of your life, even planning to settle for a marriage without love, and…"

She stopped abruptly, looking horrified at herself. Probably knowing she'd gone too far.

Landon's heated anger turned cold. He could almost taste the bitterness on his tongue. He'd been fool enough to tell Violet things about himself that he'd never told anyone else, and at the first opportunity, she'd used that knowledge to betray him.

"Landon, I'm sorry. I didn't mean… I shouldn't have…"

Violet was holding out her hand to him, but he turned away. He couldn't stay here any longer.

Heedless of her words, he stalked out.

Violet stood there, gripping the table with both hands. What had she done?

She'd let her shaky emotions get the better of her, said things she shouldn't have, and now Landon was gone.

She took a deep breath, then another, reaching out in silent prayer for strength and clarity. She shouldn't have thrown his own actions back at Landon that way.

But at heart, she knew what she'd said was true. Landon had let his guilt over his sister's death affect every other aspect of his life. Unless he could manage to forgive himself, how could he ever have a deep relationship with anyone?

He couldn't. And after what she'd done, even if he could, it would never be with her.

Now that their relationship was broken beyond repair, she knew just how much she'd grown to love him.

She pressed her hand against her heart, trying to deny the pain.

"Violet?" Maddie came in from the kitchen. "What's going on? The volunteers are starting to come in. Where's Landon? I thought he was in here."

Violet blinked rapidly. She wanted to collapse in tears or crawl into a hole and stay there, but she couldn't do either. She had a job to do. No matter how much she hurt, she had to go on.

"We had a quarrel," she said, the words blunt because she had to get them out quickly. "He left."

Maddie reached out to her, obviously wanting to comfort her but probably not knowing how. "What did—" She stopped, cleared her throat, started again. "You don't want to talk about it now. We'll talk later. Listen, if you'd like to go home, we have enough people here to help."

Violet shook her head, knowing she couldn't do that, but loving Maddie for offering. "No, it's all right. I'll be better off here."

"Okay." Maddie's expression was troubled. "But if you change your mind, just let me know."

"I won't." She managed a smile.

Maddie patted her hand. "Everybody quarrels. Don't take it too seriously. Landon will probably be back, ready to make up before you know it."

She nodded, because it was easier to agree than to say what she knew to be the truth. Her relationship with Landon was over before it had a chance to begin. Now she'd have to learn to live without him.

Chapter 15

They'd had more youths than ever at Teen Scene tonight. That surprised Violet. Were they all coming out as a show of support? If so, perhaps the vandals had actually done them more good than harm.

Like Joseph in the Old Testament, telling the brothers who had sold him into slavery in Egypt that though they had meant their action for evil, God had used it for good.

Sometimes it was hard to see God working in a difficult situation…like Belle's injury. So she was glad to be able to rejoice in this one, at least.

A few kids were starting to filter out the door as the clock counted down the time to closing. Headlights from parents' cars passed the windows as rides home appeared to collect the teens.

Violet had managed to keep thoughts of Landon at bay by staying busy, but soon she'd have nothing to do but think and regret.

Violet glanced into the kitchen to see that Maddie and her helper were just about finished clearing up. They'd stopped serving food a half hour before closing, so the kitchen volunteers wouldn't get stuck with cleanup after everyone else had left.

Maddie saw her and waved. Then she came over, scanning Violet's face. "Are you okay?"

"I'm holding up," she said, grateful for the concern. "We had a great turnout tonight."

"Yes. Too bad Landon didn't stick around to see it." Maddie's annoyance with him showed in her voice. "The kids really cleaned us out in the kitchen. Why are they always so hungry?"

"It's the natural state of teenagers," Violet said, trying for a show of cheerfulness she didn't feel. She glanced toward the outside door and frowned. "That's Tracey's father coming in. I wonder why."

She started toward them, seeing Tracey's dad scan the small group of kids who were still playing basketball. Then his look seemed to move on to the knots of chattering girls on the gym balcony. Concern deepened on his face. Obviously, Tracey must not have been ready for pickup at the appropriate time.

She grabbed Maddie's arm. "Look over there—the man in the denim jacket. That's Bob Benton, Tracey's father. Will you tell him I'll go find Tracey and send her out?"

"Sure thing. I'm done here." Maddie waved thanks to her helper and started toward the door.

Violet walked back through the games room, vaguely anxious. It wouldn't be the first time that a parent, tired of waiting, had come in to haul a kid out, but Tracey wasn't careless about things like being where she was supposed to be. If anything, she was overly conscientious, maybe because she was worried about her family. Still, there was a first time for everything, so the saying went.

Violet had been able to find some reassuring information for the girl after she'd confided her worry about being taken back to Mexico by her mother. Still, the attorney she'd talked to had said it wasn't very clear-cut, especially if a parent left the country with a child and then refused to return. At this point, all Violet could do about the situation was pray and try to be available if and when Tracey wanted to talk.

Tracey wasn't in the games room. Reminding the kids who were still playing that it was time to wind things up, Violet crossed into the social room, but it was empty already.

Worry edging along her nerves, Violet looked in the restroom and the adjoining hallway. Empty.

She went back through, automatically checking the other doors, but all seemed as it should be. They had to have more than one exit available, of course, in case of emergency, but the kids knew they were not to go up through the church for any reason, and she hadn't heard the bell that would sound when that door was opened.

She checked the rooms again as she walked back through, her concern growing. By the time she reached Bob Benton, it had reached the level of worry.

Maddie, standing with Tracey's father, turned to her as she approached. "Mr. Benton says Tracey was supposed to meet him at quarter 'til in the parking lot, but she never came."

Violet faced the man, a rough-hewn cowboy type who wore a worried frown at the moment. "Is it possible that Tracey could have misunderstood something about the arrangements, Mr. Benton? Maybe thought she was supposed to ride home with someone else?"

He shook his head. "I always pick her up. Are you telling me she's not here?"

"I've checked all the rooms, but let's not panic. We'll look again, but the first thing to do is see when she checked out." She turned to Harriet, who had been manning the door.

But the older woman was shaking her head already. "I've been over the list a dozen times already, Vi. I've got her checking in at seven-ten, and nothing afterward."

"Maybe you missed her," Bob said.

Harriet might have been offended at the suggestion, but her face softened in sympathy when she looked at him. "I couldn't have, and that's the truth of it," she said. "I haven't left my post for a second in the past hour."

"And I saw her more recently than that," Maddie put in. "She came to the pass-through for a soda, and we chatted a few minutes."

Violet thought about the conversation she'd had with the board in regard to handling just such an emergency. The possibility had seemed so remote then. Now she was glad they'd put policies in place.

"Harriet, call Pastor Jeb. And nobody leaves until you've talked to them in detail about when they last saw Tracey Benton. Those who remember seeing her should wait here in the gym until we have a chance to talk to them. If any parents are upset by that—"

"I'll deal with them." Harriet's expression was grim, and Violet knew no one would get past her.

"Maddie, Bob, we'll start working our way back

through the rooms. Check every place, and ask all the kids who are still here if they remember seeing her and who they saw her with. It's always possible she slipped out somehow to go home with a friend." That was the most reassuring thing she could think of to say.

Maddie and Bob Benton nodded, and they split up to work their way from one kid to another in the gym. Leaving the gym to them, Violet went on into the kitchen. Nobody was there, but she checked the pantry just the same. An upset teenage girl might look for a secret spot to cry.

There was nothing in the pantry but brooms and the usual paper supplies. Frustrated, she took another look around and headed back to the games room. She hadn't thought to check the tiny office area, and she should.

Ten minutes later, Violet was no further along than she had been. She went back to rejoin Harriet at the door. As she entered the gym, she saw the other adult volunteers questioning kids. When Violet reached Harriet's table, Pastor Jeb was coming in, with Landon right behind him.

Her heart thudded uncomfortably, but she forced herself to walk toward them. "Pastor Jeb, I'm glad you're here." She nodded toward Landon.

"Maddie called me," Landon said shortly. "She knew I'd want to know. Any news?"

"Nothing. I just don't understand how Tracey could get out of the center without our knowing."

She glimpsed movement from the corner of her eye and realized it was one of the boys Landon had played basketball with. He was looking at Landon, and something in his face told her he wanted to speak to him, but the kid backed away when he saw her watching him.

She nodded toward the boy, her gaze meeting Landon's. "It looks to me as if Tommy Fisher wants to talk to you," she said quietly. "He's bound to be shy about being involved in anything, but if he knows something, he might tell you."

Landon hesitated, as if getting information from a reluctant thirteen-year-old was not something he felt capable of. Then he moved casually toward the boy.

Praying silently, Violet watched them, trying not to let the boy catch her.

Please, Father, if he knows anything that will help us find Tracey, let him open up. Help him to see that her safety is more important than any teenage code of silence.

Landon put his hand on the boy's shoulder, bending over to talk quietly to him. After a moment, the two of them walked toward Violet, Landon's hand still on Tommy's shoulder.

"Tommy says he might be able to help." He patted the boy's shoulder. "You can tell us, whatever it is. You want to help us keep Tracey safe, don't you?"

Tommy nodded, staring down at his frayed sneakers. "I don't want to get nobody in trouble," he mumbled.

Bob Benton seemed to think that was directed at him. "I'm not looking to punish Tracey," he said. "I just want to find her and get her home to her mama."

"Come on, Tommy." Landon urged gently. "You heard. You're not getting her in trouble. You're helping her."

Tommy sniffed, and Violet suddenly realized he was on the verge of tears and didn't want anyone to know. "I heard them talking before Tracey came in." He jerked his head toward the door. "Out in the alley."

"Heard who?" Landon urged. "Who was Tracey with?"

Tommy sniffed again. "Sam. Sam Donner."

Violet heard the sudden intake of Landon's breath and saw him stiffen. He was undoubtedly thinking what she was. What if Sam had been drinking?

"What were they going to do?" she asked. "How did Tracey get out of the building?"

A tear slid down one cheek, out of Tommy's control. "I heard him tell her to go out that back door that goes into the church. He done somethin' to the bell so it wouldn't ring. Said it'd be a good joke. He'd be waiting in his car, and they'd go for a ride."

"Had he been drinking?" Landon's voice was incredibly harsh, and Tommy recoiled.

"It's okay, Tommy," she said quickly. "You can tell us."

"I dunno. Maybe." He shrugged, studying his sneakers again.

"Do you have any idea where they were going on this ride?" Her thoughts ran rapidly over the places where teens were known to congregate.

"That's all I know, honest, Ms. Vi. Can I go? My mom's gonna skin me if I'm not home on time."

"That's okay, Tommy. You can go home now." She touched his shoulder lightly, wanting to ruffle his hair but knowing he'd think himself too old for that gesture. "You were a big help. If your mom gives you grief about being late, I'll tell her what happened, okay?"

Tommy nodded and then bolted away from them. But he stopped at the door. "I hope Tracey's okay," he said, and darted out into the dark.

"We'll have to start looking for them," Pastor Jeb said. "If that boy's been drinking, Tracey shouldn't be in a car with him."

"If I catch up with him, he's not gonna be going with any girls in cars for a while." Bob Benton's big hands curled into fists.

"We need to get moving," Landon said abruptly. "Go in pairs, so one person can drive while the other one looks for any sign of them."

Pastor Jeb nodded. "Right. Harriet, you'd best call Sheriff Cole and get his people out. You can send the rest of these kids home. Now pair up, everyone."

"Violet, can you come with me?" Landon's voice was as impersonal as if she were a stranger. "I don't know the area, and you do."

A thousand reasons why that wasn't a good idea crowded Violet's mind, but Tracey's safety was more important than her feelings. She nodded and followed him out to his car.

By the time they were pulling out of the lot, other duos had started getting into cars. She glimpsed Harriet at the gym door, talking to a group of concerned parents. If she knew her town, there would soon be a number of people out looking.

Tracey would undoubtedly find it embarrassing that half the town knew what she'd done, but that was part of living in a place like this—you didn't get any anonymity. But you did get a lot of people who cared what happened to you.

"Which way?" Landon said, his voice clipped.

"Turn right, then right again. We'll head out to Blue Lake. That's a popular place for kids to go and park."

He followed her directions without comment, but by the time he was on the road out of town, he couldn't seem to keep quiet any longer. "What would possess her to go off with a boy like Sam? You'd think she could see him for what he is."

At least he was accepting the fact that Tracey bore some responsibility for her actions, which was more than he'd done in regard to his sister. Did he realize the dichotomy in his attitude?

"Tracey's been vulnerable lately. She probably liked the attention from an older boy. Girls do stupid things sometimes, even though they know it's wrong."

"Vulnerable how?"

"Tracey hasn't told me the whole story, but I do know her parents have been fighting. She asked me if she'd have to go back to Mexico if her mother wanted to go."

Landon shot a look at her. "You didn't tell me that."

"There wasn't anything you could do, and she only told me on my promise to keep quiet. Which I'm breaking." She shook her head. "But this situation is too serious for keeping secrets now."

Landon nodded, his profile stern in the dim light. "How much farther is it?"

"There's a turnoff to the right about a mile down the road. It's just a lane, so you'd better slow down."

Landon's hands were tight on the wheel, but he slowed down as she'd said. Soon she spotted the end of a fence that marked the lane.

"There—right where that white post is." She gripped the door handle as he turned down the narrow, rutted lane. "If they are there, what are we going to do? We can't force Tracey to go with us."

"She'll come." Landon's tone was faintly threatening.

They bounced in a rut, Violet's head nearly hitting the roof of the car. Just as she thought her bones were going to shake apart, they emerged onto the roughly cleared space that overlooked the small, man-made lake.

As she might have imagined, there were three vehicles parked there, spaced apart. She eyed them quickly. "I don't think they're here. Sam drives a beat-up, old black pickup."

"He could have borrowed a car." Landon slid out, taking a flashlight. "Are you coming?"

Obviously she was. They approached the first car, Violet feeling a bit of trepidation.

At least the kids in the car didn't react violently when Landon tapped on the window with his flashlight. The driver rolled the window down.

"We're not—" he began, and then stopped. "What's going on, man? You're not the cops."

"I'm looking for Sam Donner. Have you seen him?"

The boy's gaze slid away from Landon's. "Can't say as I have."

Violet stepped forward into the light. "Jesse Halstrom. I'm surprised to see you here." She waited a second, letting him register the fact that not only did she know him, she had been his Sunday School teacher last year. "What were you saying about Sam Donner?"

Jesse cleared his throat. "Hey, Ms. Vi. I... I was just going to say that I spotted that rattletrap he calls a truck headed down Goose Hollow Road maybe an hour or so ago. Going way too fast."

Landon headed for his car. "Come on."

"Thank you, Jesse." Violet hurried after him.

Landon took the road Violet indicated, trying not to let his anxiety affect the pressure of his foot on the gas pedal. They wouldn't do anyone any good if they had an accident.

Violet was on her cell phone talking to the reverend, who was coordinating the search. "All right. Thanks, Pastor Jeb. We'll be in touch." She cut the connection.

"Any news from the search party?"

"Nothing yet. So far we seem to be the only ones with a lead."

He nodded. "How far ahead is this road?"

"About another mile."

Something about Violet's voice made him glance at her. "Aren't you sure?"

"I'm sure about where the road is," she said. "I'm just wondering if we're scaring ourselves unnecessarily. After all, we don't have any proof that Sam's been drinking."

"Are you willing to take that chance?" he demanded.

"No, of course not. I guess I'm just trying to find some hope to cling to. Even if Sam was drinking, that doesn't mean he'll have an accident."

So she knew that was his fear. He gritted his teeth, never wanting to live through that particular pain again. Tracey wasn't his sister, but he'd still feel he'd failed her if the worst happened.

"You couldn't have known this was going to happen," Violet said, as if she knew what he was thinking. "You don't know these kids anywhere near as well as I do, and I had no idea Tracey was interested in Sam Donner."

He glanced at her, hearing the guilt in her voice. "You couldn't have known, either, Violet. Don't beat yourself up over it." The anger he'd felt toward her earlier was subsiding, drowned in the more immediate emergency.

"There's the turn," she said, leaning forward and pointing.

He swung into the road. It pitched sharply downward, the trees thick on either side. It was like falling into a well. He couldn't see anything except the short stretch of road within range of his headlight beams.

"This is a terrible road." Violet stated the obvious. "Better slow down—" Her voice choked on the word.

And then he saw what she had, and his own throat seemed to close. A vehicle, off the road, half in a gully, hood against a tree, its headlamps slanting upward to stab the sky.

Chapter 16

Landon was out of the car almost before he'd brought it to a stop, leaving the door swinging. Violet grabbed her cell phone, calling 911 as she ran toward the pickup. She rattled off the directions, reaching Landon's side with the dispatcher's assurances ringing in her ears.

"They're on their way," she said. "Tracey?"

"I can't see her." Landon handed her the flashlight and yanked at the door. It stuck, and he braced his foot against the frame and pulled. The door shrieked and opened.

Heart pounding, wordless prayers forming, Violet aimed the flashlight beam into the truck.

Sam Donner blinked against the light, blood trickling from a gash on his head. He groaned. "Wha...wh..."

Violet could smell the beer from outside the pickup. She flashed the light over the rest of the interior. Tracey wasn't there.

"If she was thrown out—" Landon muttered, fear in his voice. He grasped Sam's shoulder. "Where's Tracey? Answer me. What happened to Tracey?"

Violet caught his hand, his pain pummeling her as well. Landon was reliving his sister's death—how could he help it in circumstances like this?

"Don't, Landon." She pulled his hand away. "We don't know how badly he's injured. Let me."

For a moment she thought Landon wasn't even hearing her. Then he stepped back and she edged past him.

She touched Sam's cheek, fearful of a head injury. He wasn't in immediate danger of being hurt worse, so they probably shouldn't try to move him.

"Sam," she said urgently. "Sam…listen to me. Where's Tracey?"

"T-Tracey?" he muttered.

"Tracey Benton. You left the church with her. Where is she? Was she in the truck with you?"

He didn't answer. This was useless—they should start searching. Where would Tracey be if she'd been thrown out?

"Where is she?" Landon demanded. He sounded as if he had control of himself again.

Sam seemed to rouse. "Tracey." He frowned, his head moving side to side. "Said I was drunk. I'm not. Let her out."

A wave of relief swept through Violet. "Where, Sam?" She patted his cheek. "You're hurt, but the ambulance is on its way. Now tell us where Tracey got out so we can find her." She could already hear the siren, coming ever closer.

Sam's eyes closed. If he didn't answer they'd be left searching the county for Tracey, not knowing…

"Jenkins' Mill," he muttered. "She got out."

"Where's Jenkins' Mill?" Landon growled. "She's out there by herself. Anything could happen."

Violet wanted to protest that this was Grasslands, not the city, but bad things could happen anywhere. She stepped back as the sheriff's car, siren wailing, pulled up, closely followed by the EMTs.

"The mill is on the edge of town. We'll find her."

A few minutes later they were back in Landon's car headed for town, leaving Sam in the capable hands of the EMTs.

"At least this might force Sam to get the help he needs," she said.

Landon's hands tightened on the wheel, and she knew he was seeing the boy who'd been responsible for his sister's death instead of Sam. Fresh pain pierced her heart. What could she say to him?

"Let's hope so," he said finally. "We're almost at the edge of town. Keep looking along the road."

Landon slowed the car, and she focused on the area ahead of them, watching for any sign of movement. No one seemed to be out in this area at night—it was mostly businesses, closed at this hour.

They were nearing the church when she grabbed Landon's arm. "Look, there. In the doorway of the flower shop."

Landon braked, stopping at the curb. Tracey huddled forlornly against the flower shop door, arms wrapped around herself.

Thank You, Lord. Violet slid out and approached Tracey, struggling to get her voice under control before she spoke.

"Hey, Tracey." She put her arm around the girl. "It's all right. We're so glad to find you."

Landon approached cautiously. "Are you okay, Tracey?"

Tracey nodded, wiping tears away with her palms. "I... I'm sorry. I didn't know what to do."

Violet hugged her. "It sounds to me as if you did just right. You realized Sam had been drinking and you made him let you out."

"I'm so ashamed." A fresh bout of tears flowed. "I sneaked out of Teen Scene and now you'll never let me back in again. It was too far to walk home, and I couldn't find any place open to call. I was afraid to go to a house where I didn't know the people...and I didn't know what to do!"

The litany ended on a wail, and Tracey buried her face in Violet's shoulder and sobbed.

Violet couldn't help but smile at Landon even as she tried to comfort the girl. The recital was such a mixture of woes that she didn't know where to begin dealing with it.

Landon's face was unreadable in the dim light. He pulled out his cell phone.

"Listen, Tracey." She held the teen by both shoulders. "You made a mistake, okay? And you're sorry. You handled it well, once you knew you were in too deep. That's the important thing. Now Mr. Derringer is going to let the people who are searching know you're okay, and then we're going to take you home."

Tracey's lips trembled. "Daddy will yell, and Mama will cry, and—"

"I promise, if they do, it's only because they were scared to death something bad happened to you." She kept her tone firm and practical, sensing that was the best way to deal with Tracey's overflowing emotions. "Come on now." She piloted the girl to the car.

Landon slid behind the wheel. "The sheriff is calling off the search party, and Tracey's father will meet us at their house."

"What about Sam?" she asked.

Tracey leaned forward in the backseat, distracted from her own misery. "Did something happen to Sam?"

"He wrecked his truck," Landon said. "The EMTs took him to the hospital, but they don't think it's anything serious."

"I told him he shouldn't be driving. Maybe, if I hadn't got out, he wouldn't have crashed."

"Don't think that way." Landon spoke sharply, probably out of his own memories. "You did the right thing. If you hadn't gotten out of that pickup, you'd be the one on the way to the hospital. Or maybe the morgue."

"Landon…" Violet intervened.

"It's true, and Tracey needs to understand that." He was uncompromising. "Listen to me, Tracey, because I know what I'm talking about. My sister Jessie was just about your age when she got into a car with a boy who was drunk. But she didn't have your common sense. She didn't get out, and she died because of that. So don't ever think it would have made a difference if you'd stayed."

He'd actually spoken of his sister. Violet's emotions tumbled and she fought to stay in control.

"I… I'm sorry." Tracey's voice was very small. "About your sister."

Landon nodded, and they rode the rest of the way to the mobile home park where Tracey lived in silence, except for the necessary directions.

Violet studied Landon's face as they went up the walk with Tracey, but he had his stoic mask on, not giving anything away. This night had put his deepest grief through the wringer, and she wasn't sure how he was going to react to that. He must be tempted just to get into his car and hightail it back to Fort Worth, in order to forget she and this place ever existed.

Landon declined the second cup of coffee that Maria Benton tried to force on him. He was never going to sleep tonight as it was. He'd have headed out once they'd delivered Tracey to her parents, but Violet clearly had something on her mind.

Now Violet sat on the threadbare couch, reaching out to pat Tracey's hand where she sat with her mother's arm around her. "I'm sure you'd like for us to get out of here," she said. "But I think there's something we should bring out into the open before anything else happens."

Tracey's parents exchanged glances. "I don't understand," Maria said. "Tracey was very foolish, but she's okay now."

Violet leaned toward the girl, her gaze on Tracey's face. "You need to talk to your parents, Tracey. Tell them what you've been worried about."

"Tracey?" Bob Benton touched his daughter's cheek lightly. "Honey, what's wrong? What's Ms. Vi talking about?"

Tracey shook her head, lips pressed together. Then the tears started to flow again.

"I heard you arguing." Tracey looked at her mother. "I heard you saying about going back to Mexico. I don't want to. I don't want to leave Daddy and my friends... and my school."

Landon could see by the parents' expressions that they had no idea Tracey had overheard them.

Bob Benton sat down on the coffee table in front of his

daughter, taking her hands in his. "Tracey, honey, you've got it all wrong. We weren't talking about splitting up." He looked at his wife. "You have to tell her the truth."

Maria's dark eyes, so like Tracey's, were brimming with tears, but she nodded. "I love you and your daddy," she said softly. "I love our lives here. But a piece of my heart is still in Mexico." She stroked her daughter's hair. "You see, I have another daughter. Your half sister. She is almost eighteen now, and I haven't seen her in so long. It tears my heart to bits to think of her never knowing you."

Tracey's eyes were round. "But...you never told me."

Maria wiped her eyes. "I was afraid if you knew I had left her behind with her grandparents that you would be afraid I could do that to you. I thought I was doing what was best."

Secrets. Landon glanced at Violet. Secrets had torn her family apart, and only the good Lord knew if that could ever be made right.

"I have a sister." Tracey seemed to be trying the words on for size. "What's her name? What does she look like? Why can't she come here and be with us?"

"Miranda," her mother answered. "Her name is Miranda. She lives with my parents, and they are Mama and Papa to her. She would like to come here, maybe go to school, but the immigration..." She stopped. "It's so hard, and it takes money."

Pain tightened Bob's face. "I'd do it if I could, honey. You know that. But we're barely getting by as it is."

Landon's hands tightened on his knees. He had been so blessed financially that it seemed unfair when others had so little. But he could at least help with part of the Benton family's problem.

"The foundation I work with has a good immigration lawyer," he said. "He deals with things like this all the time. Will you let me contact him for you?"

"We don't take charity—" Bob began.

"Not charity," he said hastily. He'd seen that kind of pride before, and he admired it. "But the attorney will do the work up front, and you can pay him back over time. It would be like a school loan for Miranda. Most kids get those now."

The stubborn pride melted from Bob's face as he looked at his wife. "We…we'd be awful grateful."

"No need," Landon said, rising. "I'll be headed back to Fort Worth tomorrow, and the lawyer's office will be in touch for the information they need sometime next week. Okay?"

Bob nodded. Tracey and her mother were both crying again. Landon looked at Violet and nodded toward the door. There was nothing more they could do here, but with any luck, Tracey and her family were going to be all right.

He wasn't so sure about himself. His emotions had been turned inside out by everything that had happened. He needed time to sort everything out, time to be sure that what he was feeling for Violet was real.

He thought about what Violet had said to him…the truth that had come out when she was angry. Maybe, real or not, it was too late.

Sunday morning. Landon had heard the church bells ringing from his hotel room. He should have gone to church. Or he should be on the road back to Fort Worth.

He didn't want to do either of those things. He wanted to see Violet, to tell her what he felt. The trouble was that after a mostly sleepless night, he didn't seem to be any closer to an answer now than he had been before.

Finished dressing, he picked up his suitcase and walked down the stairs. Maybe going back to Fort Worth was the best solution. Once he was busy with his normal routine, maybe his feelings for Violet would take their proper proportion.

He'd reached the car and was putting his case in the back when he realized people were coming out of the church down the street. Violet's church. If she saw him...

But it wasn't Violet who was walking quickly toward him. It was Maddie.

She reached him, slightly out of breath, and let her gaze shift from him to the suitcase and back again. "Going somewhere, Landon?"

He definitely didn't want to talk to Maddie about his feelings for Violet. "I have work waiting for me back at the office. And now that your brother is here, you don't need me."

Maddie raised her eyebrows. "If I didn't see it with my own eyes, I wouldn't believe it. Landon Derringer, running away."

"I'm not running away." He tried to grab hold of his temper before it cut loose. "I just think it's for the best if I leave. Besides, you're the one who keeps telling me to butt out of your business. I should think you'd be glad to see the back of me."

"Maybe, maybe not." She tilted her head to the side, looking at him as if she hadn't seen him before. "What's more important to me right now is how Violet feels. Have you even said goodbye to her?"

He turned away, slamming the trunk lid. "I'll be in touch. I just think—"

"You just think you might actually have to risk showing your feelings if you hang around here any longer," Maddie snapped. "Well, go ahead, if that's the most important thing to you. But you'd better think about what you'll be losing if you drive away now. It might be more than you're willing to risk."

He opened his mouth to respond, but it was too late. Maddie was striding off down the street, anger showing in every click of her heels.

Landon got into the car, venting a little temper of his own by slamming the door. Maddie might think she had the right to meddle, but she didn't. This was between him and Violet, and he wasn't going to jump into anything until he was sure he was right.

That temper lasted him about ten miles down the road toward Fort Worth. Then he slowed. And stopped, hands grasping the wheel. He stared out at the rolling grasslands on either side of the road, but all he could see was Violet's face, all he could hear was her voice.

Running away, Maddie had said. He was running away rather than facing the risk of showing his feelings. Was that really the way he wanted to live his life?

Little Maddie had done some growing up since she'd met her twin. She was no longer the kid who'd cried over her lost job and said yes to marriage because she didn't know what else to do with her life.

And maybe, just maybe, she knew what she was talking about. He pressed on the gas, turning the car in the middle of the empty road, and headed back toward the Colby Ranch.

Chapter 17

Violet heard a car coming down the lane. Lupita would have Sunday dinner on the table in a few minutes. Who would be coming to call now?

She leaned toward the window to look out, and her heart nearly stopped. It was Landon.

Maddie glanced over her shoulder, and then gave her a smile that looked rather like the expression of a satisfied cat. "He's here to see you, not me. Better go out and meet him. I'll make sure no one bothers you."

She sent an accusing glance at her sister. "What did you do?"

"Nothing." Maddie sounded way too innocent. "Go on, now." Maddie gave her a push toward the door.

By the time Violet reached the porch, Landon was getting out of his car. He stood for a moment, looking at her with an expression she couldn't interpret. Then he came quickly to her.

"Is there someplace we can talk? Alone?"

If he'd come to tell her he was going to Fort Worth and not coming back, she'd better hear it with no one else around. "Let's walk over toward the pecan groves. It'll be cooler under the trees."

She led the way, and Landon walked beside her, not speaking. The longer the silence stretched, the more difficult it would be to speak at all.

And how could she say anything, even if she could find the words? Last night Landon had basically walked out of her life. Did she dare to believe that anything had changed?

They reached the shadow of the trees, and Landon turned to face her.

She took a breath. "Landon, I'm sorry. What I said about your grief—it was inexcusable. I shouldn't—"

He put his finger on her lips, silencing her. He was very close in the dimness under the trees.

"Don't, Violet. Don't be sorry, because everything you said was true."

"I was still unkind to say it. I had no right to strike back at you that way."

"You had to." His hand moved, the back of his fingers gentle against her cheek. "I wasn't seeing it for myself, was I? I've spent all these years rejecting God's forgiveness, trying to make up for losing Jessie by sponsoring charities, but never letting my heart be touched." He shook his head. "Until I came here, and started to see what helping people really meant. Not just throwing money at a problem, but putting your heart on the line."

She couldn't let him denigrate the good he'd done. "You've helped so many people, Landon. No matter what your motives were, you helped them. That's important."

He was shaking his head again, but this time she thought it was in wonderment at himself.

"Ever since I met you in that coffee shop, you've been turning my perceptions upside down. You've been hammering my locked heart open. And yesterday—" He stopped, and a shudder went through him.

She spoke quickly, not wanting him to relive it. "It was a close call, but Tracey is fine. Maybe this will even be the wake up Sam needed. And with your help, the Benton family will be all right. That's a pretty good payoff for all the worry we went through." She tried to smile, hoping to relieve the pain she feared still lurked inside him.

"Tracey took care of herself. She did the right thing. If Jessie had done that, she'd be alive today."

"You can't change the past," she said, her voice gentle. He was referring to his sister by her nickname now, she noticed, as if he could open up his memories to the child she'd been long ago.

"You're right." He touched her face again, and his fingers were warm on her cheek. "Neither of us can do that, any more than the Bentons can. All we can do is forgive and move on."

She put her hand over his, pressing his palm against her skin. "If you can do that now, then everything has been worth it. Even if…"

"Even if what?" Landon leaned closer.

"You…you said you were going back to Fort Worth." She didn't want the pain to show in her voice, but it did.

"Not for good," he said quickly. "Not unless you want me to stay away."

Her heart seemed to have gotten stuck on the fact

that he was coming back, and it was singing so loudly in her ears that she could barely think. "I… I don't."

"I thought I needed time," he said. He took both her hands, holding them between his as solemnly as if they were making a vow. "But your sister told me I was running away because I was afraid to risk showing my feelings. Maybe she was right. Maybe that was why I was so eager to keep everyone at arm's length, why I was even ready to settle for a marriage without love."

He was quoting her words back to her. "I'm sorry… I shouldn't have said that. I didn't mean to hurt you."

Landon dropped a kiss on her fingertips. "It was worth any hurt it caused me, because it made me look at myself. You and Maddie between you made me see what I was doing. I'm ready to take the risk now. I know it hasn't been very long, but when it's right, you know it. I love you, Violet, more than I can say."

Her heart seemed to be beating somewhere up in her throat, and she could swear she heard songbirds singing in the trees. But maybe that was just the sheer joy that was rushing through her. She looked into his face, seeing the love that shone in the depths of his eyes, and she knew it was for real.

"I love you, Landon." She would say more, but his lips closed on hers. Tenderness flowed through her, seeming to touch every cell of her body. His arm went around her, holding her close. She had never felt so cherished, so loved.

Finally, Landon drew back, still holding her in his arms. His face was so open and relaxed that her breath caught. This was how he looked with all the barriers down.

"I hate to say it, but I do have to go back to Fort

Worth for a day or two. I have to deal with some business and get the immigration attorney started on the Benton situation," Landon went on, not waiting for a comment. "And there's something I have to show you."

"Show me?" She looked up at his face, puzzled.

"Something that comes with a confession. You know that photo of your family that I had enhanced for you?"

She nodded, bemused at the change of subject.

"Guess I was being a little overprotective," he said. "Annoyingly so, I think you could say."

"What did you do?" It surely couldn't be anything that bad.

"The enhanced photo brought up an address on the mailbox. An address in Fort Worth. I was afraid you and Maddie would rush off half-cocked and get yourselves hurt, so—"

"So you deleted it on our copies." She glared at him, but he looked so contrite that her heart wasn't in it. "Interfering. Bossy. Annoying," she said.

"Guilty on all counts. Forgive me?" He leaned closer, so near that his warm breath touched her cheek.

"As long as you promise not to hide anything else from me for my own good," she said firmly.

"I promise." His lips brushed hers. "As long as you promise to include me in any plans you make for the future."

That was an easy promise to make, Violet knew as his lips found hers again. She wrapped her arms around him, holding him close. Their lives had taken some odd twists and turns, and all of those hadn't been unraveled yet. But God had brought them through to the place they really belonged—with each other.

Epilogue

"Let me see it again." Maddie grabbed Violet's hand to admire the ring Landon had given her. "That Landon doesn't waste any time, does he?"

"That's what Jack keeps saying." Violet pulled riding gloves on, hiding the ring for the moment. "'You've only known him a month. Why do you want to get engaged?' But when you know it's real, you know."

"I guess so." Maddie sighed. "It makes me think I'm missing something. Something I never felt with Landon."

Violet smiled at her twin. "It will happen for you. I know it. Now, if we're going to go for a ride this morning, we'd best get moving."

Maddie nodded. "I think we have a few too many things on our to-do lists. Decide on the right nursing facility, follow up that clue to the house in Fort Worth, to say nothing of renovating the guesthouse so that it's suitable for a newly married couple…"

Violet nodded, glancing toward the guest cottage. According to Landon's plans, it would soon be doubled in size. Her heart seemed to swell at the thought of living there with him.

"I'm just so relieved that Landon doesn't want me to move to Fort Worth. Given Mom's situation, I wouldn't want to be that far away, and there's the produce business to run, as well."

"Landon has telecommuting down to a fine art, as far as I can tell," Maddie said. "Even if he has to go into the city every week or so, at least this way you don't have to give up your work. Speaking of which, it's about time I started looking for my next job, whatever it's going to be."

"I wish you didn't have to leave here to find it." They had gotten so close in the last month. Violet hated to think of being without her.

But Maddie didn't seem to be listening. She was looking toward one of the small barns, her hand shielding her eyes from the sun. "Who is that with Ty Garland?"

Violet followed the direction of her gaze. Ty was there, all right, standing by one of the pens that contained a sow and her babies. But there was a child with him.

"I guess we'd better find out." She headed for Ty with Maddie right beside her.

Ty looked up at their approach. "Violet. Maddie." He nodded, his normally stoic face very tense.

"Morning, Ty. Who's this?" Violet watched the little girl, who looked about eight or so, approach the pen and then turn away, wrinkling her nose.

"Sorry I didn't have a chance to talk to you about her, Violet. That's Darcy. My little girl."

Violet hoped her face didn't show how shocked she was. She'd known that Ty had been married—a marriage that ended when his wife left him. She'd never heard anything about a child.

"She's adorable," Maddie gushed. Not knowing what a surprise this was, Maddie could sound perfectly normal in her response. "With that brown hair and brown eyes, she looks just like you, Ty."

Ty nodded. "Guess she does, at that." He sounded faintly surprised, as if that hadn't occurred to him.

The little girl—Darcy—had wandered along the fence, tapping it with a stick as children always seemed to do. Ty looked as if to be sure she was out of earshot, and then he turned back to them.

"Thing is, I never even knew I had a kid. My ex-wife made sure of that." Bitterness threaded his voice. "Now she's gone and I'm left with a kid I don't know who's never been out of a city in her life. What am I going to do with her?"

Violet's heart was touched by his turmoil, and she could see that Maddie felt the same. "You're her father. She'll feel a connection with you. That's what's important now. We'll all help her feel at home here. And once school starts, she'll have friends and new activities."

"I s'pose. Kids have gone through worse and come out okay, I guess," he conceded. "But I can't work and watch her at the same time until school starts. And where am I going to find a good sitter who can take care of her on such short notice?"

The idea popped into her head with such ease it was as if it was meant. "What about Maddie?" she proposed.

"She's here, and she was just saying that she wanted a job."

Maddie's eyebrows lifted. "That wasn't exactly the kind of job I had in mind." But she was smiling at the little girl.

"You're great with kids," Violet reminded her. "I've watched you with them at Teen Scene. It's the perfect answer. You'd be helping Ty, and it means you'd stay here for a while longer, at least. I'm not ready to lose my twin yet."

Maddie's smile turned to a mischievous grin. "I'm in. But it's possible Ty doesn't want me."

They both looked at Ty. He seemed torn between emotions, doubt about Maddie battling relief at the simple answer to his problem. "I guess we could give it a test run. Maybe until school starts, anyway."

"It's a deal," Maddie said promptly.

Violet could breathe again. She wasn't going to lose her twin. With Maddie here, together they could work on the fragile bond that was beginning to weave their family back together at last.

* * * * *

Brenda Minton lives in the Ozarks with her husband, children, cats, dogs and strays. She is a pastor's wife, Sunday-school teacher, coffee addict and sleep deprived. Not in that order. Her dream to be an author for Harlequin started somewhere in the pages of a romance novel about a young American woman stranded in a Spanish castle. Her dreams came true, and twenty-plus books later, she is an author hoping to inspire young girls to dream.

Books by Brenda Minton

Love Inspired

Mercy Ranch

Reunited with the Rancher
The Rancher's Christmas Match
Her Oklahoma Rancher
The Rancher's Holiday Hope

Bluebonnet Springs

Second Chance Rancher
The Rancher's Christmas Bride
The Rancher's Secret Child

Martin's Crossing

A Rancher for Christmas
The Rancher Takes a Bride
The Rancher's Second Chance
The Rancher's First Love

Visit the Author Profile page at
Harlequin.com for more titles.

HER RANCHER BODYGUARD

Brenda Minton

To those who persevere.

To my family and friends, for the support and prayers.

And to Melissa and Giselle. Without you, I'd be
a mess. Thank you for everything!

Who shall separate us from the love of Christ? shall tribulation, or distress, or persecution, or famine, or nakedness, or danger, or sword?

—*Romans* 8:35

Chapter 1

From bodyguard to babysitter. Boone Wilder leaned against the exterior brick wall of a closed boutique store in a pricey part of Austin, Texas. The sun had set more than an hour earlier and the temperature had cooled to a balmy eighty degrees. Not bad for early September. But he wished he was at home in Martin's Crossing sipping iced tea on his front porch and not standing in front of a clothing store in Austin on a late-summer evening.

He should have argued a little more when his partner Daron McKay had asked him to take this case. Daron knew the subject and knew she wouldn't listen to him. The third partner at MWP Bodyguard Services, Lucy Palermo, was Boone's backup. Daron had joked that Lucy couldn't take lead because Lucy would just shoot the client if she got on her nerves.

Lucy hadn't found that statement as amusing as Boone and Daron.

At the moment his client was across the street in a

trendy café, sipping coffee and oblivious to his presence. That was how her dad, William Stanford, wanted
it. Boone's job was to keep Kayla Stanford out of trouble, without her being aware. He'd been following her
for a week now, close enough to keep her safe, far
enough away that she didn't have a clue.

He'd like to keep it that way, with her not knowing of
his existence. He was supposed to interfere in Kayla's
life only if she appeared to be in danger, or if she appeared to be on the verge of creating a scandal. Those
were her father's directives. Boone had talked to Kayla's
half brother Brody Martin, who had assured him that
she had a way of generating controversy.

A group of people were walking down the sidewalk.
He stepped back, leaned against the wall and pulled his
hat low. He touched the brim as they walked past, just
to be gentlemanly. One of the women, a little older, and
wearing too much makeup, winked and then grabbed
the arm of a friend. They smiled and talked loudly about
his jeans and cowboy boots, their voices echoing against
the brick buildings on each side of the street.

As he watched for Kayla Stanford to leave the café,
Boone planned what he'd say to Daron. Yeah, this was
a good job and the big fat check they'd been paid was
welcome. But this was not what Boone had signed on for
when he, Daron and Lucy had started their bodyguard
business a little over a year ago. So far they'd managed
to build a decent business by protecting politicians and
doing security at various functions. Those were the jobs
they trained for. The three of them had served together in Afghanistan and they'd formed a bond.

Kayla Stanford, half sister of the Martins of Martin's

Crossing, was trouble. She needed a babysitter. Boone just didn't want to be that guy.

Unfortunately he was.

Across the street the neon open sign went off in the café. He headed down the sidewalk, keeping an eye on his target. The place was still lit up inside. Most of the customers had long since left and he could see Kayla standing near the door with a group of friends. Her dark hair was pulled up in one of those messy buns his sisters loved, and she wore a dark red dress that was too short. His granny would have told her some nice lace around the hem would look pretty. He grinned at the thought.

Then Kayla kissed cheeks, hugged friends and did a cutesy finger wave. As she walked out the door, her smile faded away. That didn't surprise him. He'd done some digging, talked to her family in Martin's Crossing, read some headlines. He'd learned a lot from the articles, from pictures in society columns. Most of the articles were about her antics, her beauty and her style. But he'd seen more. He'd noticed dark shadows under her eyes. He'd seen desperation. Everyone thought she had it all, but he thought she had less than most.

And she covered up her unhappiness by acting out. A couple of months ago, it was a slow-speed chase with the police.

The only time she kept to herself and stayed scandal-free was when she visited her siblings in Martin's Crossing. He'd never seen her in his hometown. She stayed at the ranch, holed up with her half sister Samantha Martin. Soon to be Samantha Jenkins.

Across the street she glanced around, and then walked down the sidewalk in the opposite direction. He'd guessed wrong. He'd thought she would cross the street and head for her car parked at the end of the block. When he glanced across the street, he noticed a shadow moving from the dark recesses of a building. Someone else seemed to be watching Kayla Stanford.

So much for an easy babysitting gig.

Someone was following her. Kayla walked faster, not taking time to glance back over her shoulder to see if she could get a look at the man. For two months, the feeling would come at the oddest times. The uneasy feeling as she walked down the street. The prickling of fear when she walked through the door of her apartment.

At first she'd convinced herself it was her imagination. And then she'd told herself it had to do with her lifestyle. She'd been partying hard for a few years, trying to numb herself against pain and anger. But a few months ago she'd quit everything, just to convince herself she was in her right mind and not imagining things.

The footsteps drew closer, speeding up to match her own hurried steps. She'd panicked when she first realized she'd gone in the opposite direction of her car. The farther she went, the darker it seemed to get. These weren't the streets she wanted to be on late at night, alone.

She reached into the purse that hung close to her waist. Her fingers curled around a small can. She turned, prepared to scream, to fight. Before she could do either, a fist connected with the side of her jaw. She jolted back, trying to stay upright. A rough shove and she fell backward, landing hard, her head hitting the brick building at her back. She caught a glimpse of blond hair and glasses. But the features were a blur.

Blinking, she fought to stay conscious. She heard a shout. Heard footsteps pounding. A hand reached for her arm. Unwilling to go down without a fight, she sat up, aimed and sprayed.

"Oh, man, you sprayed the wrong guy." The words sounded as if they were coming through a tunnel. She tried to focus but her eyes were burning and her head throbbed.

"Go away," she managed to croak out.

"Babysitting. I'm reduced to babysitting a woman who can't even spray the right man." Hands were on her arms. A face peered into hers. "Sorry, but I'm not going away."

"I'll spray you again." She meant for the words to sound strong but they came out garbled and weak. She was still sitting on the sidewalk, her head resting on her knees. She took a deep breath that did nothing to ease the stabbing pain in her back and the headache that had clamped down on her skull.

"Take a deep breath," he ordered, ignoring her threats. Strong fingers felt her back. She winced. Those same fingers moved to her scalp. She let out a yelp. "Relax. And drop the pepper spray. I'm the rescuer, not the assailant. He's long gone."

She blinked a few times, trying to focus on the stranger looming over her. Tall and lean with ropy muscles, the man fit the "tall, dark and handsome" label to a T. He wore a dark cowboy hat, T-shirt and jeans. Something he'd said sank in. "Babysitting?"

"We've been hired by your father to keep track of you. And it looks as if you need us more than he realized."

"I can take care of myself." Her vision swam a little as she rubbed her jaw, wiggling it to make sure it wasn't broken.

"Of course you can take care of yourself. Do you know who that was?" he asked.

She shook her head and the movement cost her. The pain radiated from her head down. Her stomach wasn't faring much better.

The man looming over her dialed his phone. "Lucy, can you pick us up? About two blocks down from the restaurant….No, I'm not fine. Neither is she. She's got a pretty good gash on the back of her head. And she sprayed me with pepper spray….Stop laughing. I'm going to have to take my contacts out so you'll have to drive us to the hospital."

After ending the call he swiped a finger across each eye and tossed contact lenses she couldn't see. But she did see that his eyes were watering and he tried to wipe the moisture with the tail of his shirt.

"Big baby," Kayla muttered. She felt a little bit sick. The world wasn't quite as sharp as it should have been. She wanted to tell him but she couldn't get the words out.

"Can you get up?"

He squatted next to her and peered at her face. His features swam. She tried to shake her head but that resulted in a wave of nausea. Something pressed against the back of her head. She tried to push his hand away but he couldn't be budged.

"You're bleeding," he said.

"I'm going to…" She didn't say more. The world went dark and the last thing she remembered were strong arms picking her up as he yelled for Lucy to open the door.

* * *

Kayla came to as they were pulling up to the hospital. From a distance, she heard voices. They were discussing her father and being hired to keep her out of trouble. That was all she'd ever been to her father. Trouble. She struggled to sit up, pulling free from the arm that held her close.

"You're not trouble," he whispered. The words, the way he said them, took her by surprise. She wanted to believe him.

She sat up, closing her eyes when the world spun a little bit out of control. The back door opened and night air, humid and warm, clashed with the air-conditioned interior of the SUV.

"Come on, sunshine, let's get you checked out."

"How do I know you're not the one I should be afraid of?" She scooted toward the door where he stood.

He gave her a sympathetic look and she noticed that his eyes, dark brown and thick-lashed, were still red and watery from the pepper spray.

"I guess you'll have to trust me. As a rule, muggers don't typically take their victims to the emergency room." He reached for her, holding her steady when she wobbled. His hands were strong, calloused and strangely gentle.

"I'm going to park and I'll meet you inside," the woman driving the SUV called out. "Are you going to be okay, Boone?"

"I can't see much but other than that, great. Don't be too long," her rescuer responded.

"Your name is Boone?" Kayla asked as he led her toward the entrance of the ER.

"Boone Wilder."

"I've heard that name before." She had to stop for a second. Her head was pounding and she felt sick.

"I'm from Martin's Crossing." He slipped his hand from hers and put an arm around her back. "Are you going to make it?"

"Of course. I don't even need to be here."

"I think we'll get a second opinion on that."

"I could refuse treatment," she said as they headed up the sidewalk toward the entrance.

"Yeah, you could. But it's hard to refuse treatment if you're unconscious."

"How did you become my babysitter, Boone Wilder?" She blinked away the blurriness and kept walking, aware that he was studying her as if he thought she might fall over.

"Your father hired our bodyguard service to keep you out of trouble for the duration of this election. I don't think he realized you were actually in need of a bodyguard. Any idea who that was back there?"

"Not a clue."

"But since you were armed with pepper spray, I'm guessing this wasn't random?"

"It's been going on for a couple of months." She stopped as another wave of dizziness hit, making her vision swim.

Without warning she was scooped into his arms. Again.

"You don't have to carry me," she protested, albeit weakly.

"No, of course not. But I also don't want you passing out in the parking lot. Relax. You're not as light as you look."

"Charming."

He flashed white teeth and a dimple. "I try."

She felt him limp a bit as they headed toward the door. "I can walk."

"Probably."

To distract herself she studied his face. Lean and handsome, but rugged. She had never been attracted to the type. As she perused his features she noticed a scar on his cheek. It was a few inches long and jagged. There was a similar scar on his neck, just above his collarbone. Without thinking, she touched it.

He flinched.

"I'm sorry. What happened?" She pulled back, suddenly unsure.

"Nothing personal," he growled. "But it isn't any of your business."

"Of course it isn't. I'd love to tell you my life isn't any of your business. But I guess my dad has taken that right from me."

"And if we hadn't been there tonight?"

She shivered and his arms tightened. They walked through the doors of the ER and he settled her in a wheelchair that had been left near the entrance. She brought her legs up and huddled tight to warm herself. Boone pushed her to the front desk. There were questions to answer, paperwork to fill out, and then they were directed through double doors where a nurse met them.

"Right this way." The nurse motioned them to follow her to a room midway down the hall.

"She's cold. Can you get her a blanket?" Boone said as he pushed her into the room.

"I should call your dad," he said to her.

"Don't bother." Kayla blinked away tears that she

told herself were the result of the blow to her head and nothing more. "He's out of town."

"Still," he said, sounding insistent. She wished he'd go away. But if he did, she'd be alone. She was tired of being alone.

What did that say about her life, that she was so lonely she wanted this man, this stranger, to stay with her? There was something comforting about his presence.

"I'll call your sister, then," he said. He pulled off his cowboy hat and brushed a hand through short, dark hair. His eyes still watered.

"You should get your eyes cleaned out," Kayla offered.

The nurse gave him a good look as she helped Kayla onto the bed. "I'll have an aid flush your eyes out. Right now let's get you settled. I'll be right back and we'll get you changed into a gown."

Kayla gripped the edge of the bed as another wave of dizziness hit. "I'm sorry you've been dragged into this. And for the pepper spray. I'll pay to replace your contacts."

"No need to apologize." His voice rumbled close by. She felt his hand on her foot. He was removing her shoes. First one and then the other. She forced her eyes open and watched him. He was looking down so she had a view of the crown of his head, of his dark hair.

"Thank you." She managed to get the words out, closing her eyes again to block his concerned expression and the tumultuous emotions that bounced around inside her.

Needing someone was not her thing.

"You're welcome," he said, standing up. "Is there anything else I can do?"

She shook her head, the movement costing her. She put a hand to her temple. "Make this headache go away?"

He put a hand on her shoulder briefly. "I'm sure they'll give you something."

And then he was moving toward the door and the nurse was there, agreeing that they would get her something for pain.

"I can't," Kayla tried to explain. The nurse gave her a curious look. "No narcotics."

Boone Wilder, babysitter, bodyguard, whatever he thought of himself, stopped at the door. "I'll be here when you get back from CT. And we'll have to call the police and file a report."

The door slid open and his partner stepped inside. She wasn't tall but Kayla got the impression this woman with her long dark hair, dark eyes and pretty face could intimidate almost anyone.

"Kayla Stanford, this is Lucy Palermo. We're partners in MPW Bodyguard services." Boone waved at the other woman in introduction.

"Palermo. Wilder. What does the M stand for?" Kayla asked as she leaned back on the bed.

"McKay. Daron McKay," Boone said.

"Of course." She covered her eyes with her hand to block the bright fluorescent lighting. "Our dads have worked together in the past."

"That's what Daron told us," Lucy said with just the slightest Hispanic accent.

The nurse rested a hand on Kayla's arm. "Time to get you into that hospital gown."

"We'll be out in the hall," Boone said as he settled his hat back on his head.

"You don't have to stay," Kayla shot back, knowing he wouldn't listen.

"You can't get rid of us that easily."

Of course she couldn't. And even though she'd said the words, she didn't mean them. Even strangers who had been paid to keep tabs on her were better than nothing.

She was so tired of being alone.

Chapter 2

Sunshine streamed through the bedroom window of her apartment. Kayla closed her eyes and wished away the brightness. Worse, someone was singing. She put a hand to her head where it ached. Minor concussion, staples in the back of her head and a bruise on her shoulder. The doctor last night had told her she was fortunate. It could have been worse.

The police report they'd taken after the CT scan and stitches had furthered that theory. They wrote it off as an attempted mugging. She'd allowed them to think so. Fortunately Boone Wilder hadn't been around to add his opinion.

But he was here now. She was sure it was him singing about sunshine.

She groaned, rolled over and gingerly pushed herself to a sitting position on the edge of her bed.

"Welcome back to the land of the living." Lucy Palermo's softly accented voice took her by surprise.

Kayla turned and saw her sitting in the chair in the corner, a book in her lap. Her dark hair was braided and she wore a T-shirt and yoga pants.

"I suppose that's a good thing," Kayla said as she stood. "Oh, wow, standing is overrated."

"Take it easy." Lucy rushed to Kayla's side.

"I'm not going to fall." Kayla took a deep breath. "I'm going to take a shower."

"I'll be here if you need anything."

"I don't need anything," Kayla said, then she sighed, because it wasn't the other woman's fault. "I'm a grown woman and I should have a say in whether or not I allow bodyguards to follow me."

Lucy shrugged. "I agree. Unfortunately that isn't up to me."

The singing grew louder, and Kayla cringed. "Does he have to sing?"

"Yeah, unfortunately he does. You'll get used to it. Or buy earplugs."

She made it to the door of the bathroom but hesitated at the opening. "Is that bacon I smell?"

Lucy rolled her dark eyes. "Yeah, he insists on a big breakfast every morning. Do you want to eat before you shower?"

"No, that's okay. I'm not hungry."

Dark eyes swept her from top to bottom. "You might not be hungry, but you look as though you haven't had a decent meal in weeks."

"I don't think my dad hired you to make sure I eat."

"No, I guess he didn't." Lucy opened her book and let the subject drop.

Kayla didn't want food. She closed her eyes and counted to ten as she leaned against the door frame.

But she'd have to count to a million to get through this, through strangers in her home, through the fear that stalked her every day, through the cravings that still dogged her at times. Through the emotional roller coaster of losing the mother she hadn't ever really known. Could you lose someone you never had?

The aroma of breakfast invaded her senses. The bacon smelled so good. She tried to remember the last time she'd had a decent breakfast, something other than a doughnut and coffee. Or just coffee. She couldn't remember.

"I'll be out in ten minutes," she told Lucy as she closed the door behind her.

Fifteen minutes later she emerged. Boone Wilder in jeans, a T-shirt, cowboy hat and no shoes was standing in her kitchen at the sink washing dishes. She glanced past him, to the full pot of coffee, the plate of biscuits and the pan of gravy.

He tossed her a smile over his shoulder. "Hey, sunshine, 'bout time you crawled out of bed."

She glanced at the clock. Barely eight in the morning. "It isn't as if I slept until noon."

"No, I guess not. Grab some breakfast. We have a lot to do today."

Her mouth watered. She shook her head. "I don't eat breakfast."

He looked at her in mock horror. "What? It's the most important meal of the day."

Was he always this cheerful? She shook her head and ignored the tantalizing aroma that filled her kitchen. She rarely cooked, and if she did it was a frozen dinner, something on the grill or takeout reheated in the microwave. Boone Wilder was filling a plate with biscuits, gravy and bacon.

He shoved the plate into her hands and nodded toward the seat on the other side of the counter. "Eat."

She lifted the plate to inhale. "You made this?"

"Of course."

She took a seat on the opposite side of the counter. "What is it we have to do today?"

He poured her a cup of coffee and slid it across the counter. "First, I need a tux."

"Why, are you going to a wedding?" She eyed him over the rim of her coffee mug. She hoped he was the best man, not the groom.

"Nope, I'm taking you to the ball, Cinderella."

"Sorry, but no. I'm not fond of the wicked stepmother."

"But I'd make such a snazzy Prince Charming," he said as he lifted his coffee cup in salute. "Do you have something against the prince, the singing animals or wicked stepmothers?"

"All of the above." She gave him a long look that forced a sharp comment. "Especially handsome princes with cowboy hats and big smiles."

"Ouch." He touched his hand to his heart. "Sorry, but we don't have a choice."

"Then, tell me what we're really doing because I'm too old for fairy tales."

"We're going to your dad's fund-raiser. I'm supposed to make sure you show up and that you behave."

She took a bite of biscuit. "He knows me so well."

That was what this was all about. It wasn't about her safety. It was about his campaign. His career. And making sure she didn't mess up either one. She was twenty-four years old and he still doubted her ability to be a Stanford. Truth be told, she doubted it, too. If he hadn't done the DNA test, she would have been positive she wasn't his offspring, so different were they.

She was her mother's daughter. The embarrassment. He'd never actually called her that. Her youngest half brother, Michael, had. She'd heard him tell a friend to ignore her, that she was dropped off on the doorstep as a baby and her mother was insane.

"You okay?" Boone Wilder's voice was softly concerned, taking her by surprise.

She looked up from the empty plate and gave him her best carefree smile. "Of course. I'm just deciding what to wear."

"Of course you are."

"We could let him know I have a concussion and maybe he'll let us off the hook."

"I already tried that. He said if you can walk, he wants you there."

"Of course he did. Dear old Dad, he's all heart."

He refilled her mug, then his. "For what it's worth, he did sound concerned."

"Did he?" That was a surprise. She carried her plate to the sink and rinsed it. "Where's Lucy?"

"On your patio. She said you have the best view in the city." Boone took the rinsed plate and opened the door of the dishwasher.

"I'm sorry about last night. I'm sure you didn't plan for a fun Friday night at the ER."

"We were working. So nothing to apologize for."

Of course. Her dad was probably paying them a decent amount for their babysitting services. "If you have your measurements, we can send out for a tux. No need to go shopping. And I already have a dress."

"I do have my measurements. But I'd give anything to not go shopping."

She noticed he rubbed his shoulder as he said it. Her gaze was drawn again to the scar on his face, and then lower to the one on his neck.

"Shrapnel," he said.

She met his dark gaze. "I'm sorry, I didn't mean to stare."

"No one ever does."

"Iraq?"

"Afghanistan." He set his cup on the counter. "About that monkey suit I have to wear..."

She nodded and headed for her room and her cell phone she'd left there. When she walked through the door of her bedroom, she noticed the bouquet of flowers on her dresser. Her dad had probably sent them. His way of being there when he wasn't.

She found the card buried amid the blooms and opened it.

You shouldn't have run, because now we're going to play dirty. Your secrets remain secrets. We get the money. Tell your father.   .

She grabbed the flowers and hurried from her room, carrying them in front of her. She ignored Boone as she opened the trash can and shoved the flowers inside, vase and all. She ripped up the card and tossed it in, shuddering as the scraps of paper fluttered among the bloodred blooms.

"What's that all about?" Boone's voice rumbled in her ear. She shook her head, unable to answer.

He reached past her, retrieving the pieces of card.

"Who delivered these?" he asked as he pieced the card together on the counter.

"Like I know? I was sleeping. You were here when they were delivered." Her voice shook. She really didn't want to sound shaky or afraid. She didn't want to give this unknown person that kind of power over her.

"No, actually, I wasn't. The flowers were on your dresser when we got here last night. You were pretty wiped out and probably didn't notice."

"They were in here already?"

"Yeah, darlin', they were here. On your dresser. You didn't know you had flowers?"

"No. I didn't know."

"Well, that's a problem," Boone said, as casual as if he was talking about the weather.

"So what do we do?" Lucy asked as she walked in from the living room.

"We go on about our business." Boone shrugged as he said it. "And we all sit down and get honest about what's going on here. Your dad said he wants you front and center at campaign events. And you're trying to push this off as an overzealous admirer. Neither of you is being honest. What secrets is this guy talking about?"

"I don't know. Maybe my drug use. Most people know about my mom. Maybe this person believes there's more to her story. I don't know."

"I'm not buying any of it." Boone grabbed a ziplock bag out of a drawer and brushed the pieces of note into it. "We'll see if we can salvage any prints."

"I didn't know that they were contacting my dad," Kayla said. She tried to remember something, anything about her attacker.

"He wanted to protect you. You were obviously trying to protect him," Lucy chimed in.

"Yes, we're all about protecting one another." Kayla walked away, unwilling to dwell on the pain of knowing how untrue those words were.

Boone followed her out to the deck. She walked to the ledge and looked out over the city of Austin. It was an incredible view. She blinked back tears that threatened to blur her vision. She would not cry.

A hand, strong and warm, rested on her shoulder, pulled her a little bit close, then moved away. She found herself wanting to slide close to him, to allow the comfort of his touch to continue. She could use a hug right now.

Great, she was getting sappy. She could imagine the look on his face if she told him she needed a hug. He'd get that goofy grin on his face and pull the Prince-Charming-to-the-rescue act. No, she didn't need that.

Take a deep breath. Blink away the tears. Be the Kayla people expected.

"We should order that tux now. Wouldn't want to disappoint my father and show up in jeans and boots. And ruin his black tie affair."

He laughed. "No, we wouldn't want to do that. Glad you're back, Stanford. I would miss this sweet sarcasm if it got all mixed up with other emotions."

"Yes, I do like predictable."

He tipped back his black cowboy hat and winked. "Predictable is one thing you're not."

That evening Lucy drove them to the clubhouse of the Summer Springs Country Club. "I'll be waiting out here for you all. Try not to get in trouble."

"Because Lucy doesn't want to have to shoot anyone," Boone quipped, hoping to lighten the mood. He winked at his partner and she grinned back. "We'll be good, Luce. And keep an eye out for our blond and handsome friend who likes to leave roses and concussions as a calling card."

"Will do, partner."

Boone opened the door and then stepped back to allow his date to exit the vehicle. She wore a black evening dress, with pearls around her neck and all that dark hair pulled back in some kind of fancy bun.

"You clean up pretty good, Kayla Stanford." He offered her his arm and she settled her fingers on the crook of his elbow. "You smell good, too."

"Charming."

"That's *Prince* Charming to you."

She sighed. "Are you ever serious?"

"I thought you were cornering the market on serious. And I have to say, I'm a little disappointed. You're not living up to your reputation."

"I'm turning over a new leaf," she offered. He didn't push. He'd seen the book for the twelve-step program in her apartment, worn with pages dog-eared. He got it. They all had stuff they had to battle.

"Well, then, let's do this." He led her toward the entrance of the stone-and-stucco building. People were milling about at the entrance. Security checked IDs at the door.

Kayla tightened her grip on his arm.

"You okay?"

She nodded and kept walking. "I'm good. I really dislike these functions. I always feel like I don't belong. You know, square, square, square, oval."

"You're the oval?"

A hint of a smile tilted her pretty lips. "Yeah, that's me."

"Well, tonight you're with another oval. Have a little faith, Kayla."

"Faith?" She smiled at that. "Now you sound like the Martins."

"They're good people."

"Yes, they are. They've all accepted me. Helped me."

"If the Martins like you, then you've got decent people in your corner." He patted the hand on his elbow.

She shot him a look. "Let's not get all emotional, cowboy. You're my bodyguard, not my therapist."

"You got that right." Boone took a quick look around. Because he was her bodyguard, not a therapist. And definitely not her date.

This wasn't new territory for him, slipping into the role of fixer. He'd learned a few hard lessons on that, the most important one in Afghanistan. He had the scars as a reminder.

He tried to remember the rules. Don't get taken in by sad stories, by soft looks or a pretty face. Definitely don't get personal with a client.

He had his own family to worry about. They needed him present in their lives, not sidetracked. Kayla needed him unemotional if he was going to keep her safe.

At the door the security detail checked their names against the list of invited guests. Boone let out a low whistle as they were ushered inside.

"Don't be too impressed," Kayla warned.

"I'm not impressed, I just didn't realize money could be wasted this way. I bet I could fence our entire property with the money they spent on these light fixtures."

She looked up, blinking, as if she'd never noticed those fancy crystal fixtures before. "I guess you probably could. We could take one with us, if you'd like?"

He laughed. "There's the Kayla I've heard so much about. What do we do first?"

"Socialize," she said. "I'm sure everyone is mingling, discussing politics and their neighbors and how to take down the person they pretend is their best friend."

"Sounds like a great time. I can't believe you don't enjoy these events."

She flicked a piece of lint off the collar of his tuxedo and smiled up at him. "I find ways to enjoy myself."

The statement, casual with a hint of a grin and a mischievous twinkle in her blue eyes, sounded warning bells. He gave her a careful look and she widened those same blue eyes in a less-than-perfect imitation of innocence.

"Not tonight," he warned.

"Spoilsport."

"No, just the guy who wants to keep you safe. I can't do that if you pull a stunt."

"I'm not going to do anything, I promise. Come with me. Time to greet my father."

She led him through double doors and into a large room complete with linen-covered tables, candlelight, a small orchestra in the far corner and of course dozens of people. Boone took a careful look around the room. So these were the people who paid hundreds of dollars a plate just to say they'd attended or contributed. Impressive.

"There's my father." She nodded in the direction of a stately gray-haired man, his tuxedo obviously not rented.

"Should we make our presence known?"

"Soon. He's talking to supporters. The woman coming up behind him is my stepmother, Marietta. My half brother Andrew is talking to that group. He's very good at being good."

She said it in such a way that meant she didn't dislike Andrew. As if his being good wasn't a horrible thing.

"We should mingle, correct?" Boone put a hand to her back and guided her around the room. She froze beneath his touch as he headed her toward a table of drinks.

"No, let's not. Please."

"There's iced tea and lemonade."

"It isn't about the drinks, Wilder. It's just…there are people here I prefer to avoid. At all costs."

"Okay. Would any of them be the one who is stalking you?" He settled his gaze on the table, on the people gathered. Most were older men, a few women. He didn't see anyone who should make her panic.

She took in a deep breath and gave a quick look around the room. "No one in that group. But I'd prefer to avoid them all the same."

"Kayla, you're here," a woman called out. Kayla turned, straightening as she did. Poised but trembling.

The stepmother was bearing down on them. Marietta Stanford was tall with pale blond hair, a pinched mouth and less-than-friendly gray eyes. Boone didn't know much about this world, but to his inexperienced eye he'd call her expensive and high maintenance.

"Of course I am. I couldn't very well stay home, could I, Mother?"

Marietta Stanford's nostrils flared. "Don't start."

Kayla smiled. "Right, I forgot. My father wanted me here. So I'm here."

Boone moved a little closer, offering the protection of his nearness. That wasn't his job, but if he was going to protect someone, he'd protect from all corners.

"Try to show some class tonight," Marietta warned. And then she smiled, as if they'd been talking about the weather. "The pearls are a lovely touch."

"For what it's worth, I think she has the market cornered on class." Boone winked at Kayla and was rewarded with a smile.

They moved away from her stepmother.

"Thank you," Kayla whispered.

"No problem. Everyone needs someone in their corner."

She nodded. "That's a novel idea. If you'll excuse me, I'm going to the restroom."

"You're okay?"

"Of course," she said as they maneuvered through the room.

For the next five minutes he stood at the door waiting for Kayla to reappear. He glanced at his watch, then smiled at the group of women who gave him cautious looks as they walked in and out.

Finally he called Lucy. "She escaped."

Lucy laughed. "Already?"

"She said she needed to use the restroom. I've been waiting here for a long time. People are starting to stare."

"I'll walk around back. See if you can get someone to go in. Maybe she's just hiding in there."

"Yeah, I will. Stay on the line."

He looked around and as he did he caught a glimpse of a familiar profile.

"Luce, see if you can find her pronto. We have trouble in here. A certain blond with glasses."

"Will do."

As he hurried across the room, someone grabbed his arm, bringing him to a dead stop.

"Boone Wilder?" The older man had a firm grip, Boone would give him that.

"Yes, sir. You must be Mr. Stanford."

"I am. And where's my daughter?"

"She's in the restroom. But, sir, I just saw the man who attacked her last night. If you don't mind having this conversation later…"

"What? Where?" William Stanford glanced around. So did Boone. There were several hundred people in attendance and it seemed that half of them were gathered in the lobby.

"Great. He's gone."

"Of course he is. Or he never existed. My daughter has a wild imagination. This isn't the first story she's created and it won't be the last."

"The attack last night wasn't her imagination. The concussion and the bruise on her jaw are not imaginary." Boone continued to watch the crowd. He briefly looked at his client. "And the letters the two of you are getting, letters you failed to divulge, are not imaginary."

A flicker of concern briefly settled in Mr. Stanford's eyes. "She's getting them, too?"

"Yes, she is. I don't want to jump to conclusions but I think there might have been more to last night's attack. It could be that their next step is to kidnap your daughter. Someone has something on you other than your daughter's very public behavior. You'd best figure out what it is."

Another man approached them, tall with graying hair and sharp, dark eyes. Boone guessed him to be in his late forties.

"Boone Wilder, this is my law partner and campaign manager, Paul Whitman," William Stanford said.

"Mr. Whitman." Boone shook his hand. It was a little too soft and a little too snaky. He refocused on his client. "I'm going to ask that you excuse your daughter from this event."

"Has something happened to our little Kayla?" Mr. Whitman asked in a voice that matched his snaky appearance. "She does tend to fabricate stories."

Boone caught a quick look between the two men. And Mr. Stanford's was a definite warning to the other man.

"Being attacked isn't a story," Boone defended Kayla for the second time.

"Then, I'm going to ask that you keep my daughter not only out of trouble but out of harm's way. I don't want her hurt."

"We might need to remove her from Austin." Boone looked down at his phone and the text from Lucy. She had Kayla.

"I need my family around me during this election, Wilder."

"Yes, sir. But you also hired me to keep your daughter safe. That's my priority here, not your campaign."

Someone called out and Mr. Stanford raised a hand to put them off. "I agree. But before you take her anywhere, you let me know. If you can't reach me, then leave a message at my office, or let Paul know."

No, Boone didn't think he'd be leaving any messages with Paul Whitman. "I'll let you know. For now, though, we're leaving this event."

"Where is my daughter, Mr. Wilder?"

"With my partner, Lucy Palermo. They're outside in the vehicle and waiting for me."

"Then, you should go," he said. "Keep her safe, Wilder."

"I'll do my best."

Boone headed out to the waiting SUV. He got in the backseat. Kayla was in the front. She didn't turn to look at him.

"Nice move, Stanford. Did you go out the window?"

"Not now, Boone." Lucy drove away from the building.

"Why not now? She's in danger and rather than staying safe, she's jumping out windows so she doesn't have to go to Daddy's fancy dinner party."

Lucy shot him a meaningful look. "Not. Now."

He raised both hands in surrender. "Fine, not now."

That was when he realized there were tears streaming down Kayla's cheeks. He sighed and leaned back in his seat, but he was far from relaxed. Protecting Kayla Stanford was supposed to be an easy job. Keep her out of trouble and make sure she showed up on time for her father's campaign events.

He hadn't considered she'd need a friend more than she needed a bodyguard.

Chapter 3

Kayla woke up early Monday morning. She blamed her new schedule on the cowboy and his partner, who had taken up residence in her apartment. They kept country hours, in bed shortly after ten and up by six in the morning.

She enjoyed sleeping in. If she didn't sleep late, there would be too many hours in a day to live, to think, to try to be happy. And to fail. Her dad had asked her to go to work for him, to use her college degree in prelaw. He'd suggested teaching if she didn't want that. She didn't want any part of her father's world. She knew it too well, knew the underhanded dealings and the backstabbing.

She tiptoed out of her room, leaving Lucy asleep on the cot she'd insisted on. Boone was asleep on her couch, stretched out, arm over his face, and snoring. She pinched his nose closed to stop the racket.

He jumped up off the sofa, gasping and flailing.

"Are you trying to kill me?"

She laughed. "No, I just wanted you to stop snoring."

"That was a definite attempt on my life. And I don't snore." He glanced at his watch. "Why are you up so early?"

"Because my apartment has been invaded and I can no longer sleep late."

"Tough, Stanford. Go back to sleep so I can sleep late."

"You don't sleep late," she accused.

"Sometimes I do. Today is one of those days."

"Too bad, because today is a day I'd like to go shopping and maybe grab some lunch."

"Have fun with that."

"You're my date," she shot back.

"No, I'm your bodyguard. There's a difference. And I think shopping is dangerous for my health."

"I need ranch clothes because you seem to think I'm going to have to be removed from Austin." She sat down in the chair across from him as he leaned back and brushed a hand through his short dark hair.

"I've seen your closet. You don't need clothes."

"Maybe not, but I can't take another day cooped up inside. Lucy has to run to Stephenville today to check on her mom. So I'm stuck with you. And we're going shopping."

"Can I have coffee at least?"

"Yes, you can have coffee. I'll even prove my worth by making it. I do know how to do a few things."

He gave her a serious look. "Stanford, I'm not the one who doubts your abilities. You are."

"Great, we're getting Freudian again. I'll make the coffee and you climb back under the rock you crawled out of."

He groaned and stood. "I was happy under that rock."

He followed her to the kitchen, and as she started the coffee, he rummaged through the refrigerator. "I should have gone to the store."

"I have toaster pastries in the cabinet," she told him.

"I'm not a fan of starting my morning with pure sugar."

She slid the sugar jar down the counter and grinned. "Go for it, it might sweeten you up."

The doorbell rang. He glanced at her, all cowboy, sleepy and a little bit grumpy. A dark brow shot up. He pushed himself away from the counter and headed for the front door. She watched from the safety of the kitchen as he looked through the peephole.

"Who is it?"

He put a finger to his lips and pointed toward the bedroom. She obeyed, even though she wanted to stay, not only to see who it was, but because he shouldn't be left alone. But the look on his face told her she shouldn't argue.

Lucy was just waking up when Kayla walked into the room.

"Who's here?" she asked, brushing long hair from her face.

Kayla peeked out the door but Lucy pushed it closed. "I'm not sure who it is," she admitted.

"Then, I doubt Boone wants your head sticking out." Then Lucy was strapping on a sidearm and slipping out of the room, leaving Kayla very much alone and in the dark.

Minutes later the door opened and Lucy peeked in. "All clear."

"Who was it?" Kayla asked as she followed the other woman to the kitchen.

"Absolutely no one," Lucy answered as she poured herself a cup of coffee. She took a sip and frowned. "Did you make this?"

"Yes."

"Don't ever do that again." Lucy poured the coffee down the drain. "There wasn't anyone at the door. There was a letter."

"Where's Boone?"

"Checking the building."

Kayla headed for the door. "Alone?"

"What do you think you're doing?" Lucy followed, pulling her back before she could reach for the doorknob.

"I want to make sure he's okay."

"And this is how it starts," Lucy said with an exaggerated roll of her dark brown eyes. "He's got pretty eyes, they say. He's a gentleman, they sigh."

"I don't care about his eyes. I'd rather him not get shot in my building." Kayla went back to the kitchen. "It would make a mess in the hallway."

Lucy laughed. "I'm not sure I like you, but you're okay."

She was used to people not really liking her. But for some reason, this hurt more than usual.

"Boone can take care of himself," Lucy continued. "He's smart and he's well trained."

The front door opened. Kayla didn't look, because if she looked Lucy would draw conclusions that weren't accurate. It wasn't his eyes, his smile or anything else. As she poured more water into the coffeemaker, she realized she didn't know what it was about Boone. She didn't really want to delve into it because it might cost her.

"I'm not sure how they're slipping out of here, but they're gone." He limped as he headed for a seat at the bar.

"You okay?" Lucy asked, as she finished making the coffee that Kayla had started.

He arched a dark brow at her.

"And you have the letter?" Kayla asked, not asking about his health. It was obviously a topic he wanted to avoid.

He pulled on latex gloves and held the letter up for Kayla to see. "Recognize that handwriting?"

"It's the same as the other letters. I don't know who it belongs to."

He slid a knife under the seal and pulled out a letter and a picture. His brows drew together as he read and his mouth tugged at the corner. Was he laughing at this, as if it were a game?

"It isn't funny, Wilder. This is my life."

He held up a picture. "Care to explain why you were crossing the border, princess?"

She leaned against the counter and buried her face in her hands. Next to her Lucy snickered. Kayla didn't blame her. If she wasn't so humiliated, she'd laugh, too. In the past she would have laughed with them. It was all a big joke. But not really. In truth it was her way of striking back at her father for hurting her.

"Well?" His voice was soft, luring her out of her thoughts.

"It was after my mom died. I went to Mexico. Two weeks of stupidity. I was slowly killing myself, intentionally, unintentionally, I'm not sure. I lost my passport."

"You could have called Daddy," Lucy said.

"I could have, but what fun would there have been in that? A friend stayed behind with me. We met some people. And somehow we ended up being smuggled across the border. The rest of our group met up with us and brought us home."

"You really think that's a game?" Lucy said sharply.

"No, it isn't a game. I'd like to think I'm a somewhat better person now. I'm still working on it, though."

Lucy raised both hands. "Yeah, okay. What about the letter, Boone?"

He spread it out on the counter. "It's a warning. Requesting the first payment or the story gets leaked to the press. And it warns us not to let you out of our sight."

"What do I do now?"

Boone slid the note back inside the envelope. "It's time to go to the police with this information. I know your father wants to keep it quiet, but someone tried to hurt you. That same someone has followed you. They've been in your apartment."

"He isn't going to agree with you," Kayla warned. "This is stuff he'd like to keep private and someone wants to make it public. Going to the police…"

"Might stop them. If it's made public, they'll stop trying to get money for secrets that are no longer secrets. Or scandals that aren't scandals, but public knowledge."

Kayla walked away, taking the darkest of her secrets with her, away from the prying eyes of two people who didn't care, not about her. They cared about doing their jobs. They cared enough to keep her safe. But her past was hers. As angry as she was with her father, she wouldn't let other people destroy him.

"Hey, we have to deal with this." Boone followed her to the deck. The sun was beating down and the concrete was hot under her feet. She sat down and he pulled up another chair to sit facing her.

"I'm not going to the police," she said, determined to have her way in this.

"We don't have a choice. I'm going to call your dad and he'll back me up on this. I don't know what it is between the two of you, but I'm pretty sure you both care more than you let on."

"Yes, we care." She looked away, to the potted palm in the corner and the flowerpot that she'd picked up at a discount store because it looked cheerful. She didn't know what it was called or how she'd managed to keep it alive.

"Are there more letters?"

She shook her head. "I threw them away. At first I just thought it was a nuisance. But then I started feeling as if I was being followed, and I'm sure they've been in my apartment more than once."

"And your dad has gotten letters, too?"

"Yeah, he's gotten letters."

He leaned back in the chair and stretched his jean-clad legs in front of him. "Well, Kayla, I guess it's time we headed for Martin's Crossing."

"Why?"

"Because I know I can keep you safe there while the police try to figure out who's blackmailing your dad."

"You can keep me safe here," she insisted, not liking the pleading tone in her voice.

"I can keep you safer on my own turf."

Martin's Crossing. She shouldn't have minded the

idea of going to the place her siblings called home. But she wasn't a Martin of Martin's Crossing. She was their half sister. The only thing they had in common was the mother who had abandoned them all.

"I guess refusing to go won't work."

He laughed at that. "'Fraid not. Before long you'll be wishing I was the only Wilder in your life."

By ten o'clock that evening Boone and Kayla were heading for the Wilder Ranch. Lucy had been turned loose to head home for a few days.

Exhausted by a day that had included police reports and long conversations with her father, Kayla slept the ride away, which helped her avoid answering any more of Boone's questions. She didn't want to explain the things best left in the past. Those subjects were walls between herself and her father. Lack of trust loomed as the largest barrier in their ever-fragile relationship.

She didn't want Boone inside those walls.

She woke up as they drove through Martin's Crossing. Her head had been at a strange angle and her neck ached. She rubbed it, aware that Boone had probably seen her drool in her sleep.

"We're home," he said, his voice softly husky in the dark interior of the truck.

Home. It wasn't her home, even though it had become familiar to her in the past year. The main street where her brother Duke owned Duke's No Bar and Grill. Across the street was the shop his wife, Oregon, owned, Oregon's All Things. Duke's wife was crafty and artistic. She made clothes, hand-painted Christmas ornaments and other pretty items. The grocery store was to the right of Oregon's. Lefty Mueller's store, where he sold wooden Christmas carousels and other hand-carved art, was to the left. Kayla was a city girl but Martin's Crossing held a certain appeal. But not long-term. Not for her.

For some reason the thought invoked a melancholy that took her by surprise, sending a few tears trickling down her cheeks. She kept her gaze on the passing scenery and brushed away the tears.

"Where do your parents live?" she asked, turning from the window and pulling her hair back from her face.

"A few minutes out of town." He kept driving, the radio playing country music and the open windows letting in warm summer air. "You okay?"

"Of course."

He cleared his throat, then let out a heartfelt sigh. "You were crying."

"I wasn't."

"I have sisters, I know tears of sadness, tears of frustration. All brands of tears."

"Okay, Mr. Tear Expert, why was I crying?"

"I'm not sure of the exact reason, but if you want to talk…"

"I'd rather not."

"Sometimes it helps," he prodded.

"Really? I don't see you wearing your heart on your sleeve."

"No, I guess I don't."

She stared out the open window, enjoying the humid breeze that lifted hair that had come loose. Outside the landscape was dark except for an occasional security light that flashed an orange glow across a lawn or outbuilding and the silvery light of a nearly full moon. Cattle were dark silhouettes grazing in the fields.

They turned up a narrow, rutted driveway. Ahead she could see a two-story white farmhouse. The front-porch light was on. In the distance she could see the dark shapes that meant numerous outbuildings.

"I hope you don't mind the country."

"It isn't my favorite."

He laughed a little. "Well, you'll either sink or swim, sunshine."

Sunshine. She'd never had a nickname. She'd never been anyone's sunshine. It didn't mean anything to him. But it meant something to her. Something that she couldn't quite define.

Sunshine was definitely better than Cinderella.

"Here we are. Home sweet home. I promise you, you're in for a real experience. We are a pretty crazy bunch."

"I can handle it."

"I'm sure you can." He got out of the truck, and she followed.

He held her suitcase and handed her the smaller overnight bag that accompanied it. "Let's get you settled."

"Don't you live here?"

He shook his head. "No. I bought a little RV. It's hooked up to power over by the barn."

"But you're going to be close by, right?" She felt as if he was suddenly drifting out of reach. She took a deep breath. He was practically a stranger. Not her lifeline.

"I'll be around more than you can stand. But I prefer my own space. I'm not much for company and big crowds. Believe me, you're going to have your share of people. You'll want solitude when you're done with this month on the Wilder Ranch."

"Month?"

He shrugged it off. "We aren't sending you out on your own until we know who is behind the threats and the attack. Maybe it wasn't the same guy."

"I kind of think it is."

She followed him up the steps and as they got to the front door, it opened. Standing on the other side of the screen door was a woman past middle age. Her dark hair was short and framed a classically beautiful face.

"You must be Kayla," the woman said, an almost imperceptible Hispanic accent, giving the words a soft lilt. "I'm Maria Wilder."

"Mrs. Wilder, thank you for letting me stay with you."

Boone's mother laughed. "Don't thank me yet. You haven't met everyone."

Boone opened the door and motioned Kayla inside. She glanced back, worried he wouldn't go in with her. But he did. The lifeline was intact.

"I'm putting you upstairs in Boone's old room. Janie is just down the hall from you with Essie and Allie. Michaela is across the hall. Jase and Lucas are on the other side of her. We're downstairs if you need anything."

"I'm sure I'll be fine. I'm so sorry for putting you out this way," she started to explain.

Maria Wilder waved a hand. "Don't be silly. We don't mind."

She led Kayla up the stairs to a bedroom that was small but bright and airy. A quilt covered the twin bed.

A rocking chair nearby had another quilt folded over the arm. Braided rugs in soft spring colors were scattered on the wood floor.

"It isn't much but it's clean. And most of Boone's smelly past has been evicted. Shoes, clothes, high school uniforms that got shoved in corners and forgotten." Maria Wilder turned down the blanket on the bed.

"It's perfect."

Boone's mother gave her a quick hug. "Are you hungry?"

"Prepare to be fattened up, Stanford."

His mother swatted at his arm. "Behave. No one likes to go to bed hungry. And young ladies don't like to be told they need to be 'fattened up.'"

"I'm fine, but thank you. We grabbed fast food on our way."

Maria made a face. "Bah. Fast food isn't real food."

"Really, I'm fine. But thank you. I'm looking forward to a good night's sleep."

Maria glanced at her watch. "You should go to bed now. Morning comes early around here."

Kayla covered a yawn. She agreed, it was bedtime. She looked at Boone, who was already heading for the door. The limp she'd noticed previously was more pronounced tonight.

"Get some sleep and try not to worry." He stopped just short of exiting.

She nodded. Of course she wouldn't worry. She was in a strange home with people she didn't know. And someone she didn't know wanted to harm her. What did she have to worry about?

"Stanford?"

She met the dark gaze of her protector.

He smiled that easy smile of his. "Don't worry."

Of course.

"If you need anything," Maria said, "don't hesitate, just ask."

They left and she was alone. What she truly needed, they couldn't give her. She didn't even know how to put a name on the empty spaces in her heart. For several years she'd filled those spaces up with anger, with rebellion and a lifestyle that had worn her out physically and emotionally.

She always wondered about the people who seemed emotionally whole and happy. How did they do it, find that happiness?

Alone she sat on the edge of the bed, her hands splayed on the cottony softness of the quilt. On the stand next to the bed was a Bible. It was small, leather bound and worn. Her gaze wandered from that small book to the needlepoint picture on the wall with a Bible verse she'd heard most of her life. "I can do all things through Christ who strengthens me."

The words were lovely and encouraging. But her heart still felt empty.

"She's a lovely girl," Boone's mom said as she followed him out to his truck. He opened the door of the old Ford and leaned against it.

"Mom, go ahead and say what you want to say. I need to get home and get some sleep."

"You need to get off your feet."

"Yeah, that, too." He took a seat behind the wheel of the truck, his hand on the key.

"Just be careful. She's pretty and lonely."

And there it was. He let out a long sigh. His mom knew him better than anyone. She also had a hard time remembering that her kids were growing up. "No need to worry. I'm going to do my job and then return her to her family."

"She doesn't have a family, not really."

He leaned back in the seat and closed his eyes. "Now I know where I get the fixer complex. From you. You're worried about me getting too involved." He opened his eyes and smiled at her. "But you know that you're just as bad."

She laughed. "I won't deny that. I look at this girl, and I see that she's lonely and hurting and could easily fall in love with her rescuer."

"I've been hired to do a job. I'll make sure all she feels for me is annoyance."

His mother patted his cheek and smiled. "You're so handsome, my son. And so clueless."

"Stop." He leaned and gave her a hug. "I'll see you in the morning."

He headed down the driveway to the RV. It always felt good to come home, even to his thirty-foot camper. The place was quiet. It had a front deck he'd built earlier in the spring. His dog was curled up on a patio chair, waiting for him. Yeah, home sweet home.

He limped up the steps and sat down on the chair next to the dog, propping his feet up on the footstool. Man, it felt good to stretch. He reached, rubbing the calf muscle of his right leg. The pain eased.

He let out a deep breath and relaxed again.

The collie that had been sleeping half crawled into

his lap, resting her head on his leg. He brushed a hand down her neck. "Good girl."

She pushed at his hand with her nose.

"You're right, time to go inside."

He eased to his feet and headed inside. The door wasn't locked. It never was. He flipped on a light and headed for the kitchen. Halfway across the small living area, he stopped and took a step back.

"What in the world are you doing in my house?" he yelled at the man sprawled on his couch.

"Sleeping," Daron McKay grumbled. "And I could sleep a lot better without all the yelling. Did you get her settled?"

Daron tossed off the afghan and brushed a hand over his face as he sat up. Boone limped across the room and settled into the recliner.

"Yeah, my mom has her. And is already worried about feeding her. And keeping her safe from me. Or maybe me safe from her."

Daron perked up at that. "Your mom is a smart woman. We should hire her."

Boone tossed a pillow, hitting Daron in the head. "Go away."

"You're the one who told me the place is always unlocked."

"I didn't mean for you to move in here. You have a place of your own just down the road. A big place. Paid for by your dear old dad."

"It's too big and empty." Daron shrugged and plopped back down on the couch. "I'll pay for the food I eat and the inconvenience."

"I like to be alone."

"I know. It's easier to pace all night if there's no one watching."

They both did a lot of pacing. For different reasons. He gave his business partner a long look and wondered just how bad Daron's nights were. Since they usually stayed out of each other's heads, Boone could only guess. And since they dealt with their shared grief, their shared memories of Afghanistan, by being men and not dealing with it, he wasn't about to get all emotional now.

"My pacing is none of your business, McKay. We're business partners, not the Texas version of the *Odd Couple*."

Daron had stretched back out on the sofa and pulled the afghan up to his neck. "You can argue all you want, but you know you like my company. And if we're the *Odd Couple*, I'm the clean freak and you're the messy one. How is our client?"

"You're the slob. And she's scared. Even if she pretends she isn't. And probably lonely. I don't know." Boone stretched his legs, relieving the knots in his muscles. "There's something she isn't telling us."

"Charm it out of her."

"You're the charming one in this partnership. I'm all business. Luce is, well, Luce."

"She's only happy with a gun in her hand," Daron quipped.

It wasn't really the truth, but they liked to tease her.

"Yeah. So you charm Miss Stanford. I'll keep her safe."

"Nah," Daron said. "I think I'll let you try charming for once. I'm out on this one. She's a handful and I'm not patient."

"I was going to make a sandwich." Boone pushed himself out of his chair. "Want one?"

"I ate all of your lunch meat. Sorry."

"I'm changing my locks." Boone headed for the kitchen, where he rummaged through the cabinets, not finding much to choose from. He grabbed a can of pasta and decided to eat it cold, out of the can.

Daron joined him in the kitchen, his face haggard, his dark blond hair going in all directions and his shirt untucked. For the supposed neat one, he was a mess. Boone accepted that it was going to be a long night. He could feel it in his bones. Literally. He could feel it in the places where skin and muscle had been ripped, in the bones that had been broken. He could feel it in his mind. And that was the worst.

For the first time he was thankful for the distraction of Kayla Stanford. And even for Daron. If he had something to focus on, he'd concentrate less on the pain, on the memories.

But Kayla Stanford proved to be the wrong place to direct his thoughts. Because when he thought about her, what came to mind was the haunted expression she tried to cover up with a smile. The way her scent, something oriental and complex, lingered in the cab of his truck. He sniffed the sleeve of his shirt, because he could still smell her perfume.

Daron gave him a long look, eyes narrowed and one corner of his mouth hiked up. "What are you doing?"

"Nothing. I smelled something. Probably you." He made a show of smelling the canned pasta. "Maybe it's this?"

"You're losing it." Daron grabbed Boone's sleeve and

inhaled. "And you smell like expensive perfume. Lucy doesn't wear perfume."

Boone couldn't help it, he took another whiff. When he did, his eyes closed of their own volition. He thought he would picture her teasing smile. Instead, he pictured the woman sitting in his truck trying to hide the tears that slid down her cheeks.

Yeah, it was going to be a long night. He had her scent clinging to his shirt and the memory of her tears. The two combined equaled disaster as far as he was concerned.

Chapter 4

Someone screamed and Kayla shot straight out of the bed, her heart racing and her legs shaking as she stood in the middle of the unfamiliar room. White curtains covered a window that revealed a view of fields that stretched to the horizon and the distant hills of Texas Hill Country. A cat was curled up at the foot of her bed. A cat?

She looked at the calico feline, white with black and orange patches, and wondered how it had gotten in here. The cat stretched and blinked, fixing green eyes on her, as if she were the interloper.

The scream echoed through the house a second time and she realized it was more of a shriek. Someone else shouted, then a door slammed. Obviously the entire family was up. And if she hadn't been mistaken last night when Mrs. Wilder gave the list of names and locations of her children, there were several of them.

Although she was tempted to hide away in her room,

Kayla dressed and brushed her hair. Before walking out the door of her borrowed bedroom, she glanced back at the cat.

"Don't you have mice to chase?"

The feline yawned, stretched and closed her eyes.

"I don't like cats," she said out loud. The cat didn't seem to care.

"I don't like them much myself. Did the screaming banshees downstairs wake you up?"

She spun to face a younger man, maybe in his early twenties. He had dark curly hair cut close to his head, snapping brown eyes, dimples and a big smile.

"I'm Jase." He held out a hand. "I'm the middle brother and also the smart one. No offense to your bodyguard."

She still hadn't spoken. He took her by surprise, with his easy banter and open smile. A few months ago she would have flirted. But she had given it up along with everything else. For the past few months her goal had been a less complicated life.

This did not fit those plans.

"I would say 'cat got your tongue.'" He glanced past her to the cat in her room. "But that's pretty cliché."

"Um, I'm just…" She couldn't speak.

"Overwhelmed?"

"Maybe a little," she admitted.

"The cat's name is Sheba. As in queen of. She lives up to it. And she wouldn't chase a mouse if it crawled across her paws. Let me walk you downstairs. There's safety in numbers. And there's probably some breakfast in the kitchen. We usually eat after we've fed the livestock."

"You've already fed the livestock? What time is it?"

He laughed. "Just after seven. And yes, we've fed, pulled a calf and gathered eggs."

"Pulled a calf where?"

He gave her a sideways glance and grinned. "Pulled meaning delivered. The calf wasn't coming out on his own so we helped the mama with the delivery. There's nothing like starting your morning with a new life. Which I guess is why I'm premed."

While they'd been talking he'd led her downstairs and through the house to the big country kitchen, where it seemed half the county had congregated for breakfast.

Boone's mom, Maria, was standing at the stove. Two young women who looked identical were setting the table. Another sister, a little older than them, was at the sink, auburn hair falling down to veil one side of her face. A toddler on pudgy legs, her curly blond hair in pigtails, was playing with bowls and wooden spoons.

"Welcome to our zoo," Jase Wilder said with a big smile that included everyone in the room. "The twinkies over there are Esmerelda and Alejandra. Better known to all as Essie and Allie, named after our grandmothers. They're not as identical as they like to pretend. In the kitchen is Mama Maria, whom you met last night. Michaela and her daughter, Molly. And my lovely sister Janie."

Janie with the auburn hair shot him a look and said nothing. Jase smiled back and answered, "Yeah, I know, Lucas is your favorite."

"Kayla, I hope we didn't wake you." Maria Wilder pointed at her twin daughters. "Those two can't keep quiet for anything."

The sister Janie half smiled her direction. "They're excited because you're staying here. And you know all about fashion. They want to enter a twin pageant in San Antonio."

"Don't let them push you around," Michaela warned with a half tilt of her mouth. She appeared to be in her midtwenties and as she spoke she reached to pick up her little girl. "If you're going to survive, you have to stand your ground and become great friends with the word *no*."

Kayla would have answered but the conversation was interrupted by the sound of the front door closing and voices raised in discussion, and then Boone along with a younger man in his late teens, and possibly their father, entered the kitchen.

The older Wilder, gray haired and thin, pushed a walker. His steps were slow and steady. He glanced up at her and grinned. She saw the resemblance between him and his eldest son.

"I'm sorry I wasn't up to meet you last night," Jesse Wilder said as he made his way to the table. "But it looks as if you're surviving. It takes some backbone and sometimes selective hearing where this bunch is involved."

Boone, wearing dirt-stained jeans and a button-up shirt, winked as he headed for the kitchen sink. "If it takes backbone, I think she'll survive Clan Wilder with no problems."

She'd been surviving for a long time. It just hadn't always looked like it to the outside world.

"The mama cow didn't make it." Boone rinsed his hands, then splashed his face. Blindly he reached around, searching for a towel.

Kayla found one and pushed it into his hands. He dried his face and draped the towel over a cabinet door.

Jase's smile had slipped away. "I thought we had her up?"

"Yeah, I thought she was okay. About thirty minutes ago she went down and we couldn't get her back up."

"She was our best cow," Mr. Wilder said. He was pale, she noticed, and his hands trembled as reached for the cup of coffee Maria set down in front of him. He hooked his free arm around his wife.

"We'll make do, Jesse. We always have." She kissed the top of his head. "And I made a big breakfast."

"Because eating makes everything better," Essie, dark haired with flashing green eyes, quipped as she brought a plate of bacon to the table. "And coffee. That's the icing on the cake of life."

And they were all talking again, laughing and sharing smiles. Kayla stood to one side, watching, comparing this tumult with her family. The Stanfords, not the Martins. Her father's family was quiet, disciplined and perfect. Always perfect. She had never fit.

The Martins were more like this family. More open. More accepting. They relied on their faith and openly shared it with others. But they never pushed. She liked that about them.

She liked them. And yet she didn't feel as if she belonged. She wasn't a Martin. She wasn't a Stanford. She was the extra, the one who didn't fit.

Her gaze slid to Boone. He was still standing in the kitchen, his arm around the sister named Janie. Kayla felt a tightness in her own throat as she watched brother and sister. He spoke quietly. Janie responded. And then a hand moved and she brushed back that curtain of auburn hair, revealing a tight, puckered scar that ran from her cheek down her neck.

Someone stepped close to Kayla, and an arm brushed hers. "Don't stare. If you want a friend, she's the best, but she doesn't like pity."

"What happened?" Kayla asked.

"She was burned in an accident years ago." Jase shrugged as if what he said was common knowledge and not heartbreaking.

Conversation ended as the family all came to the table. Boone was suddenly at Kayla's side. He pointed to a chair and then he took the one next to it, his arm brushing hers. Before she could think, he had her hand in his. Michaela, next to her, took her other hand. The family bowed their heads in unison and Jesse Wilder prayed, thanking God for their food, for their blessings, for another day to serve Him.

After they all said amen, conversation erupted again. Kayla accepted a piece of bacon. Boone forked a pancake onto her plate, ignoring her protests that she really didn't eat breakfast. But he didn't speak to her. He laughed at a story his brother Lucas told. He shook his head at the twins when they told him they were going to try team roping.

There was much laughter and teasing as the family consumed the large breakfast. Kayla ate, not even realizing that she'd cleaned her plate. She felt as if she were in a foreign world here. Austin, just about an hour away, seemed as though it might as well be on a different planet.

When she'd discovered she had a bodyguard, she hadn't expected this. He should be in the background, quietly observing. Her father was a lawyer and a politician; she'd seen bodyguards and knew how they did their jobs. And yet here she sat with this family, her bodyguard talking of cattle and fixing fence as his sisters tried to cajole him into taking them to look at a pair of horses owned by Kayla's brother Jake Martin.

A hand settled on her back. She glanced at the man next to her, his dark eyes crinkled at the corners and his mouth quirked, revealing a dimple in his left cheek.

He opened his mouth as if to say something but a heavy knock on the front door interrupted. He pushed away from the table and gave them all an apologetic look.

"I think I'll get that." His gaze landed on Kayla. "You stay right where you are until I say otherwise."

"They wouldn't come here," she said. She'd meant to sound strong. Instead, it came out like a question.

"We don't know what *they* would or wouldn't do, because we don't know who *they* are. Stay." He walked away, Jase getting up and going after him.

Kayla avoided looking at the people who remained at the table. Conversation had of course ended. She knew they were looking at her. She knew that she had invaded their life.

And she knew that her bodyguard might seem like a relaxed cowboy, but he wasn't. He was the man standing between her and the unknown.

Boone stepped to the window before going to the front door. He moved the curtain and peeked out. Jase was behind him, of course. Little brothers could never mind their own business.

"I didn't ask for backup," Boone said as he let the curtain drop back into place.

"No, you didn't. But we're brothers."

"It's just Jake. He must have found out she's here."

Jase had the nerve to turn tail and run. "Have fun with that. I think it's my turn to do dishes."

"Dishes, my—" he watched his brother head down the hall "—foot."

He opened the door to Jake Martin. He didn't remember Jake being quite so tall, or so angry. Yeah, it made him pity Remington Jenkins more than ever. Remington had fallen hard for Samantha Martin ten years ago when the two had been teens. Jake had run him out of town.

Boone wasn't a seventeen-year-old kid, and he had a job that included keeping Kayla Stanford safe. So when faced with Jake's glowering look, he just smiled and leaned against the door as if all was well. Boone had learned long ago that silence always proved successful in getting the other person to talk.

"I want to know why my sister is here and not at our place, Wilder. I want to know why we weren't informed that she might be in danger."

Boone stepped onto the porch and closed the door behind him. Jake stepped out of his way. When Boone headed down the stairs and toward the barn, Jake followed.

"Is there a reason you won't answer me?" Jake continued as Boone opened the barn door.

"Because I don't answer to you. I answer to Kayla and her father." He felt bad about that, but he wouldn't break confidentiality clauses. "I *would* like to know how you found out she was here."

"She texted Samantha."

Boone spun around to face the other man, forgetting for a second that his balance wasn't always the best. He reached for the wall and steadied himself. "She did what?"

Jake gave him a tight smile. "What, you didn't know? She's not going to make this easy for you. And I don't appreciate not being kept in the loop."

"Then, we'll sit down together, the three of us, and she can tell you what you want to know. If she wants you to be told, that is. But I can't keep her safe if she's texting everyone in the state."

A throat cleared and he sighed. Kayla was standing in the doorway, early-morning sunlight streaming behind her, leaving her face in shadows.

"I'm not a child. You can do your job, Boone, but you're not going to keep me from my family."

Frustrated didn't begin to describe how he felt at that moment. "I wouldn't think of keeping you from your family. I would like to keep you safe. And I need honesty and a little cooperation from you to do that."

"Honesty?" She narrowed those magnificent blue eyes at him. "You want honesty? I can do honesty. I honestly want to live my own life. I know I've messed up. I know they think they have something they can use against my dad. But I'd like for everyone to leave me alone. I was doing fine. I was getting my life together. I was finding pieces of myself I left behind. I was doing it. Alone. And I don't need…" She sobbed, the sound catching in her throat, and her eyes widened.

Jake shook his head. "Part of your problem, Kayla, is that you don't have to be alone. In any of this."

"Not right now, Jake." Boone knew when a woman was about to fall apart. Jake had never been soft or subtle. "Why don't you head home and we'll call you."

Boone left the older man standing there as he took Kayla by the hand and led her from the barn. She gripped his hand hard, clenching her fingers around his. He didn't really have a plan; he just knew if she was going to fall apart, the barn wasn't the place to do it. She didn't need to be where anyone could walk in. The last thing she needed was a lecture about family from an older brother who had just showed up in her life last year.

As they walked she seemed dazed, moving her feet one in front of the other without really paying attention. He kept hold of her hand, keeping her upright and moving. They ended up at his place. He led her up the steps and inside.

Thanks to Daron, the place smelled like wet dog, dirty socks and burned eggs. She wrinkled her nose but didn't say much. He pointed her toward the sofa and she complied without argument.

"Do you want something to drink?"

She laughed at the question. Boone brushed a hand across his face and shook his head.

"Iced tea?" he offered the second time around.

"Thank you." She sat curled up on his sofa, legs tucked beneath her. She reached for the afghan, sniffed and tossed it back to the opposite end. "You have a dog."

He laughed. "Yeah, I have a dog. And I have Daron McKay. Both of them shed, smell and leave messes."

What had started as laughter on her end suddenly turned into quiet sobs as he poured the tea. He grabbed two glasses and headed her way. She didn't cry pretty. Or maybe she didn't cry often and so this was the proverbial dam bursting. He sat down next to her, placing the glasses on the coffee table.

She didn't look like a woman who wanted a hug. She was stiff and curled into the corner of the sofa. He let her be because his sister Janie was like that. She wanted to do it all herself, alone, even grieve. He was his mother's son, so it was hard for him to let someone grieve alone. He wanted to wrap his arms around the person and he wanted to make it all okay.

Kayla elicited that response from him quicker than he would have imagined. She was about as broken as a woman could get, hiding all of that destruction behind her brazen actions and big smiles.

He wanted her pieced back together and whole.

Not that it should matter to him. She wouldn't be in his life that long. He guessed it was a little like his Scout leader used to say about a wilderness camping trip. Leave it better than you found it.

He'd like to leave Kayla a little better off when they parted ways.

Next to him, she'd stopped crying. She shifted, moving toward him by slow degrees. When her head touched his shoulder and she sighed, he came undone just a little. Expect the unexpected, that was what he knew about her. This softness would definitely qualify as unexpected. She melted against his side, her arm digging into his ribs just the slightest bit. He shifted and somehow that put her a little closer rather than putting distance between them.

Her face was in the crook of his neck, her breath warm, her touch light. And then she shifted a bit more, and her mouth touched his. This was crossing the line. He had that thought just as her hands moved to his shoulders, turning him to face her.

She brushed her lips over his, hesitant and seeking. The third time he fell into the kiss, giving up a little control. Her hand, soft and timid, was on his cheek. He pulled her a little closer and her hand slid to the back of his neck, her fingers skating through his hair.

Outside the dog barked; a truck door closed. He pulled away. She moved back, her eyes bright.

He started to apologize but she shook her head. "Please don't say you're sorry. Even if you are. I've felt empty for so long, Boone. I've raced through life trying to fill up the empty spaces. I've kissed men who meant nothing and made me feel nothing. You have no idea how much I needed that kiss. I needed to know that I could still feel."

What could he say to that? He sat back on the sofa and closed his eyes.

"I'm not sure I want to be your experiment, Kayla."

"I know. I'm sorry." She waited until he looked at her and then she grinned, a little mischievous and kind of sweet. "But it was a good kiss. I mean, if you're worried or have doubts, you shouldn't."

Boone grinned.

"I'll apologize now for the text to Samantha." Their shoulders were touching, her fingers laced through his.

"I don't mind if you call your sister. But we have to keep communications to a minimum so that it doesn't leak out that you're here. Family. No one else."

"Got it. Family. No one else."

The front door opened. Man, he'd forgotten all about that truck door a few minutes ago. He moved quickly, pulling his hand from hers. Kayla remained seated, as if nothing at all had happened.

Daron stepped into the camper, pulling off his hat, swiping a hand through his hair. He stopped when he saw the two of them.

"Oh, I didn't realize we had company." Daron stood

in the center of the room looking from one to the other of them. "Kayla, it's been a while."

"Daron, I wish it had been longer."

Boone looked at them. "I have to agree with Kayla on this one. What are you doing back at my place?"

Daron shrugged and headed for the kitchen. "I skipped breakfast."

"I'm sure my mom has leftovers," Boone offered.

"No, thanks. I don't want to impose."

"You're imposing now. And shouldn't you be at the office?"

Daron pulled a container of juice out of the fridge and took a drink from the carton. He swiped a hand across his mouth and set the juice on the counter. "You know that our clients don't show up at the office. They call or email us. I've got one on the line right now for Lucy. I'll keep you posted on that."

"Good to know. Kayla and I were just heading out. We're going to visit her sister."

"That's good. Have you heard anything from the police today? I called her father. He hasn't had any threats in the past couple of days. He's been making a list of people who might dislike him enough to hurt him or his family. He'll give us a copy and the state police and FBI will get copies. I told him to think beyond the people who dislike him the most. Sometimes it's the least likely person. Someone only slightly offended but more than slightly deranged could be our man. Or woman."

"I think that narrows it down to almost everyone he knows," Kayla quipped.

Boone took hold of her arm and pulled her out the door with a parting shot at his partner. "I guess you plan on being here when I get back?"

Daron saluted as he opened the microwave. "Looks that way."

"Good, then we'll take shifts at my folks."

Daron grunted a response and Boone closed the door before he could form an objection.

"Why shifts?" Kayla asked as they headed toward his truck.

"I want to make sure one of us is watching you at all times."

"You shouldn't have to lose sleep," she insisted. "No one knows where I'm at."

"Let me do my job, Kayla. And you could help by not sending texts to anyone other than family."

"Right. I'm your job. I'm sorry."

Great. The kiss hadn't even been his idea, and yet it still felt like his mistake. He guessed he could tell her the kiss hadn't left him empty, either. No, he wouldn't go there. Better to let sleeping dogs lie, and pretend kisses like that hadn't happened.

Chapter 5

Somehow they ended up with the twins, Essie and Allie, riding along to the Martin Ranch. And that meant switching to an extended-cab pickup. The girls climbed in the back. Kayla took the front passenger seat and tried to ignore the man behind the wheel. Which wasn't an easy thing to accomplish.

Because breathing meant noticing. When she inhaled, she caught his scent. He smelled good. He smelled of the outdoors, clean soap and spicy aftershave that reminded one of spruce trees and autumn. She turned her attention to the window and listening to the twins discuss a horse. Allie wanted to team rope. Essie was the aspiring model. They were compromising. Both would team rope. Both would enter the beauty pageant in San Antonio.

They were sisters the way she hoped she and Samantha would become sisters. They were on their way to that kind of relationship. Even if they were twenty-some years late to the game. This past summer they'd painted Sam's kitchen together. They'd been together when their mom had gasped her last breath and went on to whatever eternal reward might have been hers.

That death had hit them both hard in different ways. Sam had felt abandoned by their mother, Sylvia. Kayla had as well, but she'd been fortunate to have found her mom sooner. And for a short time she'd been the daughter, the one person in Sylvia Martin's life who knew her and loved her and felt loved by her.

With her passing, Kayla had been forced to take a long, hard look at her own life.

The rewind hadn't been pretty to view.

"Kayla, do you think emerald or ruby would be perfect for our gowns?" Essie asked from the backseat.

Kayla smiled back at the girls. "Either. Or maybe both. You don't have to match, do you?"

The girls looked at each other, eyes widening. "Perfect," they said in unison.

"Too easy," Boone grumbled. "Don't expect it to always be like that. They came out of the womb tugging hair and screaming at each other. Mom said if I'd shared a cramped space for nine months, I'd be a little testy, too."

The twins disagreed. "We love each other. We just have different opinions," Allie leaned forward to explain.

While the banter continued. Kayla's phone buzzed. She pulled it out of her pocket and read the text.

Poor little Kayla, her daddy didn't believe her and thought she was crying wolf. Maybe we should tell the world and then someone might believe you. Your bodyguard, for instance.

She went cold and her lungs wouldn't draw in a breath she desperately needed. The twins were still talking, although the conversation buzzed from far away. Boone said her name, not once but several times. She rolled down the window of the truck and threw the phone, watching in the rearview mirror as it bounced along the pavement of the country road.

"Oh, boy," one of the twins said in a low whisper. "So maybe just drop us off at Oregon's shop. We can get a ride home."

"Good idea," Boone said.

They got to town and he pulled onto the main street of Martin's Crossing. He parked in front of Oregon's. The sign in the window said it was open. The twins bailed out the back, quiet as mice.

"We're going back to get that phone."

"No." She shivered in the air-conditioned cab of the truck. "No, we're not."

"What was it, then?"

"I don't want to discuss it with you. It's a private matter between my father and myself."

"We need that phone. That's our only link to this guy. If he keeps telling us what he's thinking, we might be able to catch him. He might slip up eventually and give himself away."

"You're a bodyguard, not a cop."

"Honey, I was the toughest of cops. I've policed the world and hunted down terrorists. I promise you, I'm more than a bodyguard."

She shrank inside herself, wanting to be alone. She

wanted to get away from him and the temptation to tell
him all of her sorry secrets. Because he might believe
her. He might. But what if he didn't? The little girl inside her still cried for someone to trust. And she didn't
want to misplace that trust.

"We're going back for the phone," he insisted.

"Fine, go back."

"Tell me what happened." His voice had grown
harder, more insistent.

"I can't. Just get the phone and tell my father that I
didn't do this."

"You tell him. It seems to me that a little communication in this family of yours might be just the thing."

"Some parents don't want to communicate, Boone.
Don't come at me with family advice when you live up
on Walton's Mountain with homemade bread, church
on Sundays and all of that encouragement."

He pulled to the side of the road where she'd thrown
the phone. "I was wrong. You know how to communicate."

She closed her eyes. "I'm sorry. It isn't you that I'm
angry with."

"No, I didn't think it was."

He said it so gently that her heart tugged at her, telling her to trust. She closed her eyes, trying to get a
grip on that wild part of herself that wanted to outrun
the pain, that wanted to push away anyone who tried to
break through her defenses. She was so tired of fighting.

She was in over her head with this man who caused
that shift in her emotions. What did the client develop
with the bodyguard? Patients and caregivers developed
the Nightingale syndrome. Captives developed Stock-

holm syndrome. What did she have? The Kevin Costner syndrome. She smiled at the thought.

Handsome bodyguard, strong but wounded heroine. She laughed out loud. As he stepped out of the truck to retrieve her phone, he glanced back.

"You find this amusing?"

She shook her head. He was going to think she'd lost it.

"No, it isn't. I'm just trying to find humor in a really rotten situation."

He returned a minute later with her phone, and he tossed it to her as he got behind the wheel. "What's the big secret, Stanford? What didn't your dad believe?"

"You didn't have the right to read my texts," she told him.

"I do have the right. I thought this was just an easy gig, follow the heiress and keep her out of trouble. Instead, I'm fighting to keep you safe from a stalker, and from yourself. So if I have to read your texts in order to do my job, I will."

"Some things are private. Why do you limp?"

"Some things are private."

"What happened in Afghanistan, Wilder? Why do you live in a camper and not with your very awesome family? Why is Daron holing up in your place and not the big mansion his daddy bought so he could play rancher?"

"Watch those claws, Stanford." He pushed his white cowboy hat back a smidge on his head, giving her a better look into his dark brown eyes.

"I'm just saying, we all have secrets."

They sat there in the truck on the side of the road. "Let me tell you something about secrets. Secrets get people hurt. Or worse, killed. I'm trying to protect you, but I can't do that if you don't tell me what's going on."

"Could we please go now?"

He pulled onto the road.

"I can't do this, not yet." She needed time to be strong, and then she could tell him. Or tell someone. She knew it would come out. Sooner or later it was going to be revealed. If not by her, then by the blackmailers. How did they know?

"Okay. I'm not going to push." He pulled onto the road that led to the cottage where Samantha lived.

They drove past Duke and Oregon's house. The truck bounced and bumped along the rougher dirt portion of the road. In the distance she could see the roof of Brody and Grace's house. She shifted to look at the profile of the man behind the wheel of the truck. Boone Wilder. He'd been in her life only a week. She didn't owe him her story.

But she did wonder how it would feel to tell him, to have him listen and understand. How would it feel to have someone tell her they believed her?

"My dad and I are going to have to talk. We've been sweeping things under the rug for so long. And now it looks as if someone is going to force us to face this."

"Talk to him, then. Whatever it is, the power these blackmailers have over him is the secrecy and obviously the lack of trust between father and daughter. Take that advantage away from them and they fail."

"You make it sound easy."

"Tell Samantha. She can help you." He pulled the truck up behind her sister's truck.

Sam waved from the arena where she was working her barrel horse. She'd tried to teach Kayla to ride. It had not been a great experience. But she thought she might like to try again. Because riding meant trusting.

If she could trust a thousand-pound animal, maybe she could trust her father. She could trust Boone. She could trust her heart.

Boone watched from a distance as the sisters talked. They were full of smiles and hugs. Then they walked together, the horse trailing behind them. From a distance he saw Kayla run her hand down the neck of the horse. He smiled. Maybe he'd give her riding lessons. That would be a way to pass some time.

His phone rang. He pulled it out of his pocket and he wasn't surprised that the call was from Kayla's father. He answered.

"Did my daughter get a text?"

Hello to you, too. Boone grinned at his own humor. "Yes, sir, she did. She isn't in the mood to talk about you or to you. I think that's a mistake. These blackmailers know your secrets. Or at least they think they do. I know the goal is to catch them and put a stop to this. But as long as you're keeping your secrets, they have all the power."

A deadly silence hung between them for a long minute.

"Don't tell me about power, Mr. Wilder. I know all about power. And don't tell me what I already know about my daughter." There was a break in either the connection or the other man's voice.

"I'm just saying…" Boone began. But then he didn't know how to continue. Everything sounded like an accusation, and that wasn't a bodyguard's place.

He glanced in the direction of the corral, where the

sisters were talking. This simple babysitting job was taking on levels he hadn't expected, and didn't want.

"I'm going to hunt these men down," Mr. Stanford was saying. "I'm going to make them pay."

"It sounds as if you might want to deal with a few other things first. What is it you didn't believe?"

Mr. Stanford said a few choice words followed by, "Do your job, Wilder. You were hired to be a bodyguard, not a family counselor."

Boone brushed a hand through his hair and let out a long breath. "I'm sorry, that was uncalled-for."

"You bet it was. If you don't want to lose this job, remember who is paying your salary."

Boone nodded and kept the phone to his ear. Because the salary was important to him. As much as he didn't want the money to be important, for his family and for the Wilder ranch, it was. They had medical bills to pay and kids to put through college. His career was the only thing between them and financial ruin.

"I'm protecting your daughter. I'll leave it to you to find the people threatening her life."

"I expect you to keep Kayla safe, out of trouble, and get her to my town hall meeting in San Antonio this Friday."

"We'll be there."

The call ended. Boone shoved the phone into his pocket and headed for the corral and the horse that Kayla was climbing on top of. Keeping her safe meant keeping her from falling off that crazy animal of Sam's. The horse was sidestepping, aware of the novice crawling on his back as if she was hanging on to a high wire and about to fall.

"Stanford, sit up straight and take a deep breath."

He spoke quietly for fear of startling the already antsy animal. The horse hopped a little. "Sam, you have more sense than this."

Samantha, blonde, proud and unwilling to back down, arched a brow at his comment. "I know what I'm doing, Wilder."

"Of course you do. You're going to get her thrown."

"Thrown?" Kayla asked with not a hint of fear. No, instead she seemed to take his comment as a challenge. She took the deep breath and visibly relaxed. "I'm not going to get thrown. I'll have you know, I've been riding since I was twenty-four."

Both sisters laughed. He didn't.

"Fine, cowgirl, go on." He made a shooing motion with his hands. "Show us how it's done."

"The horse is tired. He'd prefer to just stand here. But thank you."

Boone took the reins from Sam, eased Kayla's left foot out of the stirrup and replaced it with his. Deep breath, he reminded himself. And then he was in the saddle behind her. The horse took off.

"Move your other foot," he told her.

She did and he slid his right foot into that stirrup. His arms were around Kayla and he wrapped her hands around the reins.

"What are you doing?" She sat poker stiff in front of him, bouncing like mad in the saddle as the horse trotted around the arena.

"Stop bouncing as if you're on a pogo stick. It's a horse. There's a beat, a rhythm. Hold the reins easy, not tight, not loose. Got it?"

"No, I don't *got* it. I don't ride, Wilder. I'm a city girl.

Remember? I shop. I go out to dinner. Green Acres is not the place for me."

He leaned into her back and for some crazy reason brushed his lips across her ear. "Smell the country air. Feel the horse moving beneath you. Green Acres is the place to be. Farm living is the life for me."

She laughed a little and he felt her relax. He guided her hand, showing her that she didn't have to pull the reins, just let them brush the horse's neck and the animal would turn away from the pressure. A light touch of the reins against the left side of the neck and the horse turned right. She rode him toward the first barrel and eased him around it.

He could feel the tension evaporating from her body. She was letting go. She was trusting the horse.

"Your sister is giving us the stink eye," he warned.

"Of course she is." Kayla reined the horse to the right and headed for the gate.

"You're a pro already." Boone let his hands settle on his legs. "It's as if you've been riding since you were twenty-four."

She glanced back over her shoulder, her smile sweet, her eyes flashing amusement. She kissed his cheek. It was a quick brush of her lips, like a butterfly landing but then moving on. But he felt it.

All the way to his heart.

Chapter 6

"I'd rather be anywhere other than at a town hall meeting listening to my father tell people he is going to make things better for a community." Kayla placed a hand on Boone's arm as he guided her down the steps of the Wilder home. He cleaned up well.

She wasn't about to tell him that, though. In the past week she'd come to the conclusion that her Kevin Costner syndrome might be more than her imagination. It was easy to be attracted to a handsome bodyguard, especially when he was a gentleman.

What she had to do, quite often, was remind herself that he was being paid to care about her. There might be a connection between them, but it would soon end. He would get a sizable check from her father. Then they would go their separate ways. He would stay on this ranch, raising cattle and training horses, and maybe someday he'd marry and have little Wilders. She would go back to… She didn't know what she'd go back to.

"Will you always do this, Boone?" she asked as he helped her into the black SUV, Lucy driving again.

He climbed in next to her. "Do what?"

"Ranch? Be a bodyguard?"

He removed his black cowboy hat and placed it on the seat between them.

"I guess I'll always be a rancher," he answered.

Lucy cleared her throat but didn't comment.

"What about you, Stanford? What are you going to do with your life when this is all over with?" Boone asked as the SUV got on the highway, headed in the direction of San Antonio.

What *was* she going to do with her life? She had thought more about that recently than she had in years. Being the thorn in her father's side no longer appealed to her. It had worn her down, pushed her to do things she couldn't undo and woke her up at night feeling a lot of regret.

"I have a degree in early childhood education," she admitted. "Once upon a time, I was a little girl who dreamed of being a teacher."

"Maybe you should pursue that dream," Lucy chimed in, no longer the silent observer. "I mean, it would be easier, wouldn't it?"

Kayla watched the landscape of Texas Hill Country fly past her from the tinted window of the SUV. Autumn wildflowers dotted the landscape, as did an occasional farm or aging barn. The patchwork of the countryside, greens, autumn browns, was dotted by the occasional small town. She had seen the sky view from a plane and that was what it always reminded her of, the patchwork quilts Grammy Stanford had loved so much. She wondered what had happened to those quilts.

"Still with us, Stanford?"

"Lost in the countryside," she answered. "Teaching. I don't know if I'd be a good teacher."

"Never know until you try."

"True. I never thought I'd like a cowboy," she teased. He laughed. "And do you?"

A choking sound came from the front seat and Lucy glanced back. "Don't encourage him."

"I won't. I wasn't speaking of any particular cowboy, Boone. My brothers are ranchers and cowboys. I am a little bit attached to them."

"There's hope for you yet, Stanford." He said it with an easy cowboy grin and a sparkle of mischief in his eyes.

It was easier when he called her Stanford.

The traffic got heavier as they drew closer to San Antonio. There were more houses, more businesses, more people. Her heart got heavier, too.

"Don't worry, we're with you," Boone said about thirty minutes from their destination, a hotel near the River Walk.

"I'm not worried. I've done so many of these events in my life, I'm used to being under the microscope."

He adjusted his tie. "I'm glad you're used to it."

She reached to fix his tie. "You've gotten it all crooked. Leave it. Or take it off. You look fine without it." She loosened the tie to pull it over his head. He looked fine in jeans, boots and a button-up shirt with a sport coat. He'd draped the coat over the back of the front passenger seat, but she'd seen it on him back at the Wilder ranch.

"Do I look fine, Stanford?" he asked with a wink.

"I told you not to encourage him," Lucy warned.

Kayla didn't answer. Soon she'd have to leave the safety of this SUV and brave her father's world. She wished she could face that world with something more than the false bravado she cloaked herself in. She longed to make eye contact with her dad and have him give her a look of encouragement. Or even love.

It seemed as if they'd been strangers for her entire life, but it had really been only in the past dozen years that things had fallen apart. Before that, she had been his little girl, going to work with him, sitting on his lap before bedtime. He'd been a good dad to a little girl who had been left on his doorstep by a woman who wasn't capable of living in the real world.

He'd married Marietta when Kayla was five. They'd gone from the two of them, father and daughter to a family of three. And soon after, Andrew came along. And then Michael. Not that she pictured herself as Cinderella. She had never thought of herself as the tragic fairy-tale heroine. Marietta hadn't banished her to the attic or forced her to do hard labor. She just hadn't wanted to raise someone else's child.

But she wasn't a terrible person. Kayla wondered how things would have been different if she'd told her stepmother what had happened and not her father ten years ago.

"We're here," Lucy informed them as they turned onto a side street, then pulled into a crowded parking lot. "And I'm only warning you once, Kayla, no stunts like the last time."

"Thanks for the warning."

"Okay, ladies, let's be friends." Boone opened his door and took a quick look around the area, then he reached for Kayla's hand.

A few minutes later they were inside the hotel and being directed to the conference room her dad had rented for the occasion. She found the term *town hall* amusing. Shouldn't it be in a town, held in a hall of some type and not in a luxury hotel, so that only certain people could attend?

"You know, he wasn't always this way, my father." She stood next to Boone as they waited for the elevator. He focused briefly on her and then past her.

"No?"

"Stop looking around as if you're afraid someone will jump out of a potted palm," she told him.

"I'm sorry, but I'm afraid of palms. And I'm trying to keep you safe. So your father hasn't always been like this?"

"No. A long time ago he cared about the people who came to him as clients. He would tell me about them, about their troubles, their lives, and how he wanted to make things better for those people who trusted him."

"What happened?"

She had to glance away from him, from dark eyes that saw too deeply. "Money. Power. A business partner who didn't have the same moral compass."

"Paul Whitman?"

She shuddered at the mention of the name. "Yes, him."

"Met him. I wasn't impressed."

The elevator opened and they stepped on. As the doors closed, another man rushed to jump on. Kayla slid a little closer to Boone and felt his strong hand on her back. He looked down at her and one side of his mouth tilted. He was all confidence.

"Afraid of elevators?" he asked as they went up five floors.

"Only sometimes." She gave the man standing in front of them a pointed look.

"This one seems to be safe. Look, it even has an inspection sticker. And besides, what do you have to fear when I'm with you?"

"Nothing, of course." She meant it, she realized.

The other man got off the elevator on the sixth floor. Without a backward glance he was gone. Kayla let out a sigh.

"I don't want to live my life like this."

"I know you don't," Boone said, pausing as if he meant to say more.

"What?"

"You have choices. This will end soon, and then you can find out what you do want from your life."

"Easy words."

The elevator stopped at the eighth floor. He led her off the elevator, cautiously looking both ways before he put a hand on her arm and guided her in the direction of the conference room.

"It isn't going to go on forever." He spoke quietly as they neared the room from which they could hear the steady hum of conversations.

"I know."

Her phone chimed. She pulled it out of her purse. She would have hid it from Boone, but he was there, leaning over her shoulder. The screen of the phone was still shattered. But the words of the text were clear.

Your dad had his chance. Tomorrow's paper should be interesting.

"It looks as if he's upping his game," Boone said as he took the phone from her trembling hands. "Let's find your father."

"I should go. I should just leave and make this campaign easy for him."

Boone led her into the conference room and through the dozens of people. He seemed relaxed, and she realized that was his persona. Good-natured cowboy. But she saw the clench of his jaw, the way he constantly searched the crowd for danger. Danger. Someone wanting to hurt her. She'd lived her life laughing at circumstances, pushing the limits. She'd never thought of danger. Not like this. Never had a person want to harm her or destroy her father.

She edged closer to her bodyguard, thankful now that he was in her life, that her dad had known this would be necessary.

"There he is. And from the way he's looking at his phone, you're not the only one being texted." There was a hard edge to Boone's voice. It sent a chill up her spine.

This man knew how to protect.

"Get her out of here," her dad said quietly, moving them away from the crowd as they reached his side.

"I'd already made that decision. But I want to make sure you have a security detail of your own and a plan for whatever is going to be released to the paper tomorrow."

"Of course I don't have a plan." Kayla's father swiped a hand over his short, graying hair. "No one has a plan for blackmail, Wilder. And yes, I have a team of people. I don't need your help in this. I need to know that you're keeping my daughter safe."

And then Kayla's father looked at her. His eyes softened. "I never wanted to see you hurt this way. I don't even know what went wrong."

"Dad, you do. But this isn't the place to talk about that."

He paled and his gaze shifted to look past her. "God help us. Kayla, someone knows."

She fought the sting of tears and the emotions that tightened in her throat. She wanted him to believe her. She wanted him to be her father again and protect her. The past came back, all of the pain, the anger, the betrayal. Because she saw that look in his eyes all over again and she didn't know if he'd ever truly believed her.

"Knows what?" Boone's voice slid through the haze of pain.

"This doesn't concern you, Wilder. Just take care of my daughter."

"Yes, Boone, you take care of his daughter. He can't. He doesn't have time. He doesn't have the courage." She turned and walked away, ignoring her father, ignoring Boone as he called out to her to wait for him.

Pain waits for no man.

"Go with her," William Stanford ordered as Boone paused for a moment, waiting for more answers.

Boone shot him a look that he knew wouldn't quell the man or put him in his place. "Sir, I don't have a daughter, but I wonder if maybe you should be the one going after her."

"I have a job to do here, Wilder."

"You have a daughter walking out that door, and I think she's your responsibility."

"I'm paying you—"

Boone cut him off. "Yeah, a lot of money to do that for you. I get it. I'll go after her."

He hurried after Kayla, who had almost reached the door. As he ran, he tried to come up with a plan, because there was a lot going on that he didn't have answers to.

"Wait," he called out as she went through the door and headed left instead of right, toward the elevator.

She paused but didn't look back. She stood still, her shoulders straight and her head high. He walked up behind her but didn't touch her. Instead, he let out a sigh and waited. She needed a lot more than him.

He called Lucy. "We're heading down. No need for you to come up. We're going back to base."

"I don't want to go," she finally spoke. She wasn't crying.

"What do you want to do?"

She shrugged, her back still to him. He kept his distance, giving her space. "I don't really know. Six months ago I would have hopped a plane somewhere. Or I would have done my best to embarrass my father and make him pay. Now I don't know."

"Come on, we'll go home. Mom will make you some of her famous hot cocoa, and maybe she still has some of that banana bread."

"Hot cocoa would be nice," she whispered.

"Yeah, she'll ply you with cocoa and you'll feel as if she's the best friend you've ever had. I think you could use that friendship tonight, Stanford."

She nodded, acknowledging without admitting. She turned to face him, no tears, just stark pain, the kind that made him feel it in his own heart. Pain and betrayal.

They left the hotel in silence, made the ride all the way back to Martin's Crossing in the same way. Lucy would occasionally give him a questioning look in the rearview mirror. He could only shrug because he didn't have answers, only questions and maybe suspicions.

He tried to think of a scenario when his own dad wouldn't move heaven and earth to be there for his daughters, for all of his children. He tried to think how it would have felt if he'd been in that bed in an army hospital and he hadn't woken up to find his dad sitting next to him.

When they pulled up to the Wilder Ranch, the house looked half-asleep. It was barely ten o'clock but the Wilders believed in early to bed and early to rise. He opened the SUV's door and stepped out, giving Kayla room to exit the vehicle without touching him, which seemed to be her wish. As she walked toward the house, he waited, leaning against the driver's door. Lucy had opened the window.

"Well?" she asked.

"Another text. Something to be revealed in the morning paper. I think it's a serious bombshell. Father and daughter were at odds and she seemed to need something from him."

"Fathers aren't superhuman. They let their children down sometimes, Boone. You're spoiled. Your father is one of the best."

"I know, Luce. I'm sorry."

She raised a hand. "This isn't about me. She's a mess and I think we're in over our heads."

"Why do you think that?"

"Because she doesn't need a bodyguard. You know it and I know it. They need a family therapist and a good private investigator."

"You're probably right," he agreed.

She gave a roll of her expressive dark eyes. "I'm always right."

"Do you want to stay here tonight?" he offered.

"Nah, I'll be fine. Mama is determined to take those bulls to that buck out in Arkansas. I'm going to help her load in the morning."

"She's a strong woman, your mom."

"Yeah, she's my hero." She restarted the SUV. "Boone." She paused and he looked back. "Watch yourself."

She touched her heart and then she shifted into Reverse and left. Great, just what he needed was Lucy all emotional and compassionate. He'd have to tell her tomorrow that he didn't need her to get all girlie on him. That would get her back on track.

Kayla had gone inside. He followed, finding her in the kitchen with his mom, the way he'd known she would be. He watched as the two of them mixed ingredients for Mexican hot chocolate. It wasn't even heating yet but he could smell the vanilla and the touch of cinnamon. Or maybe it was his imagination. He joined them at the stove, taking the place next to his mom and not Kayla.

"Make yourself a bed on the sofa, son." His mom patted his cheek. "You look tired."

"I'm good."

Her brows arched. "Of course you are. You're like your father, always good. Even when you aren't."

"Is Dad okay?"

She stirred the cocoa and the water that would help ingredients dissolve. "He says he is, of course. But I saw him today rubbing his chest. I worry."

He kissed the top of her head. "Of course you do. I'll see if I can't get him to go to the doctor Monday."

"Thank you," she spoke softly. "And you, my son. You've been going nonstop. You're limping. Take care of yourself, yes?"

"Yes," he agreed.

Kayla had sent brief glances his way as he and his mother talked to each other. He saw a hunger in her blue eyes. He knew that a moment like this was what she needed. His mom would give it to her, in spades. He'd do the guarding. His mom would do the heart work. It worked best that way. It kept him sharp and focused on the job he needed to do.

Time to make his escape. "I'll have a cup of that cocoa and then I'll leave the two of you alone. Girl talk is not my thing."

"No, you're more about the conformation of a good horse and which cows drop the best calves," his mom teased.

"A man has his priorities."

"I'll bring you a cup of cocoa. There are sheets and blankets in the hall closet."

That was his mom's way of dismissing him. He took the out she offered and left the two of them alone. The idea of getting off his feet made it easier to agree.

It didn't take him long to make up a temporary bed on the sofa. His sister's crazy cat, Sheba, appeared at his side. She gave him a long, unblinking look, then focused on his bed. Without an invitation she stretched, and then leaped. She curled up on the pillow and looked for all the world as if she thought it belonged to her.

"I don't think so, cat."

She exposed her belly for him to pet. He obliged and

then moved her to the end of the sofa to a throw pillow that must have been placed there for her. She curled up on it and seemed perfectly content.

Boone raised his left pant leg, rubbed the aching muscles until they relaxed, and then he unhooked the prosthetic leg. He placed it on the floor under the coffee table. It was computerized, a complex thing that adjusted to his gait. He didn't want it stepped on or broken.

He rubbed his leg and stretched, and then he grabbed a pin off the table and rolled up the leg of his jeans to secure it.

"Boone?"

He looked up. "Stanford."

He looked down at his leg and then back to the woman standing in the center of the living room, a cup of cocoa in a hand that trembled. She was going to spill it on his mom's new carpet.

"Don't spill that," he said quietly, bringing her back to earth.

She managed to get the cocoa to him without spilling it. "I didn't know."

"You didn't need to know."

"Of course." She sat next to him. The room was dark except for the soft glow of the porch light through the window. The cat's purring broke the silence. It felt too intimate but he didn't know how to say it without drawing attention to the fact.

"Afghanistan?" she asked, bringing the subject back to his leg.

"Yeah, Afghanistan."

Silence again, other than the purring of Sheba.

"So we all have secrets," she finally said.

"Some secrets are dangerous. Some are just nonissues. This happened a few years ago. It's just a part of my life now, and unless the skin breaks down, I'm good. I don't classify it as a secret."

"My secrets, my life…" She broke off, shaking her head.

"You don't have to tell me your secrets, Kayla. It isn't necessary. Unless you want to. And if you talk, I'll listen."

She grabbed the hot chocolate from his hands and took a sip, then she held the cup. He'd meant for her to share hot chocolate and secrets with his mom. Maybe he should remind her of that fact. His mom was the listener. He was the bodyguard.

"My dad's campaign adviser has been his law partner for years."

"Mr. Whitman."

"Yes."

"I see." He retrieved the chocolate from her and took a drink but he gave it back when she reached for it.

His mom appeared in the doorway of the living room. She stood for a moment watching the two of them and then disappeared again, leaving him to be the one who listened to secrets. He had a feeling the secrets were going to make him want to hurt someone.

They sat in silence a long time. At some point she set the cup down and reached for his hand, lacing her fingers through his. Upstairs someone was watching a late-night show, and the sound of audience laughter carried. Sheba continued to purr. And in the kitchen he could hear his mom washing dishes and the radio playing gospel music. She loved her alone time at night.

"My dad didn't believe me." The words were whispered but they sounded loud in the quiet of that room.

Her fingers tightened on his and she leaned a little in his direction. "He was my dad. I trusted him. He should have trusted me. Instead, he told me he couldn't believe I'd make up something like that about a man who would do anything for me."

She laughed a humorless laugh. "Do anything for me. Which is funny, because Paul Whitman made me promise not to tell, but before that he'd promised he'd do anything for me. And if I told, he'd make sure no one ever believed me again."

"Someone should have believed you," Boone said as she tried to pull her hand from his. But he couldn't let her go. He couldn't let her run. "I believe you."

"Yes," she whispered on a broken sob. "Someone should have."

She pulled free from his hand and he let her go, let her curl up inside herself on the corner of the sofa, the cat pulled close for comfort. And this was why Kayla Stanford fought everything and everyone. She was broken and trying to trick the world into thinking she was whole.

He reached for her but she shrank from his touch. He picked up the blanket he'd left folded on a nearby footstool, covered her and stood. He balanced next to her, looking down at a woman who appeared confident but was hiding a hurting kid deep inside. The girl who had needed her father's protection was still seeking that security from him.

"I'll do whatever I can to help you," he promised, knowing he shouldn't. "But right now, I'll get my mom. She's not going to leave you alone tonight."

She nodded, brushing hair back from her face. "Boone, thank you."

"You're welcome."

He made his way from the room, hopping on a right leg that had adjusted and gotten stronger over the past few years. He made it to the kitchen and his mom gave him a look.

"Crutches, Boone."

"Too much trouble. You're needed in the living room. I think I should go and leave the two of you alone. But I'll apologize now for the long night you're going to have."

"Don't apologize. You see, when someone is hurting they are like a sore. It can only hold the pain so long and then it's going to erupt."

"I'm not sure if that's the most beautiful way of putting it, Mom, but I guess it's accurate."

She shrugged and handed him a plate of banana bread. "Eat something. Kayla will be fine here. Don't try to go home like that. Crutches, son."

He kissed her cheek. "You're the best."

She smiled up at him. "And you are a good son. You have a good heart."

"My heart is intact, don't worry."

She picked up another plate. "So you say. But you know, someday your heart is going to…"

"Good night, Mom." He headed for the closet in the utility room. "Crutches in here?"

"Yes, they are. I'm only saying…" she started again.

"Mom, this isn't the time. You can trust me to know my own heart. I'm happy with my life the way it is right now."

"You're not getting any younger." The words followed him out the back door. "Hey, you left a leg in my living room."

"I'll get it tomorrow."

He would never call himself a chicken, or even a coward, for running. He would call himself wise. He would call leaving at that moment self-preservation. Because his mom had two sides. The side that wanted to protect her son and the side that thought he would be happiest if he married and gave her grandchildren.

And he knew that Kayla needed more tonight than he could give. She needed to be held. She needed to cry. She needed to hear from a woman who had survived that she would survive.

No, he would never call himself a coward. He was the guy who would be sleeping in his truck, making sure no one set foot on this property and that no one hurt her again.

Not even him.

Chapter 7

Kayla managed a few hours of sleep after a lot of crying and a lot of talking with Maria Wilder. It had felt good. For the first time in ten years someone had listened and believed her. She'd told Boone's mom about being a little lost in her early teens. Her dad had been busy with his career. Her stepmother had been busy being his wife and a mother to her two boys. She hadn't signed on to raise his daughter. There had been nannies for that. But nannies weren't mothers. They didn't explain what a girl growing into a woman needed to know. And they didn't take the place of a father who was suddenly too busy.

Kayla had been a victim in the making, the girl no one was really paying attention to. And Paul Whitman had known. He'd watched her drifting from her family. He'd offered rides home from school, a movie. He'd offered her time. He'd taken advantage and left her with no one to turn to.

She was the victim. At some point during the night, Maria Wilder had finally convinced her of that fact. And for the first time in years she felt the pieces fitting together again. Not whole, but closer than she'd been in a long time.

She sat up and looked out the window. Boone's truck was parked in the drive. She leaned over the sofa, and saw the prosthetic leg he'd left behind. It was an amazing piece of equipment, even attached to the leather cowboy boot. He would need it this morning.

She slipped her feet into her shoes and then grabbed the blanket, slipping it around her shoulders before she headed out the front door. Boone's dog, Sally, was sitting at the edge of the porch. The collie followed her down the steps and across the yard.

When she got to the truck, she tapped the boot against the window. He woke up with a start, reaching for something in his glove box. And then he saw her. He slid a hand across his face, rubbing the shadow of whiskers that had grown overnight.

He was beautiful, she thought. He was more than a handsome cowboy with dark eyes and dark hair, his skin bronzed from a life in the sun. No, he was more than that. Because of the kindness that settled in his eyes and the roguish smile that sometimes caught her by surprise.

But he was temporary. Yet this temporary stop in his life might have changed her life. Maybe that had been God's plan all along.

"You have my leg," he mumbled through the closed window of the truck. She opened the door.

"I thought you might want this." She handed it over.

"Yeah, I might. Did you get any sleep?" he asked.

"A little. No one else is up."

"It's Saturday. They might sleep in a little. Want to help me start breakfast?"

She glanced from him to the house. "Yeah, sure."

He pushed the door a little wider and hopped down from the truck. She glanced down, surprised that again she couldn't tell he wore the prosthetic.

"Amazing, isn't it?" he asked, lifting one leg and then the other.

"Very."

"And you have questions?"

Of course she did. "How did it happen?"

He tugged the blanket up around her shoulders. "That's a long story."

"It's none of my business."

"No, it's okay. It's just that it was another time, definitely another place and maybe another me. Daron and I wanted to help a family. A mother, a little brother, a sister."

She heard the catch in his voice and she touched his arm. He stopped walking and looked down at her. "Boone, I'm sorry."

He continued walking. "Me, too. The boy approached us one day and told us there were men in his mother's house and he was worried. I don't know, maybe he was telling the truth and he was afraid or maybe it was all a setup. I'll never know because the IED went off as a group of us headed that way to see if we could help. One of our guys died in that explosion. He left a pregnant wife behind. His little girl is three now."

"You didn't hurt them."

"No, I didn't. But I could have been more perceptive,

could have been more focused. We'd gotten too relaxed, maybe. I don't know."

He led her through the house to the kitchen. Jase was already up. He was starting a pot of coffee and eating a snack cake.

"Hey, didn't realize there was anyone else up," he said.

"I was in my truck. Kayla was on the sofa." Boone grabbed a carton of eggs out of the fridge. "I'm going to make scrambled eggs, toast and bacon. You eating with us this morning, Doc? Or was that chocolate cake it for you?"

"Yeah, I'm eating if you're cooking. Does Kayla cook?"

She laughed at that. "No, Kayla has never cooked."

"Then, Kayla should learn," Boone quipped. "Today is the first day of the rest of your life."

"Dramatic," Kayla informed him. "But I will learn to cook. After all, someday I'm going to be on my own. No one will be around to fix me omelets or biscuits and gravy."

Boone shot her a look as he pulled a big bowl out of the cabinet. "Going to be a teacher, are you?"

She managed a smile. "Yeah, I think I will be."

"Good for you," Jase said as he tossed her a snack cake.

"Drop the cake." Boone pushed the bowl and the eggs in front of her. "Get busy, Stanford, you have a lot to learn."

"I know how to crack an egg."

"Yeah, but can you get it in the bowl without the shells?"

She shrugged. "I guess we'll find out."

Boone left her to it and he started the bacon frying. Jase pulled up a stool and watched. She cracked an egg on the counter and pulled it apart over the bowl. Of course part of the shell fell in. Jase didn't say a word. He just handed her a fork and took another sip of his coffee. She gave him a warning look when it seemed he might change his mind and say something.

After a few tries she got the hang of it and managed to hand over a bowl of eggs, sans shells. She gave Boone a smug look. He handed the bowl back to her.

"Whip them up with the fork and add some milk," he ordered.

"I thought that was your job."

He shook his head. "Nope, you're making the eggs. Someday you might have a classroom of hungry kids. What are you going to feed them?"

"Schools have cafeterias, Wilder."

He just went back to his bacon. She gave Jase a pleading look. While Boone's back was turned, Jase took the bowl and the fork and whipped the eggs. She got the milk from the fridge and Jase added the right amount and handed the jug back to her.

He didn't even turn around. "Jase, let her do it."

"Eyes in the back of his head," Jase grumbled as he handed her the fork and pushed the bowl of eggs in her direction.

Kayla managed a shaky laugh. She hadn't expected to laugh this morning. Not today, when her life might become a newspaper headline. Not today, when that same story could destroy her father's career. She cared about that more than she'd expected to. She didn't want him hurt. As much as she'd tried to hurt him with her actions over the past few years, she didn't want this to be the thing that ended his career.

"Hanging in there, Stanford?" Boone took the bowl of eggs from her.

She watched as he poured them into a skillet. "Yeah, I'm good. I guess there isn't going to be an Austin morning paper around here?"

He laughed, a husky sound that shouldn't have sent shivers down her spine. "No paper here. But we'll take a look at the internet."

"Want me to get my computer?" Jase offered, already off the stool.

"That would work." Boone waited for his brother to leave the room and then he faced her again. "So you're really okay?"

"I woke up this morning feeling like a new person. Or maybe a person with faith. I expected that to get me through the day, but it isn't going to be that easy, is it?"

He opened his arms, a startling invitation that she found she couldn't refuse. His arms, strong and comforting on a morning when she was starting what appeared to be a new life but with the old life still needing to be dealt with. She stepped into the circle of his embrace and he pulled her close. It was a brotherly, comforting hug, but it included his strength, his scent, his warmth. Before he let her go he kissed her near her temple. She drew in a breath at the gesture, so sweet.

"You're dangerous, Wilder."

"No, ma'am, I'm about as dangerous as a newborn puppy."

She laughed at that. "Yes, exactly. Everyone wants a puppy."

Jase returned with the computer, giving them each

a careful look, shaking his head as he sat back down. He opened the laptop and fired it up. "Looking for anything special?"

"Yes, and private." Boone took the computer and did a quick search as she looked over his shoulder.

The story was front page in the politics section. There was a picture of her at a party, wild-eyed, unfocused. The headline said Poor Little Party Girl.

"They did it."

"Yeah, they did. But let's read it all and see what we're dealing with." He spoke quietly, his arm coming around her, pulling her to his side. Together they read the article that told of secrets and a father who turned his back on his daughter.

"They didn't give up the whole story," Boone spoke quietly. As though he thought a loud voice might shatter her. It wouldn't, though. "They're holding on to the rest. It's their ace. They've got your dad's attention and now they'll set the hook and reel him in."

"I need to call him. I need for him to know that I wouldn't have done this to him."

Boone turned her to face him. "He needs to call you and tell you that he should have been there for you. He should have believed you. He's not the victim, Kayla. Don't treat him like one."

She shivered, although she wasn't cold. Boone wrapped her in his strong arms. "The story is still yours. They didn't reveal it and you still have time."

"How much time?"

Boone shrugged, his arms still around her. "I'm sure they'll contact your dad today."

"I should go home."

"No, you shouldn't. You're staying here. You're safe

here. They want money, Kayla. But they also seem to want revenge. They're striking out, targeting you, because they know you're important to your dad."

"Right," she whispered, for the first time letting go of the newfound strength and faith. She felt weak down to her toes.

"You are important to him."

"I'm going to stir the eggs," Jase said. Kayla looked up, seeing concern in his brown eyes. She'd forgotten his presence.

"I'm sorry, Jase. You don't need this on a Saturday morning."

He winked. "I'm not worried about myself, Kayla."

"What do we do now?" she asked Boone.

"We talk to your dad. We see if his men have any clue who we're dealing with."

"And we eat a good breakfast. It's the most important meal of the day." This from Jase. Humor laced with a thread of concern, enough to ease the tension the tiniest bit.

They made it easy to smile, this family that had faced their own hardships but seemed to keep moving forward with smiles and love for each other.

A little over a week ago she'd been upset by this invasion of bodyguards into her life. A lot could change in a week. A person could change. Her heart could change.

And that opened a whole new world of possibilities.

Boone left the house after breakfast. His mom and sisters had Kayla busy, enlisting her to help prepare the twins for their pageant. He still didn't get the pageant, but Essie had explained about the scholarships and cash prizes.

Boone left them to it and headed for the barn and work he couldn't put off any longer. There was some serious bush hogging that needed to be done on a back field that had been overtaken by weeds during the hot, dry summer when it seemed weeds flourished and grass didn't. They also had some fence to fix and some calves to tag.

Jase and Lucas caught up with him when he was almost to the barn and thinking he might have a few minutes to himself. Lucas was talking about the Martin's Crossing Annual Ranch Rodeo that would be held in a week. He had signed them up for team penning and calf branding. He said it would be a good time to get those new calves branded. Jase and Boone just looked at each other and kept walking.

"What? Are we not going to participate this year?" Lucas kept at them, running backward in front of them to get their attention. "Are you going to let the Martins win again?"

"No, Lucas, we won't let the Martins win. No one lets them win. They just do it because they're good."

Lucas jerked off his hat with the bluster and energy of a teenager. "Oh, come on. We could beat them if we tried."

"We haven't been practicing. So it seems to me that not only do we not want to lose, we don't want to look like fools." Boone pushed his youngest brother to the side and Lucas moved in next to him as they walked.

Boone got it. He knew how hard it was for their little brother. A lot had changed in the past few years. Boone had been gone, and then he'd returned home injured. Their dad had suffered a massive heart attack. That had left Lucas as the youngest boy, and the one not getting what the rest of them had: all of their dad's time and attention. It was the little things that mattered; Boone knew that. Which was why he was here, helping out.

"We can practice. We should start this evening," Lucas pushed.

"The Martins practice every day," Jase reminded.

"We used to. We can get back to it," Lucas pressed further. He wanted the old days back again. Boone wanted that, too. He'd like to just focus on the ranch, and not this crazy burning-the-candle-at-both-ends thing they were all doing. Jase in college and still living at the ranch, trying to keep everything running. Boone working the bodyguard business and the ranch. Lucas just trying to still be a kid.

"We'll practice tonight, Lucas," he promised. Even as he worried about what would possibly interfere, his phone rang. "I have to take this. Jase, check the tractor. Lucas, get ear tags and whatever else we need."

He lifted his phone to his ear. "Mr. Stanford. I guess you saw the news?" Boone answered as he walked away from his brothers.

"Yes, Wilder, I saw the news. Where's my daughter?"

"She's fine, sir, in case you were wondering."

There was a long pause. "Boone Wilder, I'm going to tell you this once. I do care about my daughter. And I don't owe you any explanations."

"No, sir, you don't." Boone leaned against the fence, watching cattle graze. They'd had to cut the herd to pay medical expenses when his dad had gotten sick. They were rebuilding it. And he wasn't going to lose this job. His family was counting on him.

He thought of Kayla. She was counting on him, too. He wasn't sure what he could do for her, but for whatever reason she'd been brought into his life and his home. People had been praying for her, he'd known that. Maybe this was the way God answered, the way she got help from people who cared.

"Mr. Wilder, I'm talking to you."

Boone cleared his throat. "Yes, I'm sorry, sir. You were saying."

"My daughter is important to me. I—" There was a heavy pause. "I made a mistake."

"I see" was all Boone could say.

"I'm going to withdraw from this campaign before they can tell everything. *If* they know everything. My investigators believe that someone who knows our story might be working for another candidate and this is how they're fighting. It's dirty, but I won't let them run my family into the ground."

"If this was just about politics, would your daughter be in danger?"

"They've definitely crossed the line. But I'm not going to pay them."

"I'm not sure your daughter wants you to quit the campaign, sir. She seems to remember a man who, at one time, wanted to help people."

Man, he'd just done it again. He couldn't seem to stay out of hot water with this guy.

"Wilder, you're fired."

"I understand."

"Bring my daughter back to Austin. We'll get another service to protect her."

Boone rubbed a hand over his face and sighed.

"Sir, I understand how you feel, and I have to apologize. But in all honesty, I think your daughter wants the best for you. And I think you want the same for her.

She's safe here. This is not the time to surround her with strangers and leave her on her own."

"Then, what do you suggest I do?" This time the voice had softened, making it a legitimate question, one of a concerned father.

Boone bit back about a half dozen less-than-decent replies and softened it down to one. "Maybe you should talk to her."

"I'm dealing with a lot here, Wilder." The other man let out a long sigh. "I'm going to be meeting with the police and my PI this afternoon. I have to stop this before it goes any further. But I'll be down there in a few days. Keep her close and keep her safe."

"I'm keeping her safe. That's why you pay me."

"Yes, and don't forget it. Next time I won't be so forgiving. Next time you're out of a job."

"I understand."

Boone slipped his phone in his pocket and turned to find Kayla standing a short distance away. "My dad?"

"Yeah."

She had changed into jeans, a T-shirt and what looked like a pair of Michaela's hand-me-down boots. Her dark hair was braided on the side and hung down over her shoulder. She looked like a country girl. And she looked relaxed.

"You don't have to handle him for me," she said. "My father, I mean."

"I know. But there's no sense allowing him to run you over."

"I rarely allow that, Boone."

He took a step toward her. "No, you don't. So what are you doing out here dressed like that?"

"I'm going to help you. Your mom is reading to your

dad. Michaela ran into town with Molly to have a play-date. The twins have Janie cornered, doing something crazy to her hair."

"Janie will regret that. I let them do my hair once and ended up with highlights."

Her blue eyes sparkled with amusement and she reached out, brushing her hand down his cheek. "I like you. I didn't plan on that."

He hadn't planned on liking her, either. But then he hadn't known she was hiding this strength, and the flashes of humor. He hadn't planned on this crazy need to keep her safe, and to make her smile more often.

Warning bells went off in his head, telling him to get it together and reminding him she was just a job. She had a sad story but she was strong. She'd survive. She didn't need to be rescued. She needed to be kept safe.

He couldn't keep her safe if he got sidetracked, distracted.

"Say something," she said, looking a little worried, staring up at him.

What could he say? He was protecting her and some-day soon she wouldn't be his client any longer. She'd go back to her life. Maybe she'd leave here a little a little happier and a little more whole.

"I like you, too," he finally said. And then he cleared his throat, uncomfortable with words that sounded as if he might have said them on the playground in grade school.

She snorted a laugh. "Said like a man who doesn't want to say too much."

"I'm your bodyguard, Kayla. And you've been on an emotional roller coaster for the past few weeks."

"More like for ten years. And you're right, I'm sorry. I was hoping we could be friends."

He could give her that. "I think we can be friends."

"Can I take a ride on your little green tractor?" She pointed to the tractor coming around the side of the barn, Jase behind the wheel.

"That I think I can arrange. I'm going to bush hog."

"Bush hog?" Her eyes narrowed. "I'm from the city, you have to explain."

"The mower attached to the back of the tractor. We're going to mow the field, cut down weeds and small shrubs."

"Oh, sounds like fun."

"It isn't," he assured her as they headed for the barn.

"About my dad. He knows?"

Boone adjusted his hat to shield his eyes from the sun. "Yeah, he knows. He said he'll pull out of the race before he will allow the rest to come out."

"He said that?" She sounded surprised.

"Yes. I also told him that I didn't think you'd want him to quit. That you want him to be the politician you believe he could be. The man who helps people."

"Ouch."

"Then he fired me."

Her eyes widened. "What? He didn't."

"He did. But I talked him out of it."

She slugged his shoulder. "You are a miserable creature."

"He's coming down to see you. Maybe in a few days."

She walked away from him, toward the tractor. Jase was climbing down, leaving the door open.

"Hey, Kayla. Did you come out to help with the cattle?" He tipped his hat back and gave her that big grin of his. Boone shook his head. One of these days his little brother's flirting was going to land him in hot water.

"Actually, I'm going to help bush hog." She glanced back at Boone. "Right?"

"If you say so." He wasn't going to argue. He stood back and watched as she managed to climb up into the cab of the tractor. "Don't touch anything."

"Like this?" She pushed a button. And then she shifted.

"Kayla, I mean it."

Suddenly the tractor was moving. Jase jumped back, leaving room for Boone to take a running hop, grab the handle and climb the steps. He slid into the seat beside her and brought the tractor to a stop.

"That. Wasn't. Funny."

"Sure it was." She pulled down on the brim of his hat. "The panic in your eyes was priceless. I've driven a tractor, Boone. My brothers are the Martins. Brody taught me last year. And I know what a bush hog is. You're more gullible than you look."

"You're more trouble than *you* look," he quipped.

"You two going to kill each other?" Jase hollered up.

"Maybe," Boone said as Kayla leaned and said, "Of course not."

"I'll let you all decide. I'm going to saddle a horse, and Lucas and I will bring in the calves that need to be tagged. When we get that done, we'll be on the fence."

"Tell him work first, rodeo later," Boone called out to his brother's retreating back. Jase saluted and kept walking. Boone closed the tractor door, and the inside of the tractor turned into a quiet cocoon with country music playing softly on the radio.

"Not a lot of room in here," Kayla said. She shifted over, giving him a little more of the seat.

"No, they don't make tractors for two."

"They should if they're going to write songs about them."

He laughed and kept driving. "So Brody taught you to drive a tractor? Brave."

"He's my favorite."

"He's a good man."

A little while later she asked, "Is he angry? My dad, I mean."

"He's angry at the people who are doing this. Not you. He wants you safe. The problem with people like this, Kayla, is that they're desperate. And you never know what a desperate person is going to do next."

"I know."

"I'd like to stay with Sam. I know that isn't safe. But she's my sister. And she's a good shot."

"That isn't going to happen. We can visit tomorrow, maybe, after church."

"Okay."

They reached the field that needed clearing. He stopped the tractor and sat there for a minute.

"Seems a shame to cut that down, doesn't it?" he said.

The field had been overtaken by wildflowers. Butterflies hovered and a few tiny songbirds flitted from bush to bush. He cut the engine to the tractor and opened the door. Fresh autumn air swept through the cab.

"I think I'd rather take a walk in it than see it cut down," Kayla told him with a hopeful tone in her voice.

And he caved. "Let's go."

He climbed down and then held up a hand to help her. She didn't take the offer. She jumped down in a second, standing next to him. Her hand slipped into his, an easy gesture that shouldn't have taken him by surprise. But it did. In more ways than one.

"Maybe we could cut it after the first frost," he conceded as they walked.

"Good idea."

They walked as far as the creek. It was slow going. The wildflowers and weeds really had taken over. But it was wild and beautiful. This was what he'd missed about hill country during those long, dusty, hot months in Afghanistan.

The creek was running low, the way it usually did in the fall. He stood back and watched as Kayla slipped off her boots and rolled up the legs of her jeans.

"It's going to be cold," he warned.

"I don't care." She tiptoed into the water. "I've always wanted to do this."

"Your bucket list must be interesting."

She stood there in the ankle-deep water and his heart kind of lurched. She waded back out of the creek. She took the hand he offered, then sat down on the bank of the creek, pulling him down with her.

"My bucket list," she said. "Yes, it's interesting. I think at the top of the list was finding my family. And somehow finding myself again."

"Better than a trip to Paris."

"Been there, done that, Wilder. What about you?"

"Never been to Paris. Never really wanted to go. Getting this ranch back in the black. Making sure my dad is healthy again. I guess those are on my list."

"Those are goals, not a bucket list. You have to have one."

"Okay. I'd like to climb a mountain in Alaska. Maybe

go deep-sea fishing. And I've always wanted to kiss a pretty girl while sitting on the bank of this creek." The words rushed out, making him feel like all kinds of a fool.

"So let's check that off our list today, Wilder." She leaned in, brushing her lips against his. "Because I think that might have been on my list, too. Kissed by a cowboy."

He could have backed away. He probably should have. But her fingers slid across the back of his neck and he took the invitation. She tasted like sweet tea and sunshine. And her hands on his neck gave him crazy thoughts.

He tugged that braid that hung down her shoulder and pulled her a little closer. His fingers wrapped around the braid, lifting it to inhale strawberry-scented shampoo.

"Kayla," he finally managed to whisper. "This is going to get us into all kinds of trouble."

"I know," she agreed.

"I'm the person trying to keep you safe, and I can't do that if I'm caught up in this, whatever *this* is."

"I'm sorry, Boone. I know this is wrong. I know this is the last thing you want or need." Hurt laced her tone. And hurting her was the last thing he wanted to do.

Which was why he had to back away and keep his focus. He'd never lost focus on a job this way before. Never been tempted the way she tempted him. He liked her. It all came down to that.

"This is the last thing *you* need, Kayla." He laced his fingers through hers. "We've got to keep you safe. And you have a life waiting for you."

She closed her eyes, her face caught in the sunshine. He leaned closer to her, but they didn't touch.

Her response came a few minutes later. She opened her eyes and looked at him. "My life does seem as though it's been on hold for a while. But this is what I do. I rush into things. I rush because I want to feel."

He nodded silently.

"But you're right. I'm sorry for putting you in this position, that you have to be the person telling me to back off."

"Kayla, it isn't all you."

She sat up, her hand covering his. "Please don't do the 'it's not you, it's me' lecture."

With that he stood, holding out a hand to help her to her feet. "We should head back to the house and help the guys. And I'll try not to be embarrassed when I tell them I couldn't bear to cut down a field of wildflowers."

And he didn't know how to distance himself from the woman at his side.

Chapter 8

Kayla watched from the sidelines of the somewhat weathered and worn arena where the Wilders were practicing for the ranch rodeo on Saturday evening. Lucas had insisted she come. They had one week until the event. They could do this, he'd insisted. Lucas was the family cheerleader. The one trying hard to get back what had been lost in the past few years.

She understood Lucas. She knew that drive to get back what she'd lost.

She hopped off the fence and went to sit on the low riser next to Maria and Michaela. Jesse Wilder was near the chutes coaching his children from a chair they'd brought out for him. She could hear him calling out to Lucas, his voice weak. Jase had a calf down and Janie was holding the branding iron, a circle W that had been used on the ranch since the first Wilder had settled in this area.

"Lucas, if you're going to brand calves, you have

to be ready," Jesse Wilder called out, this time a little louder.

Lucas rode up on his horse, a pretty bay, black mane plaited in thick braids from her ears to the base of her neck. He must have spent hours doing all of that braiding. Kayla had to give him kudos for patience.

"Dad, I know what I'm doing." Lucas stayed in the saddle, swinging a lasso easily. He shot a look in the direction of his twin sisters. They were on their horses in the arena, but doing more laughing than working. "But you know we should just lock up those two and leave them at home."

"They're a part of this ranch, son."

"Then, Kayla should be out here with us. If she's staying on the Wilder Ranch, she should be one of the Wilder hands at the rodeo."

Gray haired but still charming, Mr. Wilder shot a look in her direction. "Well, Kayla?"

"No, thank you. There's no way I could help sort or brand calves. Or even stay in the saddle."

Jesse slapped his leg and laughed. "Oh, Kayla, I don't think you have enough faith in yourself. I bet you could outride this banty rooster son of mine."

"Hey," Lucas called out as he was riding away from his dad. "I resent that."

Mr. Wilder gave her a wink. And then he rubbed his chest, causing Maria to come up off the riser and head his direction.

"Jesse?"

He smiled up at his wife, but even Kayla could see that the gesture was a little less than genuine. "I'm good, Maria. Relax."

"I can't relax. You've been doing that too often lately."

"And I'm fine. Go sit with the girls. I'm going to give Lucas some tips on this branding business."

"You'll tell me if…" she started.

"If I need to be hauled off to the hospital, I'll let you know. But for now, sit down."

"You try my patience, Jesse." Maria leaned to kiss him. "I need you on this earth with me."

"I'm not going anywhere."

Maria gave him a long look. "Promise?"

"Promise."

She left him to go sit on the risers with her daughter and granddaughter, though reluctance was written all over her face. Kayla held on to that tough but bittersweet moment between husband and wife. A real ache settled in her heart, a need for something genuine and lasting.

She started back to the risers and the other women but was stopped by Boone.

"Hey, don't run off, Stanford." He was leading a pretty gray horse, the animal leaning in close to him. "I brought you something."

"I think you have the wrong woman." She backed up against the fence.

"Oh, no, I don't. We could use an extra hand for this rodeo." He pushed back the brim of his cowboy hat and a corner of his mouth tilted in a charming grin.

"Don't you try to charm me into this."

He leaned a little close. "Is it working?"

"Not at all," she said, but her heart disagreed. She was definitely charmed. His eyes were dark and a five-o'clock shadow covered his cheeks.

He wore his jeans low on his hips and his T-shirt

hugged his shoulders. A silver chain with a tiny cross hung around his neck.

"Not even a little?" he teased in a quiet, husky voice.

"Not enough to get on that horse," she told him.

He laughed and took her by the hand. "Climb on, cowgirl. Let's get this show on the road."

"I can't ride."

"Yes, you can." A truck pulled up the drive, distracting them. She exhaled a relieved breath as Samantha's truck stopped next to the arena. Both Samantha and Brody climbed out of the truck. Brody, lean and dark haired. Samantha, blonde and confident. They were Kayla's siblings. Sometimes she had to stop for a minute and adjust all over again to the reality that she'd had this family all along and never knew about them until the past year. It was Brody's determination that had brought her into their lives.

Brody hurried forward and hugged her. "Hey, little sister. I've been thinking you might call me."

"I'm sorry, I should have."

Brody switched his focus to Boone. There was a sharp look between the two. "Boone."

"Brody." Boone just grinned. "As you can see, she's safe."

Brody gave her another look. "Yeah, I can see. So care to tell me what's going on?"

Samantha let out a long sigh, because she was used to these men. "Stop circling like old tomcats and remember that you're friends and on the same side. And, Kayla, feel fortunate you haven't put up with this your whole life."

Kayla pretended that was how she felt: fortunate. "What brings the two of you out here?"

Brody shot her a look. "You, of course. We're having lunch at Duke and Oregon's after church tomorrow. We'd like for you to join us."

"We'll be there," Boone answered for her.

"We?" Brody asked, one of his brows lifting.

"Where she goes, I go." Boone leaned against the saddle of the horse he'd led over. "Where I go, she goes. And I'm not passing up lunch at Duke's."

"Well, isn't that…" Brody started.

Boone stared him down. "That sounds like a man doing his job."

Brody chuckled.

Kayla took the reins of the horse Boone had brought for her. "If I'm going to learn to ride, we should get started."

From the arena, Lucas shouted at Jase. The gray gelding next to Kayla startled. Boone reached for the reins and got the animal back under control.

"Those two brothers of mine," he muttered. He met her gaze and winked. "Brothers can be a real pain."

Brothers. Bodyguards. Yes, men could be a pain.

Boone's phone rang. He gave her an apologetic look and walked away. Samantha stepped forward, taking the reins from her and leading the horse a short distance from the arena.

"Come on, sis. If you're going to ride this animal, you have to get on his back. It works best that way." Sam shot her a cheeky look. "And keep your mind on the horse, not other things. Being distracted is a sure way to get tossed."

"I'm not distracted," Kayla assured her sister.

Sam's glance slid past Kayla, and she knew exactly who her sister thought might distract her. Boone.

No, Boone wasn't a distraction. He couldn't be. He was doing his job, keeping her safe. And as soon as the blackmailers were caught, she would go back to her life, back to Austin.

She belonged in the city. She couldn't wait to get back to her life. Not to the old life, but to the new one she planned on making for herself.

She definitely didn't need distractions.

Boone walked away from the arena, listening to the man on the other end of the phone tell him exactly what he'd do to Kayla Stanford, to her old man and even to Boone's family if someone didn't pay up. The stakes were being raised. The price was being raised. They had one week to come up with the money or the next article in the paper would give all of the details. And if that didn't convince Mr. Stanford, then they'd start playing rough.

It took everything Boone had to stay calm, to not yell at the man on the other end. The last thing he needed to do was get emotional, to show his hand. Calm, steady breaths. He listened as if they were talking about the weather.

"Interesting story, bud, but I'm kind of busy here." He grinned as he said it, as if the other man could see.

"Your old man is sick. And I'm just going to take a wild guess and say you're getting attached to your client."

He drew in a sharp breath at the mention of his dad. His gaze drifted toward the arena. His family was a short distance away, completely innocent, not a part of the Stanford family drama. But he said nothing. This wasn't going to get under his skin.

"Got something to say, Wilder?"

"No, not really. But I'll pass on your message to Mr. Stanford."

"You do that."

The phone went dead. He slipped it in his pocket and turned back to the arena. Brody appeared out of the shadows.

"Interesting phone call?" he asked.

Boone shrugged. "I guess you could say that."

"Threats?"

"A few. Nothing to worry about."

Brody walked next to him. "You look worried. If you're worried, then I guess I have a right to be."

"You can do what you want, Brody."

Brody stopped walking. "Boone, we're friends. We've been friends a long time. This is about my sister."

"Now they're threatening my family," Boone admitted. "And I'd say it's a matter of time before they threaten yours."

"Then, I guess someone needs to figure out who it is."

"Mr. Stanford has the police and a PI team on that. My job is to keep your sister safe."

"Can you keep her safe when Samantha has her out there in the arena, sorting calves?"

He glanced that way. Samantha was on his horse. She was riding next to her sister, the two of them laughing and carrying on like kids. He guessed they were more alike than he'd realized. Both were a little reckless, grabbing at life and running headlong into danger.

"She'll get thrown." He headed for the arena with Brody not hurrying behind him.

"She might, Boone, but she'll learn. We all learned by taking our falls and getting back on."

"Right, but I'm supposed to keep her safe. Not help her get her neck broke."

"Calm down." Brody laughed as he said it. "You're losing focus."

"I'm not." He started to defend himself, but then realized maybe he was. The call had rattled him. Seeing her on that horse, reckless but carefree, that rattled him, too.

And in the next instant the horse shied to the right and he watched as she toppled, landing hard on the packed dirt of the arena.

He was over the fence and heading for her as she sat up, shook her head and looked around as if she wasn't sure where she was. Samantha was off her horse.

"Crazy. Both of you are just crazy." He lowered himself next to her.

"Get a grip, Boone." Samantha reached out a hand and pulled her sister to her feet. "You okay?"

"Sore, but I don't think anything is broken." Kayla rubbed her shoulder. "I didn't see that coming."

Boone stood, looking at the two of them. He saw resemblances. He saw differences. He felt something crazy deep inside that shouldn't be there.

"Of course you didn't see it coming. You were distracted." As he said the words, they hit him hard, reality shaking him to the core.

"She's fine. You're fine, right?" Sam asked.

"I'm fine."

Jase appeared at his side. "Anything broken?"

Kayla shook her head. "I hit my shoulder, but I think it's okay."

Jase touched her arm, touched her shoulder. Boone

fought emotions that he wasn't about to put a name to. Lucas rode up, whistling, long and appreciative.

"That was quite a buck-off, Kayla."

She grinned up at him. "Thanks, Lucas."

"I think we should call it a night," Boone suggested. Not only because of her fall but because he had a strange feeling that they were being watched. The hairs on the back of his neck stood up and he couldn't quite dislodge the fact that someone knew too much about all of them.

"Let's go inside for tea," Jase offered, shooting Boone a questioning look. "Me, Lucas and the twins can get these horses cooled off and put up for the night. You all go on in."

"Thanks, Jase." Boone reached for Kayla but she was already moving ahead of him, her arm through Samantha's. Brody stepped in next to him.

"I remember the first time she showed up at Jake's. Crazy in that red convertible of hers. She's changed a lot in the past year. Having family has done that for her." Brody glanced around as they walked. "Do you think you're being watched?"

"Why do you ask?"

"Because I know you well enough to know that look in your eyes. You're cautious, Boone, but you're watching everything all at once."

"I'm doing my best." Ahead of them, his mom was helping his dad up the stairs. Michaela and Molly were waiting for them up ahead. "I think Kayla and I need to sit down and make a list of people who might know..."

"Know what?" Brody asked, his trademark smile dissolving. "What aren't you telling me?"

"Nothing. Someone knows how to get under her father's skin. We need to figure out who that person is."

"And you're not going to tell me anything else?"

Boone watched the front door close behind Kayla and Samantha, leaving him and Brody standing in the front yard alone.

"No, I'm not going to tell you anything else."

"The story in the paper implied there's more. Now you're implying it, too. If there's something that needs to be dealt with, maybe you should tell Kayla's family."

"Brody, that isn't my place and you know it." He headed up the steps and Brody followed. "I'm keeping her safe."

"Yeah, I know you are."

They entered the kitchen to find Kayla sitting on a stool, an ice pack on her shoulder. Boone removed the ice and pushed up the short sleeve of her T-shirt to take a look. He touched the bruise that had developed and she flinched.

"Ouch, Wilder."

"Sorry, Stanford. That's going to hurt tomorrow."

She moved, dislodging his hand. "Why do people always say, 'It's going to hurt tomorrow'? You know something? It hurts right now."

"I guess we just want you to know it's going to be worse before it gets better," he shot back.

She rolled her eyes at him, those big blue eyes. "Thanks, Wilder, your encouragement means everything."

Her voice sounded too tight, too emotional. He wanted to laugh it off, make it all a joke.

"That's what I'm here for," he said.

"I'm glad we all know why we're here," Brody Martin said as he pinned Boone with a look. "Wilder, the reason you're here is to keep my sister safe."

Boone leaned against the counter, crossed his arms over his chest and glared at Brody. Obviously Brody had forgotten that Boone was a few years older, and a few inches taller. It hadn't been too many years ago that the two of them had gone at each other. With Brody on the losing end of the fight. All in good fun, of course.

He winked at Kayla, then turned his attention back to her brother.

"I think you can go home, Brody. We're good."

"You have someone helping?" Brody asked.

"Daron. I'm assuming he's at my place and if not, he'll be back soon. And we'll see you all at church tomorrow."

Brody shifted his attention from Boone to Kayla. "You're sure you're okay?"

"I'm good, Brody. I'm sure that it won't be the last time I get thrown."

Brody leaned against the counter, looking down at her. "I don't mean getting tossed, Kayla. I want to know that you're okay and if there's anything we can do. You have family now."

"I'll let you know. But you should go. Grace will be wondering where you are," Kayla stated with simple ease. And it was enough to get Brody's attention. It even put some kind of strange smile on his face that Boone never would have pictured there. It was the look of a man completely in love with his wife and baby.

Boone pushed down a strange spike of jealousy that he hadn't expected. He didn't need complications. He glanced around the big country house at the family that depended on him. His mom was in the kitchen, making a batch of brownies with Molly's help. Michaela was holding her daughter as Molly stirred. The twins were in the living room arguing, as usual. It was his family that kept him grounded, kept him here doing what needed to be done.

His gaze connected with Kayla's. Their smiles touched in a way that nearly undid him. It felt as if she'd reached out and brushed his heart with that smile.

He wasn't a poetic sort of guy, not normally. But it moved him, that smile of hers. Boone walked closer to her. She glanced up at him, her eyes widening.

The gesture didn't go unnoticed. Of course it didn't. Not with his mom and sister present. Not with Samantha and Brody Martin standing not five feet away. And yet, even with everyone around them, he couldn't help but brush his fingers across hers, a brief gesture that seemed to suck the air right out of him.

From across the room, Brody cleared his throat. "Well, if you've got things handled here, I'm heading home."

"Things are handled," Boone assured his friend.

"Yeah, it looks as if they are." Brody headed for the front door, Samantha trailing next to him with a last look back and a smile for her sister.

Boone walked them out, because he'd been raised to be polite. And because Brody and Sam had been friends of his for years. Things would get back to normal. Kayla would go back to her life in Austin with occasional visits to the Martin ranch, and her family. Boone would see her from time to time. Or not.

He was almost thirty, and for the first time in a long time, that "or not" part bothered him. He didn't know how Kayla had managed to twist him up like a ball of twine in just a couple of weeks, but she had.

There were a whole lot of reasons the two of them

were a bad idea. She was city. He was as country as they came. He was her bodyguard. She was his client. This was just about the worst time for him to feel as though he wanted to take this girl to dinner, maybe more than once.

Chapter 9

Sunday morning Boone left the rest of his family fighting over the two bathrooms they shared and headed for his RV. It was the best kind of fall morning, a little bit cool and the smell of drying grass in the air. On a morning like this one, he could almost forget the troubles knocking at their door. He could let himself forget about unpaid medical bills, his dad's health problems and the complication that was Kayla Stanford.

He took a deep breath as he walked the worn path, Sally coming to greet him with a low and familiar woof. He ran a hand over her head. In response she gave him a soft look of loyalty. "This is why you're the woman for me, Sally."

A familiar Ford King Ranch was parked in front of his RV. "But you could be a better guard dog and run him off," he told her. She trotted off, completely oblivious.

As he walked up the steps of his trailer, he glanced at

his watch. He had thirty minutes to get ready, and Daron had better not be hogging his bathroom. His mom had given him the warning look before he'd headed out. They weren't going to be late today, she'd informed them all at breakfast. Because the Wilders did tend to be late. Often. There were a lot of them and that meant fighting over bathrooms. Even with the schedule their mom had posted on the fridge, they were always trying to sneak in during someone else's allotted time. They were a rowdy bunch, he guessed. And probably something of a novelty to someone like Kayla Stanford.

The smell of burned eggs greeted him as he walked through the door of the trailer. Great, Daron was cooking again. That never ended well. The kitchen was a mess. There were dirty dishes, a pan in the sink with scorched scrambled eggs, and something that looked like it might have been sausage was in the dog's bowl. The dog whined and then nudged at what appeared to be a burned offering.

Loud, off-key singing overwhelmed the music on the radio. The dog looked up at Boone, one ear lifted.

"He has to go, right, Sally?" Boone asked the dog.

The singing stopped. A few minutes later Daron walked down the hall, his hair still damp. "Oh, hey. I didn't know you were back. I made breakfast."

"Yeah, I know. The government called. They asked that you stop making weapons of mass destruction."

"Very funny."

"Seriously, don't cook again. Ever. My mom made a five-course breakfast."

Daron tossed his towel over the back of a chair and reached for his boots. "I'm not going to mooch off your parents."

Boone gave him a look.

Daron laughed it off. "I don't mind mooching off you. You're my friend."

"That's debatable. I've got to jump in the shower and get ready for church. Why don't you button that shirt and pretend you're civilized. You can ride with me to church and join us for lunch later."

"I think God and I have other things to work out," Daron grumbled as he headed for the door. "I have to make a run to Austin."

"Maybe you ought to stop that running. Slow down a little."

Daron stopped at the door. "You fix yourself, Boone Wilder. I'll fix me."

"Yeah, okay." Boone sat down to remove his prosthesis. "So how is she?"

"She?" Daron stood with the door open. "I don't know who you mean."

"Can we stop dancing around this subject? Emma. How is she?"

Daron glanced out the door, his smile long gone. "Poor. Alone. And doing her best to raise Jamie."

"He should have married her."

"He's dead, so no reason to throw stones now."

Boone conceded that point. "Yeah, I know. She still chasing you off the place with that rusted-out shotgun?"

Daron grinned. "Yep. She says I don't owe her anything. I think I do."

"We all feel as if we owe someone, don't we?" Boone stood, holding the edge of the table to balance.

"I guess we do. Who do you owe?"

Boone turned away from his friend. "You'd better go."

"Yeah, all right. Be careful. I'll be around tomorrow to give you a break."

"That would be good. I've got to get some work done around here."

Daron waved a hand and walked out the door. Boone watched from the kitchen window as his friend climbed in his truck and headed off down the drive, throwing a little dust and gravel in his wake. After a few minutes he hopped down the hallway, trying not to get caught up in Daron's pain, in his past.

They all had stuff to deal with.

When Boone pulled up to his folks' house shortly before ten, the family was spilling out the door and heading for the big van that hauled them all. He parked behind the van and got out, wincing a little at the jab of pain he hadn't been expecting. His sister Michaela shot him a look. With a grin and a wink he pushed aside her concern and headed for Kayla. She was waiting her turn to climb into the van.

"You'll be riding with me," he informed her.

She gave him a dark look, her blue eyes arctic. He just smiled, because he knew that would rile her more than anything he had to say. She was a tall woman, he realized, not for the first time. Tall and too thin. Her dark hair was pulled back and wispy curls framed her face. But he was her bodyguard, not her date.

"In the car, sunshine." He motioned her toward his truck.

"I'll ride in the van with everyone else," she countered.

"And make me ride to town all alone? That wouldn't be charitable of you."

She let out a sigh, the kind that was meant to tell him just how put out she was. But when he put a hand on her arm to guide her to his truck, she went with him. A quick glance back, he caught his mom's gaze on them, her eyes narrowed. Yeah, she would worry. He wished he could find a way so that she could do less of that. He would like to give her a year of no worries, for anyone or anything. It wasn't realistic, he knew that, but it seemed like worry should be equally distributed. One woman shouldn't get more than her share.

He opened the truck door for Kayla but she didn't get in. Instead, she gave him a more pleading look, the kind that tugged at a guy's heart. "Please, just let me stay here. I'm not going to leave."

"I'm not worried about you leaving, Kayla. I'm worried because someone is stalking you. I don't want you hurt."

Her eyes widened, telling him more with that look than she'd told him with words. She didn't expect him to care. When was the last time she expected anyone to care? She bit down on her bottom lip, then turned to get in the truck. "Boone, don't act as if this is more than a job."

What was he supposed to say to that?

"Kayla, this *is* more than a job. And I'm not going to let anyone hurt you."

"Too late," she whispered, then climbed into the truck and reached to close the door.

On the way to church Boone tried not to think about those two words she'd spoken. *Too late.* That had opened up something. He could see it in her expression, in the tension of her shoulders.

The last thing he wanted was to be the person who hurt her.

They pulled up at Martin's Crossing Community Church. The parking lot was overflowing and someone was ringing the bell. He parked and got out, but he was starting to feel as if this was a bad idea.

When he opened her door she looked up, one tear trickling down her cheek before she swiped it away and put on a big smile.

He'd spent a few years getting his life together and not getting involved with anyone. That tear sliding down her pale face just about undid all of his resolve. Yup. He was involved, no two ways about it.

"Don't worry, I'm not falling apart." With those words she got out of his truck and took his hand.

Boone led her through the front door of the building. As they walked past a pew he noticed a box of tissue. He grabbed the box and handed it to her.

"The whole box?" She laughed, but it was shaky. "I'm not going to lose it. It's nothing, so don't get all he-man on me."

"I just thought you might want to blow your nose. You're a mess."

She laughed again, but the laughter didn't stop the silent fall of tears sliding down her cheeks.

"Stop laughing like that, Stanford. You'll have people convinced you like me."

She pulled a tissue from the box and wiped her eyes. "I doubt it."

"Okay, they'll think I made you cry." He led her to an empty pew and motioned her in ahead of him. "People see what they want to see."

She gave him a long, careful look. "What do you

think they see, Boone? When they look at you, what do they see?"

Good for her, turning the tables on him. "They see a guy who takes his family and his career very seriously. A guy who can keep you safe."

"I believe that, too."

The way she said it surprised him. And worried him. He didn't want to let her down.

The pew filled up. Which meant she had to move closer to Boone's side. Closer to the protection of his body, to the scent of his cologne. Closer to a realization about herself. For years she'd been running from her pain and herself. It had taken this situation, this man, to force her to confront the past. He'd helped her open up because he knew how to be quiet and listen.

There was no way to run, not this time.

After her mom's death she had run from her siblings, from the very people who could have helped and would have been there for her. She was her own worst enemy. She knew that about herself. There might be a stranger threatening to expose secrets, seeking money, but the things she could have and had done to herself were far worse.

That was then. This was now.

When she'd returned home from that trip to Mexico she'd entered rehab. Twelve steps to a new life. One step closer to God. It hadn't been easy, laying down everything before God: all the dirty little secrets, her shame, her anger, her pain.

But God already knew. Or so she'd been told. He knew her heartache. Knew her past and her future. Her sponsor had told her that God could make something beautiful from the ashes of her life.

That same sponsor had given the analogy that she should see herself as a broken vase. God was the glue to put her back together. Kayla thought it was a sweet story, but in truth there were pieces missing, so how could she ever be truly whole?

The service ended with a prayer. Kayla bowed her head and closed her eyes, needing that moment to pull herself together. She knew how to smile and pretend none of it mattered. She knew how to act as if it hadn't touched her at all. But she needed a minute to pull on her all-smiles mask.

But the service had touched her. It had felt like a continuation of her talk with Maria Wilder, when Maria had prayed with her and told her to give herself and God a chance. Maria had also told her to forgive her dad. Forgive him, not just for him, but for herself. She had shaken off that suggestion. She was too angry to forgive. He didn't need or want her forgiveness because he didn't believe he'd done anything wrong.

A hand tightened on hers. As she stood, Boone's hand went to her back. It felt strangely protective. And she noticed he was on alert. His eyes darted to the back of the church and quickly took in the crowd.

"Do you think my stalker is going to show up here? In the middle of Nowhere, Texas?" she asked as he guided her through the church.

"I'm not taking any chances." He pointed. "There's your sister."

"Oh, that's right, lunch. We don't have to go."

"No, we don't. But we're going. I'm not letting you out of lunch with your family."

"I don't want to keep you from your family."

"You're not keeping me from anything, Stanford. There're so many of us Wilders, Mom won't notice one or two of us missing."

Samantha was upon them, her smile bright, her hug long and suffocating. "I was afraid you'd skip out on us."

"I wouldn't dream of it."

"Oh, yes, you would." Samantha gave her another quick hug and then directed her attention to Boone. "You look, glum. No offense."

"Sam, if I took offense every time you ran me down, I'd be hiding in a corner somewhere trying to find my self-esteem."

"The two of you are coming over for lunch, correct?" Sam asked.

Boone didn't respond. He gave her a look, letting her know it was her decision to make.

"Yes, we're coming over." Kayla let her gaze slide to Boone. But he wasn't paying attention, not to her. He was watching the dwindling crowds, attentive and focused.

"Earth to Boone," Kayla teased.

He flicked her a look, accompanied by a frown.

"He's playing bodyguard," Kayla said in a stage whisper.

Boone gave her one of his well-meaning looks. She found them entertaining. This one told her he had a job to do. And she wasn't helping.

"I do take my job seriously, Stanford. And in case you forgot, this isn't a game."

"I know, I'm sorry."

Samantha cleared her throat. "Okay, then, we'll see the two of you at Duke's?"

"Yes, at Duke's."

Kayla would have said more to her sister, but Boone took hold of her arm and guided her toward the side exit, not the main doors.

"What are we doing?" she asked.

"Changing things up." He kept walking, his hand firm on her elbow.

"Boone, stop. You're starting to scare me."

He didn't slow down. "You should be scared."

"Why? I have you, right? You're the best. And whoever is doing this is just out for money. They aren't after anything else."

He kept walking, not answering her questions. When they got to the back door of the church, he stepped out first, looking both ways. He pulled her close to his side. "Stay close with me, Kayla."

"I'm with you."

They headed for the truck, not stopping to talk to people who called out. She tried to wave, to smile an apology. He didn't give her time. When they got to his old truck, he pulled the door open and practically lifted her inside.

"What is wrong with you?" she asked as he got behind the wheel.

"I got a text."

"You could have said something."

He started the truck and backed out of the parking space. "I didn't really want to take time to explain to you that we need to leave."

"What was the text?"

"The person who texted me knew what you were

wearing and wanted to prove, they said, that they could get close to you."

She shivered, even though she tried to tell herself she wasn't afraid. For weeks she'd been telling herself this was all nothing more than an overzealous prankster. But it wasn't. Someone out there wanted to hurt her. They wanted to hurt her dad.

"It has to do with money and politics. So why doesn't my dad just pay them off?"

"Because they won't stop, Kayla. They'll take the money, and next time they'll raise the stakes. They'll always want more. They'll always want another payday. The only way to stop them is to figure out who they are."

"Someone my dad knows. Someone who knows me. Someone who wants him out of the race. But how do they know? It has to be someone close to our family. Or someone who worked for my dad."

He glanced her way just enough to give her a reassuring look. "We'll figure it out."

The drive to the Martin ranch was too quick. Kayla's brain was still scrolling through people she knew, or people her dad had known. Suspicions landed on those closest to her. Even her little brother Michael became a suspect. She couldn't imagine him doing this. He might want to hurt her, but never their father.

"You okay?" Boone questioned as they got out of the truck at Duke's house.

"I'm good, just thinking. Or trying not to think."

His hand was on her back. "Let it go for the day. You're safe. Your dad is safe."

"Is he?" And did she care? She'd spent so many years

telling herself she didn't. But what if something happened to him?

"He's safe. He has a great team of security people surrounding him."

"Right, of course he does."

They were met at the front door by Oregon, Duke's wife. Her daughter, Lily, popped up behind her. Kayla greeted them with smiles and hugs. They were her family. Lily was her niece. There were other nieces and nephews. It was amazing that these people were her family. And she loved them.

They were pieces of the broken life that was being made whole.

"Come on in." Oregon led them through the sprawling, two-story farmhouse that she and Duke had remodeled. "Duke's on the grill out back. The others are sitting on the patio. It's such a perfect fall day."

"Would you like to see our new kittens?" Lily took hold of Kayla's hand. "They need homes."

"I'm not sure if getting a cat is a good idea right now," Kayla said, but her objections were ignored. Lily led her through the house, away from Oregon and Boone. "They're in the laundry room. I convinced Dad they have to be inside."

"But they don't?" Kayla guessed.

Lily grinned. "Not at all. But they're cute and the little kids love them."

She was petting a pretty gray ball of fluff when Samantha found them.

"Don't let her trick you into taking one of those kittens home," Sam warned.

"I'm not a cat person," Kayla felt confident in saying.

"Of course you're not." Sam picked up a dark gray

tabby and held it close. "This one is mine. Not that I need another cat. Remington said we aren't even married and we already have a zoo."

"He loves you so much, he'd let you bring home a zoo," Kayla countered. "Another month until the wedding."

"I know. I thought I had months to prepare and then I woke up and realized I have days."

"Weddings and babies," Lily groaned. "This whole family is obsessed with weddings and babies. You know, there are teenagers. We live. We breathe. We were here first."

Sam ruffled their niece's dark hair. "Yes, Lily, you came first. We need to go. Lunch is ready."

Lunch was typical of the Martins, Kayla thought. There was a lot of laughter, a lot of talking. They ate outside where there were a couple of patio tables and plenty of chairs. Jake's wife, Breezy, sat down in the seat next to Kayla, a plate balanced on her lap and a glass of iced tea in her hand.

Kayla liked Breezy. She was earthy, quiet and genuine. And anyone could see that she was exactly what Jake Martin had needed. He was the serious older brother.

"You know, when this is over, you could always stay here," Breezy said, just as Sam arrived with her plate. Boone was a short distance away talking to Remington and Brody about the upcoming ranch rodeo and Lucas.

When Lucas was mentioned, Lily's eyes lit up. Oregon noticed it, too. She didn't look as amused. Lily was young. Too young for Lucas. That didn't mean she couldn't have a crush on the younger Wilder.

"Kayla?" Breezy cleared her throat.

"Sorry, just thinking. And I'm sure I'll just go home to Austin and go back to my life when this is all over." Back to what life? She looked up, saw the same question lurking in the eyes of her sister and sister-in-law. The life that was going nowhere? The life that counted for nothing?

"That sounds promising," Sam said with her customary honesty and a touch of sarcasm.

"Thanks," Kayla shot back. "Actually, I do have this pesky little degree in early childhood education. I could finish up, get certified and be a teacher. If there's a school that would have me."

From a short distance away Boone heard and arched one dark brow. She glared and went back to the conversation with her sisters. Oregon had joined them. She pulled up a chair and sat down.

"Martin's Crossing has a nice school," Oregon offered.

"I don't think Martin's Crossing is ready for me," Kayla answered. "And I'm not sure if I could live in the country. I've always lived in the city. It's just who I am."

This time she avoided looking at Boone, because she didn't want to see his reaction to the conversation. It shouldn't matter what he thought.

But deep down, she knew that it did.

Chapter 10

Kayla was up at sunrise Monday morning. Early to bed, early to rise seemed to make Kayla Stanford healthy, happy and wise. Because she was happy. It was the strangest thing, to be here in the home of strangers, dependent on their kindness and charity, and yet she was happy.

She slipped out of her room just as Janie was coming out of her bedroom down the hall. Janie, always quiet and self-conscious. Kayla smiled at the younger woman.

"I'm getting used to this 'crack of dawn' business," Kayla said as the two of them walked downstairs together.

"I would love to sleep late," Janie responded. "I try, but I can't. I'm just used to being up early."

Maria Wilder was already up. She had a pot of coffee started and she was sitting at the kitchen table. Janie gave her a look, because Maria sitting down was unusual.

"Mom, you okay?"

Maria nodded. "I'm good. Maybe a little under the weather. I think I have that virus Molly had last week."

Janie put a hand to her mother's brow. "You're warm. Go back to bed."

"I have too much to do," Maria argued.

"And you have a house full of daughters who can do those things. The guys are working cattle today. The twins are upstairs practicing their pageant walk." She laughed at that and so did Maria. "Go back to bed. Let us be in charge for once."

"I can help," Kayla offered. Both Janie and Maria looked up. Kayla smiled, enjoying their looks of astonishment.

"Of course she can," Janie jumped right in. "We'll thaw something out for dinner, get the laundry going. Trust us."

Kayla grinned at Maria. "Yes, trust me."

Maria reached for her hand. "I do trust you, Kayla. Completely. So I'm going back to bed and I'm leaving the two of you in charge. Michaela has work today, so Molly will be here with you."

That seemed to take Janie by as much surprise as it took Kayla. "Molly?"

"Yes, your niece. Have fun."

Maria left the two of them standing in the kitchen looking at each other. Kayla laughed first.

"We're babysitting."

Janie shuddered. "Molly is a terror."

"I heard that." Michaela entered the room with her daughter. Molly waggled along next to her on pudgy legs, her blond hair in pigtails. She looked like a little darling. But then she smiled and all orneriness broke loose.

"Mom's gone back to bed. She has Molly's virus. We told her we'd hold down the fort today." Janie held a hand out to her niece. "So you're staying with us, Mols."

Molly didn't look thrilled.

"Mom is sick enough to go back to bed?" Michaela picked up her daughter. "That's unheard of."

"She deserves a break," Janie countered. "Molly, do you want oatmeal for breakfast?"

"Cookies." Molly grinned as she said it.

"No cookies." Michaela handed her daughter over to her sister. "Do not let her have cookies for breakfast. I have to run. Keep an eye on her. Do not let her out of your sight."

"Because I'm twenty and obviously don't know that." Janie snuggled her niece. "Go."

Michaela left, giving them each a warning look before heading out the door. Janie immediately passed the toddler to Kayla.

"Cookies," Molly said with a toddler lisp.

"I don't think we should have cookies for breakfast." Kayla held the little girl close.

The doorbell rang. Janie peeked out and then opened it. "Hey, Daron. Long time no see."

Tall, with sun-streaked hair and an air of confidence that he'd probably possessed since birth, Daron McKay was not on the list of Kayla's favorite people. Older than her by five years, they'd seen each other at social functions their fathers had insisted they attend but they'd never been friends. "Surprise," he said. "Kayla, don't look so happy to see me. I'm giving Boone a break. He's working cattle with the boys. I'm on Kayla duty."

"You're just in time for breakfast," Janie offered. She headed for the kitchen and Daron motioned for Kayla to go first. "I'm going to make pancakes."

"I love pancakes," Daron called back to her. He stepped close to Kayla. "I talked to your father this morning. I want you to look at some photographs from old news stories. This person seems to have been around when you were in Mexico, and also Florida. Maybe you'll recognize someone."

"Sure." Kayla shifted Molly to her left hip. The little girl patted her cheek and kissed her.

Daron grinned. "I wouldn't have guessed you for a kid person, Kayla."

"Me, neither. She just doesn't know any better."

"Give yourself a break, will you?" he spoke sharply. "You've gotten used to being down on yourself."

"Yeah, I guess I have." She nuzzled the little girl in her arms. "Maybe I am a kid person."

He winked and took Molly from her. "Maybe you're a person who fixes me breakfast."

"Don't push it."

It was noon when Lucas and Boone came in for lunch. Jase had class on Mondays, so it was the two of them trying to separate calves that were ready to be weaned. Then they were heading back out to work on some fence that was starting to lean. Boone pulled off leather gloves and tossed them on the table. He glanced from Daron to Kayla.

"Have you showed her the photographs?"

"Not yet. She's been babysitting." Daron got up from the table. "I'll get my computer."

"Babysitting?" Boone asked as he pulled lunch meat

out of the fridge. He eyed the slow cooker. "Where's Mom?"

"She's sick," Kayla explained. She pulled plates out of the cabinet. One for him. One for Lucas. "Janie and I are taking care of things."

"Where's Janie?" he asked.

"Trying to get Molly to take a nap."

Lucas laughed as he put a sandwich together. "That's not going to happen. That little girl has more energy than all of us combined."

"Mom's sick?" Boone asked again, his brows drawing together. "That never happens."

"Molly had a virus. They think your mom has the same."

"And Dad?" Boone asked as he sat down at the table with his plate. Kayla sat next to him.

"We took him lunch a little while ago. He's up and around but sitting with her. I think they're enjoying a quiet day, just the two of them."

"Yeah, I guess that isn't something they get too much of. Time alone."

Daron returned with his laptop. He set it on the table in front of Kayla. She glanced up, wishing this whole mess away. Before she could say anything, Janie appeared with Molly. The little girl was clinging to her neck and wiping tears off her cheek with a pudgy hand.

"She won't take a nap."

Lucas stepped into the room. "You just figured that out? She is not a napper."

Molly lifted her blond head off Janie's shoulder and pinned Kayla with her big eyes. "Kayka."

Janie handed the little girl over. "You're the new favorite."

"But I'm—" she held the little girl close "—not a kid person. Really."

Boone picked up his plate and carried it to the sink. "I guess you are now, *Kayka*."

Daron booted up his computer. "Here, babysitter, have a seat."

She sat next to him, Molly against her shoulder. Boone pulled out the chair on the other side of her. Lucas and Janie made excuses about other things to do. Janie was going to fold laundry. Lucas thought he'd work with his horse while he waited for Boone.

"I pasted photos so I have them all in one file." Daron opened the folder and slid the computer in front of Kayla.

As she clicked through the photos, the little girl in her arms grew heavier. She shifted the sleeping child, Molly's head resting against her shoulder.

"So much for not wanting to take a nap," Boone said. "Do you want me to take her? I can put her on the sofa."

"No, I have her." She wouldn't have thought it could happen, but Molly had snatched up a piece of her heart. Holding her felt good. She inhaled the sweet scent of baby shampoo and brushed her cheek against Molly's soft hair.

"That's how it happens, Stanford. They lure you in when you're least expecting it." Boone leaned in to look at the pictures, but his shoulder brushed hers. She could have told him that Molly wasn't the only one luring her in. He was doing his share, and so was his family.

She would eventually have to leave this sweet place, and she knew that she'd miss it. Miss this family. Miss Boone.

"Whoa," Daron said as she clicked through pictures.

"What?"

"Back that up. Tell me who that is, around the bonfire."

She looked at the picture, a group of people around a fire. Big deal. Daron pointed. "That one."

Her heart stammered a little as she studied the picture. The face familiar, but not. She met Boone's gaze and he shrugged. Daron tapped the screen, making the image larger.

"I've met him but I can't remember his name. But I do know he's the nephew of Clarence Jacobs," Daron said quietly, letting it sink in.

"Clarence Jacobs is running against my dad. But I don't know him. So he wouldn't know anything about me." She closed her eyes, trying to force calm, trying to remember.

Boone took Molly from her arms and this time she let him. He soothed the little girl with softly spoken words as he carried her from the room.

"What would he gain from this?"

Daron leaned back, still looking at the photograph. "Money. But I can't imagine he needs any. Retribution?"

"For what?"

"Do you remember meeting him, Kayla?"

She closed her eyes, trying to bring back memories of that night. "I don't know. I must have, but I don't remember ever having a conversation with him. And it isn't as if I tell complete strangers what happened to me."

Or did she?

"It's great that she recognizes him and he's connected to politics," Boone said as he walked back into the room. "But you need more than that to arrest a guy for assault and extortion."

"Right." Daron attached a portable printer to his computer. "I'll take this to town and we'll see if we can't tie Mr. Wonderful to the phone calls, to the attacker, or even put his location near here."

"I don't even know his name," Kayla said. "I wish I could remember. A person should remember something this important."

Boone pulled her close, his arms strong. She leaned her head against his shoulder. She'd like to think she was a different person now. If she could believe anything about herself, she would believe that she was someone a man like Boone Wilder would take home to meet his family. Instead, she was the person hiding inside their home, hiding her real self, and trying to be someone they could accept.

"Stop," he whispered close to her temple, his breath soft against her skin.

"Stop what?"

Daron packed up his computer and the portable printer. He looked from Kayla to Boone, his eyes narrowing. "I'm heading to Austin. You've got this?"

Boone nodded, his chin brushing the top of her ear. "We're good."

He left with one last look for Boone. And Kayla knew that look. He was warning Boone to not get emotionally involved. Because she wasn't good for someone like Boone.

"Stop," Boone repeated, tightening his arms around the woman he held.

She turned in his embrace and looked up, her blue

eyes tangling with his. A man could get lost in those eyes of hers.

"Stop blaming yourself," he continued. "Stop this trip into the past. It'll get you nowhere."

"But I can't undo who I was or the choices I made."

"No, you can't. But you can move forward. I think you have a clear idea of who you want to be. I think you've always known that person, but you tried to destroy her. Maybe you thought you couldn't be her."

"That woman would have been crushed by…" She shook her head and stepped away from him. "It was easier to pretend it didn't hurt."

"But it did hurt. You can't pretend the pain away, Kayla. You have to confront it. And you have to give yourself a chance to live."

"I know." She brushed a hand over her face. "But I'm tired, Boone. I'm so tired. I thought I'd escaped that life, but it came after me."

"We'll conquer it again. And again, if we have to. We'll keep conquering until you're free of it."

"What if I'm never free?"

He brushed a hand down her arm and she sighed at his touch. That encouraged him. He pulled her close again. "You are free. 'Whom the Son sets free is free indeed.' Kayla, you're free from the past. You've been redeemed. That doesn't mean you won't have battles. We all have battles."

She placed a hand on his cheek. "You have battles?"

"Yeah, I have battles."

He battled guilt. He battled his brain, making him think and rethink that day over and over again. People had been hurt and a man had died because Boone had trusted a kid. What kind of world did we live in that you couldn't trust a child?

Yes, he had battles. But the person he'd had to learn to forgive the most was himself.

He knew Daron fought the same battles. His guilt kept him tied to that day, to memories of a woman and to the life of another woman.

"I'm sorry, I shouldn't have forced you back there, Boone."

He blinked away the images of that day in Afghanistan. "I'm good."

Her smile was timid and sweet, shaking something loose inside him. For a dangerous minute he forgot that he was standing in his mother's kitchen, where any number of people could interrupt. It didn't seem to matter when she stood so close he could smell strawberry shampoo.

His hand went around her waist. His lips touched hers. She tasted like lemonade and sugar cookies. Her hand touched his neck, pulling him a little bit closer.

The kiss lingered, then she pulled away but stayed in his arms. She whispered, "We shouldn't do this."

"You're probably right." He let out a shaky breath. He knew it was wrong.

Focus, Boone. He gave himself a mental shake.

He told himself he wasn't going to fall for a client. He wasn't going to fall for a woman who had no interest in country life. The woman in his arms came from a life of wealth, of ease. She'd been raised in mansions, given every opportunity. His life was all about making do and keeping the ranch going. Opposites might attract, but that didn't mean they fit into each other's worlds.

Footsteps, heavy and too obvious, grew closer. He

stepped away from her. A second later Lucas appeared, his cheeks a little bit red. They'd been caught. It was obvious from the look he gave Boone that his little brother wasn't happy that he'd had to leave the room and come back a little louder and more obvious.

"You ready to get that fence fixed?" Boone asked, happy to go along pretending nothing happened.

"I've been waiting on you."

"I'm heading that way now." Boone raised his hand but stopped himself. No, he wouldn't touch her cheek, or her arm. He wouldn't notice that mischievous gleam in her eyes. "I'm locking the doors. See that you keep them locked."

"Got it." She saluted.

He shook his head and headed out the back door with his brother. Lucas shot him a disgusted look as they walked the worn path to the barn.

"What?"

"What if Mom had walked in?" Lucas asked.

"This is the problem with being a grown man living too close to his family. I'm almost thirty, little brother. I think I can handle myself without your lectures. I don't think Mom would get too upset if she saw me," he said.

"If she saw you kissing Kayla in the kitchen?" Lucas shot him a knowing smirk. "Yeah, she'd be upset. Kayla is her little pet, big brother. Hurt Kayla and you'll be up a certain creek with no paddle."

"I'm not going to hurt her. I'm going to keep her safe and get her back to her life in Austin. End of story."

"These things never end well, Boone."

"There's nothing between us."

Lucas reached in the back of the old farm truck and

pulled on a pair of leather gloves. He shook his head and went back to digging for tools. "You're a fool."

Yeah, maybe he was. Maybe he'd started off on this job with all the right intentions and somewhere along the way he'd tripped up.

He pulled keys out of his pocket. "Get in the truck. We have fence to build."

Lucas was smart enough to choke back a laugh as he got in the truck. Boone shot him a warning look. By the time they finished building fence this evening, that laugh would be long gone. He'd make sure of it.

Chapter 11

It was close to sunset when Boone and Lucas showed up at the house. They stomped into the kitchen, dirty and looking worn out. Kayla sat by the patio doors reading a book but put it away to watch the two brothers. They scrambled to get to the sink, pushing each other away, then fighting over a towel. Boone gave Lucas a mild shove and told him to go take a shower.

"I will, because unlike you, I have a life." Lucas poured himself a glass of tea. "I have a date tonight."

"You're going to break Lily Martin's heart," Boone teased.

"She's thirteen!"

"Thirteen-year-old girls have hearts, too, you know," Kayla spoke up, reminding them that she was there. They glanced her way, Boone grinning and Lucas frowning.

Lucas wiped his face with the towel and hung it on

the cabinet door. "Yeah, but I haven't done anything to make her feel this way."

"You exist. She's thirteen. Someday she'll understand that thirteen is a child compared to your what? Eighteen?"

"Nineteen, thank you very much. And Lily is a sweet kid. But she's still just a kid." He shot past them to the door, as if he couldn't get away soon enough. "You all have a great night. I heard the twins say they were going to a movie. Michaela was going to pick Molly up and go out with a friend. Who knows what Janie does?"

"Janie went to a small group meeting," Kayla offered. "I helped your mom fix soup and sandwiches for her and your dad."

"Sounds as if everyone is taken care of. See you all later." Then Lucas was gone. Leaving Boone and Kayla alone.

"I need to get cleaned up and get off my feet," he said as he sat down at the table with her. "How about we go to my place? I'll fix us something to eat. We can watch movies."

"You don't have to do that. I can heat a bowl of soup and just go to bed early."

He pushed himself to his feet. "Kayla, I know you didn't expect to live here for a month. But I'm not going to stop doing my job. You're not staying here alone."

No, she didn't think he would let her get away with that. But putting a little distance between them wouldn't be such a bad idea. Especially when he had that soft, vulnerable look around his eyes. It was a look that would make any woman cave.

"I'm not alone," she countered.

"Come on, we'll take my truck." He pulled out his keys and motioned for her to follow.

She wasn't winning this battle. But being with him felt dangerous. Almost as dangerous as whoever was stalking her. She shook off that thought. He wasn't a danger to her.

Only to her heart.

She'd never known anyone like him. Her world had been so shallow, filled with men who were useless, with relationships that went nowhere and experiences that left her empty and searching for more.

"Okay, we'll take your truck. Do you want me to drive?" she offered as they headed out.

In answer he tossed her his keys. "Go for it. Can you drive a standard?"

"A what?"

"Don't mess with me, Stanford. I'm too tired." But there was a light in his eyes, a glint of humor.

"Yes, Wilder, I can drive a standard," she assured him.

A few minutes later she climbed behind the wheel of his precious truck. It started and she eased off the clutch as she hit the gas. The vehicle lurched a little and Boone reached for the door.

"You said you could drive it."

She eased the truck forward, avoiding further lurching and bucking. "I didn't say I was any good at it. I just said I could drive it."

The truck jumped forward and died.

Boone leaned back in his seat. "Okay, put it in First." She did.

"Start it with your foot on the clutch and the gas. Ease off the clutch. Ease. That means slowly."

She did as he told her. "I know what *ease* means."

He glanced her way, the look in his espresso-colored eyes warmed her heart. "Stanford, you've never eased through anything. You rush into every situation full throttle."

"I believe in getting things done."

"I'm sure you do. Park close to the RV. I don't know if Daron will be home tonight."

"Home?" She took the keys out of the ignition. "Does he live here, too?"

He waited until they were climbing the steps to answer. "That depends on what you mean by *live*. I didn't ask for a roommate and he hasn't been invited to live here. He just shows up and sometimes forgets to leave."

His collie, Sally, hurried to his side, nudging against him as he unlocked the door. He pushed it open and the dog ran inside.

"Don't mind the mess. Daron thinks he's the neat one. He's not. And this place just isn't big enough for two. It's barely big enough for one."

"I like it," she responded.

Boone headed for the bedroom at the back of the RV. "I'll be back in a minute."

Kayla spotted the empty dog dish. She filled the water bowl and then dug around in cabinets until she found dog food to fill the other bowl. Sally gave her a suspicious look but accepted the food.

Boone returned a minute later, the left leg of his jeans pinned and crutches beneath his arms.

She stood there, unsure. "Are you okay?"

He grinned up at her. "Stanford, I'm okay. Fixing fence isn't exactly the easiest activity. But it's done."

"If you're sure." She wasn't. "I could make us some soup."

He stood. "Please don't. I'm fine. And I can fix us something a lot better than soup."

He glanced at the sink full of dishes. "Another Daron mess. Do you like omelets?"

"Do you have cheese?"

He opened the fridge door. "Yes, I have cheese."

"Then, I like omelets."

She ran water into the sink and watched as he cracked eggs into a bowl. He added peppers, mushrooms, ham and cheese. She leaned against the counter and watched.

"Do you want toast with this?" he asked as he poured the eggs into a pan. "The bread is in the cabinet. Butter is in the fridge. I think my mom put some of her home-made strawberry jam in there, too."

"Sounds perfect." She found the bread, and then the butter and jam. "Your mom is an amazing woman."

He dropped bread into the four-slice toaster. "Yeah, she is. She's strong."

"She's raised strong kids."

"Yeah, she has. We're a wild bunch but our parents have managed to survive us. What about your family?"

Good question. "We're not close. Growing up, my dad spent most of his time at the office. It was always about the next case. My stepmother was busy climbing the social ladder as he climbed the career ladder. My brothers had their own lives."

"Sounds lonely," he observed.

"Yes, I guess it was. I thought it was typical. It was what I saw in so many of the families around us and so I didn't see it as dysfunctional."

"I guess you wouldn't if it was all you knew."

The toast popped up. She buttered it and spread jam. Boone lifted the pan and slid the omelet onto a plate. He cut it in half with the spatula and moved part of it to the second plate.

It was a strange, domestic moment in that tiny kitchen. They were close, too close. They were close physically and emotionally in ways she wasn't prepared for. As they brushed shoulders moving around the kitchen, she held her breath. Boone leaned his crutches against the counter and his hand touched her waist.

"You make it hard to breathe, Kayla." His voice was husky and close to her ear.

"Breathing is so overrated," she tried to joke.

"I've always found it to be pretty necessary to life." He slid his lips across her temple.

"The eggs will get cold."

"Yeah, that would be bad." He let go of her. "We should definitely eat."

She picked up the plates and carried them to the booth-style table. "I saw juice in the fridge. Do you want that or something else?"

He hopped to the fridge and pulled out the orange juice. "You?"

She nodded and took the juice from him. She poured two glasses. They sat down together at the table, Boone across from her. Sally sighed and stretched out on the floor. She looked up at them, her head resting on her paws.

"You know, you could press charges," Boone spoke as he polished off his eggs and toast.

"We have to know who it is before we press charges, don't we? We can't just assume Jacobs is involved?"

"That isn't what I meant. Kayla, press charges against Whitman."

Her lungs were suddenly starved for oxygen and she blinked back tears welling in her eyes. It took her by surprise, those tears. She shook her head. He reached for her, grasping her fingers in his, grounding her.

"No one would believe me. It's been ten years."

"No statute of limitations for the assault of a child."

She pushed her plate away. The dog whined and stood, coming to rest her head on Kayla's leg. Absently she stroked Sally's head, looking into the animal's eyes.

"My dad would never forgive me. It's over. It was ten years ago."

Anger tightened Boone's mouth into a harsh line. "Kayla, what if there are other victims?"

"This isn't the conversation I want to have."

He stood, looking down at her, his features softening. "I'm sorry. You're right."

She followed him to the sink with their plates and when her hands were empty she reached for him, hugging him from the back, burying her face in his shirt. He didn't move. He let her take that moment to find strength in him.

How in the world did he get himself in these situations? Good thing his cell phone came to his rescue. He stepped away from her and answered.

"Daron?" He leaned against the counter. And Kayla had put some breathing room between them.

"I have a few pictures I want Kayla to look at. The PI William Stanford hired has put the son of an ex-employee of her father and the nephew of the other senatorial candidate together."

"Okay." Boone glanced at Kayla. She'd started washing dishes, pretending she didn't care about the conversation. "When will you be here?"

"An hour," Daron told him.

"We'll be at my place." Boone sat down at the dining table.

"The two of you are there?" Daron said with a hint of amusement.

"Yeah, the two of us. See you in an hour. Drive safe."

Kayla sat down across from him. "They have something?"

"The son of an ex-employee of your dad. He's friends with Ken Jacobs, Clarence Jacobs' nephew."

She buried her face in her hands and shook her head. "I don't know what I've done, Boone. I have blank spaces in my memory. I'm not proud of that. I'm not proud of who I've become."

"It isn't who you've become."

She looked up. "Really? Easy for you to say."

"It was a side trip. You aren't stuck there forever."

"I hope you're right."

"I'm right," he assured her. "We'll figure this out, get you safe and then you can go find the person you were meant to be."

Looking at her from across the table, the dim lighting of the RV leaving her face in shadows, he couldn't help but think that he'd miss her. He'd never missed a client. He'd liked a few. He'd worried about a couple.

He wasn't too worried about Kayla. She was strong. She would do something with her life. She'd probably have that career as a teacher. She'd get married and have kids. That thought took him down back roads that he shouldn't be going down, picturing her holding a pretty little girl in her arms with dark hair and blue eyes.

"I'm not sure who I'm meant to be, Boone." Her voice shook a little. "I've been on such a crazy journey in the past year and it seems as if it all led me here, to Martin's Crossing. I know I have to go home. Face the past. Figure out what to do in the future. But being here has meant everything."

"Then, you use it as a stepping-stone."

She nodded, resting her chin on her hands, her elbows propped on the table. "Your family has meant the world to me. I'm sorry that things started out so rough. I was difficult."

Now he laughed. "Difficult?"

Her mouth tilted on one side. "Yes, difficult."

He just stared at her.

"Okay, more than difficult. I didn't want a bodyguard. I didn't want to be thrust into the middle of your family, because I knew I wouldn't fit."

"You've done okay for yourself, Stanford."

"Thanks." She stood up. "Coffee?"

He started to stand. She put a hand on his shoulder. "Let me," she said.

"Taking care of me, Stanford?"

"Yeah, Wilder. I guess I am. Don't tell anyone, but I'm going to miss you. And I'm going to hope I can become the type of woman that a man like you might love someday."

The words echoed between them. Her hand dropped from his shoulder and she stepped back. The distance she put between them was more than physical. There were things he could say, should say, to make her feel better.

But she was still a client. She was still looking for herself and her past. She was still the city girl who thought she didn't fit in their small town. He still had a bucket list that didn't include things like visiting Paris, but instead was all about taking care of his family.

"I can see you want to say something, Boone. Please don't. Don't reassure me or tell me what you think I want to hear. I know who I am and where I've been."

He reached for her hand and dragged it to his lips against his better judgment. Her eyes closed.

"I'm in over my head, Boone."

"Me, too."

"It's just the situation," she told him. "This is what happens when two people are thrown together in a dire situation. But we'll be fine. In a few months you'll be protecting someone else. I'll be working on that teaching certificate. We'll see each other at Duke's and we'll share stories about what we've been doing."

"Are we breaking up, Stanford?" He tried to keep his tone light.

"Don't be ridiculous. How could we break up? We're not a couple. I'm just saying, this isn't real. Every woman you ever protect is going to fall for you."

"Is that what's happening?"

She swallowed, then faked a smile. "Stop."

"Okay, but for the record, I don't have relationships with clients."

"Right. Silly me."

He stood, balancing, reaching for her. "There's nothing silly about this. Or about you."

She moved out of his reach. "I'm making coffee now."

The dog growled. Boone shot the animal a warning look. "Sally, it isn't an argument."

Sally stalked to the front door, the snarl coming from

deep down in her chest. Boone flipped off the light and moved to the cabinet. He motioned for Kayla to get back. He doubted she'd listen, but maybe this once.

He unlocked the drawer and pulled out his weapon. Kayla's eyes widened and she shrank into the corner of the kitchen. Sally was at the door, her growl low and menacing. He might have thought it was Daron if the dog had just barked. But Sally reserved that special growl for intruders and varmints of the two-legged variety.

Boone moved forward. The doorknob jiggled. He hadn't locked it. Of course he hadn't. He never locked the door.

"Bathroom," he ordered in a whisper. He heard her scurry down the hall, heard the bathroom door close and lock.

The front door eased open. These people were idiots. They knew he was in here. They knew the lights had gone out after the dog growled. And they were still going to come in.

Boone slid against the wall and waited. He guessed they had him at a disadvantage. His prosthesis was on the other side of the room. His crutches were in the kitchen. But it didn't take much to see he had them outsmarted.

They were inside. He could see that they were young. What did they think they were going to do, take Kayla out of here? Over his dead body.

"You boys always go about breaking and entering? You know, out here in the country, we're usually packing." He said it low, and about as threatening as his dog's best growl. Sally had moved in next to him and that growl had gone way down deep in her chest. That

was the growl that said she'd take the head off any var-
mint that crossed her.

"Dude," the kid started.

"Son, don't you *dude* me again. Put your hands up
and we'll see that no one gets hurt."

"We're just going to take Kayla Stanford with us.
We aren't going to hurt her." The taller of the two took
a step forward.

Sally leaped, teeth bared. Both of them ran. Boone
grabbed his crutches and did his best to catch up. He
guessed they wouldn't be taking Kayla anywhere. But
he also had hoped he'd be giving them a free ride to
the county jail.

Headlights flashed up the drive. He hit Redial on his
phone and Daron answered.

"They're heading through the east field. Two of
them." He stayed on the porch. No way was he catching up with anyone.

"Stay with Kayla," Daron yelled as he jumped from
his truck.

"Got it. I'll call County and have them head to the
county road." Boone dialed 911 as he watched Daron
take off through the field.

There was no moon. The countryside was dark. He
gave information to the 911 dispatcher and then he
stepped back inside the RV. Sally had gone with Daron.

"Kayla?" He flipped on lights as he headed down
the hall. The bathroom door was still locked. "It's me.
Open the door."

She was leaning against it. He could hear her breathing. He put a hand on the door and felt it shift.

"Open up."

"Give me a minute," she whispered.

"One minute and I'm coming in."

She opened the door. She didn't fall into his arms. She didn't touch him. She walked past him, down the hall to the living room. He followed, tossing the crutches in a corner and sitting next to her, but not touching her.

"I recognized his voice," she finally said.

"That coffee's done. Let me get us a cup."

She nodded. He got up and made his way to the kitchen. He poured two cups. When he turned she was standing next to him. She took one of the cups and poured in a few spoons of sugar.

This time she sat in the middle of the sofa. He sat next to her, their shoulders brushing. He stretched, rubbing the muscles of his left leg.

"You're okay?" she asked.

"Yeah, just muscle pains after a long day. You recognized his voice?"

She set her coffee on the table. "Yeah. After all this time, it took hearing the voice to jolt my memory. They were in Mexico. The night I crossed the border. They were younger than me. The senator's nephew hit on me. I'd forgotten. It wasn't one of my best nights. But I do remember telling him I wasn't interested. He tried to force the issue but a friend of his pulled him back, told him to go home to his mommy. He told me he'd make me sorry. It seems so silly now. It was just a stupid bonfire. He's a kid. Why would he do this?"

"Money and bruised ego."

"I guess."

The door opened. Daron walked in, gave the two of

them a look, shook his head and made for the coffee-pot. "They got away. But I got a description of the car."

"Kayla remembers them." Boone recounted what Kayla had shared with him. "It should be enough to at least bring them in. If the police get a search warrant, they might find some of the burn phones. And she recognized a voice."

"It was Ken Jacobs," Kayla explained.

Daron leaned against the counter with his cup. "Let's move this party to the main house. These two aren't your garden-variety criminals. They aren't thinking. That makes them dumb and dangerous."

Boone pushed himself up from the sofa. "I've got to change and put things back together. The two of you go on to the house. And call Lucas. See if he's there. He can lock doors and make sure the girls are all accounted for."

"Boone, with that many sisters it's a wonder you sleep at night," Daron joked as he was pulling out his phone.

Kayla didn't move. "We can wait for you."

Of course she would say that. He grabbed his prosthesis and headed down the hall. It didn't take him long. New liner. New sock. He changed to tennis shoes because even he wasn't that attached to boots.

When he walked back to the living room in athletic shorts and tennis shoes, Kayla gave him a long look. She whistled.

"Not bad, cowboy."

"What does that mean?" He opened the door and stepped out on the porch, motioning her after him.

"I've always been a leg girl," she said.

"Well, I'm half the guy for you."

"You aren't half a man," she said.

Daron pushed past them. "Get in the truck. We know this isn't over."

Chapter 12

Kayla put on the coffee the next morning, then watched as Maria started cooking French toast. Sausage was already sizzling in a skillet.

"You're okay?" Maria asked. She handed over a fork. "I'm going to let you cook the sausage."

"I can do that."

It was just the two of them. Kayla knew she would miss these early mornings. She would definitely miss the Wilders.

Maria put the French toast on a baking sheet. "Well?"

"I'm good. It's been a crazy few weeks. I know it hasn't been easy for you, to have an extra person underfoot."

Maria waved off the comment. "Oh, honey, you're no trouble. We have so many kids in this house, what's one more? I'm only sorry that your time with us will come to an end soon."

"Me, too," she admitted. When she'd first come here,

she never would have imagined this being the scenario at the end of her stay. "I've learned so much, Maria. Not just how to cook. But whatever faith I came here with, it's grown. I feel as if I can move forward. It's been a long time since I've felt this way."

Maria hugged her tight. "I'm so glad to hear you say that. I hope you know that our door is always open to you, Kayla. You've become a part of our family and I hope you'll visit. Often."

"Thank you." Kayla glanced at the clock on the stove. "The twins want to go shopping today. Their pageant is in six weeks and they're afraid I won't be around to help."

"Those girls. Don't let them push you into going if you don't want to go."

Boone limped into the kitchen and leaned heavily on the counter. "Oh, don't worry. It isn't Kayla who's being pushed into going shopping."

Maria patted his cheek. "Poor Boonie."

Kayla raised her brows at the nickname. "Boonie?"

"Only my mom gets to call me that." He poured himself a cup of coffee. "Don't burn the sausage, Stanford."

She turned the sausage. "I won't. *Boonie.*"

"Thanks, Mom." He headed for a stool and sat to watch them finish breakfast.

"You should tell the girls it isn't a good day," his mom said. "They'd understand."

"This is important to them."

"Yes, it is. But it isn't more important than your life."

"I think we can go without you," Kayla offered.

"Nice try." Boone winked as he lifted his cup of coffee to his lips. "We leave in an hour."

A few hours later they were walking through the

mall. Essie and Allie were all energy and no focus. Essie, sometimes a little quieter than her sister, Kayla thought, tried to calm her twin. Boone followed them, watchful and attentive.

"We need a plan." Kayla had never been in a pageant, so she had no idea what that plan would be.

The girls started to talk at the same time. Kayla opened her mouth, unable to get a word in.

"Okay, girls, listen to Kayla." Boone grabbed both twins by the arms just as they were about to hare off to a shoe store. "Because I'm not going in every single store in this mall."

"You need evening gowns, right? And jewelry."

"Yes." Allie, the blue jeans, cowboy boots and T-shirt twin, was all giddy at the mention of jewelry.

"This way." Kayla motioned for them to follow. She glanced back at Boone. "You got this?"

"I've got this." He gave her a tight grimace that she thought was meant to be a smile.

"Of course you do." Overnight she'd told herself that she'd be leaving soon and he'd be nothing but a bright moment in her life, sweet but in the past.

And she didn't want him to hurt.

"Keep walking, Stanford. I'm good."

She reached for his hand. "I'll walk with you."

"You're only encouraging them," he grumbled.

"I don't think they need any encouragement."

He pulled her a little bit closer to his side. "Yeah, and neither do I."

The shop they entered sparkled with lights, gowns of all colors and sizes and costume jewelry. Boone shuddered a little.

"This is the kind of store that gives a man hives," he said.

"And you act so tough. There's a bench inside. For men forced to shop with sisters."

"I'll be here at the door. I would say to take your time but I'm afraid you will."

"I'll try to hurry them," she offered. "And you're not okay."

"No, I'm not. But today isn't the day to worry about it. I'll get it taken care of tomorrow."

"Tomorrow is the ranch rodeo."

"It is. Just shop and let me do my job."

She nodded and backed away, from him and from what she was feeling.

Allie waited for her midway through the store. She had a gown of deep burgundy held up against her. "What do you think?"

"Gorgeous. Perfect color. You should try it on."

Allie looked down at the gown. "Really? I don't know. We have a budget. We've saved for this, but we can't go crazy."

"Try it on." Kayla pulled a similar gown, same color but a little different design, off the rack. "And your sister should try this one."

Essie suddenly appeared. She took the dress and held it up. "It's beautiful, but I don't know."

"Try them on."

She watched them go into the dressing rooms, then she stopped at the register, where she handed over her credit card. "I'm paying."

Because this family had done so much for her. They'd shared their love and their faith with her. She wanted to give back.

Allie came out, the dress soft and shimmering. "It's gorgeous, but we can't. If we could find something similar but less expensive."

"Allie, get the dress. It's beautiful. And I've found jewelry that will look beautiful with it. I want to do this for you."

"Mom would never let us accept it," Essie said as she walked out of the dressing room.

"It's a gift," Kayla insisted. "Come on. We can't keep your brother standing out there much longer."

Essie shot a concerned look at Boone, standing at the entrance of the store. "I think he must have pressure sores. It hasn't happened in a long time. But the weather is changing and he's been going nonstop."

"What does he need to do when this happens?" Kayla asked as she followed them into the dressing room area and stood outside the rooms where they were changing.

"He needs to go in and get checked. But he needs to stay off it, and probably not wear the prosthesis for a few days."

They were paying when Boone left his post at the door and hurried toward them. He was on the phone, his mouth a grim line. Kayla stepped away from Essie and Allie. They were busy telling the cashier all about the twin pageant.

"What's wrong?" she asked.

"Dad. They think he's having another heart attack. Jase is driving him to the Braswell hospital."

"Let's go." She signed for their purchases, ignoring the look Boone gave her. "Come on, girls, time to head out."

"What's up?" Essie asked as she and Allie moved to Boone's side.

"Your dad is having chest pains," Kayla explained. "We're going to meet them at Braswell."

Allie slipped her arm through Boone's. "He's okay, isn't he?"

"Of course he is," Boone reassured his younger sisters. "He's fine. He was talking. Jase is there."

Kayla gave the three of them space. Boone noticed. "Stanford, I'm still paying attention. Come here."

"I can't catch a break with you." She moved ahead of the three, leading them through the crowded mall, mindful of Boone's lagging pace. They had a long walk to get to the parking lot.

She hurried ahead of them, ignoring Boone when he told her to stay with him. She grabbed a wheelchair, paid the fee and headed in his direction. He shook his head.

Essie pushed him toward the chair. "Get in, big brother. You're slowing us down."

"I'm the bodyguard," he mumbled.

"And you're guarding us. But you can't do it if you end up in the hospital." Allie kissed his cheek. "Don't worry, you're still tough. No one will argue with that."

Kayla ignored the look he gave her. She grabbed the handles and pushed. He yanked off his cowboy hat and looked back at her.

"This isn't necessary," he grumbled.

"It is. You're in pain. Your sisters say the longer you walk like this, the more damage you can do. And we're in a hurry."

She expected him to be upset but he reached back and touched her hand. The gesture undid her but she kept moving forward. She wondered what he'd do if she stopped in the middle of the mall and kissed him. Because she really wanted to. She wanted to kiss him until she was breathless. She wanted promises from him.

And she'd never wanted that from anyone else.

Boone led his sisters and Kayla through the Braswell Doctors Hospital. His dad had been put in the cardiac unit. As they were heading out of Austin, Jase had called to let him know it had been a mild heart attack, but they were keeping Jesse Wilder at least overnight.

His mom met them as they were coming down the hall. She looked pale. And tired. He didn't like that everything had been piled on her shoulders while he'd been in Afghanistan, and then while he'd been recuperating. All that he'd done in the past couple of years had been to make things a little easier for her, and for his father.

"He's going to be fine," she told them. She squeezed his hand and then hugged his sisters. She didn't exclude Kayla, pulling her close.

The hug Kayla gave in return was one of comfort. For his mom. She was a giver, Kayla was. She just hadn't realized it before.

"Of course he's going to be fine," Kayla assured his mom. "Have you eaten?"

"I couldn't."

"I'll get you something. If there's a cafeteria. Or I can take Boone's truck. I'll bring something back for all of you."

"Stanford," Boone warned. She gave him an innocent look. "You're not going anywhere alone."

"I'll be fine," she assured him. Her arm was still around his mom.

"Don't worry about me. Go in and see your dad,"

Maria encouraged. "He was worried. He knows Lucas is looking forward to the rodeo tomorrow. And he doesn't want you distracted from your job."

"Those are two things he doesn't need to worry about," Boone told his mom.

The twins had already gone into their dad's hospital room. He could see that all of his siblings were gathered inside, making the room crowded.

"Go on in. I'll go see if Samantha is working," Kayla said, walking away from his mom.

"Stay inside. And keep your phone with you."

"Will do, Wilder," she answered.

She pulled her phone from her pocket as she left. Boone's mom touched his arm. He managed a quick smile and then he led her into his dad's room. Jesse looked up, his smile weak, but he wasn't as pale as he'd seemed for the past week or so.

"You know, Dad, you could have all of this attention at home. You don't have to come here."

His dad's mouth twisted in a crooked grin. "I didn't plan on it being a family reunion."

"No, I bet you didn't. How are you?"

His dad rubbed his chest. "Better. How are you?"

"I'm good, Dad."

"We're not going to miss that rodeo tomorrow."

"Dad, that's the last thing we need to be worrying about," Boone said as he moved closer to the bed.

"No, it's the one thing to worry about. This rodeo means a lot to Lucas. To all of you."

"Yeah, so does your health. And this won't be the last rodeo."

"No, I guess it won't. But if there's a way, I want you all in it."

For Lucas. Boone got that. "I know."

Jesse reached for his wife's hand. "Take your mom down and make her eat."

"I'll try."

"Jesse, I'm not hungry," Maria assured her husband, softening the words with a kiss on his cheek. "The kids went down to eat. Jase brought me back a salad."

Boone made eye contact with his brother. Jase shook his head.

"I want you to take care of yourself, Maria." Jesse patted his wife's hand.

Boone pulled up a chair for his mom. "Sit. I'm going to find Kayla and we'll bring you back something to eat."

"I could go," Michaela offered. He noticed she was alone.

"Where's Molly?"

"With Breezy Martin. She's fine. I'm going to head that way soon. Essie and Allie can go with me. Janie is going to stay here tonight. With Mom."

Boone's gaze landed on Janie. She was sitting near the window, a book in her hand. She always had a book. Sometimes he worried that she lived her life through fiction and avoided real life.

He didn't know how to help her. For that matter, how did he help Michaela move on from her divorce? How did he help the twins to stay grounded, and Lucas to feel as if he wasn't the son who had been skipped over?

His mom was still standing. He glared at her, pointing to the chair.

She sat down but she gave him a look that he knew well. The one that said he was trying her patience. He leaned down to kiss her cheek, softening her mood the way he'd always done. He'd been told he'd been doing it since he was a little boy. If he tried her patience, he knew it just took a hug, a kiss on the cheek and she melted.

"I'll be back."

"We'll be fine," she assured him.

He left, stepping into the hall. Out of eyeshot from the others, he leaned against the wall and took a deep breath. He let it out slowly, letting the pain go with it.

"Hey, cowboy, having problems?" Samantha had walked up, taking him by surprise. Kayla wasn't with her.

"Where's your sister?"

"You're so charming," she teased. "She went to get your mom something to eat. But first she came to find me because she said you're stubborn."

"I'm just fine." He took a step, pretending it didn't hurt.

"Yeah, she told me you'd try to deny it. And she was right. Come upstairs. We have a doctor on duty and he said he'd look at it. We want to make sure you don't have an infection. I'll get you crutches to use and you can give it a rest for a day or two."

"Sam, I don't have time for resting."

She took hold of his arm and led him to the elevator. "You also don't have time to be in pain. Come on."

An hour later he was on crutches and heading back down to his dad's room. Kayla met him in the hall.

"Samantha found you?" She smiled as she asked.

"Yes, she found me." He motioned her toward a waiting room. "Sit with me."

"Is this going to be serious? Are we breaking up?" she teased.

"Kayla." He didn't know what else to say. She was joking. He knew it was her way of hiding from the pain.

"Okay, so this *is* that moment. It's been fun. We'll see each other from time to time."

He kept walking and she followed, still talking about how life would be when she left. He opened the door of the waiting room and she entered ahead of him. He was relieved to see the room empty.

She sat and he took a seat across from her.

"So?" She looked up, her blue eyes a little misty.

"Daron is coming to get you. If I can get Mom to leave, he said he'd drive her back to the ranch, too. He's going to stay with you all tonight so I can stay here."

"I see. And then?"

"Your dad is coming to see you tomorrow. I think he wants to take you back to Austin. They feel sure they're going to have these guys in custody in the next few days."

"So it's really over."

"Almost. You can go back to your life."

She gave him a thoughtful look. "No, I don't think so. Not the life I've been living. The past year or so has been a journey and I think it's brought me to this place, to a new understanding of myself. I'm not going back to that, I'm going forward."

"I'm glad, because you deserve more than you've allowed yourself to have."

"I do, don't I?" Her smile was genuine now. "Thank you, Boone. Your family has meant a lot to me."

The words were all making sense. This was what they were supposed to say. *It's been nice. Things will be better.* But the words weren't right.

Nothing about this moment felt right. Boone stood, because he didn't know what else to say, other than goodbye.

Chapter 13

William Stanford showed up in Martin's Crossing Saturday morning. The limousine was black with tinted windows. His bodyguards didn't wear cowboy boots. Kayla stood on the front porch of the Wilder home, uncertain and a little uneasy. Her dad walked up the steps and pulled her into a hug.

"Dad."

"Kayla, I'm glad you're okay."

The words seemed genuine. "Of course I'm fine."

"We should talk," he continued. "Is there somewhere we can go?"

"There's a bench out by the barn, if that's okay."

They walked, not talking, not touching. It had been a long time since they'd been close. Hugs were in the past, in her childhood. Shared secrets had never been a part of their relationship. He'd been busy. She'd been angry.

She hadn't forgiven him because she hadn't wanted

to give him that gift. But now she saw that forgiving was for her, to give her the ability to let go.

"I forgive you," she said as they sat down on the bench.

He looked surprised.

"You let me down and you didn't protect me. I've been angry with you for a long time. I was hurt. I felt betrayed. I felt as if I had no one."

He adjusted his tie, something he'd always done when he wasn't sure what to say. She waited, because the next words had to come from him. She was out of words. She needed his.

"You're right," he finally said. "I fired Jim. We met last night and I told him he was no longer needed. I also asked him to leave the law firm."

A year ago she would have told him too little, too late. Today she took his hand and gave it a light squeeze.

"Thank you." She drew in a breath. "Dad, I have to go to the police. About Paul. I'm sorry. I know it will hurt your campaign. I don't want to do that, but I can't let him hurt anyone else."

There was a long silence between them. She braved a look at her dad. He was clenching his jaw. His gaze was on the field, on cattle grazing.

"You're right," he finally said. "I don't want scandal. But it isn't scandal. It's justice."

Her heart thumped hard, working through the fear. Ten years. She'd been fighting and she'd been alone for ten years. She wanted to hug her dad, to pretend those ten years hadn't happened. It seemed that even with forgiveness, even with his apology, she still had a lot to work through.

"I'm not going back to Austin," she told him. "I will

someday. I just can't go back today. Or this week. I need to stay here and help the Wilders. They've opened their home and their lives to me. I want to give back a little of what they've given."

"I don't understand."

"Boone's dad…" She paused. "Mr. Wilder had a heart attack. I don't want to leave until he's well and back home."

"I understand that they've been good to you, Kayla. But I think it's time for you to come home. There's going to be a lot of damage control that needs to be done in the coming weeks before the election."

"I understand, but my life is about more than your political campaign, Dad. For years I haven't really been a part of your life or your family. I get it. You didn't expect a child from your relationship with Sylvia. You certainly didn't expect me to be dumped on you. But I'm tired of not really being a part of your life." Her hands trembled and she clasped them together.

"You're my daughter," her dad finally said. "I'm sorry if you felt anything other than loved."

"Thank you."

He stood, tall and imposing. She got up, facing him, almost as tall and every bit as proud. He gave a curt nod. "One week."

"Thank you. And when I come home, I'm going to do what you need me to do. I'll attend your campaign events. I'll avoid trouble."

A hint of a smile tugged at his mouth. "I'm not sure you can do that."

"I'm not, either, but I'm going to try my best."

They walked back to the house. Not arm in arm. It was too soon for that. But they were on the mend, she thought. And maybe the healing would spread to the rest of their family. She thought of her little brother, Michael. They'd never been close. Maybe they could find a way to at least be friends.

After her dad left, she went inside to find the twins. They were sprawled on their beds looking at fashion magazines. When she entered their room, they looked up, clearly surprised to see her.

"Weren't you leaving?" Essie rolled over and sat up.

"I'm staying. Your mom is going to need help here." She shrugged. Did she really think she could help Maria Wilder?

"Boone is going to be surprised." Allie was still looking at a magazine. "So what do you plan on doing?"

"I thought we should clean the house. And maybe start dinner."

Essie tossed her magazine on the bed. "Seriously?"

"Yes, seriously. We can start soup for dinner."

Allie put aside her magazine and sat up. "Do you know how to make soup?"

"Allie, I have a smartphone. I can do anything."

Two hours later they were in the kitchen together, rummaging through cabinets, positive they had made the best gumbo in history. Allie took a taste with a spoon.

"It's spicy," she said. "But a good kind of spicy. Not the kind that makes your eyeballs sweat."

"Sweaty eyeballs?" Daron walked into the room. "That sounds appetizing."

"We made gumbo," Allie informed him. She held out the spoon. "Try it."

"Hey, not bad."

Suddenly there was a commotion at the front of the house. Voices. Footsteps.

"They're home," Allie called out as she hurried from the room. Essie followed.

Kayla remained in the kitchen. Daron had taken a seat and he shot her a look, one brow arched. She gave the look right back.

"I thought you'd be glad to head back to the city."

"I will be. But I wanted to repay Maria. She's been wonderful to me. And she's going to need some help around here."

"She has four daughters."

"I'm aware of that, Daron. But I wanted to do something for them."

He held up his hands in surrender. "Gotcha."

She turned the flame under the soup down. "Maybe I should have left."

"No, you shouldn't have left. They'll be glad you're here. And I'm sure if you keep cooking like that, you will make things easier for everyone."

The family returned to the kitchen. Essie and Allie were practically pulling Maria. Boone helped his dad to walk, holding his arm and guiding him to a chair. Michaela and Janie followed.

Jase and Lucas had been home all day. They were moving forward with their plans for the rodeo. Jesse had insisted that his sons still participate.

Daron got up, giving his seat to Michaela, who held a sleeping Molly. Kayla watched from the corner of the kitchen. She had the gumbo simmering and the rolls in the oven baking. Essie began to make lemonade.

She should leave and let the family be alone. She started to tell Allie that the soup was done and that the rolls would have to be taken out in five minutes. Boone moved to her side, preventing her from escaping.

"You've been busy," he said in a quiet voice.

"I wanted to be here to help," she explained. He caught her gaze, holding it, that half tilt of his mouth distracting her.

"That's good of you. But you should have gone back with your dad."

She managed an easy smile. "Trying to get rid of me, Wilder?"

"No, just trying to keep you safe and help you find your way back to your life. What if you get stuck here in the country, making casseroles and cleaning bathrooms?"

"There are worse things."

He pushed his hat back on his head and leaned against the counter. "For what it's worth, I know my mom appreciates you being here."

She waited, wanting him to say more. But he didn't. They were from different worlds and this had all been temporary. All of it. Her time with the Wilders, and her time in his life.

Bright lights illuminated the Martin's Crossing Saddle Club arena. The stands were packed. The adjacent field was crowded with horse trailers and pickups. Boone backed his gelding out of the trailer. Lucas already had his horse out, saddled, and was warming up in the open area next to the arena.

He didn't want to be here. Not tonight. But his dad had insisted. They were doing this for Lucas. Boone, Jase, Lucas and Janie were riding for Team Wilder. Michaela was in the stands with the twins and Molly.

Kayla was standing next to the truck. His mom had insisted she attend, even though she'd wanted to stay home with his parents. He slid his gaze her way but didn't linger there too long. She was leaning against the truck, in jeans, pigtails and Michaela's hand-me-down boots. He knew she could afford a pair of her own. She probably had a half dozen pairs in that fancy apartment of hers in Austin.

But she liked those worn boots of his sister's.

He led his horse to the side of the trailer and tied him up. Kayla settled on the wheel well of the trailer to watch.

"You're still limping," she said, her tone casual.

"Yep."

"Should you be doing this?"

He pulled a saddle out of the tack compartment of the trailer. "Yeah, I should. There are times you have to do what needs to be done, Kayla."

"I know."

He placed the blanket on his horse's back and then the saddle. She continued to watch. He tightened the cinch, adjusted the stirrups and then gave the cinch another tug to make sure it was snug.

"What events are you entered in?"

"Branding," he started.

"For real?" she asked, her eyes widening.

He grinned at that look. "Not for real. There will be a pen of calves. We'll rope them by number and bring them to the branding area and mark them with chalk."

"Okay, and then what?"

"Steer doctoring and team penning."

"And at the end of the night, if he wins, he gets to dance with the girl of his choice."

He turned, wishing for once that Remington Jenkins wasn't back in the area. In a matter of weeks he would be Kayla's brother-in-law. He and Samantha Martin were getting married.

"I don't think there's a dance." Boone slid the bridle over his horse's head. "Who do you have on the Jenkins team, Remington?"

"Ah, but there is a dance. The Carter Brothers are playing after the event and they've set up a dance floor," Kayla said.

Boone ignored Kayla. "Your team?"

"Myself, Sam, my brother Colt and Bryan Cooper. He's Breezy's… I don't know, I guess he's nothing to Breezy. But her biological sister is a Cooper, adopted by them years ago. Bryan is her brother by adoption?"

"Confusing," Boone said. "But I've met him. Good guy. Spent some time in South America on the mission field?"

"That's the one. The Coopers are a big family, from northeast Oklahoma." Remington turned his attention to Kayla. "So, little sister, aren't you riding?"

"I don't think anyone wants that," she said with a quick laugh. "The goal here is to win, isn't it?"

Remington laughed and pushed back his hat. "Yes, I guess it is. Give it time. You can't hang with this crowd for long and not be a part of things like this."

"Maybe someday," she answered.

Boone settled his gaze on her. He could see it happening. When those boots felt as if they belonged on her feet and the jeans were worn from ranch work and not by a trick of manufacturing.

"I'd best get back to my crew." Remington tipped his hat. "I'm sure we'll see you at church tomorrow."

From the arena, the MC announced the first event. Calf branding. Boone untied his horse.

"Walk with me?" he offered to the woman standing by his truck looking a little unsure, as if she'd suddenly realized she didn't belong here.

She nodded and walked alongside. His big chestnut moved in too close, nudging him. Cin, short for Cinnamon. The horse had the worst name around.

The quiet between them didn't feel settled or peaceful. He wasn't sure what to do about it, how to fix it. Or even if he should. Maybe it was better this way. To everything there is a season, his mom had always told them, people came and went. There were seasons even for friendships, she'd told them as kids, when a friend moved, a breakup resulted in a broken heart, when they'd lost grandparents.

This had been Kayla Stanford's season in their lives. He had thought it had been mostly for her, to help her face her life. But today he'd seen things in a different light. She'd grown up, and been there for his family.

"I'm going to leave Monday," she said as they approached his family. Janie was on her horse. Jase and Lucas were messing with Lucas's mare, picking her front hoof. She'd probably picked up a stone.

"It isn't goodbye," he said to the woman at his side.

She looked up at him, the borrowed cowboy hat leaving her face in shadows. He moved the brim of that hat, giving him a better view of her face, her eyes. He considered kissing her, but the good sense he'd been born with prevailed. This wasn't the time or the place.

"I know it isn't," she responded. "I'll be around. I'd like to think we've become friends. Even if you were against babysitting me back when this all started."

"We're friends," he assured her.

She stood on tiptoe and kissed his cheek. "Go beat those Martins."

He moved to the right side of his horse, definitely the off side for mounting. But he and Cin had gotten used to it. He swung into the saddle, settling in the seat and steadying the horse, which shifted beneath him.

"Don't worry, we'll teach 'em how it's done." He tipped his hat and she laughed.

Lucas moved his horse around to Boone's left. The four of them rode toward the gate. Kayla went off to sit with her family. Breezy, Oregon, Lily and the younger children. He glanced her way one last time.

Sometime during the branding of their third calf, he looked up again and realized she was gone.

Chapter 14

Kayla's phone had buzzed. When she looked down, the text glared up at her, making her blood run cold. But she'd managed to smile and pretend everything was fine. She told Breezy she was a little cool and was going to grab her jacket out of Boone's truck. Instead, she'd gotten behind the wheel of the truck and guided it out of the parking lot, careful to ease off the clutch, conscious of the large stock trailer on the back.

Her phone buzzed a second time. They wanted to know if she was coming. Alone.

She texted that she was.

She drove out of the rodeo grounds and onto the highway, the trailer jerking the truck, making it a little harder for her to ease forward the way Boone had taught her. It would take her at least ten minutes to get back to the Wilders. She texted again, telling the person on the other end to be patient. She was coming. She'd do whatever they said.

A smiley face was the response. Daron had been right. These guys were young and dangerous. She kept driving, the truck feeling heavy with the trailer on the back. Or maybe it was her, feeling weighted down, as if she couldn't move fast enough.

The slower speed gave her time to think, time to plan. But she didn't have a plan. She only knew that she wouldn't let anyone hurt Maria or Jesse Wilder.

She pulled up to the farmhouse. The place looked sleepy and innocent, as if there couldn't possibly be anyone here threatening her or the family that had been so good to her. She got out of the truck and closed the door quietly, hoping she could make a circle of the house and see if she saw anyone. She remembered that Boone had a gun in his RV. The door would be unlocked.

She took a dozen steps and someone grabbed her.

"Don't move. Don't say a word."

She nodded.

"I've been waiting for this day for a long time. You thought you were too good for me, didn't you, Kayla Stanford? You told me I was a stupid kid. But look who is going to win."

"I can't look. You're behind me."

"You don't need to see me. I'm so unimportant to you, you didn't even think that I might be the one pulling the strings, making you and your daddy dance. But I'm going to show you. I've sent the article to the paper. Tomorrow morning everyone will know about Paul Whitman."

"He's no longer working for my father," she countered.

"I don't really care about him. I care about you. I care about your father's money. He fired my father. No explanation, just told him he wasn't needed any longer. Because of that my father started drinking and never stopped. He died last year."

"I'm sorry." No one should live like that. Or die like that. "Blane. That's your name, right? Where's Ken?"

Hadn't she read somewhere that if you make a personal connection with an attacker, it softens them? She glanced around looking for the other man and didn't see him.

"Don't worry about where Ken is and don't try to act as if we're friends."

"Are the Wilders okay?" she asked, desperate enough to continue trying the friendship tactic.

"They're fine. We tied them up. They haven't done anything to us. We just wanted you."

"Okay, you have me. Where are we going? Where's your friend?"

"He's getting the car. We parked on the side road."

"What are you going to do with me?" She glanced around, hoping to see an escape route. She saw Sally, Boone's collie. The dog was easing out of the shadows, the snarl low in her chest. He didn't hear the dog.

"Ransom," he said. "We figure you're worth enough to get us out of the country. But first, we'll have some fun."

"Good. I do like a decent party."

In the distance she heard a car. His friend maybe. Sally came closer, her growl a little louder.

"I'm about sick of that dog." He pulled a gun. She elbowed him in the face as he took aim at the collie. The bullet went wide. The gun flew from his hand. A car came up the driveway.

She broke loose and ran. She wouldn't go to the

house. She couldn't put Boone's parents at risk. Instead, she ran for the RV. Inside it was dark and quiet. She locked the doors and leaned against the paneled wall, waiting for her heart to return to normal.

Blue lights flashed across the walls of the camper. Outside she heard Sally give one sharp bark, asking for the door to be opened. Kayla unlocked the door and let the dog in. And in the dark she saw a shadow, and then a figure emerged.

"It's me." Boone stepped forward, limping up the steps of the camper. "You're okay?"

She nodded, unable to speak.

He took off his hat and tossed it on the patio table. "Kayla, I…"

"I didn't want them to hurt your parents."

He brushed a hand down his face. "I'm so mad at you, I don't know what to say. You could have gotten yourself killed."

"But I didn't."

"No, you didn't." He shook his head. "I can't think straight right now. But your father is on his way. He's taking you back to Austin, because I can't have you here if I can't keep you safe."

"But you got them."

"Yeah, I got them. But right now you're not safe from me. I don't know if I want to throttle you or kiss you."

"Kiss me?" she suggested.

He shook his head. "Come on, my mom wants to see with her own two eyes that you're safe."

She reached for his hand. He wouldn't take it.

"Not right now," he said. "You should have trusted me."

"I know. But I didn't want anyone to get hurt on my account. I wanted to protect you all."

"I do the protecting around here. I don't need you to protect me."

"No, you don't." She walked next to him back to the house.

"Your brothers and sister are here." He nodded, indicating the yard full of trucks.

"Great."

"You have a lot of explaining to do."

"They said to come alone," she tried to explain.

He shook his head. "You have us for a reason. You don't have to do things alone anymore. You especially don't have to give in to the demands of blackmailers."

"They said the story is going to be in the paper tomorrow."

He stopped her, his hand on her arm. "Maybe it is. Maybe it isn't. But you're going to survive that. Your father will survive it. You have to trust the people in your life."

"I know."

Then she was surrounded by family. Boone walked away, leaving her to her siblings. Jake took control, telling her to get her bag. Her father could pick her up at the Circle M Ranch.

She allowed Jake to walk her out the door and down to his truck without a goodbye to Boone.

She took the handkerchief he offered as they drove away. Somehow she would come out of this stronger than ever. She knew that. Someday soon she would thank Boone for giving her the opportunity to find herself.

But today was not that day.

Boone woke up to early-morning sunshine filtering through the miniblinds. He rolled over and almost fell off the narrow sofa of his RV. Sally whimpered and scrambled to stay on the cushion. He glanced down at her.

"What are you doing on the couch?"

In response she slid off and curled up on the floor.

"You going to sleep all day?"

He jumped at the familiar voice. "What are you doing here?"

Daron was stretched out in the recliner.

"I thought you might need backup. By the time I got here, everyone was gone or asleep. You didn't hear me come in."

"I'm going to change the locks."

"You won't do that. You'd miss me."

"I wouldn't." Boone sat up, stretched and reached for his crutches. "I've got a doctor's appointment this morning."

"Yeah, I heard. Want me to drive you?"

"If you would. Have you talked to Lucy?"

"Yeah, she's good. She's in San Angelo on a job."

"Gotcha. Have you talked to Mr. Stanford today?"

Daron headed for the kitchen and started the coffeemaker. "Yeah, he's glad this is over. The article did come out. It made him look bad, but the real criminal is Mr. Whitman. Kayla is going to press charges. I guess you didn't think you could tell me about that."

"No, I didn't. She told me in confidence."

"She doesn't confide in a lot of people," Daron said as he leaned against the counter.

Boone opened the fridge. He pulled out a package of sausage and found a clean skillet.

"You could do the dishes today," he told Daron.

"Yeah, I will. Or hire someone. Do you think the twins would want to earn extra money?"

Boone put the pan on the burner. "The twins always want extra money. But I'm not going to pay them to clean the RV."

"Then, I will. About Kayla. She's going to be okay. I think she'll be better than ever. It's you I'm not so sure about."

"I'm fine." Boone poured the coffee that had brewed into his cup. He lifted the cup to salute Daron.

"I don't think you're fine, Boone. I think you got too close."

"You're not the head of this organization, Daron. We're partners. You're definitely not my boss or my mom. I don't need your advice."

"No, but you do need your head on straight for the next job."

"My head is on straight."

Daron grabbed a spatula and flipped the sausage. "You're right. I'm out of line. What time is your doctor's appointment?"

"Ten."

"So do you love her?"

Boone stilled, then pointed at the door. "Get out."

"Listen, if you need to talk…"

"I'll get a therapist if I need to talk."

"Boone, it wasn't your fault. The kid, he had us all fooled."

"The kid was a pawn." Boone said the words clearly, not allowing emotion to get the best of him. "And why do you think everything goes back to that day?"

"Because it does. We all relive it every day."

"Do you?" Boone leaned against the counter and

watched his friend fry sausage until it no longer resembled food.

"Yeah, I do. I convinced James he should go with us. I'm not sure what we thought we were going to do."

"We thought we would check it out and then go back with a plan to extract those guys."

"But they were waiting for us," Daron said.

Boone looked away. He didn't want to see the nightmare relived on his friend's face. He didn't want Daron to see it on his. They couldn't talk about that day without experiencing it all over again. The explosion. The heat. The screams. The pain.

"We made a stupid pact, while you were in the hospital." Daron turned off the pan. "Protect others. Live our lives for the brother we lost. We were a lot younger then."

"We were young." They'd been twenty-five. Not really that young, he guessed. But young enough to think they needed a pact to honor their fallen friends. If James wasn't going home to his family, Daron and Boone would never have families. Except that Daron had promised James he'd keep an eye on Emma and Jamie.

"If you love her, you should go for it, Boone. Don't let her get away."

Daron handed him a plate with a few burned sausages.

"I'm not sure what I feel." Boone sat down at the table. Daron sat across from him. "You know the emotions in situations like this aren't always real."

"Yeah, you're right, not always. It's a job and we can get caught up in some stuff. But you've always kept your emotions separate from the job. This time you didn't."

"No, this time I didn't. She took me by surprise, Daron. I didn't expect her. I didn't expect to feel this way."

"Don't let her get away," Daron said off-handedly as he stood and dumped sausage in the dog's dish. "I'm going to Duke's for breakfast."

"Good idea."

Don't let her get away. He brushed off the advice. They couldn't build a relationship on what they felt in the middle of a crisis situation. Kayla had depended on him to keep her safe. He'd felt like the man rescuing her from danger and from herself.

In time they'd come back to earth and see the relationship for what it was. Temporary. And if he missed her for a little while, that was normal.

They'd felt a bond only because he was her bodyguard and he had liked playing the hero.

They just needed time to realize that their relationship had been built on close proximity and the situation they'd been in.

But in truth, he couldn't imagine a time when he wouldn't think about her. What was he going to do about that?

Chapter 15

Kayla stood next to her father when he was sworn in as Texas state senator. The next day she left for Martin's Crossing.

Samantha and Remington were getting married at the end of the week. Kayla wouldn't miss that wedding for the world. She pulled up to her sister's small house and for a moment sat in the truck she'd recently traded her car for. Samantha walked out the front door, waved and then headed her way.

"Well, look what the cat dragged in." Sam leaned in the window and kissed her on the cheek. "I'm glad to see you. I need help packing."

After the honeymoon Sam would be moving to the Jenkins ranch. Kayla had asked to stay in this house on the Martins' property. She was going to apply for a job at the Martin's Crossing Consolidated School. She was going to live in the country. She'd already sold her condo. She'd traded off her convertible. She had a pair of boots that were meant for the farm, not the club.

She would see Boone. Often. Her heart beat faster on that thought.

"I'll do whatever you need me to do," she assured Sam as she climbed down from the truck.

"I'm glad to hear that. I've got so much to get done. And tonight is the family dinner at Duke's. So you're just in time."

"I'm not sure I'm ready to go to town," Kayla admitted as they crossed to the little cottage that she'd come to love.

She immediately plopped on the oversize sofa and grabbed her favorite afghan. It felt so good to be home. She smiled up at her sister, and for a minute she forgot her loneliness, the emptiness that sometimes caught her by surprise.

"Why?" Sam moved a box and sat on the chair, pulling it close to the sofa so she could put her feet on the coffee table.

"Because I'm not ready."

"You're going to see him eventually. And you know that you want to see him."

"I know. But it shouldn't be so hard. It was a month of my life. Barely. It wasn't exactly a relationship that we broke off. I shouldn't..." She sighed.

"Miss him?" Sam gave her a sweet smile. "But you do. Because it doesn't matter why you were together. What matters is how you feel. How do you feel?"

"I miss him. Every day. I thought it would get easier. I thought it was just a fluke. But it wasn't."

"Call him." Sam tossed her a phone.

She tossed it back. "I'm not calling him. He hasn't called me. How pathetic would it be to call him? But I would like to see his family. I would like to know how his dad is doing."

"Jesse is great. They put in a couple of stents, changed his medication and he says he hasn't felt this good in years."

"I'm so glad to hear that."

"But you're not going to call. You know, you could call Maria and ask how they're doing. It doesn't have to be about Boone."

"I should call. But who am I to them? No one really." She buried her face in her hands. "I sound pathetic. I'm not a pathetic person."

Samantha tossed a pillow at her. "You're a dork. You're trying to convince yourself that you didn't fall in love with Boone. And while I can't imagine loving him, I get it that he might be appealing to someone else."

"He's amazing."

"Spoken like a woman in love."

"I don't have time for love. I've wasted years of my life. It's time for me to focus on real things. Getting a job. Living a decent life. Going to church with my family. If I toss a relationship into that mix, it's just going to confuse things."

"Or make everything fit together a little better."

"Go away."

"Help me pack boxes. You promised."

Kayla shook her head. "I do not remember making that promise. And he hasn't called me. That should tell me something, right?"

"Yeah, that you're both dorks." Sam headed for the kitchen. "Come on, we'll make a casserole. Potatoes make everything better."

* * *

Kayla rode with Sam to Duke's that evening. It was dark when they pulled into town, and obvious that the town was gearing up for the Christmas season. Lights twinkled in the trees along Main Street. Homes and stores were decorated. The nativity had been set up in front of the Community Church.

A few years ago Oregon's dad had slept in that nativity. He'd said if a stable was good enough for his Savior, it was good enough for him.

There was already a crowd at Duke's No Bar and Grill. Kayla strode through the door with Sam. It felt odd to be back, and to know that she belonged here. This was going to be her home. The people waiting at a big table in the center of the dining area were her family. She stopped, taking it in, letting it become real to her.

"You okay?" Sam asked as they walked to that table.

"I'm good."

Remington was there. He stood to hug Kayla and then he reached for Sam, holding her close, their lips brushing lightly.

"Three more days," he whispered.

"And I'll be Samantha Jenkins."

Kayla glanced away because it was too much. She was happy for her sister. But she was feeling sorry for herself. Years ago she'd thought about marriage. She'd dreamed of the man she'd marry, the house they'd live in, even the names of their children. That young girl had dreamed big. There had been mansions and maybe a prince who rescued her.

But then everything had changed. She'd lost her trust. She'd lost track of that innocent girl who dreamed big. She'd been racing through life not allowing herself to think about a future with happily-ever-afters.

"Sit down." Brody pulled on her hand. "And try to relax."

She sat by her brother, and he put a comforting arm around her shoulder.

"I am relaxed." She even managed a smile as she said it.

"Yes, you look relaxed. Do I need to hurt someone for you?"

She shook her head. "No, I'm good. It's just strange, being back. And I'm going to live here. It's a big step."

"You're a country girl at heart. You'll adjust."

Of course she would. She always adjusted. She'd always been good at reinventing herself.

Boone pulled up to Duke's. It had been a couple of weeks since he'd been home so he should have kept on driving. But after playing bodyguard to a Saudi prince for several days, he needed a few minutes to relax. And he needed a piece of Duke's chocolate-cream pie.

As he walked through the door, he realized he should have kept on going. He saw her immediately. She was laughing at something Brody said. But it wasn't her real laugh, not the one that lit up her eyes. It was the laugh that said she was trying hard to fit in.

He wondered if anyone else knew that about her.

Maybe pie wasn't such a great idea. He reached for the door but a hand on his shoulder stopped him. He didn't look up to many people, physically, but he had to look up at Duke Martin.

"Change your mind, Boone?" Duke's hand was still on his shoulder and there was a challenge in his eyes that was unmistakable. "Never figured you for a coward."

"Not a coward, just a man in a hurry to get home. I thought I'd get a piece of pie. To go."

Duke's mouth twisted and his eyes lit with humor. "Sorry, but I don't have pie 'to go.' Pie can only be eaten in house this week."

"Guess I'll come back next week."

"Have a seat, Boone. I wouldn't want you to look yella."

"I'm not yella." Boone headed for a booth. "And the word is *yellow.*"

"Yeah, but when you're calling a man *coward*, you say *yella.*" Duke grinned. "Sounds better that way."

Boone sat at a booth and took off his hat. He brushed a hand through his hair to smooth it down. He was exhausted. And now he was confused. She was here. He hadn't expected that.

And he hadn't expected the emotional punch to the gut.

Duke sat down across from him, placing the pie on the table just out of reach. Ned, the best waitress in Texas, hurried over to fill his coffee cup. She gave them both a "don't make trouble" look and left.

"You look awful." Duke's hand was on the plate. "As if you really need this pie."

"What I need is for you to stay out of my business."

"But if your business pertains to my family, then it becomes my business."

"Duke, I have to get home. Either give me the pie or don't."

Duke slid the pie in front of him. "What's your hurry? Don't you want to stay and visit? Sam is getting married this weekend. We're having a family dinner. You look as though you could use a good meal."

"I'll have a meal when I get home. And I'm not going to invade your family dinner. I have a family of my own. And from what I hear, a pinkeye outbreak to deal with tomorrow."

"I hear your dad is up and around, doing better now."

"He's doing much better."

Duke sat there, silent, watching him eat the pie. Boone felt about sixteen. He now understood how Remington had felt when the Martins had run him off their ranch a dozen years ago. That had been the first time Rem had tried to date Samantha Martin. It hadn't gone well.

Boone wasn't dating anyone. He definitely wasn't going to start dating clients. When he, Daron and Lucy had started the business, they'd verbally agreed that dating clients was off-limits. It was unprofessional. It created problems.

Big problems. Such as the one he was facing now. He hadn't dated Kayla, but he'd definitely crossed lines. And those lines had led him to this place.

"I have to go."

"Yella."

Boone grabbed his hat and stood. "No, I'm not yella, Duke. I'm a man with a family and a business."

When he walked out the door, he inhaled cool autumn air. It felt good to be back in Texas. He'd spent two weeks in Southern California. It had been hot and dry there. The prince had been a pain. A guy who drove fast and lived faster.

Boone enjoyed the quiet, slow pace of country living. He wouldn't trade Texas for anything. Not even a Bel Air mansion and a Ferrari.

He stood in front of his truck for a long time, staring at Duke's.

Chapter 16

She'd held her breath when he first walked through the door of Duke's. And then she'd held it a little longer while he'd sat at the table with her brother. She'd wanted him to say something. He hadn't. So she'd laughed and talked with her family and pretended it didn't hurt.

It had been an eye-opening experience, though. In the five minutes he'd stayed in the diner she'd realized the truth. She'd been a client to him. Nothing more.

"Ten, nine, eight…" Next to her Brody was counting down.

"What are you doing?" she whispered. Jake was saying something about Sam and Remington and their lives together.

He grinned. "You'll see. Two. One."

Boone pushed open the front door and stepped back inside.

Brody chuckled. "Known him all my life. He can't stand to be called a coward. And he doesn't back down."

Kayla really disliked family at that moment.

"My guess, sis, is you're about to tell us all goodbye."

"I doubt that. I ordered one of Duke's black and bleu steaks, and I plan on eating it."

Boone crossed the diner, and when he reached their table, he looked like a thunderstorm about to break.

"I need for you to come with me," he said to her in a low voice. Everyone was watching, though. Not one person in the suddenly quiet diner had missed the order.

"I'm having dinner with my family." She managed to sound in control. At least she thought so. "And I don't like to be ordered around, Boone."

He briefly closed his eyes. "Can I please have a moment of your time?"

"Now, wasn't that sweet?" Brody said. "I think you should go with him before he tosses you over his shoulder and goes all caveman on us."

Both she and Boone gave Brody a look he didn't need interpreted for him. Kayla pushed back from the table.

"Five minutes, Boone."

"Ten," he said. He took her hand and led her from the restaurant.

They walked in silence to the park, Boone practically dragging her along with him. Christmas lights twinkled on the trees. A speaker played Christmas music. In the distance she heard a train. Boone still held her hand but his touch had gentled.

"Boone?"

Before she could ask what he wanted he pulled her into his arms.

"Don't talk." His mouth lowered to capture hers in a desperate kiss.

His lips moved over hers and his hands splayed

across her back. She didn't feel trapped. She felt complete. For the first time in weeks she didn't wonder. She only wanted. His love. Him.

His lips stilled but his mouth hovered against hers. She felt his smile.

"I missed you." Finally the words she'd longed to hear. "I couldn't drive away from Duke's without holding you, without kissing you. I'm sorry."

"Don't be sorry." She leaned into his shoulder and brushed her lips against his shirt. He smelled so good. Like the mountains and autumn. "I missed you, too."

"How long are you here for?"

"Forever," she answered, her face still buried in the crook of his neck.

"Forever isn't long enough," he told her. "I need more time with you."

"I'm not going anywhere. But what if—"

"No," he said with a voice that shook. "Don't say anything. What I feel has nothing to do with being your bodyguard. It has everything to do with love. I love you, Kayla. And I want more than a few weeks in your life."

She trembled in his arms, thinking about his words. Thinking about forever.

He hadn't planned to put it all out there. He'd gone back into Duke's determined but not knowing where that determination would lead him. He'd only known that he needed to hold her. He had needed to kiss her until the emptiness he'd felt since she'd left went away.

He hadn't expected that one kiss would make him want more. He hadn't planned on any of this, not really. But she was in his arms, her eyes shining with emotion that he had to guess meant she felt pretty strongly about him.

And he wanted to marry her. He guessed it was way too early for proposals.

"Say something," he whispered against her hair. "Don't leave me hanging, Stanford."

"Kayla Wilder. I like the way that sounds."

He picked her up and twirled her around him. It wasn't a proposal, but he knew when it was meant to be. He put her back on her own two feet and kissed her again. She wrapped her arms around his neck and held on, as if he was her lifeline.

"I love you, Wilder." She whispered the words a few minutes later. "I'm so glad you're in my life."

"I'm glad to hear that, Stanford. Because I plan on being in your life for a long, long time."

He led her back into Duke's, back to her family. But this time he stayed. He let the Martin brothers tease him. He endured the looks from the women.

Kayla sitting next to him was all that mattered.

Epilogue

Kayla walked out of the school on a sunny day at the end of May. She'd been a substitute teacher since December. Last week the school had offered her a permanent position as a second-grade teacher.

She had found herself in Martin's Crossing. She had a career she loved. She had a home, the cottage Samantha had vacated. Duke had given her a pretty bay gelding.

She had a man who cherished her. And she loved him right back. He had texted her an hour earlier asking her to meet him after school. He wanted to take her on a date.

He was waiting in the parking lot. Gorgeous. He was absolutely gorgeous. Even from a distance she knew she could drown in his espresso eyes. He had a dimple in his right cheek that she enjoyed kissing.

He smelled like mountains and autumn air. And in jeans low on his hips and a T-shirt that hugged his shoulders, no one was more gorgeous.

"You coming with me, Stanford?" he called out from the tractor he'd driven to town to pick her up in.

"I'm coming, Wilder." She crossed the parking lot as he got down from the tractor to open the door for her. "My chariot awaits. This is going to be some date."

"Honey, we do things right here in the country." He winked as he said it and he climbed up in the seat with her. "Do not touch anything."

"I wouldn't dream of it." So she scooted to the far side of the tractor.

Then he kissed her. "I've been waiting two days for that. You aren't going to deny me."

"I wouldn't dream of it."

They drove out to the Wilder ranch, cars passing them one at a time. He pulled onto the drive and through a gate. She remembered this field. They'd been here before. Last fall when he hadn't cut down the wildflowers.

"I brought a picnic from Duke's." He pointed to the bag of carryout food on the floor.

"Sounds perfect."

The tractor chugged along over rolling hills. When it got to that same back pasture, he stopped. Bluebonnets spread out before them, making a carpet of wildflowers.

"Isn't this something?" he asked. "They've been blooming for a while. I should have brought you sooner."

"No, this is perfect."

They climbed down from the tractor and he led her through the field of flowers and down to the creek.

"There's nowhere else like it."

"No, there isn't." She turned to look at the field behind them, captured in late-afternoon sunlight. The bluebonnets stretched to the base of the distant hill.

"I'd like to build our house here," he said. The words hung in the air, like the sweet scent of wildflowers.

"*Our* house?" She looked up at him, sensing the moment, her heart skipping along in agreement.

"Yes, *our* house." He spoke as if he was talking about the weather. She wanted to hit him.

"When would we build this house?" She tried to match his tone of indifference.

"We could start in a month or so and have it finished and ready to move into this fall."

"This fall? But aren't you forgetting something?" she asked, as serious as she could be when she saw the teasing glint in his eyes.

"Have I forgotten something?"

She nodded, her breath catching as he reached for her.

His hand brushed down her arm and he took her hand in his. And then he went down on one knee and smiled up at her, that mischievous light in his dark eyes turning to something warmer and undoing her composure.

"Kayla Stanford, will you marry me? And live here in this field of bluebonnets? We could build a big house and fill it with pretty little girls and ornery boys. If you'll just say yes."

He pulled a ring from his pocket and held it up, waiting.

"Yes. Oh, Boone, yes." She pulled him to his feet and he slid the ring on her finger. "I want to marry you. I want to have a farmhouse and babies. With you."

He kissed her then, and she sank into his embrace. She was home. And she couldn't imagine being anywhere but in his arms.

* * * * *